Turncoat[1]

By Viktor E. Krabin & William D. Arand

Copyright © 2023 Arand Publishing LLC
Cover design © 2023 Arand Publishing LLC
All rights reserved. No part of this book may be reproduced in any form or by an electronic or mechanical means - except in the case of brief quotations embodied in articles or reviews - without written permission from its publisher.
The characters and events portrayed in this book are fictitious. Any similarity to real persons, living or dead, is purely coincidental and not intended by the author.
Copyright © 2023 Arand Publishing LLC
All rights reserved.

Dedicated to:
My wife, Zoe, whose support throughout my writing process has been unwavering and resolute, and without which I would never have gotten this far.
To Will, whose mentorship throughout this book and my others has been invaluable.
And last but not least, my unhinged group of friends who are a constant source of information and inspiration.

Special thanks to:
Shel
Henry
Doc
Jack

Thank you to my Patrons, whom are belligerent and numerous, keeping my head in the game during the writing process. Your value is immeasurable, and I cannot do this without you lovely cats.

1205, a passing Fnord, aaron clark, Adam Rosenberg, Aetharan, Alex, Alex, Alex , alex phillips, Alex W., Alexander, Alexander Anderson, Ambiguously Anonymous, Andrei Olkhovskiy, Andres Rama, Andrew Fraser, Andrew Weaver, Ang3lusMortis54, Anonymous , Anthony Dunn, Arbiter58, Arctic Wolf, Arkon, Art Art, Azrael 11197, Ben Foard, Ben S., Benno McKinley, BlackBlood25, blackwolf393 , BobbyBoi105, Brendan Latta, Brigid, Bunten44, calum , cameron armstrong, Cameron Brown, Car Crash, Chad Arrington, Charbz, Chris, Christian SÃ¶bbe, Christopher B., Christopher Burns, Civer , Clinton wertzbaugher, Cody , Coleman Dillon, Colt, Concerned Person, crowdedstorm, csky dub, Daan de jong, Dak the Purifying, Daniel, Daniel , Daniel Brown, Daniel Knight, Daniel Sekeres, Darren Stalder, David Bueno, David Ellis, David Middleton, Dennis Altman, Dennis Hornsby, Devin Hamilton, Devin Hamilton, dink, Diokana, Dominik L, DOORDAY , Dragonkain, Driango , Ebondragon , ed, EDWARD , einar, Elric Jeffers, Emmanuel Dixon, Eric Davis, eric penn, Erik Houk, Erik Martinez, Ethan Quarello, F0ZYWOLF , Fabien Larco, FalconHalo , Fishinabarrel Jr., fishy 2.0, Fjord, Gadfium , Gage Scott, Gaunt, Geodux ,

Gibborim, Gingiberry, Glenn Merlin Hinkley, Grantes, Greg Michael, Grudge, Guini, GunNut42, Gunz442, Gustavo, Harrison, Hayden Hodge, Heato3N, HereForHFY, Hugo Kater, Huntsman 921, Huntsman225, iamontheinternet, Ian Cook, Jack, Jadon Du preez, Jakub Habina, Jakub StachoÅ"„ jal leo, James, James Bickford, James Bush, James Fidler, James G., Jazuz, JD, Jeff Fischer, Jeffrey Gonzales, Jeremiah Paltridge, Jhomtaz, Jo Richard, Joe, John Hewitt, John O'Connor, Jonathan Campbell, Jonathan de Jong, Jos Mar, Josh Adams, Joshua, Joshua Vreeland, JR9364, Justin Colt (J.C.) Williford, Kade Richard, Kimaen, Kimber Grey, King Jerkera, Kittora, kohl thaler, Konrahd_Verdammt, L H, Leo, LG, litebrite, Logan, Losferado, Lucas Roddenby, Lucifer Diavolo, Luis lopez, luke, Luke N, M. Ryan, MACDADDY_hero, mailmindlin, Mal'Thrrox, Mango_bomb, Marc-olivier Bergeron, Martin, Mason Olson, Matt Miller, Matthew Tarbard, Maxim Leone, Maxwell Christie, May Raven, MegaPanda37, Megathor3978, Mest63, Michael, Michael Bloom, Michael Nohaile, Michael Tomlin, mickg, Mikey The Wolf, Mittens, Monty, Mr. S, MWA-PL, Nathan Male, Nathan Parrish, Nekomancer, Nevercroft, Nicholas Shastany, Nick Archer, Nick Fish, Nicolas Gilliam, Noctema, Noremac236, NorthBoundAndDown, NotBahroo, nym, Okedra Renn, Omar Dahami, OrangeSpaceProgram, Pat, Patrick, Peter Liu, Phil, Phillip Layton, Phillip Mackintosh, Pizzaline07, PNova, Pointedmoss, Powurdone,

PsyduckScientist, puggle522., Pwntatochip, quinn mackay, R. Alexander Spoerer, Raider Mileghere, Randomanon, Randy, Raraki Kraken, Raul Salazar, Raymond Mouton, RedneckTurbineTech, Ricktor Blackwell, RocketDoge, RokiSKB, Ryan, Ryan Barkenhagen, Ryan Fuller, Sam Berry, Sam Frye, Sam 'Rio' King, SarcSorc, Saxdasm, Scott, Scott Sherrett, Sdff, Seamus Cook, Sean Choi, Sean Graham, Sean Gregory Murray, Sebastien Perreault, Seiryn, Seth Griffith, shamokin 73, Signal_0, simeon turner, Simon Ellison, Simon Kowalski, Skais, SpaceCacteye, Spyglass, stacksonstacks04, Steven Shelley, Taylor Hayes, Telclivo, The Walrus Transcendent, The_Kriegsman, TheAceGamingDemon, theunluckydie, Thragnar, throwaway493, Timothy Rhodes, Tom Roose, TopBat, trugearhead81, twigkid, Tyler Stokes, Tyler Warburg, Uglymud, Undead Gunsliger, Valek Azogoth, Vash, VeritableCalamity, Vitus Mägele, Walter Manning, Wellaleb, Wherecrab, WhiteBoy35, Will, William Arnold, William Christian, william hambleton, William Martin, Winston Smith, WolfKnight22, Wraithman147, Xcerpt, XD3TH, Yannick North, YourAverageNutcase, Zach Stone, Zach Taylor, Zertreix ~ADM, ZodiacalLight, zombiegamer 101

SOVEREIGN VERSE NOVELS:

Viktor E. Krabin NOVELS:
Turncoat's Truth

Arand/Darren NOVELS(In Suggested Reading Order):

The Selfless Hero Trilogy(Arand):
Otherlife Dreams
Otherlife Nightmares
Otherlife Awakenings
Omnibus Edition(All Three)

Dungeon Deposed Trilogy(Arand):
Dungeon Deposed
Dungeon Deposed 2
Dungeon Deposed 3
Omnibus Edition(All Three)

Fostering Faust Trilogy(Darren):
Fostering Faust
Fostering Faust 2
Fostering Faust 3
Omnibus Edition(All Three)

Super Sales on Super Heroes Trilogy(Arand):
Super Sales on Super Heroes 1
Super Sales on Super Heroes 2
Super Sales on Super Heroes 3
Omnibus Edition(All Three)

Wild Wastes Trilogy(Darren):

Wild Wastes ✓
Wild Wastes: Eastern Expansion ✓
Wild Wastes: Southern Storm ✓
Omnibus Edition(All Three) ✓

Remnant Trilogy(Darren):
Remnant ✓
Remnant 2 ✓
Remnant 3 ✓
Omnibus Edition(All Three)

Monster's Mercy Trilogy(Arand):
Monster's Mercy 1 ✓
Monster's Mercy 2 ✓
Monster's Mercy 3
Omnibus Edition(All Three)

Incubus Inc. Trilogy(Darren):
Incubus Inc
Incubus Inc 2
Incubus Inc 3
Omnibus Edition(All Three)

Swing Shift Trilogy(Arand):
Swing Shift
Swing Shift 2
Swing Shift 3
Omnibus Edition(All Three)

Right of Retribution Trilogy(Arand):
Right of Retribution
Right of Retribution 2
Right of Retribution 3
Omnibus Edition(All Three)

Super Sales on Super Heroes second

Trilogy(Arand):
Super Sales on Super Heroes 4
Super Sales on Super Heroes 5

Wild Wastes second Trilogy(Darren):
Wild Wastes 4
Wild Wastes 5

Save State Hero Trilogy(Arand):
Save State Hero 1

System Overclocked Trilogy(Darren):
System Overclocked 1

Veil Verse Novels:
Cultivating Chaos(Arand):
Cultivating Chaos ✓
Cultivating Chaos 2 ✓
Cultivating Chaos 3
Cultivating Chaos 4

Chapter 1

Jeremiah Carcano grimaced as he shoved the dismembered arm into a large black garbage bag. He shook the appendage to the bottom before twisting the plastic around and tying a knot in the bag itself.

He cast the remains onto a large pile of other assorted bits and pieces, stacked in the living room of the upscale two-story house.

Sighing loudly, he stepped over to the box of additional bags and retrieved two more.

Jeremiah stooped and picked up a large number of assorted entrails - from which of his targets it had originated, he wasn't sure. However, it had managed to escape cleaning so far, and he stuffed it into one of the sacks. He also grabbed the severed head of the monster-fucker herself.

He stared into the dead woman's lifeless eyes with a scowl. It always made his stomach a bit queasy when he was forced to eradicate the victims of the scourge.

And that's what this woman was, a victim.

He took a brief second, rolling his tongue around in his mouth as he stared into a photo proudly displayed on the coffee table. The woman clutched the arm of a dark-haired man, smiling brightly. Her lacy, white dress, immaculately coiffed hair, and vibrant red lipstick, contrasted wildly with the severed head he held in his hand.

"How'd you let it get this far, lady?" Jeremiah shook his head, dropping the last of her into the bag before twisting and tossing it. He made a mental note to say a prayer for her immortal soul later, in the hopes that maybe, just maybe, she could be redeemed.

To the monsters, humans were and always would be one thing above all else: Food.

He glanced down to the horrendously mutated abomination that had maliciously conned the woman into believing he was capable of love, of common decency.

It was vaguely human-looking, even now in this hideous state, somewhere between two extremes of natural.

The Were-Hyena had been in the process of transformation as soon as Jeremiah had breached the house, entering under the rather ironic guise of a pest exterminator. The woman had so kindly opened the door and invited him in after he informed her of a nearby outbreak of rodents, and that he would like to check her house for any contamination.

Perhaps that was it then, naivety. At least she hadn't had to suffer, as the silver spike had pierced her brain stem before she'd realized that she was under attack.

"And you…" he growled darkly down to the very-dead Were beside him, kneeling to remove an oversized, exaggeratedly long arm. He placed the serrated blade of the medical saw against the upper bicep of the beast and began to draw back and forth. "Because of you, a perfectly good soul is sent to the One and All, stained and unclean."

Jeremiah shook his head slowly from side to side, frowning grimly as the limb came free. To think that even two years ago, he'd had no idea of the darkness that lurked on the edges of society, no idea of the massive, looming axe pointed down at humanity's neck.

Everything was true, apparently, all the legends his mother had told him of as a small child.

He'd been taken advantage of in much the same way as this young lady. The disgusting creatures many times wore the face of humans, much as the alluring Vampire that had so easily swayed his youthful eyes.

Of course a twenty-one-year-old at a bar would be enraptured by a woman so far out of his league paying him even the smallest hint of attention.

God he was a fool then.

Much as this naive young woman had fallen for the bog-standard tall, dark, and handsome shtick, so too had he been drawn back to the tall, pale redhead's lair on the promise of company. Then, of course, he'd been imprisoned, drained to his limit repeatedly, and rarely saw the light of day until someone had come to his aid.

Jeremiah let his mind wander as he finished his stomach-churning task, bagging up the remains and folding the plastic sheet up into a tight bundle before it, too, went into a bag.

After a quick scrub on the two remaining patches of blood to finish getting the floor clean, done easily with a light dose of bleach, he went and stood by the door.

He inspected his handiwork. As far as he could tell, everything looked alright.

Do it right, or do it twice.

He let the mantra circle about in his thoughts as he slowly paced from one end of the home to the other.

After a full circuit, he felt satisfied.

With a nod of his head, he grabbed the first of many bags and hefted it to his shoulder before opening the front door.

The day was bright and sunny, like it seemed to always be in Larimer around this time of year.

Jeremiah frowned and blinked up at the sun before glancing down to his blue coveralls. The name on the right breast of the shirt matched the company logo on the van parked outside.

He crossed the manicured green lawn and opened the back door of the otherwise nondescript white van to toss in the bag. It hit the large, open deck with a thump.

He closed the door before returning to the house, rinsing, and repeating. Trip after trip went the same way, with Jeremiah always being on guard for anyone who might be watching.

By the time he'd finished, his face was flushed, and a good deal of sweat was winding its way from his brow.

With the final bag in hand, he tossed it in.

Letting out a heavy sigh, he closed the rear door and pulled a flip-phone from his pocket as he walked around to the driver's-side door.

Selecting the only contact in the phone, he hit the dial button.

He pressed it to his ear when he heard the line dial up, clicking audibly after only two rings. There was no voice on the other end of the line, no cheerful greeting, though someone was certainly there.

"Gawain. One, two, three, two," he stated bluntly into the line, letting the silent receiver know that he was alive and uninjured, two targets had been exterminated, the mission was completed successfully, along with the fact that he was uncompromised and requesting further orders.

"Leodegrance receives. Six, two," the garbled

voice on the other end acknowledged, giving him instructions on where to drop the van off, along with what to do after before hanging up with an audible click. Nodding thoughtfully to himself, Jeremiah snapped the phone in half at the hinge, removed the battery, and stuck the phone's remains in the center console - the cleaning crew would take care of it.

He put the van in drive and exited the cul-de-sac without another thought.
Two hours later and he was deep in the downtown area, pulling into a nondescript alley behind a butcher's shop.
Once he had it in park, he pulled the keys from the engine and stuffed them under the seat.
Pushing the door open, he quickly exited the van.
Standing there with the door open and partially shielding himself, he quickly pulled off the blue coveralls. He tossed them into the passenger side seat and practically leapt into the pair of jeans that'd been stowed in the door's storage shelf.
Which normally would have had a bottle of piss or trash, considering what he normally used that space for in other vehicles.
Now comfortably dressed in jeans and a t-shirt, he felt better already.
Jeremiah consciously ran his hands around his waist, checking that each item was where it was supposed to be on the inside of his waistband.
Satisfied that the pistol, dagger, and silver spike were tucked securely into his heavy-duty belt, he angled the mirror around till he could inspect his face quickly.
Other than his brown hair looking a bit wild

due to sweat, nothing stood out to him.

He hastily arranged several of the short locks into a less wild look, before running his fingers along his stubble.

I really should shave when I get back.

He planned out his evening activities as he stood up and walked away.

Exiting the alley, he stepped into the throng of people pushing down the street in an orderless mass of bodies that somehow managed to pour around each other without incident.

Jeremiah stared intently into the eyes of each person he passed, looking for any signs of... other.

Then realized what he was doing and stopped. Right now he didn't want to be noted as being in this area.

Someone staring you down would be noteworthy.

Two blocks down, he turned into a parking garage and looked around for a car he was certain should be here.

It was late in the afternoon, and the orange sun spilled down over the western mountains to beat back the shadows on the third story of the structure.

A truck sputtering to life nearby drew Jeremiah's eyes, and he cocked his head thoughtfully, watching the massive, ancient, square-bodied yellow truck back out of its ill-fitting space.

Jeremiah stepped to the side to let the vehicle pass before it slowed to a halt beside him.

"How much for a quick trip around the block, baby?" a gruff voice propositioned from inside while the tinted window rolled slowly down. Jeremiah rolled his eyes, fighting back a grin. "Aww shit, anyone tell you you're the ugliest hooker they've ever seen?"

"Eddie, where the hell did you get this hunk'a junk?" Jeremiah called back staring with furrowed brows at the utterly outdated pickup truck. In truth, it wasn't actually a hunk of junk, given its near-forty years of existence. It lacked the usual smattering of rust, dents, and other cosmetic damage you'd find on a vehicle of this particular age.

In his mind, he had a momentary pang of concern.

The vehicle actually stood out for the lack of wear.

"She's not a hunk of junk!" Eddie argued, folding his arms across his chest as Jeremiah stepped around the front of the truck to the passenger side door. Jeremiah pulled on the door handle fruitlessly before he looked annoyedly at Eddie. Eddie shot him a teasing smile with a waggle of his brow and slapping the dash. "Say you're sorry and that she's a very nice truck."

Jeremiah closed his eyes and inhaled deeply, a snarky reply dying on his lips. Instead, he said: "And what did you name her? I swear to god if you say some cheesy shit like Be-"

"No! I didn't name her Bessie, what kind of generic, basic-ass bitch do you think I am?" Eddie quipped back at him with a clearly fake mortified expression. Jeremiah raised his brows, waiting for the inevitable culmination of whatever bit his friend was playing at.

Probably named it something equally as stupid... like Elizabeth, or Zippy, or...

"I named her Betsy!"

Jeremiah couldn't hold in the snort of laughter that escaped his nose. He chuckled softly to himself, leaning over to the hood of the truck, and giving it several overexaggerated pats.

"I'm sorry, Betsy," he apologized, looking pointedly at Eddie, who stared expectantly back at him.

Eddie didn't unlock the door.

Jeremiah closed his eyes and clucked his tongue before asking, "Really, Eddie?"

"Really, Jerry," Eddie replied firmly but humorously.

"You're a... very nice truck, Betsy," Jeremiah added with a put-upon frown. Apparently, this was good enough for Eddie, since he leaned over and opened the side door of the truck with a broad, playful grin.

"Thanks," Jeremiah said sarcastically, climbing into the cab. "You could've just unlocked it from the start, ya' know? Could've saved the bullshit for when we get back."

"Eh, lock's busted," Eddie shrugged, putting the truck in drive. "Can't be opened from the outside. Old trucks, ya' know?"

"I swear to fuck, Eddie, please tell me you didn't trade your car for this!" Jeremiah lamented with a shake of his head.

"What? Oh no, this actually came from up top, something to do with future work," Eddie shrugged absently, turning down to the next floor of the garage. "Not supposed to touch the radio at all. Technically we're not supposed to even be driving it yet, just keeping it on ice until we get more orders but-"

Eddie clucked his tongue and bobbed his head from side to side, taking them around another turn in the garage.

"I wanted to see how she did, and boy does she purr!" Eddie revved the engine slightly with a malicious gleam in his eye.

"You're an idiot, dude," Jeremiah grunted as they pulled to the bottom of the parking garage. Eddie flicked the blinker, and they waited for traffic to clear enough to turn onto the road. "Up top's gonna skullfuck you if you get even a single scratch on her."

"Eh, might be into that, ya' know?" Eddie remarked, pulling into a gap in the traffic. "Oh, by the way, I brought your shit."

"Oh?" Jeremiah asked while Eddie shoved his arm into the small gap behind his seat and pulled out a small tan backpack. "Sweet! Thanks."

"Any time, bud," Eddie replied with a warm smile as he guided them through the sea of vehicles towards the highway. "Figured you'd want to play'n listen to something while we drive."

"You just wanna listen to my mixtape, don't'cha?" Jeremiah watched him with a squinting smirk. "Since you're not supposed to touch the radio after all."

"Always enjoyed a drive with some tunes," Eddie agreed, changing lanes. Jeremiah unzipped the front pouch of the pack, withdrawing his cell phone, iPod, and a nine-millimeter pistol in a plastic holster, before placing the backpack between his legs. He pushed the gun a bit deeper and then went to grab the media player. "Before you turn that on, boss man says we've got work coming up. He ain't told me much, but it's not gonna be the usual pest extermination."

Jeremiah froze, contemplating that.

"Something big's coming down the pipe,"

Eddie continued, turning and staring knowingly over the console at Jeremiah. "He doesn't just throw around the words 'Priority One' over nothing. So... don't get caught up in anything you can't dip out of over the next couple days."

"Understood. Any ideas?" Jeremiah acknowledged with concern twisting his expression. Priority One was usually only reserved for the kinds of things no one wanted to think about. Things that could change the organization to its core. The kind of operation that could make or break a hunter and solidify their reputation forever forward.

Jeremiah wanted that kind of recognition, even if it would extend no further than the members of the nearby detachments.

"Not a clue," Eddie replied blankly, shaking his head as he merged onto the highway. "Apparently the underground cats are talking about big changes going on in the monster world - a lot of Vamps, Weres and sympathizers have been talking up a storm lately."

"That sounds... bad," Jeremiah noted, turning to look out the window.

"That's because it is," Eddie said with a dark chuckle, before smacking the back of his hand against Jeremiah's knee. "Good thing that all you've gotta do is stick by my side when I need it."

"Like a ball and chain, brother..." Jeremiah nodded slowly, watching the cars pass by in the midday traffic. "Speakin' of ball and chain, how's Sarah doing?"

"Eh, she's doing alright," Eddie grunted, briefly looking over to him with raised brows before he turned back to the road ahead. "Pregnancy's hitting her kind of hard though. Had to call in from work a couple of times last week, just from the morning sickness wrecking her shit like a freight train. We've got an empty trash can on-call at all times by her side of the bed now."

"Fuck, sucks to be her," Jeremiah looked back to Eddie with a teasing grin. "Knew I shoulda' told her to run as far as possible when you two hooked up."

"Oh fuck you! I'm being a good husband!" Eddie shot back while they changed lanes. "I even empty the bucket for her!"

"Oh yeah. Real good for her. Doing the bare minimum," Jeremiah laughed with a shit-eating grin.

"Asshole! This is why you're always single, Jerry!" Eddie chortled back before adding with a feral smile. "Can't handle the responsibility of caring for someone else!"

"Have you met me?" Jeremiah quipped back, folding his arms across his chest. "I'm a handful to take care of on my own, I've got enough on my plate without adding a woman to the mix. Besides, I don't think there's a woman out there who could handle this kind of life."

"Keep telling yourself that, bud," Eddie remarked, turning off the highway. "You just wait, there'll be some blind chick with no hands here in a couple of years that'll fall head over heels for your dumb, ugly ass."

"Okay... I get the blind part," Jeremiah said, staring confusedly at Eddie. "But what's with the no hands?"

"No way for her to get a conclusive measurement until it's too la-"

"Fuck off," Jeremiah rolled his head back with an exasperated smile as they turned into a residential street. He leaned down beneath and between his legs, pulling the backpack up to his lap expectantly. As Eddie slowed to a stop outside his apartment building, Jeremiah held his fist out to his friend expectantly.

"Take it easy, bud, stay by the phone for a bit, 'kay?" Eddie instructed with a smirk and gave him the expected fist bump.

"Yeah yeah, I know," Jeremiah rolled his eyes. "Just make sure you give me enough notice to do my hair - want my mugshot to look nice."

"Will do," Eddie nodded once before Jeremiah opened the door of the truck and dropped out with a soft pat. He slammed the door behind him with some force, before throwing the bag over his shoulder and stepping onto the sidewalk.

Jeremiah turned over his shoulder and watched the truck roll away down the street with faint rumble.

Damn thing really does purr...

He turned and headed for the apartment building, giving his car a quick look over as he passed by. Internally, Jeremiah debated making a run to the store for groceries, but decided against it - he still had leftovers, and those would do until tomorrow, or whenever he could get to the store next. He climbed the three flights of exterior stairs two at a time, and made it to his off-white painted door.

Reaching into the side pocket of his bag, Jeremiah pulled out his keys, found the right one, and inserted it into the lock.

Pushing the door fractionally inward, he hesitated.

With long honed practice, he deftly reached his arm up and disconnected a hair-thin strand of fishing line connected to a small hook at the top left corner of the door, before he pushed it all the way in.

Monsters were, by their very nature, sneaky and nocturnal. The flashbang grenade that was screwed onto two metal straps to the wall beside the door might be overkill for some, but Jeremiah didn't want to worry.

If something entered his home at night, he would know.

As well as most of the building.

It was a risk, considering some of the items he kept in his apartment, but finding a dead monster would already be a dead giveaway.

"Ha. Dead... giveaway. Besides, knowing is half the battle," he mocked, stepping fully into his apartment, throwing the door closed behind him. He set his bag down beside the bar before turning and resetting 'the Doorbell', as he called it. Meandering over to the fridge, he opened it and stared at its meager contents.

Chef's specials are...yesterday's spaghetti, a sandwich from three days ago, and...what the fuck is that?

He leaned forward to grab the tub of what he desperately wanted to believe was a salad.

"God, how long have you been back there?" He grimaced at the moldy, discolored Tupperware before throwing it in the nearby trash can. His appetite sufficiently killed by the disgusting sight, he kicked the fridge closed as he left the kitchen.

He decided to work up an appetite before trying again later, and stepped into his living room.

With a shove, he moved the coffee table out of the way, turned the tv to the local news channel, and got into a workout then and there.

Forty-five minutes later, Jeremiah stepped out of the shower, enjoying the pleasant ache of his muscles as he went to his bedroom.

He grabbed what he believed was a clean sleeveless shirt from the end of the bed, a pair of basketball shorts, and an AK-pattern rifle from beside the bed frame. After swinging the last over his shoulder, he set about making dinner. In reality, he was just reheating spaghetti from the night before in Tupperware that may or may not have been microwave safe, but dinner was dinner.

Food in hand, Jeremiah sat down on the couch, only half paying attention to the television.

Between eating his meal and aimlessly fidgeting with the rifle, he didn't hear anything form the tv at all.

Finishing his meal, he dumped the Tupperware to the side of the couch and sat there. Staring at his gun.

Blinking several times, he sniffled once and then rubbed at an eye. He didn't feel tired, but his eyes felt heavy.

Heavy and a bit raw.

Rubbing at them now with both hands, and more than he probably should, he instead closed them.

Only to open them again and find the morning sun greeting him. Spilling bright golden rays through his blinds.

It genuinely caught him off-guard.

My sleep schedule is fucked. Been happening more than I'd like to admit.

His phone rang loudly from where it lay beside his thigh, and Jeremiah rubbed the eye grit out of the corners of his eyes quickly.

"That's..."

He grimaced, not sure if he had managed to help or hinder his vision with that.

Several quick blinks later and shaking his head, he looked down to his phone.

He rolled his eyes as he saw the number.

"Wassup, fucker," he grunted into the receiver after accepting the call. "It's too early for your shi-"

"No time for shit," Eddie interrupted firmly. "How quickly can you be at the station?"

"The Station?" Jeremiah asked, pushing himself out of the couch cushion and onto his feet, which felt slightly unsteady as he worked at waking up. He set the rifle to the side across the arm of the couch. "Uh, give me an hour, do I need to bring anything?"

"Be here in half that, and just the usual," Eddie instructed before pausing and adding: "Bring your A-game."

"It's all my A-game," Jeremiah replied before Eddie grunted and hung up the line. Pulling the phone away from his ear, Jeremiah stared at it for a moment before shrugging. Quickly, he changed into a pair of jeans, a black t-shirt, and an oversized flannel jacket.

There wasn't much for him to grab - just his pistol, his backpack, and a pack of chewing gum from the counter once he decided he didn't have time to brush his teeth this morning.

As Jeremiah exited his apartment, he reset the doorbell, closed the door, and headed down the stairs to his car, hell-bent on making it halfway across town in less than twenty minutes... somehow.

Chapter 2

Jeremiah jerked the wheel to the side and sped past an old woman in a sedan. He turned to his right as he passed her and received a scowl and the middle finger from the old bat as she blurred by.

Despite the tense situation he was in - trying to make a drive that should take a little over thirty minutes in less than that - he still smirked at the grumpy woman.

He'd done it before, at the dead of night, when no one was on the roads. However, morning traffic in Larimer, even on the weekend, was oppressive and left little opportunity for long drags at breakneck speed.

Unless someone was very lucky, very stupid, or a very good driver.

Jeremiah was not a very good driver, which left one of the other two options. Given the number of honked horns and flung fingers at him as he passed, he reasoned it was a combination of the two.

Oh well.

He had places to be, and if breaking a few traffic laws was the greatest of his problems today, then he was in for a good day.

When he pulled into the lot of the 'Station' - a small, dilapidated warehouse in an industrial district of the city - he checked the timer on his phone. A grand total of thirty-two minutes from the moment he'd sat in his driver's seat was displayed on the small screen, and Jeremiah grinned.

Was it within the thirty minutes prescribed by Eddie? No.

Was it far better than he honestly expected, given Saturday morning traffic? Ab-so-lutely.

Jeremiah snatched up his phone and opened the door of the car, idly slinging his backpack over his shoulder as he approached the lackluster building.

A reinforced metal door swung open before him. Holding it open was none other than Eddie.

"Right on time," the man grinned at him and pushed a wayward lock of brown hair up under his dark grey watch cap. "C'mon in, they brought some real heavy hitters for whatever the fuck this is."

"They haven't told you?" Jeremiah asked suspiciously as he stepped through the threshold.

"Nah, been real skeevy about it too- oh- 'fore I forget-" Eddie pointed at a small tray beside the door labeled 'PHONES', the one word written in big bold letters and all in caps on a large sheet of paper taped to it. "No electronics for this one. Power off and drop 'em in."

Jeremiah reached into his pocket, powered down his phone, and idly tossed it into the pile of nearly two dozen similar devices. He squinted at the pile and turned back to Eddie.

"That's a lot of phones, bro," Jeremiah pointed at the bin with a thumb before Eddie gestured for him to follow. "We got friends today?"

"Oh yeah, apparently-" Eddie pulled open another large steel door, briefly bracing it with his foot to let Jeremiah follow. Jeremiah grabbed the door with one hand, following his friend through. "HF bigshots thought this one deserved not two, but three individual teams, and you just wait until you see the big surprise!"

"Or, and hear me out," Jeremiah replied sarcastically, trying to match Eddie's brisk pace through the dimly lit unfinished hallway. "You could just, oh I don't know, tell me what the fuck is going on before I walk int-"

He abruptly cut off as Eddie threw open the door to the main, open space of the warehouse.

Normally, at most, there would be six or less people here. Instead, there were at least thirty men and women in varying levels of combat gear standing, sitting on folding chairs, or generally milling about the open space. Some wore masks, and others didn't - or at least they had them resting around their necks and atop their heads.

Looking back now, Jeremiah realized that the watch cap Eddie wore was actually a rolled-up balaclava. He snapped his mouth shut and gazed out into the large room full of enough people to make his skin itch uncomfortably.

The more people you brought into something, the more points of failure there were.

And this looked like a lot of points of failure.

"What the hell is going on?" Jeremiah muttered under his breath as he surveyed the small crowd.

"Not totally sure, but my guess is a large operation of some kind - well above the usual single targets we go after," Eddie shrugged and pointed towards a large whiteboard beside a black van parked in the middle of the concrete floor. "Take a look at who came down from their castle on high to join us today."

Jeremiah followed his finger towards six people in incredibly heavy tactical gear. Atop their plate carriers, riot pads on their arms, legs, and pelvic area, were affixed small wax seals connected to dangling strips of fabric.

Jeremiah cocked his head to the side as he stared at the purity seals with a frown.

"The Council brought Templars into this?" Jeremiah questioned, flicking a glance to Eddie before he went back to staring at the formidable individuals. At their waists, each had a glimmering sword belted.

Knowing Templars and their gear training, they were probably as, if not more, capable with them than the rifles they carried.

"Fuck yeah they did," Eddie replied with a grin. Surreptitiously, he pointed at one of the holy warriors with his finger. "I chatted up that one for a bit, hoping to get her number for ya', right?"

"Oh yeah, it was totally about getting it for me-" Jeremiah shot back before Eddie interrupted him.

"Either way, it didn't work - she's all business. Like flirting with a brick fuckin' wall. I think we're just waiting on a co-"

"Enough of this!" one of the Templars shouted with a shake of his head and a thick Italian accent. "I am tired of awaiting profligates who laze about when summoned. I will deliver my briefing here and now - and when they bother to show up, they may receive it secondhand."

The tall, muscular man waved his hand above his head in a circular motion before stepping in front of the whiteboard with an impatient frown.

The small throng of people milling about the chamber rapidly organized themselves into small groups around the whiteboard.

Eddie slapped Jeremiah on the shoulder and led him over to their team.

"Good morning to those of you who bothered to show up," the middle-aged man in a bad mood began, looking to each group, one after the other. "I will not learn your names, however you may address me as Brother Claudius.

"We have been gifted a most glorious mission today, one that befits Gladioso's such as yourselves. I am honored to have been placed in command of this operation," effused Brother Claudius with a proud smile. He extended his palms wide to either side, as if basking in nonexistent praise. "We have located a den of mongrels that not only exist in spite of all that is pure - but also deign to commit heresy, to desecrate holy ground with foul vandalism.

"Even now the beasts consume the flesh of innocents, and further spread their foul disease to innocent souls!" Brother Claudius preached at the organized fighters. Jeremiah raised an eyebrow at the self-important tone of the man, contrasting it with the legends and tales he'd been told of Templars in the past.

Supposedly, Templars were ordained specifically to fight monsters. It was their sole purpose in life.

Usually they equipped themselves with relics, holy items, and utilized holy powers to make themselves a cut above the average human.

This was on top of the years and years of training they went through on the One and All's dime.

Jeremiah was... less than impressed with Brother Claudius and his continuing diatribe which seemed to go nowhere, even after five minutes of proselytizing the importance of their mission, of faith.

Preaching to the choir bud...just tell us what we're doing.

You're going in more circles than Eddie on a

damn hiking trip.

Unable to help himself, Jeremiah shook his head with a frown, crossing his arms across his chest.

"-Sister Elanor, if you would please deliver their instructions," Brother Claudius finally finished his speech, gesturing to a tall, lithe woman nearby - the one that Eddie had apparently attempted to flirt with.

"Thank you, 'Brother'," she tacked on the title with a noticeable edge of frustration. She stepped up to the whiteboard with a nod of her head.

Pulling up one of the magnets on the board, she set it atop a laminated sheet of paper with a clack. Doing so several more times, she'd quickly put down nine in a square.

Still not yet speaking, she grabbed a dry-erase marker off the bottom of the board and quickly began to sketch in lines.

"Just after midnight tonight, we will be stepping off to engage a Were-Coyote nest located in the eastern district of town," Sister Elanor began, stepping back and gesturing to the whiteboard, which was clearly a satellite image of an industrial building.

Small, narrow lines were drawn in across the surface of the whiteboard at the edges of the papers. Jeremiah assumed they were roads, paths, or lines of attack.

Additionally, she'd put down several notes in pen on the laminated sheets, though he wasn't close enough to read them.

Several large rectangles were also drawn onto the impromptu map, clearly denoting other nearby buildings. Sister Elanor began to draw several smaller dashed lines in sequential circles around the central objective.

"The lot of you will be establishing an inner and outer cordon, while we - okay," Elanor sighed loudly as she frowned pointedly at the three groups around her. "Who here knows what a cordon is?"

Somewhere around half of the members raised their hands, and of those, Jeremiah saw several nervous looks around the room.

Jeremiah barely held back a sigh.

He knew that Humanity First as a whole tended to recruit some... less-than-capable individuals, purely because their heart was in the right place.

Not every team leader had as high standards as Patrick, who currently stood slightly to the right of and in front of Jeremiah and Eddie.

Patrick briefly turned back to the two of them with a smug expression, as if communicating to them with eye contact alone that he had told them so.

Patrick was a combat veteran and had lost his wife to a Were attack several years before Jeremiah had his experience with the Vampire coven.

He was also the one to recruit Jeremiah after the incident, and the one to teach him the ropes of hunting as a whole.

Jeremiah, along with the rest of his six-member team, all had their hands raised.

Elanor let out a disgruntled sigh that caught when she laid eyes on Jeremiah's team. She hesitated briefly, as if to mentally check something off in her thoughts, then moved on to the rest of the group.

"To put it shortly, and with deliberate simplicity, it's just area of control. The inner circle, or cordon, looks inward for security. Outer cordon looks outward for security.

"Anything more is frivolity and a waste of words," grumped Elanor, turning back to the whiteboard.

Wincing, Jeremiah found the description indeed short, to the point of being dismissive. Though he did see those who hadn't understood, nod their heads in understanding.

Well, I mean...there's that dumb saying, right?

If I had more time, I would have written a shorter letter.

It takes more effort to explain a complex thing in a few words.

Jeremiah unfortunately quickly became lost in his thoughts. Mindlessly staring at the whiteboard and not hearing a damn thing.

"You in love or something, Jerry?" hissed Eddie, catching his attention suddenly.

He was quite literally staring at Elanor right now, without blinking.

"Like a dog on point," continued Eddie with a chortle.

"-At twelve-thirty tonight, we embark. You are dismissed. Go get geared up and attempt to rest. Team leaders, stay around for a few minutes," Sister Elanor finished her briefing by gesturing at a small vestibule inside the warehouse. "Given that we wish for you all to be as equipped for this operation as possible, we have opened our arsenal for your use - utilize what you see fit at your own discretion."

Despite feeling somewhat nervous that he'd genuinely missed most of the plan, he was at least excited about the possibility of getting more equipment.

As detachments went, Jeremiah's was decently well-equipped. But Templars were a different story entirely.

Wonder if they have a belt-fed in there?

Jeremiah's mind was churning up possibilities while he remained mostly in place. He would wait until his team was given somewhat... clearer instructions from Patrick before he went in and geared up.

Meanwhile, the other two detachments flocked and practically clambered over each other to try and get inside the small room that his team usually used for planning operations, and he watched it happen.

A frown slowly creased his mouth as he considered the situation.

Something was off. Internally, he considered the possibility that, as under-funded and under-equipped as they were, perhaps they were among the best of the organization as a whole.

"Not gonna try and squeeze yourself in?" Eddie asked, stepping up beside him and crossing his arms as he watched with ill-disguised concern. The small press of bodies finally managed to pile into the room, and the automatic door closed behind them with a small click.

"Fuck that," Jeremiah snorted, shaking his head. "I mean hell, can you imagine squeezing into your kit with everyone packed in that tightly together? I'm betting that there's gonna be... three black eyes when they come back out."

"Black eyes from what?" Eddie chuckled back, turning slightly to stare at Jeremiah with a nervous smile.

"Elbows from people forgetting wingspan is a thing. Putting on a plate carrier's gonna suck with that many people," he mimed shimmying into something, and made a small clicking noise as he gently touched his elbow against Eddie's temple. The other man shook his head slowly and rolled his eyes before sighing loudly.

"Man, I hope we get the outer cordon. It'd be nice to just run minimal, maybe an SMG at most."

Jeremiah watched his friend with a squint and a frown. He didn't want to be part of the outer cordon, he wanted to be part of the inner, or better yet, attach himself to the assault team.

He was here to kill monsters, after all.

To spend his Sunday night just staring down some boring street, watching for a car to come too close, or at best, waiting for some criminal reinforcements to try and help the den, would be mind-numbing.

There was a moment where the quiet part of his mind worried over that desire.

Then it was gone as quickly as it came, without Jeremiah even noticing it.

"Fuckin why?" Jeremiah asked while Eddie reached into his pocket and pulled out a pack of gum. Eddie shrugged, taking a stick out and offering it to him.

"Worried about Sarah, or maybe I'm just lazy and want an easy night's work," Eddie shrugged as Jeremiah accepted a stick and popped it into his mouth. "I'unno."

Something dark crossed behind Eddie's eyes, a brief flicker of hard-to-discern emotion. He pocketed the pack of gum and threw his stick into his mouth after shaking his head.

"Might be time for me to make my way outta here, at least in the everyday shit," he mused. "It's not like the benefits are awe inspiring."

"Eddie what the fuck ar-" Jeremiah cut off abruptly. Two very unhappy-looking team leads stormed across their field of view and into the small office space.

"Alright, on me guys!" Patrick called from behind them.

"We're talking about this later," Jeremiah pointed a finger at Eddie, who smiled with an otherwise unreadable expression. As they turned and rejoined their group, they made it just in time for Patrick to stop in front of the half-circle of monster hunters.

"Alright, so," Patrick started, clapping his hands once before rubbing them together excitedly. "Good news is we've been given the inner cordon. Any of you who've gotten tired of dressing up as a janitor or some shit to get jobs done, well, it's your lucky day.

"The other two detachments have been given the outer cordon, along with transportation, and that's why you saw them lookin' all mopey," Patrick added with a quiet chuckle and a small gleam in his eye. "Had to put all the shiny toys back so they could blend in."

The small team chuckled before Lily raised her hand with a smile. Patrick noticed her and pointed a finger with an expectant gaze.

"Does that mean we get to play tactical dress-up?" the older woman questioned, brushing a lock of chestnut hair out of her eye before folding her arms under her chest.

Patrick's jaw flexed and he nodded his head with a broad feral smile.

"Ab-so-lutely," Patrick nodded, his smile somehow getting deeper. "Three teams of two, and one team of one."

Ol' Patty always did love his lone wolf shit...

Jeremiah chuckled at that answer.

"Alright everyone, get geared up and pair off. We'll all be stepping out together in about ten hours. Hope you brought a book," Patrick concluded.

Chapter 3

Jeremiah lifted his head up from the buttstock of the rifle resting between his legs. He leaned back in the bench and rested his head against the back of the van instead.

Turning his head slightly to the side, he blinked rapidly as the headlights of the white van behind them momentarily blinded him.

The vehicle behind them held half of his team, including Patrick and Eddie, along with the second team of three Templars. His van currently held Lily and Carl - along with a Templar escort of their own.

"Two minutes!" their driver said over his shoulder, bringing everyone's eyes to the front of the vehicle.

The driver did a visual check of the other denizens of the cab while Lily and Carl pulled their balaclavas down over their faces.

The Templars supplied his group with some serious hardware - night vision monoculars, body armor, and short rifles decked out with expensive and high-quality attachments. In addition, he was sure that the rounds loaded in their magazines weren't the run of the mill, either.

He firmly believed that the government had their own, specialized anti-monster bullets - but good luck getting your hands on them as a normal civilian. Jeremiah looked down to his rifle and ejected the magazine before inspecting the rounds. Instead of the normal copper jacket that was part and parcel to firearms, the projectiles were a crystalline lattice, interwoven with flecks of something he couldn't identify.

He slapped the mag back in place, racked the charging handle, and closed the dust cover before double-checking his safety. The others from his cadre followed suit shortly after, the loud staccato noises of weapons being readied permeating the cab.

"At least you know how to handle those..." Sister Elanor's brassy voice broke the extended silence and lack of conversation, as her pale emerald eyes went from his weapon to his face. Her voice had a slight edge to it that he almost missed. Considering she didn't seem like the chatty type, he'd bet on her being nervous.

"You might actually survive if something goes awry," she concluded. A backhanded compliment if ever there was one.

"Eh, Patty keeps us squared away," Jeremiah shrugged before rolling his own balaclava down from under the brim of his helmet. "Spent a solid six months doing weekly range trips with him until he decided I was good enough to touch a job."

"It's good to know that at least someone keeps their team in check. Leodegrance mentioned that your group were their favorite in the area," Elanor sighed and idly smacked the handle of her submachine gun down into place.

Jeremiah flicked down his monocular, turning it on briefly to test if it worked before moving it back up. He didn't reply to Elanor's statement at first.

Instead, he merely watched her with a neutral expression while figuring out what to say. She rolled her head to the side and adjusted her hair under her helmet and met his eyes again.

"Not gonna wear a mask?" Jeremiah asked in lieu of responding to her, finally allowing the question that had been cooking in his mind for the entire way over to spout forth.

Elanor smirked at him before touching a small totem on the collar of her armor. In an instant, her face became a mottled, nonexistent mass of skin-colored nothing.

She touched the totem again and her face returned to existence with the same self-assured, haughty grin she'd had before. Jeremiah sighed loudly and shook his head with a smile that was mostly disguised by the mask he wore.

"Why am I not surprised?" he asked, as the van made a hard left turn.

"Because you wis-" Sister Elanor stopped abruptly as their radio crackled to life.

"Brothers and Sisters," Brother Claudius' voice rang in his ears through the headset. "Today we go forth to purge filth from our beautiful world. The One and All has demanded their heads as payment for their misdeeds - their abominable existence. May our blades strike true, and our bullets find new homes within their flesh."

Jeremiah snorted and lifted the headphones up to the sides of his helmet, making eye contact with Elanor as she subtly clicked her radio off.

Apparently, she feels the same way about blowhard Claudius.

He smirked and looked to the front of the van, just in time for the driver to tilt his head toward the back of the van while staring ahead.

"Thirty seconds!" the man shouted before Jeremiah looked back to Elanor, who no longer had a face.

Guess that's the end of the conversation... though it didn't feel like one to begin with.

The van began to slow down. With a steady squeal of the brakes, the vehicle came to a stop, and Jeremiah threw the back door open. He was greeted with the still night air, broken only by the soft puttering of the exhaust of the van.

As his boots hit the ground, he caught a glimpse of the members of the other vehicle disembarking as well, the remainder of his team all jogging to get to their overwatch positions.

He paused for a moment to survey his surroundings, glancing over the rooflines of the nearby run-down industrial buildings in particular.

Mostly because that's where he'd be if he was waiting to ambush someone.

They were stopped two blocks south of the objective, a last-minute change from their original plan.

The outer cordon, who had arrived and set up twenty minutes earlier, had called in an oversight made in the planning phase. Apparently, the main road they were planning on using to arrive at their destination was closed off from the north.

Thankfully, it was relatively simple to merely redirect and approach from the south, but the whole thing just sent goosebumps up Jeremiah's spine.

"C'mon Jay," Eddie said, slapping him lightly on the shoulder and nodding towards their goal. "Let's get to work."

"Uh... yeah, yeah let's go," Jeremiah stuttered, startled from his nervous scanning. He shook his head once and Eddie passed him before turning to follow the man.

"Something wrong?" Eddie asked, leveling the long rifle he was using down an alley.

"Not that I can think of," Jeremiah licked his

lips as he stared over his sights down the dark pathway ahead. He flicked down the night vision tube and tried to focus down the grainy and green space between buildings. "Something just feels wrong. I would've scrubbed it when the north was a no-go."

"Eh, seems like the Temps have a real hard-on for this den," Eddie shrugged, and stepped into the alley with Jeremiah close behind. "I don't think we've got the whole story, personally."

"What'd ya' mean by that?" Jeremiah asked, rotating at the hip as they passed a dumpster to check the shadows behind it.

"I think these 'yotes gave them a black eye, somehow. You catch that slip in the briefing about 'desecrating holy ground'?" Eddie rolled into a T in the walkway, pointing his rifle down the alley with Jeremiah moving past him, rifle level with the end of the path.

"I did," Jeremiah nodded, lowering his voice slightly as they approached their destination. Eddie walked slightly faster than him, and caught up just behind his left shoulder before Jeremiah continued: "What, you think this is retaliatory for something? Stole a relic, killed a priest or some shit?"

"Maybe. Dunno," Eddie replied noncommittally as they walked ever closer to the den of Weres. "Hey, ladder."

Jeremiah saw the small, gated-off metal structure that went up the side of a building on their right. According to the plan, their position should have been across the street, through the next alley. A small offshoot that would've provided an unobstructed view of the front of the target building.

He mentally compared their current position

with where they were supposed to be. He followed Eddie's train of thought, quietly sucking on his teeth as he considered the possibility of having an elevated position that could still watch the front entrance.

"Dinner with a view?" Jeremiah asked, slowing his steps as Eddie stepped past him. He reached into the man's small backpack and pulled out the pair of bolt-cutters that stuck out the top.

"More like dinner and a show, if the Templars are as badass as the stories say," Eddie replied while Jeremiah stuck the bolt-cutters on the lock. He braced one of the arms against his chest, or more specifically, the armor plate there, and pulled back. After a couple seconds of force, the cheap lock gave way and was severed with a loud popping noise.

"Or half as tough as Claudius thinks he is," Jeremiah muttered, stuffing the cutters into his teammate's pack. Eddie pulled open the gate after flipping the lock off with a small clatter. The hinges of the small, metal door, squeaked loudly when he swung it open and rested the designated marksman rifle in its sling.

Jeremiah waited at the bottom of the ladder, scanning the alley fruitlessly as his friend climbed the ladder. Two soft, metallic pings sounded from above him, and Jeremiah looked up to see Eddie tapping the bottom of his muzzle against the top of the ladder, signaling for him to follow.

Jeremiah lifted one foot and began to climb the ladder. His radio crackled to life.

"IC-one in position."

What were we again? IC-two, right?

"This is Brother Claudius, I understand IC-one," the man replied in his usual self-assured, haughty tone, instantly dampening Jeremiah's mood.

"We use callsigns for a reason, dipshit," Eddie grunted from the top of the ladder while Jeremiah climbed over.

"Never know who's listening," Jeremiah finished the unspoken sentence.

Eddie pivoted smoothly and moved towards the other side of the roof. Both of them hunched low as they approached the short parapet wall at the northeast corner of the building, surveying the dimly lit street below.

"IC-three in position," Jeremiah's radio crackled in his ear.

"Four, in position," Followed a brief second later.

"IC-two, ready," Eddie stated into his headset, bracing his rifle atop the wall.

Jeremiah knelt down beside him, staring at the front of the warehouse with a frown.

Supposedly this was a Were-Coyote den. And yet, no one stood guard.

While he wasn't exactly an expert on Were-Coyotes, or Weres in general, this wasn't what he'd expect from something that required his kind of response.

Things weren't matching up in his head.

"Something's fucked, dude," Jeremiah whispered, peeking at the nearby rooftops. He was suddenly regretting not hearing the whole briefing or asking questions. "Where did the Templars say they got this intel, again?"

"They didn't," Eddie growled, his head lifting above the marksman's rifle scope.

"Very well! We go forth to strike at the heart of this rot!" Brother Claudius said proudly into the line before it clicked off. Jeremiah grimaced, his heart beginning to beat ever faster.

"Fuck this, dude," Jeremiah said in a low growl, resting his rifle on the edge of the building as well. A flash of movement below caught his eye, and he instinctively turned his rifle towards the perceived threat, only to find the team of six Templars sprinting at full tilt towards the front of the building.

The group stopped and filed into an orderly line beside the front door of the compound, before one of them stepped out from the group and placed a small, padlock-shaped object around the door handle.

The figure stepped back to the rear of the group.

Then, the door simply folded itself inward noiselessly. At least, noiselessly until the shockwave of the explosive charge reached them almost half a second later. With the door now gone, the Templars filed quickly into the building.

Jeremiah listened.

And listened some more.

It was silent as a grave.

"Fuck, it's a dry hole, isn't it?" he asked rhetorically, bracing his rifle tighter against the side of the building. "This was a goddamn trap!"

"Hold on, bud," Eddie soothed, pressing the push-to-talk on his radio. "IC-two to assault team, you guys see anything?"

"Foyer is empty, pushing dee-" Elanor's voice cut off abruptly. Almost a second later, a slew of staccato pops and loud booms sounded from the front of the building. "Shit! All teams—"

"*FUCK YOU!*" screamed a voice over the same line. Someone was very close for it to transmit that clearly.

"—break contact! Shit, fuck, die!" finished

Elanor.

"What the fuck?" Jeremiah asked before a Templar was flung out a second-story window of the warehouse. He was followed by a spray of glass and other debris, landing with an inaudible thud on the street below.

"Get down the ladder, Jerry," Eddie pointed towards where they'd come from, as gunfire began to ring out all around them.

"THEY'RE EVERYWHERE!" a voice shouted over the radio, before it cut off with several rapid pops.

A wash of noise followed, the radio either being jammed or the man having just held down the transmit button in a death-grip.

Jeremiah's pulse began to pound in his ears as gunfire began to spring to life sporadically all around him.

He allowed himself a single moment to regret not having trusted his gut.

They were being ambushed.

"Get down the ladder, I'll be right behind you!" Eddie ordered with a harsh growl.

Jeremiah briefly flicked his gaze back to the front of the warehouse. Two Templars sprinted down the street, firing wildly behind them. A third was actively dueling a black-clad woman with a sword.

Jeremiah wisely decided to comply with Eddie's instructions and ran for the ladder. Vaulting up onto the parapet, he turned to see Eddie beginning to jog towards him across the roof. With a nod, more for himself than anyone else, he gripped the rungs of the ladder and began to climb down two rungs at a time.

The sound of gunfire and infrequent

explosions permeated the air now, seeming to emanate from all around them.

    Distant, close, single fire, and fully automatic. Everywhere.

    Who the fuck are we fighting?

    The fed wouldn't come down with this kind of heat, and the goddamn Weres wouldn't be smart enough to plan an ambush like this.

    Jeremiah jumped the final few feet to the ground, stumbling slightly, not used to the weight of his gear, or how bulky he felt.

    Shaking his head with a growl, he brought his rifle to bear down the alley, strafing across it while he jogged to a large metal dumpster. As he knelt behind it, watching the northern entrance of the alley, he heard a loud pinging noise above him.

    Eddie was beginning to climb frantically down the ladder, just in time for a stream of tracers to zip above his head from the rooftop across the street.

    The red phosphorus rounds streaked across the sky periodically in a strangely pretty way.

    "Shitshitshitshit!" Eddie muttered, making it to the bottom of the ladder, jumping off and sprinting over to Jeremiah's back, watching behind him. "This is so fucked! We're dead, man! Fucking dead!"

    "Let's just... try to get the hell out of here, okay?" Jeremiah replied, trying to calm down his friend. "Make it back to the vans, and jus-"

    "We won't make it! That was a fucking belt-fed!" Jeremiah jerked his head over his shoulder to stare wide-eyed at Eddie. "Those cats had a goddamn sixty! I got a peek at the other building right before they tried to turn me into Swiss cheese. Where the fuck is the outer cordon?"

    "Dunno, probably dead, or maybe they just up

an- fuck! Run!" Jeremiah jolted like a lightning bolt struck his very soul when the front of a large, up-armored Humvee, pulled up on the edge of the alley.

He spun and grabbed Eddie's "drag-handle" on the back of his plate carrier, not waiting to see if the vehicle had a turret on it or not.

"C'mon, go go go!" hissed Jeremiah all the while.

Several yards ahead was the small T-intersection in the alley that they'd passed on the way in. Eddie stumbled to his feet, being half-pulled along by Jeremiah's frantic attempt to escape.

Adrenaline forced him ever onward, as the air around him began to explode with the firecracker-like pops of high-velocity rounds breaking the sound barrier.

"Shit!" Eddie shouted behind him. It felt like something punched the back of Jeremiah's carrier like a sledgehammer.

He stumbled at full speed around the bend in the alley, bringing his rifle level with the long, dark path ahead. He saw nothing, the alley seemingly empty.

Jeremiah grit his teeth as a knot formed in his upper back, just under his left shoulder blade. He'd been hit, and was now wondering if his armor plate had caught it or not.

He turned over his shoulder as Eddie blew past him, stumbling.

"You good, Ed?" Jeremiah asked, watching the man clutch his left hand tenderly against his chest.

"No... fuck, they... fuck! My fingers!" he growled through gritted teeth. Jeremiah ran up to Eddie, stepping around to the man's front and grabbing his left hand. Looking the mangled flesh over, he found that Eddie was now missing his index, middle, and the front of his ring finger. Blood pumped through the glove, but they really didn't have time to do much for it.

Not here, with a gun truck just around the corner.

"Keep moving, we'll fuck with it when we get a moment," Jeremiah grunted and raised his rifle towards the mouth of the alley. "Stay close and I'll make sure Sarah gets to see you again. We can make it out."

Eddie's eyes were wide and fearful as he stared back at Jeremiah.

Slowly, he nodded, and Jeremiah slapped him on the shoulder reassuringly before turning back down the alley. Panning his head from side to side, he surveyed the sea of dark brick, concrete, and shadows before him.

He saw only more nothing ahead as he jogged forward.

As they neared the end of the alley, Jeremiah came to a stutter-stepping halt.

Loud, crunching footfalls and the soft whirr of machinery emanated from just beyond the mouth of it.

If he could just cross the street, pull Eddie through another alley or two, and keep mobile, they could escape whoever the fuck this was.

He hoped.

But the noise slowly grew louder.

Jeremiah cocked his head and listened, staring at the back door of the building beside him with confusion. The crunching footfalls were clearly metallic, a small squealing scrape of steel on concrete rang out with each step.

Striding around the corner came a nine-foot-tall science-fiction trope.

Decked out in what looked like heavy angled steel, reactive armor plates, and far more weaponry than he wanted to consider.

"What the," Jeremiah muttered under his breath, lowering his rifle unconsciously as a massive wall of metal and weaponry stepped into view and opened up down the street, with deep, resounding blasts of an autocannon.

The light of the muzzle-flash gave him a brief view of a black-and-red color scheme.

Then, much to his horror, the beast began to turn at the waist towards him.

His mind blanked out, as he pushed off his back foot in a sprint towards the door of the industrial building, lowering his shoulder at the last moment.

Nope, fuck that.

Fuck!

Is it the feds after all? Is this some area fifty-two, bleeding edge bullshit that they wanna test on us before-

He crashed into the door, then through it, the lock apparently giving way. Rolling onto his back, Jeremiah lifted his head up and stared through the open doorway as the hinges tried to push it closed.

Rolling onto his feet, he had just enough time to see Eddie drop down behind a small brick protrusion on the building at the other side of the alley, before the door swung shut.

Chapter 4

Jeremiah jumped up and jerked the door open.

He got a lovely view of a stream of large tracers zipping past down the alley. The beast continued firing its autocannon with steady, deafening blasts. Jeremiah grit his teeth and demanded his brain to work, to come up with some idea to help.

The flashbang!

An idea sprang to life from the sea of dumb plans that poured into his head. One of the many pieces of kit he'd taken from the Templar arsenal was a small, metal grenade. It didn't have an explosive charge, per se, but what it did have was a disorienting bright flash and a deafening bang.

Make the distraction, get Eddie in here...then what?

Jeremiah shook his head as he dug the item out of his pouches with a tear of velcro.

Eddie watched him from behind his rapidly dwindling cover, with rounds slamming into the backside of the surprisingly sturdy wall.

Jeremiah, unable to hear his own thoughts anymore as the machine continued harrying them, held the grenade before him, shaking it back and forth to get his counterpart's attention in the chaos.

Eddie saw him and nodded shakily.

Jeremiah pulled the pin and held up three fingers. He counted down to one and tossed the device out the door towards the armored monster, whatever it was.

Half a second later, and the first bright,

resounding boom sounded, somehow louder than the machine's halted gunfire.

Eddie, thankfully, had enough brainpower left to dart across the alley the moment the gunfire ceased.

Nearly the moment his foot crossed the threshold, the machine seemed to recover its senses.

A split second after Eddie was fully inside the doorway, the cannon fire began again in earnest, and Jeremiah threw the door shut.

Fuck that monster.

He squinted in confusion at the door's closing mechanism. Somehow, it'd been sheared away from the frame.

The ongoing boom and rolling thunder of the mechanized monster outside kept him from being idle.

Instead, he frantically looked for something heavy to shove in front of the door instead.

Grasping at a shelving unit nearby, he tested it and dumped it down in front of the door. A number of boxes that'd been on it slammed into the ground as well.

Jeremiah wasn't going to waste any more time with it. He wasn't sure a dainty shelf like this would hold up that machine very long.

This was all just for peace of mind rather than actual security.

He turned to get Eddie's attention to get him moving, only to find the man sliding a tourniquet up over his forearm, blood dripping steadily onto the floor.

Shaking his head, Jeremiah really didn't think that was the best idea, all things considered, but it wasn't his hand either.

"Fuck... Sarah's gonna be pissed," Eddie muttered through clenched teeth, biting the stick, pulling the strap with his good hand. Jeremiah approached him while he tried to tighten the windlass down with a shaking, unsteady hand. "We're already up to our ass in doctor's bills from the baby and-"

"I know, bud," Jeremiah interrupted him and batted his shaking hand away to tighten the tourniquet around his arm. Eddie relented, exhaling deep breaths as Jeremiah worked to tighten the tourniquet down until the bleeding ceased. "We'll make it through this. You remember that Vamp nest we took out under that haunted hotel? That was way more dangerous. It was just you, me, and Patty."

"Vamp's didn't have a fucking gundam, Jerry!" Eddie balled his uninjured fist and grit his teeth as Jeremiah torqued the windlass ever tighter. "I mean, shit, are we up against some black ops shitbirds or something?"

"Dunno," Jeremiah clicked the stick into place, satisfied with his work. "All I know is that my gut was right, and I'm gonna keep following it until we get the fuck outta—"

There was a massive boom and the wall that was keeping them safe from the metal monster shifted inward suddenly.

"Fuck, they're not going to bother with the door," Jeremiah whispered. His worst fear was indeed true. The door, the wall, and the itty-bitty shelf, wasn't going to keep that thing out.

There was another boom and part of the wall started to come down with a rattling clatter. Their time was up. It was time to go, and they had to do so immediately.

An arm smashed through the wall and started to pull down the wall itself. A great deal of it was coming down in front of the door itself.

The only reasoning Jeremiah could come up with for its actions was it was trying to get enough of an angle to fire into the warehouse itself.

Eddie and Jeremiah both had already moved to the back of the building by this point. The former with a raised pistol, and the latter with his rifle.

Neither said anything, and Jeremiah felt a lot like they were going to be attempting to fight a battle-tank.

A loud explosion lit the night sky above them through small skylight windows on the ceiling, followed shortly by the lights flickering, then shutting off.

As suddenly as the nine-foot death machine had started to come for them, it stopped. The arm retracted itself, and everything went quiet.

Leaving the two men sitting there in the dark with nothing but the silence.

Jeremiah coughed, jerked down his single night vision tube, and realized their time was up. His world became a sea of green in a small, claustrophobic circle, an inch in front of his face. He turned his head just in time to see Eddie fumble to return his pistol to its holster, pull his own night vision gear down, and re-draw the weapon.

He couldn't see Eddie's face under the balaclava, but his eyes almost glowed under the infrared vision. Jeremiah opened his mouth to make a quip about feeling like a mouse hiding from the cat, when a resounding boom sounded from the far side of the warehouse. He lifted his rifle, pointing it in the direction of the noise, before another thud sounded.

Did the damn terminator come around the other side? For fuck's sake!

A door he hadn't noticed slammed open, moonlight spilling through as two figures sprinted into the warehouse, with the second spinning around to slam the door closed behind them.

Jeremiah flicked the safety off, placed his finger on the trigger, and was in mid squeeze when one of the the newcomers spoke.

"Those mongrels!" Brother Claudius spat, spinning a small circle in place, letting the belt-fed machinegun dangle in its sling. He rested his hands atop his helmet, his face still oddly warped and blurred as if by magic.

Knowing Templars, it probably was.

"Holy shit! Am I glad to see you guys!" Eddie exhaled a sigh of relief as both of the figure's heads spun to face them. Claudius leveled the SAW at them, but the second Templar leapt forward, slapping his muzzle down.

"It's one of the detachments!" Sister Elanor hissed. Jeremiah and Eddie had both ducked briefly behind an aisle of shelves as Claudius almost mowed them down with wanton machinegun fire. "Is it just the two of you? Did anyone else make it?"

"Not that we saw," Jeremiah stepped back out and exhaled a thankful breath. "Too busy dodging gun trucks and a fuckin... gundam."

"A what?" Sister Elanor cocked her head to the side quizzically. How a person could look confused without a face, Jeremiah wasn't sure, but she pulled it off.

"Big robot-looking monster; has a cannon? You guys didn't see that?" Jeremiah asked, well aware that even he wouldn't believe himself if he didn't see it.

"No... no we manifestly did not," Brother Claudius replied, no small measure of skepticism in his voice. "Bah, it matters naught, now. Sister, you said there were tunnels we could use to escape here?"

"According to the maps," she said, clicking a small, futuristic-looking tablet off her chest before turning it on and tapping several times. "There should be a maintenance tunnel entrance somewhere over there."

She pointed deeper into the warehouse before reaffixing the tablet.

"Come then, let us be rid of this place," Brother Claudius groused, rolling his shoulders and cracking his neck. "I do not wish to suffer the failure of these fools any longer! We must report back to the cou- to command at once."

Jeremiah considered himself to be a fairly easy-going person. And yet, at every turn, this man somehow found a way to shit on his day.

Because he was fairly certain the man was referring to himself and Eddie when he spoke of the 'fools', though he could just be insecure at the moment.

"Let's get to it then," Jeremiah flexed his jaw and nodded at the man, who stared back with an appraising gaze, as if just now seeing him.

"Ah, here it is!" Sister Elanor said, having stepped several yards away. With an idle shove, she sent a pallet of heavy-looking boxes to one side.

She leaned down and pulled loose the heavy steel manhole cover as if it were made of air, dropping it beside them with a loud, clanging thud that shook the floor.

Machinegun fire began to rip through the side

of the warehouse, sending tumbling, snapping, and ricocheting rounds in every direction, as the rounds worked horizontally across the wall.

"Fuck! Really? Again?" Jeremiah shouted, dropping to the ground and crawling towards the open hole in the ground as Claudius jumped down, followed by Elanor. Eddie hunched low and ran across the short stretch of open ground.

Almost there. Just a few more feet, an-

A round snapped across Jeremiah's thigh, a searing heat blinding his nerves for a split second.

"Jay!" shouted Eddie, his legs dangling in the open hole in the floor. He began to squirm back out, pushing off with his good hand.

"Eddie! Go, I'll be fine!" Jeremiah shouted, still crawling, despite his aching ribs and stinging leg. He crawled faster as Eddie seemed to consider what to do, before he simply pushed off, and dropped into the tunnel below.

Jeremiah made it to the hole several seconds later, just in time for the door the Templars had come through to burst open behind him as the endless MG fire abated.

Taking the opportunity for what it was, he pushed to his feet and ran for the exit.

A round snapped by his head.

Jeremiah turned around and saw a figure clad in black combat gear charge into the building, a submachine gun leveled towards him.

"Fuck!" he shouted, lifting his own weapon and firing several rounds into his opponent, whose return fire struck his own armor twice.

Thankfully, his opponent hit the ground a second later, their arms coming up to try and get their weapon in position at the same time.

He wasn't really sure if he'd broken through their armor or not, but they were at least no longer an immediate threat.

Jeremiah smiled ferally at having at least managed to get his own shots in. Considering everything that'd happened, it felt like a minor victory.

"Fuck you, you big fuckin' fucker. Fuck," he spat out, even as he hopped into darkness that beckoned him, not sparing any more time. While it didn't sound very eloquent, he was rather pleased with the response despite that.

When he hit the ground, he was rewarded with his ankles screaming their wrath at having been so cavalierly used to stop his fall.

Not to mention reminded that he had a hole in his thigh.

To the point that he collapsed to his knees then and there.

He was jerked to his feet by Sister Elanor, who patted him reassuringly on the shoulder.

"Follow me," she demanded, and gave him a pull, before turning and continuing down the tunnel where Jeremiah could make out Eddie leaning against Brother Claudius. The man positively dwarfed Eddie both in height and muscle.

Nodding his head, Jeremiah chased after without a word.

For an entire hour they rambled along through dark maintenance tunnels.

Every minute that passed was an eternity as they pressed onward.

Silently marching on, or in Jeremiah's case, hobbling.

Thankfully, nothing happened.

In fact, they even made it to the city sewers themselves thanks to Elanor's mapping software without too much of an issue, other than Jeremiah having to start doing a weird hopping walk to keep up.

All throughout, Jeremiah couldn't shake the image of the mech from his mind. The idea of that mechanical death machine nearly ripping through the wall, was plastered in the back of his head like a painting.

"Manhole ahead," murmured Sister Elanor, and moved to a small ladder in the side of the tunnel. She took several steps up it and the sound of something large and heavy shifting was quite audible.

Elanor came back down after a few seconds. She let out a relieved exhale, touching the small dongle on her collar as her face returned to view.

"It appears we're under a small commercial district. Mall parking lot, it looks like. We can blend in with the locals and make our wa-"

"Fine, best we clean up and be done here," Brother Claudius declared loudly, cutting Elanor off. With a push, he shoved Eddie away and onto the ground. "There's no way you could blend in with everyone up there. You're more likely to slow us down as well."

"What do you suggest, then, 'Brother'?" Elanor asked in low tone, her eyes becoming squints. "And it isn't as if we would blend in very well either. Our gear sets us apart, would it not?"

"Well we can't just leave them here. They'll either be found by the enemy, interrogated, and killed, or be found by the police, interrogated, and jailed when they link them to the ambush," Claudius stated while deactivating his face-obscuring magic.

He didn't seem to want to respond to Elanor's point about their gear.

"Hey!" Jeremiah interjected as he crossed behind Claudius to help Eddie up. He'd broken his ankle earlier when he'd jumped, apparently landing wrong on the short concrete curb inside the tunnel. "I like to think we get a say in this. We're hurt, but we're still in this. If we're by a mall, can't we just get some new clothes, catch a cab, and dip? Like Elanor said, it isn't as if you can just march around in your kit up there."

"Far too complicated. We all left any identifying information at the staging area, did we not?" Claudius asked, not even looking at Jeremiah. "How then, are we supposed to obtain fresh clothing for the two of you? We will leave, and then you can do as you see fit."

The large man checked his watch, clearly more for dramatic effect than any form of timer.

"Oh, ten minutes or so," Brother Claudius finished, turning over his shoulder with a self-assured grin. "If the two of you have cash, or the wherewithal to sneak your way back through the city, then by all means, do as you see fit.

"I for one, do not wish to be saddled with the task of babysitting two members of the half-witted organization that managed to compromise and so magnificently dismantle an operation months in the making!"

"We didn't compromise shit, dude!" Jeremiah snarled back, placing his hand back on the grip of his rifle. "It was a fucking ambush, and those weren't fuckin' Were-Coyotes. That was pre-planned, long before I ever heard about it."

"He could very well be right, Brother," Elanor

said soothingly, stepping towards the large man with a calming gesture. "We only gave their detachments a day's notice to organize. Perhaps our sources received fa-"

"This is neither the time nor place to deliberate on the cause of failure. The fact remains that four of our order are dead because their outer cordon failed to spot a veritable army approaching us," Brother Claudius straightened himself out, looming over Elanor, who stared back at him with a frown.

"Whether or not the cells failed in their duty, it does not excuse us -abandoning- our charges!" Elanor extended her hand towards Jeremiah and Eddie as she defended them. Pointing an accusatory finger at Claudius, she continued: "Just because the solution is hard, or heavens forbid, -complicated-, is irrelevant. We still have an objective to complete, to get back to the parish and inform them of what happened!"

"Fine. This is certainly a crossroads. A disagreement that we obviously must solve right here and now. So, let's simplify things then, shall we?" Claudius asked with a grin. Something about it made Jeremiah's skin crawl.

"Exactly. We get them out of the tunnel, commandeer a vehicle, and drive to the parish. Let the bishop decide what to do with them. Simple, and out of o-"

She didn't get a chance to finish her sentence.

"You don't want to go out after us? You can go ahead of us," Claudius remarked, and jerked up his machinegun before Jeremiah could even respond. Then the lights went out with a sharp crack of the gun going off.

Chapter 5

Jeremiah tried to force his eyes open. Tried to lift his eyelids despite them feeling as if they weighed several tons each.

When he managed to see the world in front of him, he nearly just shut his eyes again.

What he'd seen was that he was surrounded by a lot of what could only be charitably described as junk.

There wasn't much light, but there was just enough that he could see the immediate vicinity around him.

Additionally, there was a near crushing weight pressing down on him.

In fact, it happened to be a rather large mound of filth that was piled up on him. In nearly every direction.

Instinctively, he tried to wrestle an arm free.

With his lips pressed tightly together, his teeth grinding together, he grunted and huffed. Pushing and shifting about whatever he could.

His whole body writhed at his command and after a few seconds he finally pulled free an arm. It came out of the disgusting mass with a shunk and a clatter of trash.

Except it hadn't really helped him much, as his arm had apparently been holding up some of the weight.

His body now ached with the weight pressed atop him. All of it focused seemingly atop his ribs directly.

Fuck...c'mon, just gi-

His left hand moved fractionally.

Then a bit more.

Then his elbow pressed against something with a lot of give to it.

Which really didn't help much.

He managed to wedge his right hand under a large, flat piece of ice-cold metal laid across his chest. It vaguely resembled either a fridge door or the top of a washing machine.

He was able to shift it back and forth with effort.

Jeremiah worked his other arm free after a minute of pumping at the metal, slowly worming it over till both of his arms were free.

At least, wherever he was, there was air, even if it stank like a dumpster behind a restaurant on an extremely hot summer day.

He pushed with all the leverage he could put into it.

When nothing came of it, he pushed some more, trying to tip the piece of quarter-inch thick metal away from him.

He'd had better success rocking it to and fro to begin with after all.

C'mon you fucking piece of shit!

His mind was screaming, even as his muscles quivered and flexed with his mental demand.

Just. Fucking. MOVE!

His final, forceful thought was accompanied by an inarticulate scream.

Followed immediately by a sudden squeal, as either the metal gave way, or finally tore free of its position.

Taking a sudden breath, and letting out a strange chuckle that sounded odd to his own ears,

Jeremiah braced himself and pushed again. This time, buoyed by his own success, he felt as if this were possible.

There was a long stretched out moment where nothing happened at all.

Then with a sudden ping, something broke.

A crack, a screech, a thundering groan of metal, and the weight from above him tipped away from him and slid into a pile of mush he was hoping his arm wasn't of inside a moment ago.

Short lived was his respite, as a pile of fetid, stinking debris spilled down onto him once again. He flailed his arms, clearing himself a hole through nearly two feet of disgusting filth.

Except he was extremely thankful for this new ocean of disgusting yuck. Even as it filled his nostrils and his mouth, as he gutturally cheered his success at having dislodged the metal press-plate of doom.

This sea of sick was goopy enough that he could move through it. Or at least, drag himself up out of it.

Clawing, kicking, pulling, he came free of the morass of muck, and into the air above, feeling a lot like a sick mole.

Sitting there, his arms resting on top of the yuck, he had a much better view of his surroundings.

Spitting, running his teeth over his tongue, and finally blowing his nose, he desperately wanted a shower.

Using his less shit-covered hand, he scraped at his eyes and managed to see everything clearly now. Or at least as clear as a trash-monster might see.

Blinking several times, he stared out into a cloudy, murky sky on the horizon.

"I…" he trailed off, his most recent memory,

Claudius' gun going off, slammed back into the forefront of his mind. "I'm alive."

He slapped his hands to his chest and head, feeling for the holes he was sure would be there.

He was decidedly whole.

If covered in filth.

A brief inspection of his torso and head with his fingertips, while pushing aside the yuck, gave him no obvious holes or bandages.

Jeremiah then looked to his hands and saw no blood there, nor any other issues.

Idly, he brushed off a very rotten banana peel from his wrist.

"Where the hell am I?" he asked no one, surveying the expansive landfill before him. Pile after pile after pile of rancid food containers, plastic, and household appliances, lay piled in thirty-foot mounds before him. The air itself stank of rot and decay, of the filth of millions compiled in a single location.

He grimaced, pushing himself up and out of the pile he currently halfway resided in.

Wriggling backwards, Jeremiah pulled his left leg up, only to repeat the gesture with his right.

It reminded him briefly of trying to walk through deep snow.

Getting up higher on his rear end, he squirmed about until he was now sitting atop the mountain of trash.

Not far off, the partially covered mouth of a washing machine was gaping at him.

Right, uh.

How about we just...

Getting his foot out of the junk, he got it into the edge of the washing machine and shoved.

Surprisingly, the machine tumbled out from

the mountain of refuse, spinning and careening down the embankment to hit the muddy ground below with a thud.

Well that sucked.

Grimacing, he set himself as best as he could for trying to get up without a ledge to stand on.

After a few more seconds of quicksand-like struggle, he extricated himself and stood.

He had his hands up to his side as if he were afraid he'd most assuredly suddenly be sucked right back down into the disgusting mound.

In that half crouch, he looked up as much as he was willing to, given the situation.

He tilted his head from side to side, eyeing his surroundings, trying to discern where in the hell he was.

There's mountains over there…maybe northern Larimer? I don't think I've seen them before. Western slope, maybe?

If it was, there wouldn't be this many trees though. Gods, who fired the gardener?

Jeremiah eyed the slew of trees that sat on the outskirts of the dump with suspicion.

Low hanging dark clouds obscured the sun above, giving him little information, other than it was sometime in the day.

Maybe I just caught the city on a rainy day, could be old GJ, just somewhere I ain't seen before.

With a shrug, he brushed his grimy hands off on his shirt, pausing as his fingers brushed across something that felt far too slick.

Dangit, what am I covered in?

He looked down and found that it wasn't that he was covered in something. It was that he was apparently wearing a suit.

Did they fucking put me in a burial suit, then dump me in the trash?

The thought came unbidden when he looked at the pinstripe black and pink jacket he wore. Or at least, he thought it was pinstripe beneath the slime he was coated nearly head to toe in.

Jeremiah began to take slow, careful steps down the pile, eying each individual item of garbage where he would place the high-end leather shoes he was surprised to see himself wearing.

When he reached the bottom, a small path between more mountains of trash, his shoes instantly started sinking halfway into the mud.

Or at least, he hoped it was mud.

Standing there, he held perfectly still, as there was an instant sensation of movement. Except it wasn't beneath his feet, it was inside of his own body.

With growing horror, he felt something shifting around in his chest. It moved like a coiled slug from his heart, down to his gut, and back up, before settling somewhere beneath his shoulder.

An ice-white pain blasted through his torso when the movement stilled, knocking him to his knees as memories that weren't his own came to him.

They began to play unendingly on the theater space of the inside of his mind and the backs of his eyelids. Too fast to really grasp and too brief for him to understand, they shot by even as he felt his body quiver with pain.

He tried to pay attention to the flashes of images, of scenes and voices he didn't recognize, while his torso burned with an unholy fire.

When the pain subsided, he pulled his knee out of the mud with a slurping squelch. He suddenly wanted to get to his feet and get out of the area. To run and flee, even if he was fairly certain the problem was inside of him.

What the fuck...

That's...not normal. Something is wrong with me.

Something...something is wrong.

His thoughts carried him as he meandered and stumbled through the sea of garbage, following the sounds of machinery.

Escaping nothing at all, given his fears.

Get out. Figure out where I am. Try to get in contact with Patrick, maybe Eddie...if he survived.

Wait...would I even want to get into contact?

They tried to off me.

Regardless of his situation, he knew his end goal. Felt it wind its ugly purpose around his heart like a coiled vine.

No, they didn't try to kill me.

Claudius did.

Find Claudius and return the favor.

Burn him and who-ever sent him to the fucking ground.

He set his feelings to words within his mind.

Traitors and those who support them don't deserve a seat at the table.

A garbage truck was visible as he rounded another pile of garbage.

It was parked beside a small shantytown of trailer-based office buildings. A small group of people in reflective vests stood around the vehicle, chatting amicably amongst themselves.

"Ayo, what the fuck?" one shouted, pointing at Jeremiah and jumping back.

"Hey, woah, dude are you okay?" a middle-aged man in a white hardhat asked, leaving the group and half-sprinting towards Jeremiah.

Jeremiah looked him in the eyes, which had narrow, slitted pupils like a serpent. His forearms were scaled with a blue-green iridescent shimmer, and small pointed ears poked out of his mop of unruly blonde hair.

Not a Vamp, not a Were…what the fuck are you?

Jeremiah had never seen whatever the hell this individual was. Some abomination of reptile and human was his best guess.

A monster is a monster. I should kill him. End his unholy existence here and now.

Too many witnesses, though. And they're human…I think.

Later, then. When I find the rest of my team… whatever's left.

"Don't touch me," Jeremiah snarled as the man extended a hand that surely only appeared helpful. Knowing monsters, he would probably just corrupt him with some form of bullshit 'death-by-touch' toxin. "I'm fine."

The man paused several feet away in his steps, watching Jeremiah with concern and confusion in equal measure. He exhaled slowly.

Deliberately.

His breath came out in a forced measure with an almost imperceptible nod of his head.

"Sorry, chief. A… are you alright?" the man added, apparently respecting the short distance between them.

"No, I just woke up in a pile of fucking trash," Jeremiah snapped, holding his hands up in front of himself in an exasperated way. "I have no idea where the fuck I am, or who the hell you assholes are!"

"This is Casey's Dump, bud," the man informed him, holding his hands up and his palms open in a calming gesture. "Off of Carson and Ringer street."

"Thanks. Never heard of it," Jeremiah replied acidly "Do one of you have a cellphone I could borrow, maybe a map of where the fuck we are?"

"Uhh, yeah. Yeah I do," the man replied with a friendly smile and a nod, but Jeremiah saw the venom behind his eyes. Of course the monster wanted to kill him. He was probably just as worried about witnesses as Jeremiah was too. "Here ya' go, pal."

The man passed a cellphone over to him. Or what Jeremiah assumed was a cellphone.

There wasn't a keypad to be seen anywhere on it. Just a black, six-inch long rectangle that reminded him of the futuristic tablet Sister Elanor had affixed to her chest.

Maybe it's a touch screen?

There were some companies putting out cellphones pretty recently without a keypad, and just a full screen.

He tapped it, and the thing lit up with a prompt to slide upwards on the screen to unlock. He followed the clear instruction and the thing opened without issue, displaying several widgets on the screen, with one of them bearing the logo of a phone.

Following his instinct, he tapped on it. It opened to a keypad, and he typed in a number he remembered vividly. Lord knows he had spent days just memorizing it from a sheet of paper before burning it.

He prepared his mental numbers, ready to deliver Leodegrance a status report, when the line clicked and screeched in his ear.

"We're sorry," the automated voice on the

other end said. "The number you are trying to reach is not in service. Please han-"

He hung up and checked the number. It was correct. He tried again, to the same result.

Fuck, did that ambush wrap up the whole organization?

If Leodegrance isn't around, that means that it probably wasn't just the Larimer group that went down. I should check the local papers, see if there's any news.

Jeremiah stuck his tongue to the roof of his mouth as he stared down at the device with a sour expression.

"Looks like they're not answering." he shrugged and handed the phone back to the whatever he was. "I'll probably just find a payphone, deal with what I've gotta' later. Thanks, though."

"No... problem?" the man stared back at him with a raised brow and a deeply confused expression before snorting and shaking his head. "Dunno about finding payphones though. Think the city got rid of 'em about a year or two ago. I mean, hell-"

The man pointed almost as a form of punctuation behind Jeremiah.

Following the long, clawed finger, Jeremiah saw a smashed payphone housing laid against the slope of a pile of garbage.

It was severely rusted, clearly in a state of disrepair before it had been ripped out of the ground and lain here.

"This is gonna sound a little odd," Jeremiah started, forcing a friendly smile to his face as unfortunately, the human contingent of this jobsite still watched him nervously from a couple dozen yards away. He looked the reptilian man in the eyes and asked, like an idiot. "But uh... what city am I in?"

"Clallam. Why, party too hard last night?" the man chuckled, watching Jeremiah with a teasing grin.

"Clallam... as in, Washington state, Clallam?" Jeremiah's jaw fell open whatching who he believed was the foreman with suspicion.

Fourteen hundred miles...how in the hell did that happen? He's gotta be fucking with me. Maybe there's some small town that shares a name in-

"Yup! Why?" the man sniffed the air briefly, rolling his head the other way. "That good-good they sell in the city fuck you up that hard? Must've been a hell of a party."

I have no clue what good-good is, but we'll go with...drugs.

"You have no idea," Jeremiah replied, licking his lips and quickly grimacing at the taste before bidding the man goodbye.

With that, he stepped around the man and headed for the open gate of the garbage facility. As he exited, the strange shifting feeling returned.

A crawling sensation inside of himself that left him feeling almost weak-kneed.

It wormed its way down his shoulder and into his arm. Like a slimy lance of white-hot pain.

He grit his teeth and grabbed his arm, trying to avoid screaming, scenes that he immediately forgot playing once again inside of his head.

Don't attract attention.

He repeated the mantra in his mind while he trudged onward, well aware of the odd looks from passersby.

Need to find somewhere to shower. Get some fresh clothes. A pinstripe suit that looks and smells like it just took a dip in the local sewer isn't subtle.*

He looked around at his surroundings and judged it to be some type of commercial park.

With a click of his tongue, he considered the standing trash, broken windows, and torn up parking lots. All the signs of something that was most certainly run down.

Joy. I'm pretty sure I'm in crackhead county.
I might actually be able to blend in here.
For the moment at least.

The pain in his arm subsided and he looked down to the sleeve of the suit jacket with a frown.

I mean, I'd blend in if you don't really look at me, I guess. Who wears a suit this dirty?
Or wears a suit at all as a crackhead.
Crackheads who wear suits are in the penthouse, or whatever.

He pulled off the jacket and stared at the small tag on the inside breast pocket.

Armanee?
Fuck.
Don't these start at like…five grand a suit, before tailoring?

He groaned and stared at the absurdly expensive suit in his hands with a frown.

Not only did he have no idea why he instinctively knew about the costs of high-end suits, he didn't know why the hell was he wearing one in the first place.

In fact, now that he considered it and looked to the streets around him, some of the names sounded familiar. Yet he swore he'd never been here before.

The last I remember, I was in a full military kit, not…this.

I should go wash up somewhere.

Maybe a river.

This part of Washington is wet as hell, if I remember correctly. I nee-

His eyes widened as they settled on a group of women on the other side of the street.

All four were tall, lithe, and decidedly inhuman.

Long, pointed ears, slanted eyes, and sharp canines, greeted him when they looked his way. They burst out laughing at something one of them said, and kept on going, as if being out in the open was the most normal of things for a monster to do.

I'm sorry, what kind of hellscape is this city?

He jerked his gaze away while thinking such, fighting back the urge to cross the street and remove the inhuman. To burn them from the land.

He shook the thoughts away.

Now was not the time to kill, to break the monsters that preyed upon humans over his knee. Now was the time to figure his shit out and find shelter, or at least a reasonable alternative.

He didn't have an apartment here, at least not that he knew of. He saw a bend in the road ahead, with a small copse of dense green foliage that to him told him only one thing.

This was where standing water was.

That meant it was his goal.

Trudging onward, he did his best to look as nonchalant as possible.

Get cleaned off.

Then...well, I don't know what, then.

Maybe crash in an alley, or a homeless shelter until I can figure out what to do.

His stomach grumbled loudly, voicing its clear

desires.

Maybe a soup kitchen.
If they even still have those.

Reaching his goal, he entered the green-belt and moved in.

He pushed his way through the brambles and brush that ran alongside the trees and was rewarded with a small, babbling brook nestled in a small, sloping valley.

Right now he couldn't tell if it was run-off from a neighborhood nearby or actually a river, but in either case, it was clean enough.

Or cleaner than his suit, at least.

He stripped off the white collared shirt after tossing the jacket against the rocks on the side of the stream. Looking down at his arms, he frowned. Shoulder to wrist, he was coated in unfamiliar, colorful, and artfully done tattoos.

Staring at a winged serpent that coiled its way down his forearm, he really couldn't process the situation any further. None of this made sense, and he was starting to earnestly doubt his grasp on reality.

Giving up on his arms, and the madness they promised him, he focused on what he could actually change.

Which was getting clean.

Kneeling down to wash himself from the still pool of water, he glanced at himself in the water. No sooner than he saw himself, he just about leapt backward.

His face wasn't his face.

The person looking back at him wasn't the one he'd seen in the mirror every day of his life.

Who he was looking at, or who was looking

back at him, was a middle-aged Asian man with soft brown eyes that had a flatness to them that left him cold. Close-cropped black hair and a trim goatee, paired with high cheekbones, actually gave him a rather striking look.

Then, the writhing sensation that felt like an icy slug at the moment returned.

Gliding its way up into his neck and leaving behind it a frozen trail.

Jeremiah let out an involuntary shriek before falling backwards. The pain had been so much that he felt his teeth snap together involuntarily, with the rest of it coming out as a low-voiced moan through gritted teeth.

He clutched and gripped at his face, feeling the muscle and bone beneath his hands shifting. Rolling back and forth across the ground, he could hardly focus on anything at all.

That disgusting and mind-rending pain had slithered its way up to reach what felt like would be behind his eyes.

As if there was something, or someone, else inside of him and it had a mind of its own. All across his face, it moved and left behind a sizzling sensation.

Somewhat reminiscent of water hitting a scorching hot pan.

He lost himself in that pain completely.

When his mind finally resurfaced from the pain-fueled haze, he could barely remember what he'd been doing.

His face and head ached terribly, and all he wanted to do was lay there and breathe.

Breathe and pretend today wasn't happening.

Thankfully, blessedly, every second he lay on his back, staring at the sky, the pain fled. Leaving him alone with only an echo of it.

An echo that was fading into the distance and memory.

He exhaled after several minutes passed.

Nothing of the pain remained and all he had left over was a lot of sweat and a feeling as if his clothes didn't quite fit anymore.

With a groan, he pushed himself to a seated position. Taking several breaths, he then got himself to a standing position.

Standing there, he hesitated. Nothing felt out of the ordinary for once.

A tentative shake of his aching head didn't surprise him with anything new either.

Emboldened, he moved back to the small pool of water.

His face was his again.

Chestnut brown hair haphazardly arranged, and just enough stubble to give him a carefree look. His blue eyes gazed back at him, as if they'd always been there.

"What the fuck?" he whispered under his breath. He shook his head. Perhaps this was all some pre-death "life flashing before your eyes" bullshit that he really didn't understand.

He groaned, blinked his heavy eyelids, and set about washing his clothes free of the stench of a mountain of garbage.

Except that, even at a tentative glance, he could tell they wouldn't quite fit as closely as they had only moments ago. That while they would be approximate, it would no longer feel as perfectly tailored.

No...that all happened...didn't it.
The question then becomes, why?

Or actually, better yet, all of it is a big fucking why.

Just, why?

* * *

"This looks like the place," Jeremiah muttered to himself, staring at the typography on the side of a run-down restaurant. "Grace Works Meal Center... damn, that's a hell of a mouthful. And a line, shit."

He'd inquired from several homeless men on his wet, chafing walk around the city, as to where he could get food.

Where he could get food for no money, that was.

The locals had all recommended this place, the only caveat was, good luck getting in. Because a local ministry ran the shop as a charity organization, and apparently, they had the best food anywhere nearby.

Near the level of an actual restaurant, supposedly.

Unfortunately, this meant the line stretched around the block most nights, and once the food was gone, it was gone. It was all limited, given that it was a community driven out-reach program.

He stared at the line of dozens that led down the block, full of haggard and weather-worn faces, contemplating how to get the best spot in line.

When he'd taken stock of all he had on him at the river, he'd found two items that could theoretically be used for bartering: a golden chain and a fancy-looking watch.

He could probably go to a nearby pawn shop

and sell the both of them for a small pittance, but he didn't know where one was.

On top of that, for some reason, there was something that he couldn't honestly discern.

He was hungry. Hungry in a way that made him feel as if his stomach was clawing at his spine. A hunger that went beyond the desire for food.

Almost in a way that didn't feel like hunger at all.

His mind had shied away from running down that thought and instead settled on, "fuck it, get food now".

He approached near the front of the line, idly rolling the small gold chain around in his caged fingers.

Just gotta find the tweaker in the bunch. The kind of person who values drugs more than food...wher-

He smiled at finding his target and coughed.

"Hey bud," he said in a rasping voice, trying to blend in while the waifishly thin man looked to him with hollow eyes. "Can I get cuts?"

"No cutting, asshole," the tweaker snorted and shook his head, before folding his arms across his chest.

"Trade, then?" Jeremiah asked, trying his best to look pressed and willing to barter his soul. "Dude, I haven't eaten in a week."

"Huh," the man snorted and raised an eyebrow. "I'm hungry too, bitch. What'chu got?"

Jeremiah put on an act, half lifting his hands to his neck, hesitating, and sighing loudly before pulling the necklace over his head.

"This is all I got man. I think it's worth something, one of my ex's gave it to me for my bi-"

The crackhead's eyes widened with glee before

he snatched the necklace from Jeremiah's hand and stepped aside in the line, opening his hand to offer up his spot with a predatory grin.

"Be my guest, bud," he offered as Jeremiah took his spot in line. He sprinted away, giggling maniacally before yelling over his shoulder. "Chump!"

Jeremiah shook his head and waited patiently for the line to inch ever forward.

Ten minutes of feet shuffling and trying not to contemplate too much, Jeremiah was at the actual front. The attendant at the door pointed over his shoulder with a thumb and let him inside the kitchen by stepping to the side.

It was packed with people at long, open tables, greedily eating away at the portions of food on their plates.

It was an odd smell that pervaded the place: a stench of unwashed bodies and freshly cooked food. He did his best to ignore the wafting scents of the patrons as he made his way to the bar and grabbed a tray.

Chapter 6

"What can I get ya'?" a chipper voice asked as Jeremiah slid down the counter with his tray in hand, eying the swath of food on display. Fried chicken, potatoes, mac and cheese, green beans, a tomato soup.

He greedily drank in eyefuls of the prospective meal before him, not even looking at the server as he already piled food onto an imaginary plate.

"Uh, can I get some... uh," he said, trailing off as he glanced up to find a red-skinned woman smiling brightly at him.

Short, black horns jutted up from just above her temples, along with long, rounded ears that sloped down and out from the side of her head. She smiled cutely back at him, giving him a view of several sharp canine teeth at the corners of her mouth.

Jeremiah frowned and looked down at the appetizing food. Then back up at the non-human woman. The idea of food continued to make his stomach gurgle demandingly, but he wasn't about to let a Demon poison his food.

He inhaled deeply, scowling at her.

"Can I get someone else to serve me?" he asked. He just didn't understand how everyone else was seemingly okay with what appeared to be an actual demon serving them mashed potatoes. The woman froze, a plastic smile etched on her face.

"I'm sorry, did I do something wro-"

"Yes," Jeremiah scowled at the woman across the counter from him. "I don't wanna start shit. I just wanna be on my way with a full stomach, not full of whatever bullshit you decide to la-"

"There a problem here?" a deep-voiced, stocky man asked, walking up beside the woman.

"Uh, he says that he wants to be served by someone else, Father Thomas," the woman replied with a nervous smile. "I can go if-"

"No, Jenny. You're just fine," Thomas shook his head and placed a large hand on her shoulder before turning to Jeremiah. "There a problem with my volunteers, young man?"

"Yes. Do you not see what I see?" Jeremiah asked, extending a hand towards Jenny with a confused frown.

"What? A young lady taking time out of her busy college schedule to feed you? To warm the bellies of the hungry masses?" Thomas folded his large arms across his chest as he watched Jeremiah with a scowl. "There a problem with a woman serving you? You know what? I'm not even going to debate this with you.

"You have two options right now, son: eat the plate of food served by Jenny with a smile and an apology, or leave this property."

Jeremiah inhaled deeply, looking briefly to the side, considering what to do.

His stomach ached. He'd been hungry before. He could handle going hungry for a night until he could find somewhere else to grab chow.

What he couldn't stomach was apologizing for standing up for his beliefs.

She wasn't human. She probably fed on pain and misery or something.

Just like all the others.

She was a monster that fed on humans, and

he was sure of it.

He set the tray down on the bar and stepped back, mentally debating leaping over the counter that instant.

In the end, he decided to not start a fight in the shelter. He could come back later, when the Demon wasn't serving food, corrupting the masses.

He walked away from the kitchen in a grouchy mood, unfed and annoyed.

Almost as soon as he left the kitchen, the insane hunger that he'd momentarily forgotten came back. To the point that it nearly knocked him down to his knees.

Except, his pride kept him upright, for better or worse.

He didn't go back for the food that his unconscious mind demanded he go beg for. To apologize and thank them, and shovel it into his face.

Panting softly, he made it out the doors and back onto the street. He stood there for several seconds and ground his teeth together.

He felt stupid and foolish.

Against better judgement, he'd squandered one of the few material possessions he'd had for absolutely nothing. Now he had nothing to show for it, and it could be very likely he might be turned around from the establishment at a later date.

Jeremiah shook his head slowly and let out a long sigh. Slowly, he started walking down along the street once again. He couldn't just stand here after all.

Once he got moving, he watched a car slowly roll by, momentarily distracted by the abysmal condition of the ride.

Didn't that model come out like a year or two ago? Why the hell does it look like it's had a solid ten years of abuse? Fuck did you do to it?

How some people could let surface rust take over a large swath of the undercarriage, the paint get scratched and dingy, and be completely fine denting a brand-new ride like that was beyond him.

I guess it's to be expected of norms.

Why would you put the effort in if you don't realize just how sideways things can go at a moment's notice?

Buying a gun and doing regular vehicle maintenance just seem like an expensive and time-consuming way to waste your hard-earned free time and money, if you don't worry about a vamp drinking you, or a Were pack breaking into your house and eating your family.

If only your average person wasn't so skittish and easily set off. With enough people, we could easily wipe out the monsters, with only minimal losses.

He snorted loudly as a drop of rain touched his shoulder. Looking up to the heavens above, he squinted when more sporadic drops of rain fell from the skies.

If the One and All is up there, he's probably laughing at me right about now.

Maybe Patrick was right, after all. The duty to act against evil exists solely for those who hear its call. For everyone else, it's just Tuesday, as they go about their blissful, normal life.

A momentary pang of sadness hit him as he thought about his team.

They were probably all dead by now, wrapped up in the ambush that had nearly taken his life too. He wondered what, if any, steps the Fed would take against the perpetrators, assuming they weren't the ones who ordered the ambush in the first place.

You died doing what you believed in, fighting the good fight.

The rain began to fall in earnest, so Jeremiah began to peer down every alley he passed - hoping to find an alcove, an unoccupied box, or just about anything, really.

That'll do.

He nodded to himself, spotting a small overhanging tin roof in the fifth alley he looked down. Half-jogging, he made for the shelter as the rain began to open up even more than it had before.

Upon the corrugated tin roof, the downpour sounded like endless, raucous applause, near-deafening in its intensity. He still sat down underneath it, taking stock of all he had on him.

There was a lingering pained thought at the fact that he'd traded an item away already and got nothing for it. Once more cursing his lack in judgement.

Followed by the grinding of his stomach eating at itself.

No weapons, no gear, not even a damned wallet. At least the watch is kinda nic-

Jeremiah's train of thought ran dry when he stared down at the maker's mark on the watch.

Okay.

How in the fuck did I afford a fuckin' goddamn Supertanker Marine timepiece?

I may not know much about suit jackets, but didn't that jewelry store in Thanton have one of these for like...thirty grand?

Fuck.

I really screwed up giving away that chain, didn't I?

Ugh.
I wasn't in my right mind.
He quickly reaffixed the watch to his wrist and leaned back against the moist brick wall behind him, the rain steadily refusing to abate.

Deciding now was as good a time as any to grab some shuteye, Jeremiah closed his eyes.

* * *

Visions flashed and fled in Jeremiah's dreams.

Nightmarish, haunting scenes that would've left him sick to his stomach. Except, in in this fevered-like stated, that sick feeling, along with the experience, fled.

Because no sooner had he experienced them than he forgot them, left only with the impressions he gained from their momentary existence.

Even as he dreamed, nothing stuck or held with him other than a general feeling.

A sickened feeling that he had seldom felt.

The feeling itself wasn't unknown to him, but it was something that hadn't truly plagued him before.

Guilt.

For his actions, and even his own existence.

Yet there was no reason for that guilt.

Nothing for it to attach to, even as the horror-parade of things tore through one side of his mind and vanished out the other.

'Please!' shouted a voice from inside his mind. It unfortunately remained with him. A voice that

somehow caused him an insane desire to curl up into himself and hide.

'Just let us leave!'

"Just let me go! I don't have anything you want!"

Jeremiah scrunched his eyelids and felt himself stir from his slumber.

The last voice wasn't the same as the pleading voice inside of his own head.

Her voice.

Wait, who's her?

The thought bubbled up from the strange place between dreams and reality. Where one could grasp at the fleeting images of dreams quickly forgotten.

"How about… nah," a male voice replied, also decidedly not a part of his dream. Jeremiah awoke to darkness.

Then, he shoved aside the long piece of cardboard that had apparently blown atop him while he slept.

It was nighttime, and the rain had stopped - leaving the world a steamy, muggy mess, that wafted a miasma of scents into his nose.

The stench of fresh and old garbage, motor oil, and city life crashed into his sinuses like a Mack truck.

"This… isn't what you want!" Jeremiah turned his head to see a woman standing in the dead-end alley, hemmed into a corner by three dark-clothed men.

Nevertheless, she stood confidently, dangling her purse at her side with a white-knuckle grip on the strap.

"Just leave me be, and we all go home safe

and sound," she offered up, as if it were the most reasonable possibility.

"Relaaaaaax, darlin'," the man in the middle replied with a malicious chuckle. "We're only muckin' about. How's about you hand us that bag, we rifle through it and get what we want, and then we can move on to gettin' what we want a second time?"

The woman stood alone. Jeremiah looked to the other end of the alley, finding no one coming to help her, even as multiple people passed by. They didn't even look down the alley.

That kind of abysmal lack of situational awareness gets you killed.

Hell, probably what happened to her - wasn't paying attention, got grabbed, and now she's in this mess.

Jeremiah shook his head, pushing himself to his feet.

Lesser men might debate with themselves on choosing a three-on-one fight against evil. He was no lesser man.

He killed monsters.

He had killed enough monsters to be well aware of an unfortunate truth, one didn't need to be an unholy abomination of hideous magic and foul darkness to be a monster.

Being evil, as these men clearly were, was a type of monster all in its own.

I shall lay my head upon the root of the tree of life.

Jeremiah breathed in, mentally going over a mantra preached by Patrick at one point.

May she see fit to spare my life, or use my blood to nourish herself.

"Ohhh yeah," one of the other men began to laugh maniacally. "That shirt looks expensive, lady, why don't you take it off?"

Jeremiah froze mid-step, looking to the abundantly normal white t-shirt the woman wore. It didn't look at all expensive to him.

"Hey, Chuckles!" he shouted, stretching his arms above his head. Jeremiah bent to his left, then his right, until he felt a small series of pops echo up his spine. He sighed contentedly as the strain from sleeping in a seated position against a brick wall faded away. "How about we all just go home, and forget about seeing any of this, alrighty?

"You and I both know how complicated witnesses make things," Jeremiah smirked when two of their number broke off to approach him.

They walked confidently, in a distinctly menacing, slow pace.

"Would you look at that, boys," Chuckles laughed, spinning a large bowie knife in his hand. Jeremiah watched it with a frown. The weapon was nearly the size of a small machete. "We got ourselves a hero!"

Where the hell do you keep that thing, guy?
That's a terrible weapon for sneaky shit like this.
Can't ditch it easy, requires a big sheath...just ain't the right tool, chief.

"You know guy, I just woke up," Jeremiah sighed loudly as the two men flanked him in a wide, ninety-degree arc. "Really don't wanna deal with any corpses today - it's already been weird enough. Do you know how hard it is to fold you guys into a sewer grate that small?"

Jeremiah pointed to a small two-by-one-foot grate nearby. Chuckles seemed unperturbed by the threat. His friend, however, hesitated, almost flinching back, watching Jeremiah with a frown.

"Oooh, man's got tough talk," Chuckles clicked his tongue loudly, shaking his head. He brushed a lock of blond hair away from his eye and pointed the knife at Jeremiah. "Big words to back up, there, fuckhead."

Jeremiah caught a view of the lone man going after the woman backed into a corner.

Hope you can survive long enough for me to kill these two yahoos.

Try and stay alive, lady.

He sent out the thought, looking back to the tip of Chuckles' knife. Jeremiah tilted his head and smiled.

"Big words need some big action, don't you think?" Jeremiah replied, watching Chuckles, the adrenaline began to course through his veins. He pulled off his suit jacket in a smooth motion and tossed it to the small piece of cardboard he'd taken a nap on. Half of winning a fight like this was posturing: fraying the enemy's nerves, forcing doubt into their minds about their chances of winning. "Let's give the lady a show, eh?"

Jeremiah forced a false, enthusiastic smile to his face, like he was happy to be here, excited to have the opportunity to fight three against one.

Chuckles hesitated ever so slightly in his steps, and Jeremiah's smile became genuine.

Nothing more was said. Nothing more needed to be said.

Jeremiah jumped to the side as Chuckles slashed out with his large knife, pushing all his force into his left leg.

He'd intended to slam into Number Two with his shoulder and send the man sprawling.

Instead, his momentum carried him to and

through the other man, sending them both sprawling and rolling into the nearby alley wall.

Jeremiah felt an ugly and dull pain in his side. Unable to check given the situation, he felt like perhaps he'd landed on something.

Instead of fussing over it, he pushed himself to his feet, just in time for Chuckles to rush up to him, at the same time bringing the knife down in an overhead plunging strike aimed for Jeremiah's chest.

With barely enough time to spare, Jeremiah brought his arms up before him, catching Chuckles' wrists and stopping the point only two inches away from reaching flesh.

What the fuck?

Jeremiah's mind was scrambling to quickly take in the situation, staring at the knife before glancing back to Number Two on the ground beside him.

The man's neck was twisted at an odd angle against the wall, a small dent in his skull was plainly visible, and the man drew in ragged, incomplete breaths.

I...I didn't...there's no way I hit him that hard. Did I?

Jeremiah set that thought aside. This wasn't the time or place for him to worry about tackling someone and inadvertently killing them.

Unnecessary roughness wasn't a thing in life-or-death situations.

Given the fact that he was currently holding off a knife pointed directly at his throat, it was a boon.

No one would be attacking him from the side, provided the woman could hold her own. Or at least, keep the other attack busy for a time.

Alright fucker!
Let's see how you handle this!
Jeremiah smiled, putting all his focus on Chuckles.

Not wanting to give up control of the knife, since that seemed like the worst possible thing to do, Jeremiah clamped his hands down. He was feeling particularly fit at the moment, and this man didn't look like he had much outside of an average man's strength.

Stepping into his opponent, Jeremiah rammed his shoulder up into the man's armpit. Stepping hard into him, he bent his waist and grunted, leveraging the man up and over his back, and tossing him bodily.

The force of the throw had surprised Jeremiah and sent him down to a kneeling position. Watching as the man went careening down the alley.

He'd momentarily had a thought to try and break the knife free from the man's grip but hadn't managed it.

The throw had happened so quickly, and if Jeremiah was honest, he had no idea what he was really doing. It wasn't something he'd done before.

"Neat trick," Chuckles said, scrambling to his feet at the same time Jeremiah did. He was watching Jeremiah with a sour expression.

Not waiting for Jeremiah, the man rushed straight ahead, with the knife held in front of himself.

So obvious and blatant was the move, that Jeremia had more than enough time to merely sidestep his opponent's blow this time rather than engage him.

"Toro," Jeremiah said with a laugh, even going so far as to slap the man on the rear end as he went past.

"Get up Beck!" Chuckles groused, kicking the foot of Number Two, as he spun back around to face Jeremiah. "Really gon' let this happen? Getting your dumb ass out?"

"Pretty sure he's dead, guy," Jeremiah added, pointing a finger at Number Two with a smirk. The man was clearly in the hazy phase between life and death. He was dead, his body just hadn't gotten the message yet.

"The fuck he is!" Chuckles shouted, slid forward, and tried to stab Jeremiah with the point of the knife this time. Jeremiah caught the man's wrists just in time to stop the weapon, the point of it less than an inch from gelding Jeremiah.

Too close! Way too close!

Jeremiah thought frantically with wide eyes, as Chuckles pulled the knife back and prepared for another stab.

Can't let this go on.

At some point either he'll get lucky, or I'll get stupid.

This situation wasn't one that could be walked away from, or forced to a rapid close.

All the options he would normally use would probably leave him with a severed femoral artery, unable to walk, or singing soprano for the rest of his life.

Most of his options were more along the lines of attacking the man's hand when he went in with the knife.

Except, suddenly, and unexpected, it wasn't Jeremiah's problem anymore.

A purse slammed with blinding speed into the side of Chuckles' head, with a thump that sounded quite solid.

The man's grip went lax on the blade and Jeremiah stood there, somewhat stunned by the sudden change. Without an outlet for the insane adrenaline rush he was going through, his body decided it was a great time to freeze.

Without moving, he watched the woman bring her handbag up, and then down atop Chuckles' face like a sledgehammer.

Jeremiah winced when he heard a -crunch- from the bag slamming home atop the man's face. Whether that was from an item in the bag breaking, from Chuckles' nose, or Chuckles' face caving in, he wasn't sure.

To be honest he didn't care either.

Regardless, the man wouldn't be getting back up anytime soon.

The bag sounded heavy after all, and he was unmoving on the ground.

Glancing toward the man who had been dealing with her originally, Jeremiah saw that he was face down on the ground and unmoving.

Somehow, someway, the woman had managed to put him to sleep.

Not really wanting to consider the situation, and with his mind partially blanking out, he didn't really process everything.

"Hell of a wake-up call, lady," he exclaimed in a lighthearted tone. She'd apparently had to kill one man and save him from another. "Thanks for the assist. My heroic plan didn't turn out so heroic in the end."

"Well. I wasn't going to just stand there. Nor do I think I could have handled all three very well. So... thanks for stepping in," she replied in an odd tone, her eyes moved to Chuckles at her feet, and she seemed to be considering his bloody face. "Didn't realize this was a dead end. Really wasn't paying attention."

"I… wouldn't make a habit of going down dark alleys at night," Jeremiah only half-lectured, since he'd also been in said dark alley. "Probably should get moving. Someone might've heard all that, and I really don't wanna end up on camera, or be here when the cops arrive."

The woman stopped staring down at the man beneath her to look up at Jeremiah with a frown, and he instantly had to quell the urge to say something stupid.

She watched Jeremiah with bright emerald eyes, set in an unusually pretty face that was twisted into an odd look he couldn't identify. She brushed a lock of pale brown hair out of her eyes, seeming to watch him questioningly.

Her face softened as she seemed to come to some type of resolution to her own thoughts.

Then, she suddenly favored him with a bright smile.

"Pretty sure that that's not an issue," she laughed softly. "Not around these parts."

"Still, you don't wanna risk it," Jeremiah argued. "They're gonna have a lot of hard to answer questions about… well… everything. Pretty sure the dude I knocked into the wall is dead, too."

"Again, the police probably won't care." the woman bit down on her tongue as she looked from one body to another. Frowning spectacularly, she rolled her eyes and chuffed. "A thirty minute plus response time won't help anyone."

"That's why I always try and stay strapped,"

Jeremiah shrugged absently as he tried to blink away a sense of vertigo that crept up on him.

"And... where was that strap a minute ago?" The woman watched him with a confused expression, her head tilted to the side.

"I uhh... left it in my other pants." Jeremiah smiled and mimed slapping his empty pockets. Clucking his tongue, he pointed at the corpses on the ground and began to turn down the alley "Anyway, I'm gonna go. Been nice meeting you, and uh, good luck with the dead guys."

"Wait!" the woman blurted suddenly, quickly coming up beside him. Jeremiah turned fractionally to look down at the brightly smiling petite lady. "Listen. I don't think a simple thank you is enough.

"You jumped in and helped me when you didn't have to. The least I could do is let you come back to my apartment, get cleaned up, and have a bite to eat."

Jeremiah blinked at the sudden offer.

Women don't just... invite the crazy homeless man in a suit back to their place for a bite to eat and a shower. She's probably just being polite.

"Thanks but it's really not necessary," Jeremiah nodded once and continued walking towards the mouth of the alley. "I'm sure I'll find my way to another cozy carboard box."

His stomach rumbled disapprovingly.

She did say a bite to eat. After the debacle at the soup kitchen, I really should find something to eat. Maybe just go back to her place, grab a couple slices of bread, and then leave.

Maybe she has a map of the city I could borrow too.

Find my way to a Templ-

Nope, can't go to the Templar Parish. Not after what Claudius did.

"Yeah, but you could either go directly to the cardboard box, or go to the cardboard box with a clean... fancy suit and a bite to eat.

"Speaking of that, I don't think I've seen a more well-dressed homeless man before," the woman replied in confusion. "Why were you in that alley in the first place?"

"Needed somewhere to sleep," Jeremiah replied simply. He wasn't lying, even if he was burying the lead a little.

A lead that he still felt was at the edge of his mind.

Like a word he'd forgotten.

"Uh-huh." she gave him a direct, knowing glare that told him that she didn't buy his story, or at least the resoundingly over-simplified answer he'd given her. "Anyways, the offer's open. Shower, food, out of the cold for an hour or two."

It didn't feel all that cold to Jeremiah.

Still, the offer was incredibly enticing. He was itchy.

And –very– hungry.

"I don't wanna impose," he offered, attempting to be polite and give her an out.

"It wouldn't be an imposition at all!" she replied with a bright smile. "I'm Ashley, by the way."

"Jeremiah," Jeremiah introduced himself, as they both came to a stop. She extended her hand to him with the same blisteringly pretty smile, and he shook it with a relieved sigh. "Lead the way, then."

Chapter 7

Jeremiah shut the door behind him, cutting off the din of televisions, shouting couples, and the general noise that pushed its way through the thin walls of the apartment building hallway.

He looked around the combination living room, foyer, and kitchenette of Ashley's apartment. It was small and cramped, even in comparison to his own one-bedroom flat back in Larimer.

Small knickknacks rested on nearly every available surface, along with various polished rocks, what were clearly travel souvenirs from foreign countries, and a solitary picture atop the shelf above a remarkably thin and large TV.

Damn, maybe I'm doing something wrong. Apparently, you can get a high-speed TV and live in a crappy part of town.

Been living my whole life wrong, I guess.

That or Clallam is just that amazing.

Then again, I woke up to a be homeless man, in a four-figure suit and with a thirty-thousand-dollar watch so... can't really talk shit, can I?

"Nice place," Jeremiah said, trying to force a kind tone into his voice.

"Don't lie to me like that," Ashley snorted and shook her head, flicking on the hallway light.

"Okay fine. Just trying to be nice," he replied with a guilty grin of his own, scratching at his side. "It's cozy, that better?"

"Mmmmm," she tossed her head from side to side, clearly considering his words with a somewhat amused smile. "Cozy is better... still think you're giving it too much credit."

"I mean, I was racked out under a piece of cardboard, in a stinking alley, about twenty minutes ago," Jeremiah shrugged as Ashley turned back to him with a raised brow. "This is a hell of a lot better than those digs."

Ashley watched him with a thoughtful expression as he stepped deeper into the apartment and poked at one of the thick, green blackout curtains.

"I suppose that's fair," she offered with a long-suffering sigh. "How long have you been in the city, by the way?"

"Why? Is it that obvious I don't belong?" Jeremiah snorted, releasing the hem of the dense fabric.

"Kinda," she replied, smile on her face becoming a smirk. "The suit is certainly nice, though out of place. Might have picked that up from anywhere. The 'Mr. Hero' act, while amusing, also wasn't really par for the course, but not that unique either."

"Honestly... what really gave it away, was you obviously have no idea where anything is."

Ashley gave him a knowing look with raised eyebrows before continuing.

"Spent the entire walk over here looking at stores, like the SpeedyStop, and any landmark you could see. Honestly, reminded me of my dad," she murmured.

"Ah," Jeremiah replied, unsure of how to respond to that statement.

"Yeah. He was always a little... on edge. But back to my question-"

"Got here today," Jeremiah replied levelly,

feeling confident in revealing at least that chunk of information. She'd already guessed as much, and Jeremiah knew that nothing could really be gleaned from that tiny puzzle piece. "From out east, a little bit."

"Well, I guessed that much. It'd be pretty hard for you to come from the west!" she stated. Jeremiah caught the slightly forced smile on her face, clearly trying to put him at ease and thrust some levity into the conversation. "So, whereabouts are ya' from?"

"Eh, Saint Anthony was my old stomping grounds, bounced around from here to there for a while, though," Jeremiah lied with a noncommittal shrug. "Never spent too long in one place."

Just play it off like I'm a drifter.

Maybe a career gambler, someone that would reasonably go from flush with cash to nothing in a night or two.

Jeremiah internally patted himself on the back as the idea solidified in his mind.

It would work perfectly.

He could shower, maybe get his clothes washed, and begin to put the pieces together before leaving the next morning, and have it be completely plausible.

"Had a bad run of luck at the tables, tried to drown it away, and woke up in the garbage dump earlier today," Jeremiah said, blending the truth with lies. "I wouldn't recommend it by the way. It's a really… ah… rotten, way to wake up."

Then again, maybe it was more truth than he wanted to admit.

He'd been tricked and outdrawn by Brother Claudius, an abysmal run of bad luck.

If she, for some unknown reason, tried to

follow his trail back to when he woke up, she would find it to be entirely true.

"I can see that," Ashley trailed with a slow nod before sighing. "Or more accurately, smell that. It certainly explains why you smell the way you do. Speaking of which, please just... don't touch anything until you shower. Or sit anywhere.

"It's nothing personal but I really don't want that stench to linger. It's not you."

"Wasn't planning on it," Jeremiah replied to Ashley's pleading smile. "Looking forward to that shower, actually. Speaking of which."

He let the sentence trail off in a clear question, briefly glancing down the short, stubby hall to the right side of the apartment.

It was barely ten feet deep and held three doors, though which one was the bathroom, he wasn't sure.

"Oh right!" she replied with a small chirp, as if her thoughts had taken her elsewhere. She shook her head and pointed down the hall. "The left door. Just toss your dirty clothes in the sink, and let them soak there for a bit if you want. Or you can throw them in the washing machine straight away. Your choice."

Jeremiah nodded, then paused. He rolled his tongue on the inside of his mouth as he thought about his problem.

"You got a book or something that I could borrow?" he asked with a raised brow, not wanting to wait the hour or so it would take for his clothes to finish cleaning, naked, in the bathroom, with no entertainment.

"Yeah, I do... why?" Ashley cocked her head to the side, her long, near-blond hair spilling over her shoulder.

"I'm wearing everything I own. As nice as it is to do laundry... well, I don't exactly know you well enough to wander your place naked," Jeremiah smiled down at Ashley as he stepped into the hallway. "Would like to have something to do while I'm waiting on these to get clean."

He pulled demonstratively at his stained and grimy dress shirt with a smirk.

Ashley bit her lower lip cutely, staring at Jeremiah's chest - more specifically, through his chest, as her mind clearly worked at solving the problem a different way.

"I think my ex left some clothes here—" Ashley began slowly, sliding behind Jeremiah while he opened the bathroom door. "Let me check if I can get you a pair of jeans or... something."

Jeremiah paused in the doorway of the bathroom, briefly stepping back to watch Ashley open her bedroom door.

He half-followed her, waiting just on the outside of the doorframe. He frowned, seeing the two windows in her bedroom were also covered by blackout curtains.

She seems to really hate the sun.

He looked around the tidy bedroom with a frown. Ashley currently rummaged through several drawers in a dresser on the right side of the bedroom, and a queen-sized bed with a blue, threadbare comforter sat on the left-middle of the room.

"AHA!" she giggled excitedly, pulling free a pair of grey-black checkered sweatpants.

Setting the pants to the side atop the dresser, she grabbed a blue oversized T-shirt from the same drawer and stacked it atop the pants before grabbing the small pile up into her arms and returning to the doorway.

She extended her arms out to him, offering the garments with a grin. "Dumbass couldn't remember my birthday, so he definitely couldn't remember to take his pants with him either!"

Jeremiah grabbed the garments with a neutral expression, actively working to stuff down his instincts.

Don't hit on the pretty girl.

Don't do it, she doesn't want to be flirted with by the strange homeless guy that followed her home.

Don't.

Flirt.

"Eh, he was dumb enough to miss out on you, then," Jeremiah replied instead. It didn't feel like flirting and was just a positive affirmation. Harmless pleasantries. "Don't expect him to be smart enough to plan ahead and get his pants back."

Jeremiah did his best to not touch the clothes more than he had to.

He had them in a three-fingered grip, far away from his body.

Ashley's eyes flicked down for a brief second before she looked back up to him and nodded her head marginally.

"Go shower, Stinky," she instructed with a grin in a humorous tone. She pointed over his shoulder.

"Right, yep!" Jeremiah replied with a thin-lipped, embarrassed smile.

Stinky was a definitely appropriate title at the moment.

He spun on his heels and stepped into the bathroom, closing the door behind him with a deep exhale and a shake of his head.

He set the clean clothes atop the porcelain throne and began to strip out of the suit.

He set the belt to the side, realizing that was not machine washable. The leather looked to be high quality, along with the brass buckle.

The best he could do for it was attempt to clean it with a smattering of water and paper towels or toilet paper.

Or better yet, Jeremiah could wash it in the shower with him.

He started up the water in the shower after a brief moment of fidgeting and figuring with the knobs.

Once again, he was abruptly reminded that he was hungry.

Hungry to the point of starving.

Such that it felt as if his stomach would try to scoop his spine out and devour it.

His body chose that moment to drive home the point, and he heard an incredibly loud rumble of his stomach as he placed the pants and underwear in a wad in the sink.

Given how the last forty-eight hours had gone, he briefly considered that it might have been a good idea to get picked up by the police.

He'd at least get a meal out of it.

He snorted and shook his head with a slow sigh, unbuttoning the collared shirt, pausing to pulled it down over his shoulders.

From his chest to his wrists, Jeremiah was covered with tattoos.

A surprise to be sure the first time he'd seen them, and more so now that they yet remained.

When he'd been gunned down in Larimer,

he'd had none.

Thinking further on that, Jeremiah looked over his body for any sign of scarring, of bullet wounds that should reasonably be stitched across his chest.

Other than the colorful, artistic sigils, paintings of mythological creatures, and a small, knotted scar he was unfamiliar with on his forearm, he had none.

What the fuck happened between then and now? Did I survive and somehow get my memories eaten?

No, no that's...that's stupid.

That's just stupid.

I'm most certainly me...but not me...and...and it's all just messed up.

And all those memories that came and went.

I can't remember them but...but I know...I feel... they were there. There's an empty space now. But there was something there.

A voice.

It was.

Jeremiah's mind slowly uncramped and he felt a moment where his thoughts ran clear. Clear and pure.

'*Just let us leave!*'

Almost immediately, the voice that had shocked him earlier shot back into his forethoughts. Causing him to wince, hunch his shoulders, and curl up closer to the sink.

Closing his eyes, he shook his head, as if he could knock the voice free.

Jar it loose.

An enormous and ugly feeling of guilt rose up in him then. That everything about him was completely wrong.

Not waiting, and wanting to clean himself, he

got into the shower.

The guilt followed him even as he got under the water and began scrubbing at himself. There wasn't the immediate release of the feeling he'd hoped for as he worked to get the stink off himself.

Instead, he tried to prod his mind into working on something else. Rather than letting it dredge up things, he put it to action.

Except that prevailing thought that wanted to pop up into the fore front of his mind was of where he'd only been the other day.

In a sewer with Edie and running for their lives.

Because at this moment, even if he wasn't dead, there was no escaping the truth that, there was the most certain possibility that no one else was alive.

That the Church of One and All maybe was exterminated to the last in the same operation.

Strangely, there was an odd feeling that popped into his head.

A grateful and glad feeling that resonated with the possibility of the Church being exterminated to the last.

It was immediately followed by him shuddering at the thought of it. By the thought that he didn't want that. That he wanted it to still be there.

Only for the guilt to instantly rise back up and nearly drag him down to his knees at the idea of him hoping the Church remained.

"Fuck," he growled in a half whisper. His only option to find out anything at all would be to contact the local parish, to find their Templar and talk with them. Talk with them about everything that happened and maybe what'd been happening.

Except, once he made contact, the chance of running into Brother Claudius or his ilk was incredibly possible.

Especially if he'd be bringing up the most certainly failed operation.

With that thought neatly severing his desire to reach out, he went back to his showering.

He leaned back into the water and began washing his short hair, closing his eyes before the water flowed over his face.

He breathed in deeply of the flowery scent of Ashley's soap.

It wasn't his brand, by any means, but it did smell a far sight better than a majority of things.

Such as, a literal garbage dump.

Or himself only a minute or so ago.

Wiping down his face, Jeremiah stared at the water spilling down the drain in the middle of the shower. As more and more grime was sluiced off his body, the dark brown, filthy water slowly lightened in color, until it was merely a pale brown, then at last, became clear.

Fuck, I was dirty. Apparently I didn't get everything off at the river.

Never taking soap and hot water for granted again.

Jeremiah decided with raised eyebrows, staring down at the drain.

A strange sad echo flickered through his thoughts.

Forlorn and lost at the idea of ever truly being clean again.

Jeremiah tried to turn his brain off.

By the time he stepped out of the shower ten minutes later, flowery-smelling and clean, his skin felt pleasantly smooth.

Almost numbed by the heat of the scalding water, though cleansed.

He grimaced, stepping up to the sink, smelling the miasma wafting from his pile of dirty laundry. He exhaled, snatching up the sweatpants and T-shirt with an internal thank you to whatever fortune was graced to him for the opportunity to put on clean clothes.

The pants felt soft against his skin, and the shirt fit him snugly around the chest and shoulders. He stared at himself in the mirror, noting with some skepticism that he actually looked good with tattoos, despite avoiding them for his entire life.

An intrusive thought sprang into his mind.

He needed a plan and a direction right now.

Spinning his wheels endlessly and fretting over what might be didn't get him any closer to answers.

Right now, he was homeless, in an unfamiliar city, with no ID, no idea what was going on, and had a score to settle with a Templar.

From there, he needed to figure out what'd happened and if there was anywhere for him to pick up from where he'd left off.

That was a plan for tomorrow.

During the daylight hours.

Tonight was a day that was done and gone.

He crumpled the clothes into a small ball in his hands, holding them far away from his clean ones, and opened the door.

Jeremiah stepped across the hall, believing that the small door directly across from the bathroom was a small vestibule that held a washer and dryer.

At least it would be the case in his own

apartment.

As it turned out, he was right.

Jeremiah dumped the clothes into the washing machine, filled it with an abundance of soap, and started the cycle.

As he closed the machine, the lingering odor was thankfully banished. Immediately replaced by a smell that practically sang to his sinuses.

Fresh-cooked food.

His gut screaming loudly, Jeremiah stepped into the living room and turned to his right.

Ashley was currently bouncing between cooking eggs on a cast-iron skillet, and checking on a small toaster oven on the counter with several slices of bread. She swayed back and forth to the beat of an inaudible tune, moving over to the fridge.

Apparently not noticing him enter the room, she bent over and inspected the inside of the near-empty fridge, continuing to sway before she pulled out the pad of butter.

He blinked once, not really understanding what was going on. Though it was a hard battle to not let his attention focus entirely on the food.

He tried coughing once to get her attention.

She didn't respond, instead turning back to the pan on the stove as if she heard nothing.

"Hey, Ashley," he tried again, getting no response a second time.

Am I getting the silent treatment for some reason?

A frown creased his face as he pondered the situation, watching her continue to listen to inaudible music.

Did I piss her off that much?

Deciding to try and get an answer, he tapped her on the shoulder. Ashley jumped slightly, before pulling a small earbud from her ear and looking at him with raised eyebrows and wide eyes. She exhaled deeply and laughed.

"Fuck, you scared the hell outta me," she smiled up at him as he stepped back, giving her a respectful distance. She was significantly shorter than him, and he didn't want to loom over her. She was already opening her home to him, so he imagined she was probably nervous at least. "I kinda zoned out there for a bit."

"Sorry, didn't mean to spook ya'," Jeremiah held his hands up apologetically before continuing, "That looks really good, by the way."

"Thank you! Not the best cook, and I'm kinda low on options," she turned back to the food with a shrug, stirring around the scrambled eggs on the pan. "But I figured you'd like something real to eat instead of the college student special of ramen."

"I'm just thankful to eat!" Jeremiah laughed, stepping around behind the small bar that separated the kitchenette from the living space. He sat down on one of the stools, ran his fingers through his hair and sighed. "Thanks for this, again. Certainly more cozy than a rainy alley."

Ashley flipped her hair over her shoulder and leaned her head to the side, pulling out another earbud before she put them both in a small, white case.

Are those...Bluetooth? Didn't that just come out? I've only seen them on big earmuffs and whatnot. Must've been expensive but...she doesn't look like she has a lot of money?

What the heck is going on?

He noted the headphones with a small frown before looking at the rest of the room.

"So, what do you do for a living?" Jeremiah asked casually of Ashley, filling the empty silence. It didn't sound like the brightest question, but the pause in conversation had him immediately on Edge.

Looking at the flatscreen TV on the wall for a moment, he looked back to Ashley.

Everything in her apartment seemed somewhat run-down.

Except the tech, which was leagues ahead of everything he owned.

Or had owned.

A clearly high-end, incredibly thin laptop sat on a small folding table in the corner of the living room, with a stack of textbooks next to it. Jeremiah continued trying to put together the odd puzzle placed before him.

Blackout curtains, fancy tech, run-down apartment in a bad, cheap neighborhood...is this a safehouse for something?

He struck that thought down purely on the merit that he was here by invitation.

Ashley seems...confident that I won't hurt her. Though, I suppose that could be because I jumped in to help her in the alley. If you can't trust someone that helps you, who can you trust?

But you can't trust someone you don't know, least of all the weird homeless dude who threw down with some assholes.

Jeremiah chewed at the inside of his lip at that thought.

"College student," Ashley chuckled, leaning over to the small toaster oven, and visually inspecting the bread after opening the front. "I, erm, go to the WSU campus a few miles away. You? Beyond the gambling and what not, that is."

Though, she clearly can fight.
Actually did better than I did in the alley.
Maybe she's just some martial-arts fanatic and is confident enough to throw down with me if things go sideways.

"It's a little complicated right now," Jeremiah replied with an absent shrug as Ashley pulled a whistling electric kettle off a small, black base. "I guess I'm kinda between jobs at the moment. Or uh, between tables."

"That does explain why you crashed in an alley," she grinned back at him, holding up a small box of earl grey tea in one hand and a glass container of instant coffee in the other. "Tea or coffee?"

"Tea," Jeremiah replied with a thin-lipped smile, wary of any instant coffee. To him, instant coffee was a crime against flavor.

"Oooh, good man," Ashley replied with a smile, turning back to her work in the kitchen. She pulled free two bags, and stuck them in pre-prepared mugs on the counter. She poured the steaming water into them, taking the time to stir Jeremiah's.

He was looking forward to the tea though, more so the meal it would come with.

The same meal which she now loaded onto a plate, piling the entire pan of eggs into the center before she pulled free the toast from the small toaster oven.

As she worked, he looked over to the window that was in the kitchen. It had a heavy blackout curtain in front of it. Behind that, was pull shades.

Behind even that, he saw that a film of some sort had been completely taped over the glass.

Allergic to sunlight, good in a fight.
Unusually strong.

Budgets for low income, but sometimes has infusions of cash enough to buy shiny tech.

The thoughts all coalesced in his mind at once as she placed the plate before him.

He said his thanks and dug into the meal while Ashley leaned against the counter, checking the steaming mugs of tea at regular intervals.

Jeremiah ate fast, wolfishly so, his aching belly demanding its payment, even as his mind settled and solidified around a singular realization.

He took a bite of the third piece of toast as Ashley brought over the mugs of tea.

She set his down before him on the counter, offering the carton of milk with raised, expectant eyebrows.

Still chewing, Jeremiah waved his hand and shook his head, avoiding talking with his mouth full.

Ashley shrugged and returned it to the fridge. Swallowing and staring down into his tea, Jeremiah watched the small fleck of white that floated at the top with a frown.

Tentatively he brought it to his lips, watching her expression curiously. He took a small, testing sip of the scalding liquid, forcing a neutral expression onto his face as it burnt his tongue.

Letting it cool, Jeremiah sampled the flavor, comparing it with the glasses of earl grey he'd had previously.

Something was off.

A hint of a slight chalky flavor permeated the liquid.

He disguised him spitting it back out as taking another drink and sighed contentedly. Now, he was sure of what she was.

Well, ninety percent sure.

Enough that it still felt like a gamble.

He forced himself to take slow, calming breaths to lower his heart rate.

He flicked his eyes up to Ashley, who watched him with a smile. Then, he chucked the contents of the mug directly at her face.

With a screech of pain, Ashley took a step towards him menacingly.

Can't hide from me, you blood-sucking fucker!

Jeremiah screamed in his mind with a snarl, shoving himself backwards off of the stool.

Chapter 8

As quick as Ashley's scowl had appeared, it disappeared. Closing her mouth with a snap, the Vampire made a sour expression, as if sucking on a lemon.

"What the -hell-?" Ashley shouted indignantly, brushing the dripping contents of the mug from her eyes. "You goddamn asshole!"

"Bloodsucking bitch," Jeremiah replied with a snarl, stretching out his shoulders, he slowly strafed to the middle of the living room. "You think you can trick me? This ain't my first time getting roofied."

Ashley stuck her tongue out the side of her mouth.

Closing her eyes, she cocked her head and sucked in a brief inhale of air. She sighed loudly and pointed towards the door.

"It's unlocked. You can leave if you want!" Ashley leaned forward, rested her palms on the counter and shook her head. "So leave then. Get the hell out!"

"So you admit it, then?" Jeremiah asked, still grinning widely.

"What? That I was thirsty?" Ashley snapped, raising her arms up in an open, aggressive question. "Yeah! I'm fucking thirsty! And you interrupted my dinner earlier!"

"So what?" Jeremiah scoffed back. "What, you just drain any dude that walks into your place like some kind of fucked up spider?"

"No! You dumb motherfucker!" she shouted back, extending her palm to the door behind

Jeremiah, clearly dismissing him. "And get the fuck out! Do you know how hard it will be to find another top like this?

"Ugh. Maybe I can get the stain out? Damnit. Damnit, damnit."

Ashley gestured to the patterned, frilly blouse she'd changed into. The last of her statement had been made almost to herself it seemed.

"I'm not going to leave a monster like you on the streets," Jeremiah straightened out and mentally prepared himself to do something that would be considered borderline suicidal. Fight a Vampire unarmed, alone, without any backup. "You might look human, even manage to pretty convincingly act human, but at the end of the day you exist for one purpose: to feast on the good, innocent people that just try to live their lives."

I can do this. She's just one Vampire.

Just gotta find something to ram through her eye socket or heart.

Where the fuck would she keep a screwdriver?

"Oh kiss my ass, you ignorant fuck," Ashley snorted and rolled her eyes. "There's exactly two ways I've eaten since I got turned, okay?

"From the blood bank, and from assholes like those in the alley. Stupid bastard."

Jeremiah watched as she held up her hands in front of herself and gestured with them as she spoke, as if explaining it to him like a child. He was not about to be talked down to by some self-important Vampire, a monster in human form.

"So no, I don-" Ashley cut off when Jeremiah charged her, dropping his shoulder at the last second to try and catch her low in the ribs.

Vampires could get the wind knocked out of

them, same as any human. With a small squawk of fear, she jumped to the side before Jeremiah slammed bodily into the fridge behind her.

Jeremiah shook his head and spun around as Ashley stared daggers at him from behind him in the living room.

"Okay, asshole," she spat, brushing a wayward lock of hair out of her eyes. "You wanna do it that way? Fine. The cops are gonna laugh their asses off when they scrape your dumb ass off my floor!"

Ashley leapt forward, throwing a punch at Jeremiah's face that he had zero chance of dodging.

Still, somehow, perhaps by blind luck, it blurred past his face as he sprang back into the small kitchenette. Her fist slammed into the fridge, denting the front around her knuckles.

"Fuck, dammit!" Ashley shouted, grabbing the refrigerator on either side and steadying it from rocking. "Nononono, please don't die!"

Ashley opened the door of the fridge quickly while Jeremiah stared at her in confusion. She sighed in relief when the light inside turned on before closing the door and turning to him.

There was rage writ large across her features now.

Oh no.

Jeremiah dove over the counter into the living room as Ashley charged him again, shrieking wordlessly.

He scrambled to his feet just in time for her to tackle him onto the small coffee table in front of the sofa, the thin, almost decorative legs shattering as they both careened to the ground.

She threw her fist down at his face after they

landed in a heap. Jeremiah caught it with his forearm, directing it at the ground by his head.

"I let you into my house!" Ashley screamed, trying and failing yet again to rain a blow on his skull. "Fed you, let you take a shower! This is why everyone is an asshole! It's like I'm not allowed to be nice!"

Jeremiah grabbed her wrist and wrenched her over his shoulder and onto the ground. He climbed atop her hips in much the same way she had been on him, and threw a punch down at her face.

It didn't connect.

He faltered when Ashley's fist connected with his ribcage, and he was flung off of her, the momentum of the Vampire-strength punch sending Jeremiah sprawling up and over the couch behind them.

Jeremiah coughed loudly, staring up at the ceiling and trying to regain his breath. He grunted, pushing himself up on his elbows, his heart pounded away in his ears.

The slug began to move around again, coiling its ugly and painful way down into his legs.

He stood shakily to his feet, mirrored by Ashley on the other side of the couch.

"You try and act all high and mighty, like you don't drink innocent people," Jeremiah growled as the pain in his gut subsided, the stinging on his ribs fading quickly to a dull ache. "Probably just gonna drug me, and then feed me to your fuckin' coven. Where are they, by the way? Shouldn't you have another bloodsucker on hand in case you meet someone like me?"

"I don't have a fucking coven, you idiot!" Ashley yelled back at him, lifting her hands, apparently throttling him in her mind. "Do you think I'd live in a shithole like this if I did?"

Jeremiah's brain froze for a split-second thinking about that. Most covens tended to run expensive, trendy businesses in his experience. Trendy businesses, wealthy businesses. Her apartment decidedly did not meet the definition of 'wealthy accommodations.'

Even for a safehouse, this stretched the limits of what many Vampires would tolerate. This was most certainly not something that a coven would want to be associated with.

Wait, she doesn't have a coven then?

"So what," Jeremiah questioned, letting his breathing slow down to quell his racing heart rate. His hands came down partially from the defensive posture they'd been in. "You just freelance and eat random people dumb enough to come home with you? Turn them into your blood-slave?"

"Oh for fuck's sake," Ashley sighed dramatically and shook her head. "And you broke my coffee table, jackass!"

"You broke it yourself!" he shouted back at her in a childish way. There was a distinct feeling like he was in the wrong here that he didn't want to consider.

This had to be just her trying to blame Jeremiah for her hunger, her attempt to drain him like a juicebox.

Or so he forced himself to believe.

"Because you're the crazy man trying to kill me!" Ashley snapped back. "I told you to get out already!"

"You're the crazy bitch trying to drug me and drink me dry!"

Ashley raised a finger, opening her mouth and closing it with a snap. As if considering his words earnestly.

"Okay, I did try and drug you, and that wasn't the best way for me to get fed, you're absolutely right," she admitted in a rush. Her words caused Jeremiah to pause yet again. He'd killed Vampires before. Several, in fact. None had apologized or shown any remorse for their actions. "But you interrupted my dinner! I was going to drink form those lowlives!

"And I'm so hungry that everything is just pissing me the fuck off! I'm starving. Literally!"

Jeremiah really didn't know how to respond to all of this. It suddenly felt less like they were fighting and more like they were having a screaming match over what to have for dinner if anything.

"The blood banks around here just hiked their prices, I haven't eaten in a week, and I'm barely making ends meet as it is!" Ashley continued in a defensive tone, staring at Jeremiah as if he were the biggest idiot she'd ever met. "I'm- I was trying to get a degree so I can make money like a normal human, just with a sun allergy. Okay?

"Is it too much to ask to just live my life without some coven asshole trying to recruit me, or you racist 'monster hunters' trying to shank me every chance they get?"

Jeremiah snapped down the immediate response of "Yes" before his mouth could spit it out. The words burned at him to be said, but he couldn't actually speak them.

Somewhere deep down inside of him, he agreed with her.

It was in fact what he'd wanted at some point

in his life too.

Before he joined HF.

Just to be able to live his life.

"But you... bloodsucking freaks don't get that opportunity. You lost that option when you decided to become the monster you are," he accused instead.

Ashley rolled her eyes, took in a shaky breath, and closed her eyes. When they opened again, her expression shifted.

"I'm a monster... a freak? Fine, fuck it, fuck you, fuck this shit!" she snarled, resolve steeling her countenance. "I'll show you a monster."

She jumped up and over the couch as Jeremiah sidestepped with more force than he predicted, launching himself several feet into the hallway.

What? Why the fuck does that keep happening?

He asked himself, scrambling to his feet while Ashley turned her head slowly towards him, her pale brown hair hanging over her face like a veil.

"I just wanted to take a little blood. Less than you'd even lose at an annual checkup," she growled as she began to walk slowly towards Jeremiah. "You'd wake up in the morning thinking we'd just had a fun night together. None the wiser, none the worse. In fact, you probably wouldn't even feel any different at all."

She began to laugh darkly while Jeremiah stepped back, realizing that this had been more than likely a complete mistake.

That if he'd taken a rational approach and maybe, just maybe, not flown off the handle, this would have had a different outcome.

I should've just smiled and not drank the tea.

"I've spent two fucking years in therapy. Two

years trying to deal with what I am, what he forced me to become," hissed Ashley.

What?

Jeremiah cocked his head to the side, even as he fidgeted with the knob on her bedroom door, having nowhere else to go.

"You wanna talk about bloodsucking leeches, you wanna talk about victims? What about Vamps like me, huh?" she demanded, closing on him.

Jeremiah slammed the thin, cheap door closed between them and scanned her bedroom for anything that could be used as a weapon. He stepped around her bed, scanning the floor for something.

The door opened as the knob itself simply crumpled under Ashley's strength.

"I've spent two years debating pulling my own teeth out!" screamed Ashley, standing there in the doorway. "Just grabbing a pair of pliers so the temptation to drain a bitch that screams at me because her coffee has cream instead of half and half would go the fuck away!"

Jeremiah spun as she stepped into the room, a wrathful scowl painted on her overly pretty face. He grabbed the lamp off of the end table at the foot of her bed and threw it at her face.

She caught it with an outstretched arm, inhaling deeply. Slowly, carefully, she set it on the bed beside her.

In a single blink of Jeremiah's eyes, she was on him, gripping his arms tightly and holding them to the sides of his body.

She opened her mouth wide, leaned in, and sank her fangs into his neck.

As the sharp pricks of fangs sinking into the space between his shoulder and neck sent alarm bells spiraling through Jeremiah's mind, he did the only thing he could think of doing.

He flopped backward and went limp.

Letting his body weight do the work for him.

Stumbling forward, Ashely's fangs came free and she went sprawling into the window behind him. Then, with a spray of glass fragments, the window shattered behind her.

Holding tight to the small cuts in his neck where her fangs had been yanked out of, Jeremiah pushed himself to his feet, stumbling to the far end of the room as Ashley struggled to extricate herself from the bent blinds and half-fallen curtain.

"You fucking asshole!" she shouted yet again, freeing her torso from the curtain and climbing to her knees. "You talk all this shit about protecting humanity, and you're not even Human? You're no different than I am!"

"I'm as Human as they come, lady!" Jeremiah shouted back from the far side of the room, the chill night air rustling the other surviving curtain.

"No. You're not!" Ashley held up a hand and wiped blood off a lip. She licked it off her finger and looked to him with raised eyebrows. "I have no idea what the hell you are, but it's not Human. You also broke my damn window."

"Technically, you broke it," Jeremiah got out in a whisper, desperate to get back to the 'try to kill each other' part of this.

He was Human.

He had to be Human.

If he wasn't, then that would leave only one option.

That everything is wrong.

The overwhelming chasm of guilt opened up

beneath him and he felt almost as if he were falling. Falling endlessly through a canyon of wrongs that he'd heaped upon others without ever truly understanding anything.

'Just let us leave'.

The whispered plea fractured his mind and knocked him out of his unwanted stupor.

With a quick shake of his head, Jeremiah looked down to the alley, the pavement five stories below. That certainly wasn't really a viable option for him at this time.

"Liar," he growled as she stared at him. "You're just trying to work your way out of this. Of what you did!"

Jeremiah ducked down and snatched one of the long, jagged shards of glass that were scattered around the room.

Was it a Vampire killer's best weapon?

No.

Would it work?

Yes, provided he could get it lodged in her throat.

It had cut his hand just from grabbing it too tightly already.

"Out of… out of what I did? No, I'm more than happy to take accountability for my actions. Can you? Mr. Non-Human?" Ashley asked indignantly, holding her arms up in frustration and shaking her hands at him. "Because, at the end of the day, I'm living with what I was forced to become to the best of my ability.

"And you know what, maybe trying to get a nip in with you wasn't the best idea either. I've already said that it was wrong for me to drug you, but there's really no going back at this point, is there,

Mr. Non-Human."

Standing there, Jeremiah gnawed at his lip.

The Non-Human comment unnerved him.

Unnerved him a way that was almost worse than the feeling of guilt had, or the plea he kept hearing in his mind.

It pushed down the very core of his existence to something else. That it wasn't as he'd always thought.

An unwanted thought popped up into his head.

Not being human would certainly explain a lot of what'd happened to him lately.

He immediately dislodged the thought, burned it, buried the remnants of it, and considered it never to have existed.

"Could I have just rolled up on you, gave you the bedroom eyes and said, 'oh hey, mind if I bite you real quick to take the edge off?' do you really think that would've worked?" Ashley extended her arms to the side, questioning him with raised eyebrows. "Really, Jeremiah, tell me how the fuck you'd insert that into a conversation. Because I'm hungry, I'm pissed, and you deprived me of the only chance I've had at a meal in days."

Jeremiah thought about that for a brief moment as the slug-thing inside him moved around suddenly.

"You can't just go around eating people, Ashley!" he replied, sucking in a deep breath of air as he thought about how to attack the Vampire across the room.

"You didn't seem very sad about the three assholes in the alley back there. Dead is dead," she replied. "Didn't you kill one yourself?"

Grinding his teeth, Jeremiah shook his head. He really didn't want to admit it, but he couldn't deny her words.

Dead was indeed dead.

Rather than let his mind dwell on that, he tested the shard of glass in his hand to see if it'd withstand any force at all.

It was sharp, but it might not be strong enough to survive being used as a weapon.

It wasn't.

The long, jagged blade, became a blunt trapezoid as it snapped in half with a small bit of pressure.

He dropped the former weapon on the ground and looked back to Ashey's pointed glare.

"What difference is there between snapping a rapist's neck and drinking them dry? Tell me, Mr. Non-Human. Tell me. I'd love to know," she demanded. "If I've only ever taken the lives of those who you yourself would have done the same to, can you claim you're better than me?"

Despite his better judgment, Jeremiah paused to give that question some thought.

Because as much as he wanted to just yell at her, he couldn't. Her question wasn't one he really wanted to answer.

Instead, a different question popped up.

If an op went sideways and I got turned...could I actually kill myself? I know that's what they always expected everyone to do, but could I do it?

He began to question himself and even more doubt crept its way into his mind.

If I didn't...what would I do?

Would I hunt Humans the same way she does? Follow the sex offender registry and just...guzzle myself on the blood of evil men?

Jeremiah looked to the side with a frown as Ashley crossed her arms again, watching him quietly. She didn't seem as intent to try and murder him at the moment.

No!

She's confusing me. I'm doubting when I shouldn't be.

Because I'm human.

I'm human.

I am human...I am...I'm —

The painful sensation that crept about inside of his body unwound itself and began to glide around inside of him.

Oozing along his aching ribs while the pain dulled, then went away.

He looked at his hand, which had been cut by the glass, finding only normal, unmarred flesh on his palm.

Am I human?

He looked to the horizon behind Ashley, the sky above the distant mountains glowing a pale orange as dawn approached them.

In the past, he'd killed humans for any number of reasons - for cavorting with Weres, for bringing Vampires their 'meals', hell, even for just committing heinous crimes against other humans that he happened to witness.

If I fight her here, hold her here. If I can just keep her away or even get her outside, this wouldn't be a fight at all.

The dawn would do my job for me.

He smiled at the thought of watching the Vampire fade to ash beneath his hands. To kill a monster like her was good and natural, the way things should be.

Something whispered at the back of his mind, something he was actively working to ignore and shunt out of his mind.

Fear and doubt.

The Church of the One and All proselytized often about redemption, of absolution and atonement.

An eerie stripe of sweat rushed down his back and he heard a pleading voice distantly, that came only from the depths of his own mind.

Then the frigid hand of guilt brushed clawed fingers across the surface of his thoughts.

"No one is free of sin," Jeremiah muttered to himself without realizing he'd said it.

In that moment he had a flash of the sewers that were so recently the crux of his life.

Of a Templar that was supposed to be the vanguard to save the world, turning his weapon on him because he was an inconvenience.

"You wanna go kill some real monsters? That's fine. I know where the coven who turned me operates! Go bother them! I'm just trying to live my damn life. Whatever's left of it at least," threw out Ashely with a hand wave at him.

Now that was a proposition that he was more than willing to consider.

But Jeremiah had nothing, no support, no weapons, not even a place to sleep. How could he begin to take on a coven like this?

He couldn't even fight a single Vampire by himself.

If Brother Claudius, a –Templar–, was evil, a traitor…is it possible that there could be one redeemable bloodsucker in the world?

If all things are in balance like the church says,

then for every spot of dark within the light, there must be light in the dark.

Though...does that mean I was a spot of dark?

Flinching mentally away from that last thought, he focused on the rest.

"You... you said you didn't want to be... what you are, right?" Jeremiah's question sprang from his mouth before he even had a chance to lock it down, to stow it away for some other time when he could seek wiser counsel. "You got turned against your will?"

"Yeah. Cops just let that bastard walk, too! Despite the fact that apparently there's this entire legal statue around turning the unwilling. Pretty sure he had money or connections. Maybe both? I don't know," Ashley gestured beside herself, glaring at him as if he were the densest object in the universe. "Trust me, I don't like the covens either - doesn't change the fact that I need to eat, and blood banks are fucking expensive!"

Expensive...expensive?

That-it-wait, are they that common place?

"Do you know how hard it is to support needing two pints of blood every week on eight bucks an hour? It sucked when I –had- a job!

"Or, better yet, how I can apply for good jobs when proper sunscreen is three hundred a bottle? So that I don't go up faster than a match?" Ashley asked, swapping from open hostility to talking to him in as if he might even commiserate with her. "It's not like I can just eat ramen like a normal college student! In fact, I miss ramen. It tastes awful now."

That was a valid point.

Wait, is it?

Yeah.

No!
No.
Maybe?

Jeremiah's thoughts screamed at each other inside his head, tripping, stumbling, and falling over themselves in a cascade of cacophonous noise.

"Help me take down the coven," murmured Jeremiah, his voice taking shape without thinking or considering the consequences of his words.

Am I really about to spare a Vampire, a literal drain on human society, purely because she said some frilly words? All because she dropped a sob story on my head in the middle of a fight?

"We work together, we go into this as neutral allies, I get some help and support with this, you kill the dude who stole your life, and then we go our separate ways. Deal?" he finished, his words running away before he could stop them.

Moron!
This is a stupid plan.
She'll just attack us anyways, won't she?

Jeremiah imagined he'd probably wake up soon enough with her fangs in his neck, feeling the life drain from his body.

You're just food to her, nothing more than an inconvenience to deal with.

Then his mind did an odd one-eighty.

She's just a monster to you. You wouldn't even spare her a moment to hear her.

Jeremiah frowned, his thoughts seeming to separate and take on differing opinions, dissociating themselves from each other.

Trying not to look as insane as he felt, he blinked, put a hand to his head, and then gave it a quick shake. With everything that'd happened to him lately, he was starting to question his own sanity anymore.

"What?" Ashley deadpanned, shaking her head and raising her hands. "No, I'm not gonna square off with a whole coven - no wa-"

"It's that or we keep going at this till one of us ends up dead," Jeremiah replied levelly. Right now, it felt more as if his words were taking him on an adventure and he didn't get a say about the tourist traps to hit on the way.

Except, even after he'd said it, he didn't exactly feel like he wanted to take any of the words back either.

The mental image of a Templar being more evil than a victimized young woman turned vampire wouldn't dislodge itself from his mind.

Trying to kill her outright, forcing the situation to a final conclusion without an in-between. That all rang a bell for him.

I'd be no different than Claudius.
Inflexible, manipulative.
She didn't want to be this.

On second thought, maybe I should just go. Sprint out of here and try to hide, never acknowledge it again.

"You know what? Fine! Fine," Ashley raised her hands skyward as if wholly done with this entire situation. "I've been wanting to pay Vasily back for what he did to me. You wanna be Mr. Big-bad-monster-hunter? Okay, but you get to feed me."

Jeremiah blinked and opened his mouth.

"Feed me! Because I don't have a damn dime to my name to pay for food. Doubly so if I'm going to have to help you at all with any sort of... any sort of... anything!" she demanded. When she put it like that, he felt somewhat cowed. "On top of that, you get to fix my window. In fact, you get to fix all the shit you broke in my apartment!

"As to feeding me, twice a week. That'd eliminate all my food costs. Do that and I'll help you hunt them down.

"Oh, and by the way, Mr. Non-Human, your blood tastes good. You might be rotten on the inside with a shit personality, but you've got that going for you."

Ashley laughed and actually smiled, if with an edge of madness in her eyes. "Like the smell of concrete after a fresh rain," she finished cooly.

"I'm not gonna let you just drink from me like a damn soda!" Jeremiah replied firmly, shaking his head and crossing his arms across his chest. "Not happening."

"Oh? You're not? Can you afford the blood bank? Your suit looked nice, but I doubt you'd care about crashing at my place if you could afford two hundred bucks a pint twice a week," Ashley quirked a brow, seeming to size him up. "Because that's part of the deal if you want my help, consider it rent for crashing on my couch. Let alone the damage you caused when I went and made you a nice meal and everything.

"If it makes you sleep better, you at least know where I'm getting my blood from. No concerns for anyone else at all. I get what I need, your conscience is in the clear, and we get to work on this."

Jeremiah sucked on his teeth, the idea of willingly letting a Vampire feast on him made him feel physically nauseous.

A place to stay, a coven to fight, someone who could literally cover my back and fight another vampire toe to toe.

She's not wrong about being able to watch her either.

On top of that...I don't have jack shit.

Ashley's rich as fuck compared to me.

"Fine. But I don't have a way to pay for what's broken. Like you said, I've got fuck all to my name," Jeremiah winced, hearing himself agree. There was no way he'd be able to afford fixing her window, door, drywall, fridge, and the other things they'd broken.

The only thing that he had was his suit, which was ruined and—

The watch.

His eyes flicked down to the watch on his wrist.

He didn't need a thirty-thousand-dollar timepiece, hell, no one needed a timepiece that expensive.

Could sell it, replace everything, fix what I can't, and still have enough left over to buy the basic needs. Not to mention, she'd help out where she could too.

If the watch was real, that was.

"Well... well... you better... figure out something, I guess," muttered Ashley, sounding considerably less sure of herself. Then she sighed and shrugged her shoulders. "I guess you could pay more in blood? I don't mind trading that for what my near nothing salary would do."

"I... think I just did," Jeremiah replied with a sigh, nodding sideways at the door to the hallway. "C'mon then... let's go."

Can't believe I'm about to go halfsies with a bloodsucking parasite.

Ashley watched him skeptically, raising her

brow and shifting the angle of her head. Almost giving him a side eye.

"So... you're not gonna try to kill me after all? I'm safe to sleep in my own bed?" she asked pointedly, narrowing her eyes. "Not gonna wake up with a stake through my heart?"

"As long as I don't wake up with fangs in my neck," Jeremiah replied in the same tone, offering her the same energy back.

He felt just as tired as she likely was.

"Well, I'd say it's time for me to eat because honestly... honestly I'm drained. You should probably eat what's left of your own meal, too." Ashely admitted with a small shake of her head. Now that he looked at her, she really did seem to be out of gas. Then she frowned and looked at him with trepidation. "You're not squeamish about your own blood, are you? My therapist told me more people than you'd think can't handle the sight of their own blood."

With that said, Ashely turned her back to him and went back down the hall.

Leaving him there, standing in the ruined bedroom.

Would it have been so bad to drink the tea, bang the vampire, ruin a bed, sleep, and bail?

The strange thought rang through his exhausted mind, leaving him with mild revulsion, and considering hopping out the window and to the ground very far below.

"Come on then, it still feels warm? I can nuke it if it isn't," Ashley called from the kitchen.

I...uh...dinner.

Dinner time.

Chapter 9

"You know what," Ashley said as Jeremiah trudged out of the bedroom and moved down the hall. "Even with all the stuff you broke, that was kinda... fun isn't the right word. Uhm, hmmm-"

Ashley trailed off as Jeremiah looked around the remains of the apartment.

The fridge was dented and twisted at an odd angle, the coffee table was splintered where the legs met the frame, and a faint breeze wafted in from the open bedroom door at the end of the hallway.

"Fulfilling? No, that's not right either," Ashley shrugged and pushed a fragment of wood away with her foot. "That's... cleansing. Yeah, cleansing feels right. Fighting with you and then screaming at each other got some of the-the tension, out."

Jeremiah watched her with bemused curiosity as she quickly tapped the buttons on her microwave.

"So... you like getting attacked by random homeless dudes in your apartment?" Jeremiah asked, humor tinging his words despite his apprehension towards this situation.

"Ha ha ha. Ha. No. I most certainly do not enjoy that.

"Especially not with all the shit we broke, or you actually trying to kill me.

"Dick move, by the way," Ashley said accusingly and turned her mouth into a moue. Glaring at him from under her brows almost. He ignored it as he picked up part of the shattered coffee table and started to clean up. "That said, yeah, it was cleansing. It felt good to just unleash it all and let loose. You know? Probably need a safer place to do it though.

"Oh! I think there's a vampire martial arts gym a mile or two away, that could be really fun, once my expenses get a bit better."

The microwave pinged behind her, and she spun around to open the door to it.

"You want to fight more? Me?" Jeremiah questioned slowly, somewhat confused by the positive response from the Vampire.

Moving the busted table top to the door, he set it up against the hallway wall. He wasn't entirely convinced he couldn't fix it now that he'd looked at it. The table legs had just been bolted in.

Even though he'd asked the question in a semi-incredulous way, the idea of fighting her became more and more enticing to him.

It would help keep his skills sharp, in addition to the fact that she wasn't human. In the past, he'd had the opportunity to spar with other people, mostly other members of his cell.

Fighting with a Vampire would push him pretty far to get better. Not to mention, he'd learn what they were capable of.

In a situation where he wouldn't be sucked dry for the slightest misstep, it might be an invaluable experience.

"I mean, if I'm gonna be helping you take down the coven, I'm gonna need to be a hell of a lot better than I am," Ashley shrugged absently and stuck down the plate of food on the counter top for him. Her eyes however, seemed to watch a place behind Jeremiah with empty eyes. "A lot better."

"Do you know how many are in the coven?" Jeremiah asked, a wave of drowsiness slamming into him like an unseen wall. He blinked slowly, briefly shaking his head as Ashley considered his question. Then, he looked to the plate sitting on the counter top and quickly moved over to it.

"I'm not sure…" Ashley replied after a few moments of consideration.

Jeremiah sat down in front of the plate and started back in on it as she thought on it. This time though, he didn't even bother with manners. It all ended up piled in the center before he inhaled it outright. "I know it's more than fifty, and they all report to Vasily, but I honestly didn't pay much attention to it. Really—"

"Did you drug the food too?" Jeremiah asked suddenly as he set the silverware to the plate. He'd let her continue on about the coven and what little knowledge she had as he ate.

At the same time, a massive wave of tiredness washed over him and made its demands quite clear to him.

He found that his eyes wanted to close on their own.

"I- what? No, just the tea. Why?" Ashley shook her head slowly as Jeremiah brought his eyes back to her face. Exhaling as his head began to spin, he stumbled over to the couch and flopped down into it heavily.

Then his ears began to ring.

"The hell is happening to me?" Jeremiah questioned in a murmur as the slug-like thing inside him began to feel like a red-hot poker, slithering up from his legs and coiling around his heart.

Burning, icy heat spilled out through his veins as Ashley took a singular step towards him with a nervous expression. Locking up, he arched his back as every single muscle in his body pulled taut, only able to move his eyes as he watched Ashley staring at him with wide eyes, unable to speak.

Jeremiah's lungs began to burn as he struggled to force in a breath that just wouldn't come.

Slowly, arduously, as Ashley said something inaudible to his roaring ears, the fire fled towards his feet. Then it moved away from his legs and slowly worked its way up his body, as the pain fled and faded to a disconcerting memory.

"No no no, don't die on my couch. That's like... my only piece of furniture right now," Ashley murmured as his ears quieted down.

"Not... dead," Jeremiah grunted in between deep gasps of air, trying to blink the haze behind his eyes away.

"Oh. Good. That's good," she replied with a sigh. While he'd been busy trying to breathe, she'd moved in close and was leaning over him with her hands on his shoulders. She hesitated a moment before she took her hands away. "You have no idea how often people shit themselves when they die, ruins the whole meal. I just can't after that. The smell is just... it's everywhere."

"Actually, I do have an idea, and oh yeah? All it takes is a little stink to scare you off? Pretty sure I stunk worse," Jeremiah leaned back in the couch and readjusted himself. He felt somewhat numb and boneless.

"I mean, yeah, you stunk pretty bad. So did they though. Not enough to take my hunger away but... poop is... it's enough to make me nauseous," Ashley added sourly before sitting down on the recliner that was next to the couch. The way she'd said it sounded rather girly for a vampire. "Not enough to stop me if I'm -really- hungry, though."

Jeremiah grunted at that, blinking as he stared at the black TV screen in front of them. The silence that stretched on felt awkward.

Even as somewhere within himself, his mind roiled at just what was happening to his body.

The need to hide away from the thoughts, to stuff them deeper within himself, still sat squarely on the forefront of his mind.

"Shiny TV," he tried to fill the silence with some form of conversation. "Wonder what's on? You got cable?"

"I might be a Vampire, but I'm not that old," Ashley chuckled as she leaned forward and scooped the remote from where it laid on the floor. "And it's really not that shiny. I think I bought it for about four hundred a few years back. It was on sale, though. Super good deal."

"Bullshit," Jeremiah scoffed, folding his arms over his chest. "I've only ever seen flatscreens like that on sale for a couple grand at electronics stores."

"What is this, twenty years ago? It's not even 4K!" Ashley continued to laugh, though she did glance at him in askance.

"4K?" Jeremiah asked, unfamiliar with the term.

"Yeah, the resolution!" Ashley turned on the television through the remote, and instead of popping up with whatever channel she was last watching, an unfamiliar user interface with a series of colored icons sprang to life on the TV.

"And I thought 1080 was high res," Jeremiah noted quietly, watching as she maneuvered through the menu. "Now I know you're bullshitting me about the price. Where, did you steal this from, one of your marks?"

"Uh, no," Ashley replied, seeming rather miffed about the accusation. "I don't even have 'marks', I just kinda... wander around alone at night until someone tries to shove me in an alley. There's always someone who wants to be awful."

"There's no way you just bought this... futuristic bullshit, for a few hundred bucks at the store!" Jeremiah snapped back with some heat to his voice.

"Futuristic? This isn't two-thousand-seven," Ashley accused him with a roll of her eyes. "What rock have you been under? Or I guess... trash heap."

Wait, what?

"Wait, what?" Jeremiah asked almost in time with his thoughts. "Ashley... what month is it?"

"Uh, it's May?" Ashley looked at him with concern clearly in her eyes. She raised one eyebrow and watched him skeptically.

"It's already May?" Jeremiah blinked his eyes and shook his head as his brain seemed to struggle with the revelation that it had been nearly a year since the operation with the Templars. "I've been out for... nine months?"

"What do you mean you've 'been out'?" Ashley questioned after a moment that Jeremiah spent staring into the space between them.

"The last thing I remember... it happened on August twenty-first. Then I woke up in the trash," Jeremiah shook his head slowly and growled. "That... That's impossible. Do you have a... calendar or something? Maybe on your laptop?"

"Y-yeah..." she paused, reached in her pocket, and sighed. "And of course the screen is cracked... whatever, add it to the list I guess."

Ashley turned on her high-end, touch-screen phone with no visible buttons, and handed it over to him. Then, she tapped on an icon that vaguely resembled a calendar and pulled up a date.

I glared at him with certainty.

It was May alright.

Just like she'd said.

Then, his eyes flicked absently to the year, glossing over it before he froze, looked back, and blinked.

Two thousand nineteen!?

"That... that can't be right. No, this is... this —" Jeremiah trailed off, his eyes wide as saucers. Something, some-one had taken over a dozen years of his memory, his life.

Gone, like those years never existed, or never happened.

"Okay, for some reason, that look scares me more than your big-bad-monster-hunter one," Ashley said, turning partially in place in the recliner to face him directly. "What's wrong now? Is it my phone?"

"The last thing I remember was in August but... thirteen -years- ago. Not last year."

Jeremiah looked up from the floor where eventually his gaze drifted to Ashley's eyes.

"You're shitting me," Ashley replied, her mouth hanging slightly open. It was neither a question, nor an accusation. It instead felt more like a plea, a hope that the man sharing a couch with her wasn't actually that crazy.

"No," he admitted, almost in a whisper, looking back down to his hands. "Wish I was. That'd make more sense."

What the hell happened to me?

"I want you to tell me everything that

happened, everything you remember up until we met in the alley," she demanded, raising her hands, opening them, and then returning them to her lap.

He couldn't tell what she was doing and just chalked it up to her needing to move in some way.

"I can't... I can tell you what happened from this mo-"

"Nope, you're telling me everything," Ashley interrupted him with a pointed finger. "You could already turn me into the PID for the shit I've done, I'm not gonna say anything to anyone.

"If what you're telling me is true, Jeremiah, then you need to trust me.

"Because right now, you seem insane.

"If you're right, then I'm probably the only thing you've got going for you," Ashley briefly ran a tongue over her canines in an idle way. Almost as if she weren't even aware of it. At the same time, she seemed to consider her next words carefully. Finally her eyes went back to him, and her mouth shut briefly. "Look. I've wanted a way back at Vasily for everything he did to me.

"The lawsuit didn't work. The therapy doesn't work. At this point, I'm only willing to work with the crazy homeless man in an expensive suit that tried to kill me because –nothing- else has worked."

Ashley jabbed a finger at him again, her eyes digging into his face as if she could force his secrets out by force of will alone.

"But that only works if I... we, trust each other. Clearly, something's... wrong with you. You think you're human, but your blood says otherwise. Apparently, you've also time-traveled, or got hit in the head really, really hard."

Jeremiah stared into the Vampire's eyes,

searching them.

He couldn't find a single trace of dishonesty, trickery, or deceit in her rather lovely green eyes. Nor could he find anything wrong in her tone.

She could've taken a bite out of me a few minutes ago when I locked up...what happened, happened thirteen years ago.

My entire team is dead, Eddie is...dead. I need to trust her, or I'm fucked anyway.

"Where should I start?" Jeremiah asked with a raised eyebrow.

"Start with... why the hell you hate Vamps so much," Ashley replied, folding her arms across her chest. "No judgement, I know there's quite a few assholes out there, but I could say there's just as many Human assholes."

"No," Jeremiah shook his head quickly. He could start near to the point she wanted though. "That story is off-limits. Just know that I was personally fucked over by a coven. When I got rescued, Patrick and Eddie found me. Invited me into their team..."

* * *

"... and then, well, Claudius turned his gun on me and Eddie. I just... wasn't fast enough," Jeremiah shrugged as he came to the end of his explanation of what was, to him, the past two years of his life. "I woke up at the bottom of a pile of garbage. That's all I know."

Well, that wasn't quite all he knew.

He'd left out the part about his hallucination of waking up as a middle-aged Asian man. And the slug-like thing that moved around the inside of his body.

"Hmmm. What about your parents? Family?" Ashley asked with a frown on her face. She'd been mostly quiet during his tale, save for a few small clarifying questions. "Even I still call, text, and try to videochat my family. I didn't hear you bring them up once."

"What about them?" Jeremiah questioned in a bored tone. "I haven't talked to them in years."

"Oh for fuck's sake," Ashley leaned back against the arm of the sofa and pressed her palms to her eyes. "I'm too hungry for this bullshit.

"No, I mean like, isn't there one of them that you can call, have them send you a bus ticket home or some shit?"

"That's... actually not a bad idea," Jeremiah acknowledged her question, somewhat miffed that he hadn't thought of it first.

Hell, he'd just called Leodegrance first thing, not even considering calling family. "I'm sure I could call... could call... I could..." Jeremiah trailed off as his mind seemed to slam face first into an invisible barrier.

Who...I could call my...my...

His thoughts were unsteady and shifting.

The more he focused on his family, on trying to remember his mother and father's names, who his siblings were, or even if he had siblings, the more his mind kicked the information away from him.

Their faces were hazy, their identities felt like they were on the tip of his tongue, just out of reach.

When Jeremiah let his brain rest, images of a snow-wrapped cabin in the mountains played behind his eyelids.

The sounds of laughter, of unintelligible

conversation around a dinner table, echoed in his ears. When he thought hard, however, it all faded to an inky grey blob of nothing.

Like the faint, untouchable memories didn't exist.

Didn't actually happen.

"I... can't remember them," Jeremiah muttered more to himself than her.

Ashley stared at him with a haunted expression, looking briefly to the side before shaking her head.

"Uh... huh... great. That's... great," she muttered to herself and let out a low cackle. A laugh that sounded somewhat crazed. "I've teamed up with the -amnesiac-, monster-hunting psychopath, to take down a coven full of kin-drinking, blood mages!

"They always said my senior year of college would be exciting. But this is just too much."

Jeremiah wasn't entirely paying attention to her, as his mind continued to struggle against the barricaded section of his thoughts.

"Ugh... this is all so fucked up. And I'm sorry, my best therapist impression sucks. I'm too hungry," Ashley sighed loudly, rubbing at her eyes and face.

She stood up from the couch, went to the kitchenette, and quickly returned with a sharp-looking knife. Jeremiah blinked at her as his mind caught up with him.

He didn't have a weapon.

She did.

Feeling himself getting nervous, he swung his feet around and planted them on the ground. In half a second, he was upright and seated now. He had his feet positioned and his weight partially shifted, as if he might just bolt then and there.

Ashley snorted loudly, simply flopping down on the sofa next to him like nothing was the matter. Like she hadn't just walked towards Jeremiah with a weapon, staring hungrily at him.

"Geez you're twitchy. I've already said I wasn't going to kill you. Now give me your arm," Ashley demanded, making an open and closed grabby hand sort of motion at him.

He watched her with narrowed eyes, slowly lifting his arm up and over to her.

"Okay... so, I think they said about... here?" Ashley reached up with the hand that didn't hold the knife and rotated his limb, so the underside of his forearm pointed at her face.

Her eyes flicked up to the TV, then down to the remote. "Anything you wanna watch? We'll probably be here for a bit. A couple of the gals in the support group have told me that this usually takes about half an hour, maybe a little longer. Might be good to turn something on."

"Uh..." Jeremiah paused, considering the question. "I mostly just watch the news. Don't really have the time to watch anything else."

"Damn, your life sucks!" she chuckled, even as she inspected his veins. "If you don't give me something to go on, I'm just going to pick a chick flick!"

The Vampire who was about to literally drink his blood, smiled threateningly at him, like this was all very normal.

Nothing about this was normal to him, though. He felt as if he were only a second away from skittering off like a spooked cat.

Still, Jeremiah knew one thing: he did -not- want to watch a chick flick.

"Eh, fine. Maybe a spy movie, action or something? I've been gone for a few years. Pick something I wouldn't have seen?" Jeremiah replied with a shrug, as his shoulder muscle began to ache from holding his arm outstretched without any support.

"Typical," Ashley snorted and shook her head. "How about a compromise? Got this cop show I like - plenty of gunfights and explosions, but also has an actual plot underneath that stuff."

"Whatever," Jeremiah grunted, looking away from her as she navigated the menus and selected her chosen option. "Let's just get this over with."

To think, he was allowing a Vampire to feast on him.

How the mighty have fallen, huh?

Jeremiah ruefully thought as he stared at the intro playing on the TV.

A sharp pain caught him off guard. Likely as Ashley stuck him in fact. Then it slid down toward the middle of his forearm. He winced, balling up his fist with a grimace.

Need to get her a sharper knife if we're gonna do this regularly.

The fuck was it, a steak knife?

The blade left his skin and Ashley sniffed the air somewhat loudly.

"Don't... fucking smell me!" Jeremiah snapped suddenly, half-jerking his arm from her grasp. With her natural Vampiric strength, she easily pulled him back.

"You don't know what you are, I don't know what you are. The more I know, the better we can figure your shit out," she explained earnestly. "Maybe one day in the future I'm at the blood bank, or someone cuts themself while I'm standing nearby and I can piece it together.

"I can already tell you're not an Elf, you're not a Troll, and you're not a Changeling, nor any of the fancy blood I've ever tried before when I actually had a bit of cash."

She flicked her tongue out and licked a corner of his wound as it began to bleed in truth now. A constant run of blood meandering down.

Resisting the urge to tell her off, Jeremiah instead turned his head slightly and ended up staring at her. Though she didn't notice at all.

She was gazing off and up into the ceiling as she moved her tongue around in her mouth and was clearly tasting him.

"But your blood... ohhh," Ashley let out a soft ecstatic giggle. She then smiled predatorily down at the wound on the underside of his arm. "It feels like it radiates magic... like the powered blood I've heard about. Maybe you're a sorcerer who never screwed around with magic before. I don't know, but I do know that I want it.

"I'm starving. I honestly considered trying animal blood I was so hungry. This is infinitely better."

Her grip turned to iron, she brought the cut to her mouth, and began to drink.

Strange, conflicting, and uncomfortable thoughts wandered their way into the forefront of his mind as she pillowed her lips around the wound, wiggling happily into the sofa for a more comfortable position.

Instead of considering them, he turned his eyes to the TV, and focused on the entertainment she'd provided.

His arm didn't even feel that heavy, considering she'd taken up the entirety of the weigh with ease.

If I'm not human...does that make me no better than her?

Am I a monster too?

He stuffed that thought deeper, trying to bury it under a deluge of surface thoughts about the characters on the mindless show they watched.

The situation felt wrong.

Domestic, even.

Not at all like the Vampire lairs full of bloodsuckers and their slaves. Like what had happened to him.

Chapter 10

Jeremiah awoke to the sounds of gunfire.

Startling awake, his eyes scanned around the room.

His heart thundered away in his chest while he found the source of the conflict.

The TV was still on, the characters locked in a gunfight, taking cover behind several parked cars.

Jeremiah leaned back on the cushy sofa with a deep, relieved sigh. His dreams had been... odd.

Uncomfortable.

Flashes of existences he couldn't properly remember, like viewing someone's daily life through a bad time-lapse.

"Mmmh," Jeremiah looked down to his lap at the soft groan. Ashley was curled up on the couch beside him, using his thigh as a pillow. She continued to murmur softly, her pale brown hair a mess of tangles.

Hard to believe she's a bloodsucking monster.

Jeremiah brushed a lock of hair out of her face.

Right now, she only vaguely resembled the intimidating woman who'd fought him last night. With that thought came what she'd said the night prior, and how she'd said it.

I wonder if what actually happened to her is more common?

Someone being converted against their will, their soul stained permanently, all because some monster took a shine to them.

Fuck that's heavy...if that bitch at the bar had had the same idea for me...I could've ended up just like her, instead of being stuck as a portable blood bag for a few months.

The thought struck a chord deep inside him, reverberating around his head for several seconds as he stared into the sleeping face of the Vampire snuggled into his lap.

If there was ever a bloodsucker, a monster capable of redemption in the end...it's the one who just wanted to live a normal life in the first place, who never wanted this for herself.

Oh get real!

Jeremiah blinked as it felt like his thoughts separated into two distinct entities.

Do I actually believe her bullshit? She's just another monster trying to lure me into a false sense of security. Once I get all nice and cozy, trust her? She'll just lock me in a box, feeding me barely enough to keep the tap running.

She's no different than Natalie. She's just using my inability to say no to the "damsel-in-distress" routine as a means to an end. It's the same as Natalie wearing her low-cut dress and pretty smile to get me back to her place.

Jeremiah squeezed his eyes shut and grimaced, trying to shake the odd feeling of having completely separate trains of thought residing in his head.

They were very clearly his, but also felt unfamiliar at the same time. As if Jeremiah just booted up a slightly different worldview into his thoughts.

Okay...something is definitely wrong with me.

A sharp pang of hunger shot through Jeremiah's gut. Licking his lips, he glanced over to the now-dented fridge.

Deciding that she might have something edible inside, he grabbed the couch pillow next to him, gingerly lifted Ashley's head, and swapped places with it. As he stood from the sofa, the Vampire made a soft grumbling noise, followed by a cooing sound.

Jeremiah snorted at the sleepy antics before moving to the fridge and opening it quietly.

Okay...eggs, bread, cheese, and...nothing else.

He quietly sighed and shrugged.

Looks like eggs and toast again. Wonder why she only has this. Is it just a stopgap in case someone else comes over?

Eh, maybe.

I could probably pull off egg salad sandwiches... yeah?

Hm.

Jeremiah set about making himself breakfast, or in actuality, lunch, according to the small digital clock on the counter.

Watery scrambled eggs and slightly overdone toast wasn't the breakfast of champions, but it would do until he could get more diverse meals.

Even then, he couldn't help but be thankful for the food regardless.

Or, as the back of his mind prompted him, more accurately, Ashley.

He set the plate down on the counter, and apparently the soft clatter of the ceramic plate on the faux wood was enough to break sleep's hold on Ashley.

"Mnn, wha-" she blinked her eyes and pushed herself up to a seated position on the sofa. "What time is it?"

"Eh, just after two," Jeremiah shrugged and turned the swiveling barstool in her direction. "So, we need to come up with a plan for today. I've got some errands to run if you want your place fixed up, and

I'm gonna need your help."

Ashley blinked slowly, shaking her head as she watched Jeremiah with a bleary expression.

"It's the middle of the night…" she squinted at him, even with the blackout curtains of her apartment blocking the vast majority of the daylight.

"No, it's the middle of the day," Jeremiah chuckled, taking a bite of the toast.

"Yeah. For me, that's like waking up at one in the morning. I normally wake up at six!" Ashley seemed to regain more of herself as time went on. "I'm going back to bed."

"Not if you want your money, you're not. Unless you know of a pawn shop that operates after dark," Jeremiah replied as Ashley paused halfway to laying back down. She rotated her head slightly, tonguing one of her fangs before sitting back up.

"Can't you just… go yourself?" she asked, frustration tinging her words.

Almost as if she were whining.

"I'm sure I could, just print me off the MapQuest directions. That being said, I think most pawn shops ask for ID when you try to sell them an expensive item. Stolen items and the like are always a concern."

"Right," Ashley replied with a frown, staring at the floor in clear consternation. "And no one prints out maps anymore - we just use our phones."

"Wou- you know what, at this point I'm just gonna stop questioning the futuristic bullshit," Jeremiah admitted with a frown. Instead, he took another bite of his sandwich. "But yeah, I probably need you to sell this for me."

Jeremiah lifted his wrist and jiggled the watch around. Ashley looked at it for a moment before turning her eyes back to him.

"You sure that's actually worth anything?" she quirked a brow suspiciously at him.

"Pretty sure, yeah," he nodded affirmatively, taking a bite of the bland eggs. "Last I checked, these went for around thirty to forty grand. Granted, that was a while ago, but it might break fifteen thousand if you play your cards right."

Ashley's eyes nearly bulged out of her skull at that revelation. Jeremiah just shrugged and took another bite of his food.

"Should be enough to fix all the shit we broke-" he began before she interrupted him.

"You mean everything that you broke," Ashley corrected with a nonplussed expression.

"Okay, I'll definitely take credit for breaking your window, but the fridge is absolutely your fault," Jeremiah offered in return, a grin creeping onto his face despite the situation.

"Oh no, you don't get to pin that on me. You dodged too quickly!" a corner of Ashley's mouth twitched.

"Not my fault you can't hit a moving target!" Jeremiah smirked when she narrowed her eyes and licked her lips.

"Not my fault the crazy homeless guy I took pity on is a walking government watch list. By the way, I think I figured out what your stroke was last night."

"Do tell," he watched her with raised eyebrows and a smirk.

"I think, and I'll have to feed from you again to confirm this, but I think it was a reaction to my… me giving you Vampirism. Your blood tasted…" Ashley stared up at the ceiling briefly before looking back at him, as if contemplating the finer aspects of blood flavor. "Dead. Not your blood itself, but like... something dead was inside it. I think when I bit you, I wasn't completely in control of myself. Your body reacted to the disease that vampirism is. That I... injected, and then your body killed it."

Jeremiah watched her nervously wringing her hands as she explained the process of accidentally infecting him with Vampirism, clearly uncomfortable.

"I'm still really new at this! The other Vamps in the support group say it's like a one in five chance, especially early on... but yeah. I think that's what it was. I'll have to call Jenny and ask what she thinks about it."

"Jenny?" Jeremiah asked with a frown. He really didn't want to bring anyone else into the circle of confusing bullshit that was his life right now, but if someone had the right qualifications to help figure out what was wrong with him, everything that was happening? Well, he could make an exception.

"Jenny... uhm, she's a friend from class," Ashley admitted, leaning forward on the sofa. "She's working on her doctorate in paranormal medicine, which as you might gather, is medicine for us paras, and just might be able to figure out more about you than I could. Unless you wanna let a more experienced Vamp dr-"

"Nope, no, uh-uh!" Jeremiah shook his head vigorously from side to side at the idea of letting someone else feed on him, for scientific purposes or not. "Med student it is. I didn't even know they had a degree of paranormal medicine."

"They do. I mean, it makes sense, given that we make up roughly a third of the population. But, okay, I'll text her and get her input on all this. So...

let's go get this watch sold, I wanna sleep in my bed as soon as possible."

Jeremiah's mind ground to a screeching halt at that revelation, barely even paying attention to the rest of what she had to say.

A...a third? That...that can't be right. That would mean...

"Holy fuck, Clallam has that big of a population? A third of the population here are Weres and Vamps? How has this city not been drunk dry yet?" Jeremiah asked with wide eyes, slack-jawed.

"Do... do you only know about Weres and Vampires?" Ashley replied to his question with one of her own, squinting at him and clearly trying to hide a smile. "I would've thought you'd know more, given that you have a mask of your own."

"A... mask?" Jeremiah was confused, as he wasn't wearing a mask right now. He didn't even have access to a balaclava in any way, shape, or form.

"Yeah... a mask. Hides you from norms, or at least, anyone without a mask of their own. See the faint sparkle around my head, looks kinda like a really faint glitter?" Ashley asked, waving a hand at her face.

As he stared more intently, focused, he, in fact, could see the faint sparkle that floated around her head, like dust in an old building.

"You've got one too, but I can't for the life of me imagine what it is, given that you don't have an ID. Most of the time it's someone's driver's license, social security card, or something like that. Anyone with a mask can see through everyone else's, at least the government-issued ones."

Jeremiah frowned, trying to imagine what

could be functioning as a mask on him.

Could this be why he'd been seeing shit since he woke up? He finally had the ability to peek through whatever shielding was used to hide from society.

But if there's so many, how have more people not been...eaten, turned, or killed by them?

That's just too much for there not to be millions of missing people, right?

"A third of the people in Clallam are monsters?" Jeremiah pressed, looking to the side as he wondered whether or not he'd genuinely bitten off more than he could chew.

"Actually, it's closer to half here. A third is more of a general estimate for the country," Ashley shrugged, as if she hadn't just dropped a life-altering revelation in his lap. "Yeah, there's all kinds of us. Trolls, Changelings, Elves - hell, I even went to high school with a Lamia! She was really sweet, but way too touchy-feely for me. I think she just wanted my heat. Like she was cold-blooded or something."

"That... can't be right. You know what. No, fuck this. I'm done with this conversation. Let's go to the pawn shop," Jeremiah didn't want to think about how he was outnumbered by orders of magnitude in this city. The last time he checked, six million people lived here.

If Ashley was right, that meant neither he, nor anyone reasonably, had the ability to stem the tide of non-Human's that was sure to spring to life from the plethora of creatures that freely roamed their streets.

With his appetite sufficiently settled, he stood up. He'd managed to clear his plate outright for the most part. There wasn't much of anything there.

He put it in the sink with a clack.

* * *

Jeremiah sat in the small park bench across from the pawn shop storefront, staring at the seemingly omnipresent cloud cover above with a scowl.

He missed the Colorado sun, the baking heat of the high-altitude rays interposed with the brisk breeze.

Here it just seemed cold and wet.

Though that was part of why Vampires liked it, he supposed, a natural sunblock.

Is that even necessary, though?

He wondered, thinking back to Ashley slathering on the sunscreen that was apparently both rather expensive, and very effective.

Can't even trust the sun to protect us anymore. A Vampire can just...walk around, live a normal life.

His eyes narrowed and followed a gaunt, greenish-skinned man with quite a few lesions on his skin, as he half-hobbled past.

He wore a blue polo shirt, khaki slacks, and munched on a bar of something. It didn't look like any protein bar Jeremiah had ever seen.

This has to be something new...something that happened in the years I can't remember.

Jeremiah crossed his arms tighter across his chest. He needed something warmer, despite the fact it was already may.

Somehow, the world went sideways in a hurry. To think, nearly a third of the population was turned in just over a decade. Though...if I couldn't see through the masks before, does that mean that...it's always been like this?

How many times have I flirted with a cute barista, or went to a restaurant with a line of cooks that are entirely inhuman?

And beyond that, the numbers wouldn't work at all.

Would they?

There's no way you could 'convert' a third of the population if what Ashley said is right. That there's a variety of other types of...of...not...Humans.

They wouldn't be turned from Humans.

They'd be born that way.

Jeremiah eyed a group of dark-skinned, long-eared women stride elegantly past. Somehow, all of them walked with poise and grace, as if the entire world was their own personal catwalk. They looked human, for the most part.

When he looked closer, he saw the multiple rows of canine teeth, the slant to their slightly oversized eyes. Clearly, they weren't human.

That still didn't change the natural reaction his body delivered when one of their number, a purple-eyed tall woman, with cascading rows of elegantly braided hair, looked his way and smiled warmly at him.

He gulped deeply as the eerily pretty woman delivered a trouser-dropping grin, batted her lashes, and waved at him as the group went past.

Shortly after they left his immediate area, the group burst out into bubbly giggles and conversation between surreptitious glances over their shoulder at him.

Women.

Jeremiah snorted and grinned back at them,

despite himself. His grin elicited another round of laughter and conversation before they rounded the corner of the street and left his view.

That was all very…decidedly…unmistakably… Human.

Jeremiah looked back to the storefront ahead of him, where he could just barely make out Ashley in the middle of a fierce debate with the store owner over the market value of his watch.

So far, they'd been to four different places.

One had outright laughed her out of the store, the second had come close to their expected offer, and was actually polite, just not willing to meet their price.

If this place failed, they'd take the hit and sell it back at the second place. Ten grand was nothing to sniff at, but fifteen was better.

The man behind the counter leaned back and crossed his arms, making a thoughtful expression before waving his hand dismissively and replying.

Ashley snapped her fingers with a broad grin, said something, and nodded enthusiastically.

The gentleman behind the counter, a broad-shouldered swarthy man in his middle-age, clearly fought back a smile at Ashley's enthusiastic "victory" in their haggling. With an ever-broadening grin, the man dramatically rolled his eyes, scooped the watch up off the counter, and went into the back of the store.

A minute or so later, he returned with a fat wad of cash. He counted it out atop the counter for Ashley to see and extended a hand to shake.

When Ashley shook it vigorously, the man lost control of his faint smile and began to laugh genuinely, waving as she left the store.

Jeremiah stood from the bench and sighed as Ashley left the storefront with a broad, enthusiastic grin - barely taking the time to look both ways before she crossed the street.

She slowed to a walk several feet in front of Jeremiah, giggling like a madwoman.

"Hehe! I got us fourteen thousand, five hundred!" Ashley blurted, holding the fat wad of hundred-dollar bills to her chest, doing a small spin in place. Jeremiah instantly flicked his eyes around them nervously.

"First of all, lower your voice," he pleaded, wondering if people were watching them now.

"I don't think I've ever held this much cash all at once!" Ashley exclaimed, decidedly not lowering her voice. "My hands barely even fit around it!"

Jeremiah stepped up beside her and wrapped his arm over Ashley's shoulder, leading her back towards her apartment.

Thankfully, she complied, even as she continued to babble happily about the wad of money clutched against her chest.

"Can you at least... stuff it in your purse? Zip it tightly and hold that?" Jeremiah questioned the woman, his eyes scanning their immediate front, while he tried to focus his ears on what was might come from behind them. "Lotta eyes here."

"Oh! Right, right," Ashley continued to giggle, even as she shoved the stack of cash into the depths of her purse. "Smart. Though, let's be real here, if someone steals from us, they're gonna have a real bad day."

"Ashley, this is America, do you know how many guns there are?" Jeremiah looked at her with a smirk. "I've killed Vamps with guns before. All it takes is a magdump in the right parts of their body, and they're done. Vampire healing is neat and all, but it has limits.

"It can't fix a brain turned to Swiss cheese by a nine-millimeter."

Ashley looked nonplussed at that revelation.

In that moment, he had an extreme pang of guilt suddenly wash over him at his most certainly abnormal statement.

Then, she frowned and looked away, as if unable to look at him. It left him feeling torn and cold at his own words.

"Forgot you're a psychopath," she muttered, now clutching the purse to her chest.

"I'm not a psychopath, I'm a monster hunter. If it eats people, it deserves to die," Jeremiah bit back reflexively.

"I thought you already established that I don't deserve to die. And here I am... I need to eat," Ashley rolled her shoulder, knocking his arm off of her.

"No, you're different," Jeremiah replied without thinking yet again.

Jeremiah exhaled and ran his hand through his hair.

"You know what, this conversation can wait until we get back," he tried instead. He suddenly realized that at this moment, he didn't have the mental footing to back up his position.

Because it didn't feel really tenable anymore.

"Yeah," Ashley replied with a morose edge to her voice. "I guess it can."

The silence that fell as they walked to her apartment several miles away felt heavy.

Like a blanket draped across Jeremiah's head.

What the hell is her problem?

Jeremiah's thoughts kept him company as they traveled.

She knows what she is, she knows she's a monster. What's the issue with me saying it? It's only natural for humans to kill the things that want to eat them. A wolf is no different than any other monster.

But...if I'm not human, if she's right about that... would I have killed me?

Jeremiah blinked away that thought, and focused on watching everyone around them as they returned home, watching for any signs of trouble.

Because the thought that came right behind that, that yawned open like a black hole wanting to pull him straight into its depths, was that he was indeed a psychopath.

His memories of his childhood felt as if they were manufactured.

The world didn't match anything that he'd steadfastly believed.

If all of that had been wrong, if everything had been him being led astray, then all he'd done was leave behind a miserable and broken life filled with the suffering of others.

Others that maybe didn't deserve it.

An overwhelming weighty sense of guilt lashed him, as if it flayed the skin and muscle from his back. Laying him open to the bone.

So deeply terrifying was the thought, the feeling, that he firmly stuck it behind himself and fled.

Ran from it in his mind as if he were in a deadly pursuit.

'Just let us leave!'

Wincing, Jeremiah recoiled and blanked out his thoughts. Even as the whispered plea clawed at what felt like his very soul.

Chapter 11

"Okay... looks like we weren't followed..." Jeremiah muttered, taking one last look into the apartment building hallway before finally closing the door. With a relieved exhale, he locked the door behind them and stretched his arms over his head. He wasn't sure if the relief was from actually making it back to the apartment, or the constant invasive thoughts that questioned everything he was. Or thought he'd been. "With that much, we should have enough to fix all the... stuff y-we broke, and still have plenty left over for the gear to pick a fight with your coven."

"Not my coven," Ashley replied, setting her purse on the counter. "Remember?"

"Eh, they made you. Even if you hate them and want 'em dead, they're still your coven, technically," Jeremiah pointed out as he flopped down on the couch. He was feeling somewhat touchy at his mind refusing to work for him, rather than against him. "But yeah. Sometime soon, we need to do some recon and observation of any locations important to them. Good old-fashioned stakeout."

"Yeah, probably," Ashley shrugged noncommittally.

Wonder what's eating her?

Jeremiah flicked his gaze over to Ashley for a scant second as she leaned against the counter, staring down at the off-white surface fixedly.

"You said you know where they primarily operate out of?" Jeremiah questioned with a frown.

"Yeah, out of the Red Lotus club...

downtown," Ashley yet again delivered just enough information to answer his question. Nothing more, nothing less, in a tone that sounded almost... hollow. She pulled out her phone and typed something into it before stuffing it back into her purse. "I'm gonna go take a shower. I texted Jenny about you, I should hear back by the time I'm out."

"Okay," Jeremiah nodded slowly as Ashley left the kitchen-living room combo, watching her go with a raised eyebrow. Clearly, something had upset the Vampire, but he couldn't fathom what.

Was it something I said?

No sooner had he finished the thought, than he knew the answer. He'd definitely said something, and he could trace it right back to the conversation.

He wasn't stupid.

It was obvious exactly where the issue started.

Saying you would murder someone outright with enough gunshots to their head was not an everyday statement. Especially when the opposing side argued that they weren't a monster at all, but just a person.

His breath caught, his teeth ground together, and he fought against calling out to Ashley to try and offer an apology. Even as he felt like it was the right thing to do, he simply refused to do it.

Instead, he just watched Ashley exit her bedroom with a small bundle of clothes, enter the bathroom, and shut the door behind her.

Realizing he'd fucked up and lost his chance, he instead tried to watch the news on the flatscreen TV.

He navigated the menus, trying to find the channel that would link him to the local outlets, when he saw a name he recognized.

An old video-sharing website that was growing in popularity in his time was apparently still around.

Denying all the intrusive thoughts that wanted to beat him down for his antics regarding Ashley, he clicked on the logo and set about surfing the plethora of videos available to him.

* * *

Ashley's phone chimed in her pocket. Jeremiah looked over as she retrieved it and looked it over.

"Okay so… Jenny is here," she said hesitantly, biting her tongue as she seemed to consider how to say whatever it was she wanted to add to that.

"Alright. You really think she can figure out what I am?" Jeremiah asked as the silence of her consideration seemed to stretch.

"If there was ever someone to figure it out, it would be her," Ashley trailed off again. "I get the feeling you're not the type to actually go through a government testing regimen to find it out either, so your option right now is pretty much just Jenny."

"You're talking a lot like you expect me to react badly to her," Jeremiah noted after watching Ashley seem to squirm underneath his searching gaze.

"I mean yeah. You tend to fly off the handle and sound like a psychopath. She's not human," Ashley said with her voice firming up quickly. Then she glared at him. "Don't try to kill her, or do anything crazy. If you do… I swear this whole partnership is over. Do you get it? Do you understand?"

"Not human?" Jeremiah asked with a flat, unimpressed stare. Getting tested by yet another non-Human felt almost worse than getting the government involved. "You're bringing another monpara, into this?"

"Do you want to know what the fuck is happening to you, or not? Can you keep all that insane shit inside your cracked head long enough for someone to try and help?" Ashley demanded defiantly. She folded her arms across her chest and stared archly at Jeremiah. "I still have enough time to tell her to turn back if you just want to sit around and suffer. Or are you going to start calling me a monster again? Something that should have her head shot to pieces?"

Jeremiah sucked at the inside of his mouth with a frown, staring at the ceiling. On the one hand, he would be allowing yet another nonhuman to be touching him. On the other, he really wanted to know what was going on with that slug thing inside him.

"Fine. I'll play nice. And... and I'm sorry... for saying what I did. It wasn't-you're not... it wasn't the right thing to say," Jeremiah ground out. While he'd thought he'd lost his chance, this was at least a moment he could make a correction in.

Even if that meant he needed to sit still on a couch while some Were, Vamp, or whatever unusual monster Ashley managed to pull out of a hat, poked and prodded him to find out the answers.

"But if she tries to pull any funny business, tries to nibble at my finger or some shit, I'm absolutely throwing hands," Jeremiah stated with finality.

"I'll let her know. Though if you do something stupid, this whole thing is off and you can go your own way with half the money."

"So... how about we all play nice," Ashley offered with a barely contained flat and unapologetic smile. Staring at him as if he were some gigantic idiot. Like he wasn't in the right to be worried about some random monster girl snacking on him with no witnesses other than the local goody-two-shoes Vampire. "I've already warned her that you can be a little... abrasive. For what it's worth, I can't blame you for being sketched out at some random person prodding at you. I wouldn't like it either. This is a good thing though."

Jeremiah huffed, but said nothing more in the end as they waited in silence for Jenny to make it upstairs. When several soft knocks sounded from the door, Ashley quickly moved behind the couch and opened the door.

"Hey Ash! Sorry, class ran late, one of the other students kept pestering the professor mid-lecture, and it ran overtime," said a soft voice.

Jeremiah watched as a hand with a set of keys wrapped around Ashley's shoulder. "You said you needed some diagnostics done on a para friend of yours that doesn't know what they are?"

"Yeah, he's been having some issues lately. Seizures, memory loss, stuff like that," Ashley broke the embrace and stepped back from the door, allowing the guest to enter.

"That's not good, I wonder if it's something to do wi... with... YOU!"

Yep...that's exactly my luck.

Because apparently, there can't be two Jennies within a twenty-mile radius of each other.

Jenny, the Demon from the soup kitchen, stared at him with a scowl.

"Hey Jenny!" Jeremiah forced a smile to his face as it looked like the woman was about to find the nearest heavy object and apply it to his face. Repeatedly. "Long time, no see."

"What the hell happened here?" Jenny blinked as she looked around the room, from the shattered coffee table, to the dented fridge, and back to Ashley. "Did he hurt you?"

Jenny stepped forward and grabbed Ashley by the chin, turning her this way and that, in what apparently was an impromptu check-up.

"Jenny, I'm fine," Ashley replied with a small, if awkward laugh.

"I asked if he hurt you, not if you were alright!" Jenny flicked an angry glare over her shoulder at Jeremiah, who worked at sitting pleasantly on the couch.

A part of him begged, wished for Jenny to lash out. To do something that would give him the opportunity to scour a literal Demon from the face of the Earth.

And more importantly, to do it in a way that placed absolutely zero possible blame on him. As much as it pained him, he needed Ashley, and the only way he could reasonably remove Jenny from the world and have Ashley even remotely support him, would be to have her attack first.

Even as the ugly thoughts passed through his mind, the same horrendous and lurking guilt that seemed to hover behind him loomed closer.

Pinning his mind to silence, Jeremiah kept smiling at the woman before she turned back to Ashley.

"I attacked him first. I was hungry and wasn't thinking properly, tried to drug him," Ashley admitted and stepped back from Jenny's searching hands. She put her hands into one another, almost like a child standing in front of their mother. "I like to think I kinda deserved the fight that came out of it since... well... yeah."

"Ashley, you can just feed from me if you're hungry!" Jenny offered exasperatedly, running her hands through her black hair before gesturing wildly at Jeremiah. "You don't have to shack up with a racist bastard just because you need to eat!"

"Jenny, it's fine," Ashley soothed, stepping over to where Jeremiah sat on the couch. "Also, did I miss something? Do you two know each other?"

"No," lied Jeremiah.

"Yes," Jenny answered at the same second as Jeremiah. "He got kicked out of the meal center because he wouldn't even let me serve him. Father Thomas threw him right out for being a dick!"

"Yeah, sue me!" Jeremiah shrugged and shot back. "Before the other day, the only monsters I thought existed were Weres and Vamps. Waking up in a new city and meeting a Demon working at the local soup kitchen isn't exactly the friendliest introduction to this shit!"

"But... you have a mask. Usually those are only given to people already in the know," Jenny frowned and tilted her head to the side, a cascade of obsidian hair falling to the other side of her head.

"Yeah, let's just add that to the list of 'weird-shit-I-didn't-know' that's been going on," Jeremiah growled out at the woman who still stood on the other side of the room. "Are you gonna help me, or just keep being a-"

A gentle hand was placed on his shoulder and Jeremiah stopped mid-insult.

"Like I said, Jenny, he can be a little... abrasive. He doesn't mind his mouth as well as he should," Ashley, much to Jeremiah's surprise, interjected. "But other than the little –incident- when we met, he's been rather helpful.

"Which, again, I was somewhat at fault for since, you know, the drugging...thing. Yeah.

"He even sold a super expensive watch for me to help make up for the damage our little disagreement caused. Now we have enough money to breathe for a bit.

"Jeremiah and I have come to an understanding, so I'm asking you, as your friend, to let his bad attitude go for now, okay?"

Jenny stuck her tongue behind her bottom lip as she looked at Jeremiah with a scowl. Inhaling, she shook her head slowly, and then nodded.

"Fine!" Jenny allowed, shucking off her backpack and setting it on the couch. "But you call me when he steps out of line. Not if, -when-."

"I will," Ashley murmured quietly from just behind Jeremiah. Jenny seemed to search Ashley's face for a brief second before she turned and began to rummage through her bag, withdrawing a small syringe, a needle inside a small, sealed plastic bag, and several small phials.

"Okay. Here's how this is gonna go," Jenny began in a sour, somewhat fed-up tone. "I've got another shift at the center here in about an hour or so. That means I need to do this quick and dirty. I'm gonna take a few samples of blood to test against other known samples in the lab. Then, I'm gonna ask you some questions about what's been going on.

"I need you to answer honestly, regardless of whatever holier-than-thou hooplah you're feeling about me, 'kay? The more honest you are, the more details I get, the more things I can correlate, compare, and use to figure out what you are. What you tell me won't leave this room."

"Anything you're looking for specifically, or do you just want my life's story?" Jeremiah questioned as Jenny affixed the needle to the syringe.

"Eh, give me the short version of the story. After I pull the samples, I'll ask specifics."

And so, Jeremiah laid all his memories out before the Demoness as she drew blood from different places on his body. Jenny was a non-stop gallery of different, expressive frowns as he introduced each relevant point of his memories, even stopping to look him in the eye quizzically as he mentioned the ten-year gap in his memories.

When he began to talk about his initial meeting with Ashley, the Vampire in question enthusiastically chipped in with extra information from her point of view.

Jenny had finished with her blood draws, and now sat on a barstool she'd pulled over, listening to the pair of them explain the events of the past two days.

"I honestly thought he was having a stroke, or some kind of allergic reaction to the sleeping pills!" Ashley helpfully chimed in as Jenny looked between the two of them with wide eyes. "I'm just glad he lived - his blood is pretty delicious if I'm being honest and... well... it's just what I needed when I need it, I guess."

Jeremiah briefly glanced over to her and back to Jenny before shrugging.

Weirdest ego boost I've ever had.

"Oookay," Jenny trailed off before exhaling through a closed mouth, making a soft raspberry. "Ash, could I ask you to step into the hallway, or the bathroom for a few minutes? I've got a couple more… sensitive medical questions I need to ask Jeremiah."

"Okay! Just yell when you need me," Ashley stood up from the couch and walked down the hall to the bathroom. As the door snicked shut, Jeremiah turned back to Jenny as a small rustle of fabric sounded.

"Ah," Jeremiah got out as he stared down the barrel of a small, semi-automatic handgun.

"Listen, dirtbag - and listen good," Jenny growled quietly, her finger on the trigger.

In the instant that Ashley had left the room, Jenny's orange eyes had begun to glow a deep, pinkish red, as ruby mist poured faintly from her mouth and nose. "I have zero issues gunning you down this very instant after what you told me, and the only reason I'm not, is that for some reason, Ashley apparently values you living. So don't move, don't flinch, don't do squat."

"You have my attention," Jeremiah replied placatingly, lifting his hands in line with his shoulders in an attempt to lessen any jumpy movements in front of the Demoness.

"Good. I don't care that you think you were some powerful, monster-killing action hero. I frankly couldn't give less of a fraction of an iota about your existence, either. But I need to make one thing abundantly clear.

"Ashley's a nice girl, and she's gone through quite a lot the past couple years. One thing she really doesn't need is you adding more shit to her plate. I can't control her life, but I can make strides to try and keep her safe, as much as I can."

"Ashley's a Vampire," Jeremiah snorted despite the loaded weapon in his face. The absurdity of getting the 'angry-best-friend' talk from a Demon, about a Vampire who literally drank criminals dry, rang somewhat humorously in his mind. "I'm pretty sure she can handl-"

"Oh I'm sure she can handle it, but she has the bad habit of trying to see the best in people," Jenny licked her lips and stared daggers into his eyes. "Even when it's not there. I'm only a text message away, and I'm not nearly as forgiving.

"If I come back and find you've pulled another stunt, or she calls me because you laid hands on her... well, do you know how easy it is to fake a toxicology report? Amatoxin ain't hard to come by, and I have needles so small that they'll never find the hole."

"Okay. Don't hurt Ashley. I got it!" Jeremiah acquiesced with raised eyebrows. "Wasn't... wasn't planning on it, not anymore."

"Mmm, so you did want to hurt her?" Jenny rolled her head to the side again as another breath of red mist poured from her mouth.

"I mean, did you miss the whole fistfight through the apartment part of the story?" Jeremiah flicked his eyes down to the gun in her hand, hoping he could disarm the woman with a bit of trickery and misdirection. "Really? You didn't even put a round in the chamber?"

"Wanna find out?" Jenny questioned as the trigger moved back fractionally. "I carry with one in the chamber everywhere I go. This city isn't kind to a woman after dark."

Okay...she's...squared away. She didn't even

break eye contact.

Jeremiah frowned at his failed attempt to bait the woman into pointing the gun away from him.

Don't fuck with the Demon lady.

"I take it I've made my point?" Jenny asked with a bright, self-assured smile. With the hand not holding the firearm, she brushed an errant lock of hair up and behind one of her horns. "Gonna play nice?"

"Yeah, nice and friendly!" Jeremiah agreed with raised eyebrows, contemplating if he was close enough to spring forward and disarm her before she could ventilate his skull.

"Great. Glad we had this 'lil chat," Jenny's smile became absolutely predatory in a way that did odd things to the back of Jeremiah's mind. "You can come back in, Ash!"

Jenny waited until the door had opened to stow the pistol in a near-invisible holster in her waistline. Jeremiah had to give credit where it was due. Not only had Jenny gotten the drop on him, forced him to submit to her demands, but she'd also maneuvered him into a situation where if he did anything, he would look like the bad guy.

That he most certainly couldn't attack the Demon who'd just held a gun to his head, was a train of thought that Jeremiah couldn't even begin to understand.

Though that immediately bled into a different thought.

One he didn't really want.

The Demon, something he thought was supposedly to be the absolute of evil, hadn't actually harmed him. She hadn't even actually threatened him over anything other than harming her friend.

A strong and strange dissonant thought rose up inside his head as he tried not to consider how this whole situation didn't match up to his expectations.

"Get all the info you needed, Jenn?" Ashley asked, rounding the corner of the hall as Jenny stood up, lifting her bag onto her shoulder.

"Yup - I'mma run these samples down to the lab and store them in the fridge," Jenny relayed with an affectionate smile at Ashley as she clearly made to exit the apartment. "I should have some results to chat with you about in a few days."

"Thank you so much!" Ashley smiled back at the Demon as Jenny opened the door to the apartment. "I owe you big time for this!"

"Don't mention it!" Jenny nodded and closed the door behind her.

Chapter 12

Jeremiah nodded politely at the hostess as he sat down at the table. The woman smiled kindly back at him, laid down their menus on the elegantly stitched tablecloth, and folded her hands in front of her waist.

"Is there anything else I can do for you?" she asked in a bright tone, looking between Jeremiah and Ashley.

"Mmm, could I have the red menu?" Ashley asked, pointedly emphasizing the word 'Red'.

The...red menu?

Jeremiah questioned internally, momentarily frowning as the hostess, without missing a beat, grabbed a red-bordered menu from the bottom of her small stack of menus.

Oh. Vamp specific menu...are they really that prevalent? Eh, I suppose we are across the street from a Vampire-owned club...probably have a bunch of regulars.

"Of course, not a problem," the hostess continued happily, turning to Jeremiah. "Will you be needing one as well, sir?"

"Nah, this one'll do me just fine," Jeremiah forced a smile to his face, internally wondering how ever deep this situation could get.

I bet they don't get their blood from particularly – willing- donors.

"Lovely! In that case, your server, Anton, should be with you shortly! I hope you two have a lovely night!" offered the hostess.

"You as well," Ashley favored the woman with a radiant smile, before turning it on Jeremiah as the hostess left their table.

"I feel kinda... under-dressed," Jeremiah noted as Ashley's smile began to infect him. She wore an elegant sapphire dress that hugged tight to her figure and flared out around her knees. The white shawl she had draped over her shoulders accentuated the almost soft glow she carried around her. "Where'd you even pull that out of?"

"Oh, it was my prom dress, and I just never threw it away!" Ashley shrugged noncommittally before looking down at the menu. "I honestly just tried it on more on a whim than anything. I'm surprised it still fits. I've grown a bit in the past few years."

Now that she mentioned it, Jeremiah did realize that it fit somewhat tightly around her hips and chest. In doing so, however, it managed to only look intentional - emphasizing the flare of her waist and swell of her bust, and prominently displaying her cleavage underneath a large emerald and gold pendant.

"That necklace certainly draws the eye," Jeremiah noted with a smirk that was met with a knowing, playful expression.

"Oh... the necklace does, does it?" Ashley asked with a raised brow and a smile.

Oh for fuck's sake, why does the world hate me?

Jeremiah fought back a grin that broke through despite his efforts.

If only you were human, Ashley.
If only.

"Well I mean, it really brings the outfit together. Dress looks good on you," Jeremiah replied, looking the menu over as his cheeks began to heat.

Jesus fuck, has this place ever even heard of a

burger?

Jeremiah kept skimming the offerings, turning the leather edge of the menu page.

Oh, there's on- aaand it's quinoa…what kind of fucking restaurant has a menu for Vampires, but makes it an act of congress to just get normal meat?

With some more searching, Jeremiah finally found the one seemingly normal item on this menu: a twelve-ounce sirloin.

But gods above, who would get a sixty-dollar steak like that?

"So," Jeremiah thought out loud, laying the menu on the table before him. Ashley peeked up and over her own menu with an expectant expression. "This place is… pricey."

"Well, it is one of the highest-rated restaurants in town… I'm honestly surprised we even got a table, with how booked it usually is," Ashley shrugged and lowered the menu enough to show a bright, fanged smile. "I blame it on us coming on a Wednesday."

"I dunno," Jeremiah looked over the balcony to the street below.

Across from them sat the Red Lotus club, a name that practically screamed 'Vampires here!' to him. The bright, artistically done neon sign in the shape of a flower bathed the entire street below in a red, hazy glow.

"Maybe they just wanted you in here. I kept getting jealous looks on the walk over. Honestly surprised someone didn't try and rob us with that rock on your neck," he murmured, his eyes moving around the street before coming back to Ashley.

The vampire had bit the tip of her tongue and clearly fought a smile before peering around them. She leaned forward and waved him over.

"It's costume jewelry," she half-giggled, half-whispered from less than a foot away. "I think I paid like ten bucks for a whole set at the Halloween store last year."

Jeremiah leaned back from her far-too-close face, sucking in his lips to avoid bursting out laughing. He could have stared at Ashley for hours without figuring out that her entire outfit was completely makeshift.

Stop flirting with the Vampire. She's just a means to an end!

He chided himself internally, even as they both burst out into infectious, quiet chuckles.

She gets to live because she's helping kill even worse Vampires.

She gets to live because she didn't deserve what happened to her!

The idle separation of his thoughts again caught him off-guard.

She's no different than you. Just another victim of a coven.

Jeremiah blinked rapidly, turning his eyes on the club they were supposed to be surveilling, to look for notable and important Vampires that Jeremiah could get an eye on and identify.

The sun had set an hour previously, and they used the excuse of the window-repair team wandering around their apartment as a reason to get out.

Jeremiah and Ashley had planned this, and he wholly expected to spend his evening watching the front of a Vampire club, taking notes and munching on food. What he hadn't expected, despite the fact that he'd been forced to obtain a dress shirt and slacks by Ashley, was for her to dress up the way she had.

A part of him recoiled at the sight of her, dressed to the nines, in a way that drew his eyes effortlessly.

On the surface, it reminded him of the Vamp that had preyed upon him all those years ago. The one who'd lured him back to her coven on the promise of a lovely night with one of the most beautiful women he'd ever laid eyes upon.

And yet there was a part of him that cried out that this was different. That she was different.

With Natalie, the Vampire honeypot, the allure had been dark, carnal - a promise of a wild and eventful night that she had delivered upon, if in a different way than he'd expected.

Ashley contrasted wildly.

Her white shawl reflected the yellow lights strung on the edge of the awning above them, giving her head an almost imperceptible halo in the faint fog that drifted in from the nearby ocean. Her blue dress was elegant, instead of the revealing, complicated black and red number Nathalie had worn.

"Aren't we supposed to be watching the club?" Ashley questioned with a faint blush to her cheeks, pointedly looking down to the Red Lotus before focusing on her menu again.

"Right, yeah," Jeremiah coughed once, realizing that he'd been staring thoughtfully at the Vampire across from him instead of watching the front of the club.

Refocusing on his part of the excursion, he observed the security by the front door, making note of the several large bouncers, along with one tall, lithe, well-dressed woman who seemed to be their supervisor.

"Good evening," a male voice broke his thoughts away from his task. "I will be your server tonight. Is there anything I can get started to drink?"

"Uh, yes, but I had a question first," Ashley nodded to the well-dressed man who stood beside their table with a notepad. "How do you source your red?"

"Ah, a discerning customer, I see," Anton nodded at Ashley with a kind smile. "All of our red is locally sourced and cruelty-free from vetted, tested, and consenting volunteers. They are well compensated, and we can provide testimonials to our methods."

"Perfect, that's what I wanted to hear!" Ashley smiled thankfully at their server. "Can I get the guardian red, then?"

"I'll have it right over," the server nodded and turned to Jeremiah. "And for you, sir?"

"Just a MacGunnea lager, please," Jeremiah answered neutrally.

"Of course. I'll be back for your meal order shortly."

With that, Anton left them alone at their table again.

"Okay, that guy right there," Ashley pointed at a man who walked into the front of the club, flanked by several women on either side. "That's Aiden. I remember him talking with Vasily about 'acquisitions', usually people they wanted to forcefully turn… like… erm- me. He was constantly at odds with Analise, about cleaning up the money for it,"

"Okay, so he's the head of human trafficking?" Jeremiah asked, staring at the blonde-haired, eerily handsome man, as he turned around to the cabal of women behind him and said something with a toothy grin. Whatever he'd said, it clearly was funny, as the entire group began to laugh before entering the establishment. "And whomever Analise is deals with the money?"

"Maybe? I honestly don't know much, just the general idea of who people are," Ashley shrugged. "I know kinda what all the higher-ups do, but not specifics."

"How?" Jeremiah questioned, his eyes moving back to Ashley.

"Vasily… kept me on a short leash after he turned me. I've heard him talk with them outside the room, but… at the time, I was mostly focused on how I could escape," Ashley nervously wringed her hands together as she refused to meet Jeremiah's eyes. "It's a little hard to worry about the ins and outs of the people keeping you locked in a bedroom, or to think about much of anything outside of escape."

"Fair, you've remembered more than I did," Jeremiah shivered as he remembered his time as a blood-slave. Comparing and contrasting their experiences internally, he had to give it to her.

She'd had it worse and seemingly did better.

"The bitch by the door is Veronique, she runs security for the club," Ashley pointed at the woman beside the bouncers. "She actually broke one of my ribs because I asked her for food."

"Okay. So we're gonna kill her from a distance," Jeremiah noted, reaching across the table and wrapping his hand around Ashley's. A small chirp of surprise left the Vampire's mouth as he held her hand and slowly pulled it back down to the table.

"We're here to look like a couple on a date. Not people scoping out the local Vamp den. Pointing at important people draws attention."

Jeremiah smiled reassuringly at Ashley, trying to quell the nerves she clearly felt about this situation.

"Right. Okay, so, how shou-" Ashley cut off abruptly, looking at a point behind Jeremiah with a clearly forced polite smile.

"We have the guardian red for you, miss," the waiter set an artistically crafted cocktail of swirling red and pink colored liqueur before Ashley, and then placed the beer in front of Jeremiah without a word. "Are you ready to order?"

"Ah, yes," Ashley smiled and briefly looked down to her red-bordered menu before continuing. "Could I get the blood sausage and pasta? With extra garlic sauce?"

"Wonderful choice!" the waiter smiled brightly at the woman before turning and favoring Jeremiah with a neutral, inexpressive stare. "And for you sir?"

"I'll have the sirloin and vegetables," Jeremiah replied with a small nod.

"Mmm," the waiter nodded and gave him a thin-lipped smirk. "I'll have that right out."

As he left, Jeremiah stared at the back of Anton's head with a frown.

"Fuck is his problem?" Jeremiah asked quietly, looking back to Ashley without turning his head.

"I think you just picked the most boring, average order on the menu," Ashley chuckled, reaching over to snatch his menu off the table. Looking through it, she grinned, looking from it, to him, and back again. "Yeah. You didn't even ask about the chef's special."

"I'm not gonna eat octopus, ever!" Jeremiah plucked the menu out of her hands. "I don't care how much anyone pays me."

Ashley snorted and rolled her eyes before a companionable silence stretched between them. As he watched the front of the club, he watched an unassuming man of average height, dark brown hair, and slim build wearing a white suit, step out the front of the club and eye the surroundings with a confident smirk on his face.

"That's... that's him," Ashley's voice became a low, dangerous hiss. "That's Vasily."

"Kinda scrawny for a kingpin," Jeremiah watched the man out of the corner of his eye. "Looks like a stray gust of wind might knock him over."

"Oh trust me, he's more p-" Ashley cut off as her eyes went wide as saucers. "He's coming over here, why is he coming over here?"

"Maybe he's hungry," Jeremiah shrugged absently, trying to outwardly remain calm as the man crossed the busy street between the club and the front of the two-story restaurant.

"Oh god, oh fuck, we need to go!" Ashley hissed, snatching up her purse. Jeremiah, again, leaned over and put his hand on hers.

"And go where?" he asked, his tone deadly serious as his apparent calm had failed to transfer to her. "There's only one way in and one way out.

"If he's coming in here to start shit, we're surrounded by witnesses. If he's coming for food, we wait for him to take a seat, pay, and try to get the fuck out as sneakily as possible, alright?"

"But... he..."

"Ash, trust me," Jeremiah soothed, using the nickname he'd heard Jenny use earlier. "I've hunted a coven before. He's not gonna make a move where he can be seen like this."

"Okay," Ashley seemed to stare into his soul with her bright green eyes, breathing heavily.

Confident that he had stopped her from doing anything rash, Jeremiah leaned back and took a long pull of his beer. A small throng of servers hustled past their table, each looking nervous and hopeful in equal measure.

He's probably a regular.

Knowing covens, he likely tips really well.

They're all hoping to serve his table, get a week's pay for a night of work.

Jeremiah took stock of the situation, glancing over to the front of the club.

Veronique stared intently right back at him.

Well shit. That's not good.

"Ashley!" A deep, sententious, eastern European voice, carried from Jeremiah's left. "It's been too long!"

Jeremiah turned towards the voice and found exactly who he expected.

Vasily confidently sauntered between the tables of customers, his arms wide to the side, as if greeting an old friend he didn't expect to bump into. Passing by one of the tables with an empty chair, he grabbed it by the back and dragged it loudly across the floor. For nearly thirty feet, in the center of the crowded restaurant floor, Vasily scraped the metal legs of the chair obnoxiously along the floor behind him.

With a small flourish of his hand, he effortlessly twirled the chair around to his front, casually unbuttoning the front of his jacket before sitting down.

Vasily turned his icy blue eyes on Jeremiah for a brief moment, running his index finger and thumb on the underside of his chin thoughtfully before dismissing Jeremiah outright.

"I had hoped to see you soon, but not in the company of another," Vasily continued, as Ashley seemed to shrink and curl in on herself. "You left in such a heartbreaking way, my dear pet - you didn't even tell me you were leaving. I worried for weeks over you!"

Jeremiah forced himself to hold back a sigh over the Vampire's sanctimonious tone, full of false sympathy and worry.

"I would have expected you to return and beg for my kindness once again, to be fed and loved as a woman of your beauty should be!" Vasily turned wrathful eyes on Jeremiah for a scant second before they mellowed and returned to Ashley. "I must confess, I am... hurt, to my very soul, that you would trade what I offered you, to spite my gift for... mmm, this."

Vasily gestured absently towards Jeremiah with a small roll of his wrist.

"I can have him removed if he is bothering you," Vasily continued confidently, not even bothering to look Jeremiah in the eyes again. "Or perhaps he might leave once you tell him what you are. Have you told him were yet, salodki?"

"He knows," Ashley muttered quietly, her eyes flicking up to meet Jeremiah's. When they met, something seemed to shift. A small spark of confidence flickered to life. "He partner-feeds me. Helps me."

Vasily chuckled loudly, slapping a hand to his chest and leaning back in his chair with an entertained grin on his face. "No no no, not that. It would be hard to keep that kind of secret from someone you care about. Does he know that you were my pet first?"

Jeremiah nearly attacked the waiter out of surprise as he placed a plate full of artfully staged, seared steak, upon a bed of roasted vegetables before him.

As his heartbeat slowed, Jeremiah caught an intrigued glance from Vasily towards him.

Ashley, again, seemed to fold in on herself by the time he looked back. As calmly as he could manage, Jeremiah pulled out the utensils from the rolled nearby cloth napkin.

He cut into the steak with the large, serrated knife that was part of the kit, and took a bite of his steak. The knife was very sharp.

"You know, assholes like you are why Vamps have such a bad reputation," Jeremiah noted, taking a bite of his steak.

"Ah, he speaks!" Vasily proudly proclaimed, turning to smile at Jeremiah like a cat playing with a mouse. "I almost thought tonight was going to be boring! You know how my Ashley is, always quiet and reserved!"

Jeremiah barely avoided frowning at that, considering in his experience, Ashley was fairly bubbly and talkative. Sarcastic, at times, to be sure, but not quiet and reserved.

"Maybe you're just really bad at conversation," Jeremiah offered, taking another chunk out of his steak.

Bait him. Piss him off.

Wait until he throws down, put the knife through his eye.

Vamp healing can't fix brain hemorrhaging.

"I can assure you, mister," Vasily trailed off,

waiting for Jeremiah to reply with his name for several agonizing seconds, before clicking his tongue and sighing. "Very well... I can assure you, Mr. Nemo, that my conversational abilities are of the highest caliber and quality. Though, clearly you have something I do not, if she dines with you outside my front door. As if I would not take notice."

"Maybe this is just the best joint in town to take a cute Vamp like Ash," Jeremiah shrugged with a sharpened smile. "Why worry about a loudmouth ex when you've got better things to focus on, right dear?"

Jeremiah hoped he could pull this off, that he could convince Vasily that they –weren't- just there to observe and stake out the club.

Just play the annoyed boyfriend routine.

Hopefully he just talks like an asshole for a bit and leaves.

Ashley's eyes flicked up from her plate of untouched food, meeting Jeremiah's gaze, as the faintest fraction of a smile touched the corner of her mouth. Vasily watched the byplay, his grin faltering for a moment before he fully turned his attention back to Ashley.

"Come back to the coven, my dear, my pet," Vasily said in a sickly-sweet tone, resting his hands on the table. "I have seen you starve, you try to rejoin the cattle, not accepting what I have blessed you with. You struggle to keep even that abhorrent apartment over your head. Come back to me, come back to luxury."

Vasily began to reach one of his hands out towards Ashley's, clearly intent on touching her.

Asshole.

Jeremiah flicked the knife into a backwards

grip and lashed out before he knew what was happening.

Instead of slamming it through the Vampire's skull, as he had planned when the Vampire approached, it slammed down and into Vasily's hand - pinning it to the table, as the now-weapon buried itself to the handle.

After the small clatter of dishes being jostled from the impact ceased, the restaurant was dead silent.

"Hmmm," Vasily noted without a hint of pain in his voice. "Interesting."

Why did I do that?

Jeremiah furrowed his brow as he stared at Vasily's impaled left hand.

Why didn't I just go for his eye?

Vasily lifted his hand up a couple inches, and the table came with it.

"Brave," Vasily said, bracing his impaled hand on the table and pulling the blade free with a small grinding noise of metal-on-wood. He examined the slightly bent knife with a frown before turning back to Jeremiah and handing it back to him, handle-first. "Behave. We are civilized here."

"Nothing about you is civilized, you bloodsucking asshole," Jeremiah snatched the weapon away from Vasily, no longer bothering to keep his composure. He continued, his words coming out almost without control. "I look forward to watching you go up in flames, you disgusting piece of shit. You're a goddamn insult to your fuckin' kind.

"You know, if I had met someone like Ashley first, I wouldn't even have hesitated about dating her to begin with. Get the fuck away from our table."

"Mmm. So it is, then," Vasily shrugged and

sighed dramatically, pushing himself away from the table. "Ashley, it has been lovely seeing you again. I ask that when you next return to my new restaurant, you only bring pets that you've house-trained. Enjoy your meal."

Vasily buttoned his jacket back up, spun, and walked away.

Periodically, he stopped at tables and offered conversation and condolences for their ruined night, gifting their meals for free. When the Vampire finally left, Ashley let loose a deep, shuddering breath of air.

"I can't believe you actually did that!" she chuckled nervously, somewhere between fear and excitement. "That was so fast, just, right through his hand!"

"I wanted to go for his eye," Jeremiah muttered, using the other, less sharp knife in the small roll of cutlery. He really didn't want to accidentally consume Vampire blood tonight. "Dunno what happened there, or how I just... went through the table."

"But you didn't see the look on his face!" Ashley hissed, a large portion of the nerves gone from her voice, replaced with giddy enthusiasm. "I don't think I've ever seen him shaken up like that before! He stared at the knife like it was a snake!"

"Bad news is now he knows I exist... should've just gone for the head and taken the jail time," Jeremiah muttered to himself, as he took another bite of the single best steak he'd ever had.

Jeremiah swallowed the bite and risked a glance to his right, over the balcony. Veronique and Vasily had made it down the club entrance, watching them with wildly different expressions.

Vasily seemed almost entertained, as he lifted

his hand and waved with false friendliness to Jeremiah. Veronique, on the other hand, stared daggers at him.

We're gonna get followed...aren't we?

Jeremiah frowned, looking back to his plate.

Shit, I fucked up...didn't I?

Chapter 13

"Thank you, have a good night!" Ashley smiled brightly at their driver - someone from a 'not-quite-a-taxi' service that Ashley had summoned, on-demand, after their run in with Vasily at the restaurant.

"You as well!" The man driving the car waved as Ashley shut the door behind her.

Jeremiah's head was on a swivel as his eyes quickly surveyed the front of Ashley's apartment building.

Vasily knew where she lived. Had always known, apparently.

He'd apparently been content to watch Ashley from afar.

Now, because of Jeremiah's outburst, the Vampire lord had a reason to come after Jeremiah, let alone Ashley. There was the possibility he'd come for Ashley if only because she was now directly linked to Jeremiah.

Gonna have to accelerate the plans, or slow way the fuck down.

Maybe just move.

Jeremiah frowned pointedly, as Ashley stepped up beside him and entwined her arm through his. Jeremiah glared down at the limb and debated pulling away, but thought better as his brain started to spin up.

Actually, this is for the best.

If Vasily thinks it was all just an act from a jealous boyfriend, it might change his methods away from a full-frontal assault.

We have to be careful and play the game until we can hit our first target.

Just look like the cute Vamp-Human couple coming home from an odd date night.

Jeremiah allowed that image to carry him up to the front door of the apartment building, even resting an arm over Ashley's shoulder as she fidgeted with the key for the exterior door.

Looking over his shoulder and doing his best to appear bored, he saw no one in their immediate area.

An occasional pedestrian walked down the street in the distance, but no people he could identify, and more importantly, no one that looked like they were observing them.

"There we go!" Ashley mumbled happily as the latch clicked. As she pulled open the door, Jeremiah stepped quickly inside the small atrium, looking from side to side. Again, he saw nothing.

"It's too damn quiet," Jeremiah muttered as the door clicked shut behind him. "Never met a Vamp that would tolerate an attack like that."

"Vasily is... odd," Ashley murmured as she stepped up beside him after locking the door. "He might not actually do... anything. I mean, he's let me stay away for about two years after escaping. And he clearly knows where I live."

"You're likely right but... it's not something I want to gamble on," Jeremiah replied with a shake of his head. "Tomorrow, we're using some of the money to buy guns and other supplies to take down a coven.

"If we have the means, and they have the stupid idea to try, we can use said equipment to defend the apartment if they send a team of bloodsuckers after us."

Ashley didn't respond to that.

"We're taking the stairs up," Jeremiah pulled Ashley off course from the elevator bay just ahead. "Real easy to ambush us when the doors open, and we won't have anywhere to go."

"But what if they're waiting for us in the stairwell too?" Ashley questioned, now freely allowing herself to be pulled along towards the building's main set of stairs.

"Easy, then we just go back down," Jeremiah stopped at the bottom of the stairwell and peered up. Seeing nothing, he began to ascend.

"I... okay, yeah, that makes sense. It's kinda like a fire, but with powerful, decades-old Vampires with assault rifles," Ashley replied with an edge of sarcasm from close behind him. "Fuckin' Christ, I never should've gone back."

"It was an oversight by both of us," Jeremiah replied, continuing to stare up the central hole in the stairwell, hoping to spot anyone loitering about maliciously. "Neither one of us knew that he owned that restaurant now, and I'm guessing that you didn't know he was that obsessed with you, either.

"We should've done a little more recon and info-gathering before we jumped in to grab a bite to eat across the street.

"Honestly, given the fact that I've done this kind of shit before, and you haven't - it's more on me," Jeremiah shrugged as they rounded the next landing, his nerves on high alert.

They're bloodsuckers. They should have sent someone after us by now.

They climbed ever higher in the apartment complex, only to find an unnerving amount of nothing.

Silence gathered between them as they climbed several more flights, and finally made it to Ashley's floor.

Jeremiah leaned slightly out of the stairwell alcove, peering down both sides of the hall.

Again, it was resoundingly empty.

He gestured for Ashley to follow him as he pushed on towards her door.

Pausing on either side of the entry to her apartment, Jeremiah watched as Ashley pulled out her keyring.

Jeremiah caught her attention and pressed his finger to his lips, indicating for Ashley to unlock the door as quietly as possible.

Slowly, cautiously, she slid her key into the lock, turned it, and opened the door a scant fraction.

If someone's going to be anywhere, they'll be inside. Push in, follow the long wall, and avoid sight lining yourself from the bedroom.

Living room, kitchen, bathroom, bedroom, in that order.

Jeremiah nodded decisively at his own thoughts and threw open the door.

The living room was empty, lit only by a small lamp on Ashley's desk.

He checked behind the counter, and was again rewarded with nothing.

By this point, his Vampire counterpart seemed to have caught on to what he was doing, and began to move fluidly down the hallway just in front of Jeremiah.

A split second before he touched the handle for the bedroom, Ashley flung open the bathroom door. Jeremiah frowned as he peered into the darkened bedroom, and flicked on the light, clearing the small apartment.

Something is wrong. Something is very wrong.

Jeremiah's tightly wound nerves leaped into the atmosphere as his heart thudded away in his chest.

"See anything?" Ashley asked from behind him, eliciting a small jump as he spun to face her.

"Uh- no, nothing," Jeremiah shook his head and took one last look over his shoulder at the empty bedroom behind him. "Looks like the window repair company did a good job, though."

Jeremiah gestured over his shoulder towards the now-fixed window, still missing one curtain.

Perhaps I just over-estimated them. Maybe Vasily just doesn't care about a boring human.

Jeremiah stepped aside as Ashley moved into the room, staring at the pane of glass with a faint smile.

Over-confident asshole.

"Wow, you can hardly tell I was thrown out of it by a crazy homeless man not that long ago!" Ashley turned a playful grin on him as Jeremiah rolled his eyes.

"I'm going to bed," Jeremiah chortled, shaking his head as he made for the couch. "'Night, Ash."

"Yeah," there was a slight edge to her voice as she replied. "'Night."

The door closing behind him felt far louder than it should have.

* * *

Jeremiah stared absently at the ceiling as sleep evaded his grasp. He'd managed to get a whole twenty minutes of sleep in just over three hours.

"Why the fuck am I adapting to her sleep schedule?" Jeremiah groused quietly, pushing his palms into his eyes. "Couldn't she just deal-"

He trailed off as he made the connection he already knew, but still irked him.

"The fucking sun," Jeremiah sighed and pushed the back of his head forcefully into the arm of the couch, as if he were trying to beat sleep into himself. "Allergic to the fucking sun. How'd you let it get this far, guy? Shacked up with a Vampire like it's completely normal.

"Well, on second thought...nothing about the past few days has been normal."

The haunting whispers and echoes of thoughts and memories he didn't want to understand scurried after him in that moment.

Jeremiah sat up on the couch with a yawn, dislodging the thoughts before they could settle into his brain.

Staring at the blank TV screen in the dark room, he was alone in his head again.

The blackout curtains managed to block out most, but not all of the light. Just enough to get a blurry idea of where everything was.

He stood up and grabbed the glass off the counter he'd acquired for water runs in the middle of the night.

"If the One and All really is up there, they've got one hell of a sense of humor," Jeremiah chuckled to himself as he leaned back against the stove. "One he-"

A loud thud shook him from his thoughts. It

was followed by a near inaudible moan and another soft thud.

Shit, they were just waiting for us to let our guard down!

Jeremiah realized the sounds were coming from Ashley's room.

Probably just rappelled off the roof, or just had a blood-sorcerer float them up to her window!

Damnit, I got complacent!

Jeremiah sprang into action, practically sprinting his way to the attacker in Ashley's room.

He flung open the door, fully ready to charge headlong into a blood mage draining her dry.

Instead, all he found was an empty room - save for a tossing, turning, and agitatedly moaning Ashley on the bed.

Spying around the room, he confirmed again that no one was there.

"No," Ashley mumbled, pushing against the blanket that covered her. "Don- I don't want to be-"

Jeremiah stared down to the Vampire, clearly in the throes of a nightmare. He snorted and rolled his eyes as his heartbeat slowed down.

Just a false alarm...damnit, Ash.

Jeremiah sighed at the Vampire, turning for the door. He'd let her ride it out, she wasn't his problem, after all.

"No, get off me!" Ashley half-murmured, half-shouted in an odd, distressed cadence that tugged at something deep inside him.

Freezing halfway out the door, he held the knob and internally debated the merits of what he was about to do.

I'll just wake her up. She can deal with anything else on her own. I can't sleep with all this racket, after all.

Grimacing, he realized that that had absolutely nothing at all to do with why he was waking her up. He could easily just wrap a pillow around his head and ignore it.

No. Even if she's just a Vampire, she doesn't deserve to suffer like this.

She'll sleep better after getting more of a chance to process her thoughts.

"Ash, wake up," Jeremiah said in a commanding tone, projecting his voice across the room.

Still, the woman in bed thrashed and murmured discontentedly.

Jeremiah rolled his eyes, stepped up to the side of her bed, and pushed on her shoulder.

"Ash, it's jus- shit!" squeaked Jeremiah.

Ashley's eyes snapped open as she grabbed him by his collar and yanked him down to the bed over her body with enhanced Vampiric strength.

He slammed into the soft surface and just barely had enough time to brace his arm across Ashley's chest as she snarled, baring her fangs and dipping her head forward towards his neck.

Her fingers dug into his biceps as she struggled mindlessly to pull herself at him, to clamp down on his throat.

Shit! This is it, she's gonna kill me now!

Strangely, the thought felt hollow and wrong despite the situation. As if it didn't line up somehow.

Jeremiah acted quickly, pulling Ashley down over his body and trying to roll atop her, hopefully getting the chance to strangle her in the process.

"Die!" she growled in a rasping, hateful voice as they rolled, and Jeremiah fell off the side of the bed.

Landing hard on his shoulder, Jeremiah scrambled to his feet and jumped back, mentally preparing himself to go toe-to-toe with a pissed-off Vampire yet again.

He brought his hands up in a defensive stance, locking his eyes to her face, as she stared confusedly around the room as if she didn't remember it.

Wild eyes full of fear cast about as Ashley began to hyperventilate, her hands shakily opening and closing like they couldn't seem to find a way to stay still.

Gone was the wrath from a mere second ago, replaced as fear, confusion, and disgust.

"J-Jeremiah?" She asked shakily, her searching, haunted eyes landing on him. "I- I…"

Ashley trailed off as the words she was about to say failed her.

"Must've been one hell of a nightmare," Jeremiah replied cautiously, dropping his hands to his sides and exhaling a sigh of relief. As it turned out, his new roommate was not trying to kill him and drink him dry.

"Yeah," Ashley gave him a one word reply as she seemed to fold in on herself, pulling her knees to her chest and resting her head atop them. "Sorry I woke you."

The apology was muffled, as she pressed her face into her knees.

"Eh, I was already awake," Jeremiah shrugged but didn't move otherwise. "I'm a little jetlagged from adjusting to Vamp time."

"Well-" Ashley lifted her head up and gave him a forced smile, her cheeks were stained with tracks of eyeliner. "Then, sorry for going full… full monster on you. Seeing Vasily again just shook me up."

"You... wanna talk about it?" Jeremiah asked, even as his surface thoughts screamed that this wasn't his business, that the damsel-in-distress routine was just that: a routine to force his sympathy.

Except that was a bit late, the routine had already worked.

"Not much to talk about," Ashley shrugged absently as she stared at a point between them, some infinitesimal speck that only she could see. "Nothing I haven't told the support group. I got kidnapped by a Vampire crime boss after matching on a dating app. I got used, bitten, and turned - then I escaped... I thought."

She gave her head a quick shake and then sniffled loudly.

"Turns out this entire time, he's just been watching me from a distance, waiting for me to come back or some stupid bullshit like that," Ashley said with a snort and shook her head again. "I wonder if he's the reason I lost my job and got expelled... they said I was stealing university property for accidentally taking a library tablet home. I even returned it, fat lot of good that did me."

That's...fuck.

Vasily royally fucked her over.

I should've just gone for the head.

I should kill every last one of those motherfuckers.

No sooner had he had the thought than he found that it felt hollow.

Since of those 'motherfuckers' was sitting there right in front of him, and the cause for his anger.

"Usually when I have a nightmare, I just call Jenny and... vomit all the words," admitted Ashley as she pressed her face back into her knees. "You can go, I'll just call her."

"No, I'll listen," Jeremiah nodded slowly as Ashley began to reach for her phone. Jeremiah stepped over to her bed cautiously before sitting down at the corner. "Ain't got nothing better to do. Having trouble sleeping myself."

"Oh yeah, need to vent too?" Ashley asked, shimmying herself to sit down beside him on the foot of the bed.

"Nah, I'm good," Jeremiah shook his head fractionally as he stared at the place where the floor met the wall. "Just some bad memories, I think... nothing special."

"It's still good to talk about them," urged Ashley, and pushed on his shoulder with hers. "Not like I'm gonna run off and tell anyone. At this point, you and Jenny are... all I've got."

"Don't you have family?" Jeremiah asked, turning slightly to look at her.

"I do but... I told them about what I was, and they didn't take it well. My parents are big into the church, and at this point I'm just surprised they haven't sicced the bishop on me," Ashley sniffled once and brushed at her nose before she got out in a hiccupping sob. "They disowned me, told me never to co-contact them again."

"Dick move," Jeremiah chuckled sadly, knowing full well that, before the past few days, he would've done the exact same thing, if not outright try and kill her.

Should always put the rabid dog out of its miser-
Jeremiah cut his own thoughts off as he scowled at the floor.

She's not a dog, she's...she can make a choice.

Even at dinner, she asked about where they sourced their blood...like a damned, oh god what are those annoying fuckers called again?

Jeremiah scrunched his mouth as he struggled to remember.

Like a damned vegan. Ashley, the cruelty-free vegan Vampire...that's a thought.

"Yeah... but hey, Vampirism poisons the soul, right? Can't have a soulless daughter! Even my sister barely returns my calls," Ashley chuckled sadly before it turned into a quiet, singular sniffle. "I remember sneaking those trashy Vampire romance novels from my high school library home, reading them in the middle of the night, thinking how cool it would be to sparkle.

"But I don't sparkle, I just... melt and eat people. Catch fire."

"Could be worse," Jeremiah added with a wry chuckle. "Could be the crazy homeless time-traveler with fuzzy memories. Could be dead. Could still be locked up with that bloodsucking monster."

"I swear. If you ever call me that again, I am going to bite you-" Ashley jabbed him in the ribs painfully with her elbow. "Clearly, you're immune. So you get to have some pain again. Call me a Vamp bitch all you wan-"

"I won't," Jeremiah nodded his head at her request with a deep sigh as a thought that had been slowly roasting away in the back of his mind made its way to the surface - leaping from his lips before he had the chance to control it. "You're nowhere near the same.

"It's like comparing a wolf to a black lab. I... I was wrong. I don't know if you're the lone Vamp with a heart of gold, or if there's others like you... But regardless of what happens, if we get killed by a Vampire hit squad or something, just know: you're better than them."

How many just like her have I killed?

The ugly thought settled into Jeremiah's head as he licked his lips.

How many monsters are just victims of actual monsters. No different than her.

Than me…

He shook his head rapidly, trying to shake off the disgusting feeling that overcame his body.

No. The chances that someone can overcome their nature, that their soul is pure enough to beat back the desire to prey upon humans is astronomically high. Some might pretend, but it's one-in-a-billion.

The thought almost made him feel better.

Almost.

It was a lie, and somewhere deep inside himself, he knew it.

"Better than them… yeah," Ashley muttered, as if hearing it from someone else was a revelation unto itself. "Coming from a Templar, that actually means something. Not just the lip-service from others like me."

"Not a Templar," Jeremiah corrected her and smiled. "Just wanted to be one for a… long time. I was part of Humanity First, one of their wetwork detachments. Granted, we all wanted to be Templars, and they did recruit from groups like ours from time to time, but no… I'm just a monster hunter."

Ashley grunted at that before sniffling and rubbing her nose again.

"Well. I guess you better start teaching me, then. Ever trained an apprentice before?" she asked, in a bright tone that sounded forced.

"Can't say I have. But we're gonna need guns, and good sleep, before we can really start to throw down with a coven more than twenty times our size," Jeremiah looked to the faint lines of orange sunlight that spilled in underneath the curtains. "So let's get back to bed, and get ready to run errands this afternoon. Here in the next few days, I'll take you to the range and teach you the same shit Patrick taught me."

A Vampire hunting other monsters...

The thought brought a smile to Jeremiah's face.

Would make one hell of a movie.

He stood up from her bed, but stopped halfway to turning for the door as Ashley's hand gripped his wrist.

"Can... can you sleep here, with me?" she asked in a soft voice, barely louder than a whisper. As she continued, her resolve seemed to steel up: "I didn't have any nightmares the other night. It's a hail-Mary, but if having you next to me makes my head shut up, then—"

Ashley shook her head and broke the sentence off cold.

"And if I wake up like that again, at least we know you can handle it until I'm back to normal," she finished.

She wants me to...sleep with her?

Jeremiah frowned as he looked back to her, smiling hopefully up at him. It was clear at the edges of her smile that Ashley was just as nervous about asking the question as he was about answering it.

Why does the helpless pretty girl routine work so well on me?

"Yeah," Jeremiah returned a thin-lipped

neutral smile as he nodded. "I can do that."

Ashley's smile brightened several thousand lumens.

She released his hand and crawled into place, organizing the haphazardly thrown covers as she crawled underneath.

Jeremiah stared at the bed as she folded back the blankets, leaving the sheet on the bottom.

It's just sleep.

He reassured himself as he climbed into bed with the attractive Vampire.

You already feed her. You know you can fight her. There's even a sheet between us, and we're wearing clothes. This is fine.

If it's fine, then why am I so...nervous?
This is fine.
This is okay.
This is..the right thing to do, right?

Chapter 14

Jeremiah took another bite of the steak-and-egg burrito while he stared at the notebook in his hands with a frown.

He'd written down an impromptu hierarchy and general role-in-the-coven list from Ashley's memory, and now had it sorted into a rough flow chart.

"I'm sorry I ever made fun of you for the whiteboard charts, Patty," Jeremiah chuckled, remembering the presentations he would get in organized, concise collages of gathered and vetted intelligence from the leader of their cell. "What I wouldn't give for one of those now. Maybe I can talk Ash into getting one for us."

He'd made Ashley a list of items to purchase and initially planned to go with her.

However, he didn't want to risk buying guns with her when he didn't have any identification.

Jeremiah knew for a fact that without a friendly neighborhood arms dealer willing to sell under-the-table, the only way to get one was with a background check.

And so, Jeremiah had to make himself scarce. Ashley would take a cab back from the store, hopefully with the gear he'd asked her to source for him.

Though, I wonder if a cab will even let her on when she's got a rifle case stuffed full of random junk.

Jeremiah shrugged and took another bite of the burrito, considering the options for how to go about dismantling the coven.

On the one hand, the prospect of just cutting the head off the snake and killing Vasily felt very correct to Jeremiah.

Unfortunately, this isn't about watching Vasily's head pop like a watermelon, satisfying as it would be.

Jeremiah sighed as he looked over the chart of eight individuals that supposedly assisted Vasily in running the coven.

We need to break it down so hard that it never tries to re-grow. If we leave two people in a power vacuum, someone will take over, and it'll be business as usual in a couple months, after one drains the other.

If we leave two dozen no-name, middle-management plebs, they'll be like crabs in a bucket.

Jeremiah chuckled as he imagined Vampires in elegant suits struggling to clamber over one another.

They'll get nothing done, and hopefully just fuck back off to nowhere. Or at least, they'll start making overt plays that get the Feds on their ass.

Jeremiah and Ashley sure had their work cut out for them and it was going to take some serious cash to fund their two-man operation.

Hopefully the first couple Vamps have some shiny shit we can sell, or just a few bricks of cash.

He bobbed his head from side to side as he contemplated the likelihood that they would have easily liquidated assets.

I say we have a fifty-fifty shot of being able to get what we need. We should hit Aiden and Analise first...

Jeremiah frowned down at the heads of human trafficking and chief of money laundering operations respectively. All they were right now, was names on a page with a general role underneath, all from memory.

This is gonna be a shi-

Jeremiah's train of thought cut off as seven rhythmic knocks sounded from the door. He glanced over at the digital clock on the counter and reasoned that Ashley could've gotten done with the errands by now.

Probably just bogged down with bags and goodies.

Jeremiah stepped around the counter and started for the door.

Extra Vampire strength doesn't mean extra Vampire hands.

"Damn, Ash, I didn- oh, hey Jenny."

"Already chatted with Ash, she'll be back in a bit," Jenny said dismissively, stepping past him into the apartment. "Got your results back."

"Okay, great," Jeremiah watched the tall Demoness walk to the counter and sit down on the barstool to face him. "What's the diagnosis?"

"That's the problem, I can't really give you one. At least not the specifics," Jenny bit her lower lip and frowned, before meeting his eyes with a shrug. "Knowing you, you're either gonna try and kill me or have an existential crisis, so I'd prefer it if you were sitting down for this. It'll give me a little more time to draw and get a sight picture."

"Ah, fuck," Jeremiah muttered, flopping down in the center of the couch. "That bad?"

"Language, and it depends on your point of view," Jenny flicked her index finger out as she scolded him. "For you, yeah, I'd imagine so. Because you don't seem to know all that much about us Paras, I'm gonna ask you some questions beforehand to figure out where I should start with all this, m'kay?"

"Oookay?" Jeremiah raised his eyebrows skeptically.

"Alright, so!" Jenny clapped her hands together, pushing them away from her body emphatically. "Have you ever heard of a created life-form?"

"What, you mean like a robot?" Jeremiah asked, scrunching his eyebrows together in confusion. He'd seen movies before that had sentient machines as part of their main plot, but sincerely doubted the validity of that existing yet.

"No. That answers one question," Jenny finished her sentence by pursing her lips and pressing her hands together. "Next question: are your memories... jumbled? I'm not just talking about your decade-or-so lapse in memory, I mean before that. Your core memories: childhood, high school, some girl that lived just down the way - any of those either blurry, out of order, or just not there?"

"Yeah, that's pretty much the conversation me and Ashley had a couple days back," Jeremiah responded, again trying to touch the intangible and unavailable memories that should be there. "It's like... I know what I think is there, but I can't actually touch it."

"Yup, that is absolutely in line with what little the tests could scrounge up, as well as my own impression," Jenny confirmed and nodded at Jeremiah before blowing out a small raspberry, clearly building up to broaching what she believed was a sensitive topic.

"Okay, some background before we begin. Wizards, Enchanters, magical beings of various types, will sometimes create servants to do their menial labor. They look like humans, act like- well, okay, usually they're whatever kinda people their makers are.

"If for instance, I had the power to make a Golem, it might just look like a Demon-Knight, but it would be created with the intent of looking like one. Lotta them enchanters get heads too big for their britches and obsess over the 'made-in-my-own-image' shtick. But that's beside the point.

"Jeremiah, I think, based on the evidence provided, that you're some kind of Created life-form."

Jenny held her hands up in front of her face in a 'what-can-you-do' gesture, as she looked at him with a thin-lipped, nervous smile.

"You don't seem too confident about that," Jeremiah tried, and watched her with a sidelong expression, hoping she was wrong.

Hoping that there was something to explain his existence and odd amnesia away.

Perhaps he'd just contracted some odd bug from somewhere.

"Yes and no," Jenny shrugged and met his eyes. "Unfortunately, there's a few problems with this diagnosis. One is the fact that your core- uh, okay, your core is like your CPU. It runs everything, and ensures that a Created stays within the guidelines set by the creator. It does a lot more, but that's a topic for another time.

"Your core is... damaged. There's fragments of it in your bloodstream, as if it was hit by a Mack truck. Usually, Golems and other Created are relatively durable and able to be repaired by their creator with ease, provided the core is intact."

Jenny moved her head about as if she were trying to dodge her own thoughts.

"Based on what I know about you and how you woke up, I think someone probably shot you and hit your core, or at least grazed it in a way that compromised your memories and caused it to reset to its last stable state.

"You just have a very shootable face, anyone ever tell you that?"

"Ah-" Jeremiah tried to interject his thoughts as Jenny continued on.

"Though, all the tests I did on your blood and core fragments had some wild results, as in, medical marvel level stuff if you were human! You're naturally resistant to toxins, infections and parasites that would normally thrive in exposed blood in a dish.

"Your cells actively continued to heal themselves outside of your body for almost a full day, and to top it all off!" Jenny snapped her fingers with a broad, bright, slightly crazy smile that sharply contrasted with her revelations to Jeremiah. "They all displayed the ability to regress and adapt to new states, like stem cells on-demand!

"Jeremiah, I don't know what cr-" Jenny cut off as the front door of the apartment opened, swinging inward with some force.

Turning his head, and only half-paying attention to the world, Jeremiah saw Ashley grinning widely, loaded down with equipment.

A rifle bag was strapped to her back, a backpack was slung over her shoulder like a purse, several grocery bags from a local supermarket hung from each hand, and to top it all off, a large, black, heavy-looking duffel bag was clutched by a strap in the same hand that held three of the plastic grocery bags.

"What in the hell?" Jenny asked, her train of thought clearly severed by the loaded-down Ashley in the doorway.

"You have no idea how many looks I got walking up here!" Ashley grinned widely at them, and her skin was faintly glistening, though whether from sweat or from the Vampire-designed sunscreen, Jeremiah wasn't sure.

"I wonder why!" Jenny exclaimed with a shocked and confused expression. "And why the hell does it look like you just raided a damn armory, Ash?"

"I mean," Ashley giggled with the same broad, playful grin etched on her face, as she closed the door behind her with a backwards kick. "I kinda did. Though, I did it with a debit card instead. The guy behind the counter gave me a bulk-buy discount!"

"Why on Earth would you buy guns in bulk? Ash, I've never even heard you talk about guns, let alone go to a range!" Jenny half-asked, half-stated in confusion. "Do you even know what you bought?"

"I do!" Ashley dropped the duffel bag on the floor beside the door with a thud that shook the room. Shucking the backpack to the ground after transferring all the grocery bags to her other hand, Ashley looked between the two of them with a radiant smile. "I grabbed everything Jeremiah thought we'd need, and we still have a few grand left over for bills!"

"Why the hell would you need- okay, you know what, lemme see what that idiot made you buy first," Jenny pinched the bridge of her nose and stood up from her barstool.

Damnit, I didn't think about how Jenny would react to the gun store run.

Jeremiah thought as she approached Ashley with an air of authority.

If she did get everything, then we should have a couple AR-pattern rifles, a sniper rifle, and a few handguns. I wonder if she got the shotgun as well, since I know I said that was more of an "If you get a good deal" kind of thing.

"Oh, don't worry about it," Ashley laughed nervously, waving her hand dismissively. Jeremiah took in a silent, long inhale of breath as Jenny froze in place - one hand on the backpack.

Jenny stared down at Ashley as she straightened out, folding her arms across her chest before turning back to Jeremiah with an expectant expression.

"Somethin' y'all wanna tell me about?" she asked, as a frown that bordered on a scowl grew to being on her face. Apparently finding nothing in Jeremiah's eyes, she turned back to Ashley. "Is he making you do this? Puttin' you up to gunnin' down people he doesn't like?"

"No, it's not that at all!" Ashley shook her head before stepping in between Jenny and the backpack. "Listen, Jenny. I'm very thankful you're helping him with his... amnesia or whatever it is, and I don't wanna ask for even more from you. Jeremiah and I have come to an... understanding. I'm okay, so don't worry about me! I want this!"

Ashley smiled beautifully, reassuringly up at Jenny, before patting her on the shoulder.

"Ash, I had a merc for a ma', I know what preparing for an operation looks like," Jenny offered in return after a second's hesitation. "I'm not gonna let you get hurt because he's got a problem with things he don't understand!"

"Jenny!" Jeremiah tried to get her attention, stepping around the bar.

"Oh no, don't you start, mister!" Jenny waggled her finger with a slightly-thicker-than-normal drawl to her voice. "I don't want Ash to end up getting hurt again just because you have beef with everyone that ain't human."

There was a distinct look of concern etched into her features.

"You're not just going to waltz into her life, shack up in her place, and smash her life back into pieces when she just got it together again," Jenny said, and turned her head slightly to stare darkly into Jeremiah's eyes. Hers were glowing a faint orange, as a pale red mist began to trickle from the corners of her mouth.

"Jenny," Ashley reached up and cupped the Demoness's cheek, pulling her face back towards hers. It was an oddly familiar and tender gesture to Jeremiah. It made his brain wonder on just what their relationship actually was.

"I want to do this. Need to do this. If you wanna help, that's fine - but what we're doing stays between us. Stays in this room, okay?

"Jeremiah has some really rough edges, but he means well. I'm not being forced, I'm choosing to throw in with him because, other than you-" Ashley trailed off as she sucked in a deep, forceful inhale that she released with a shudder. "He's all I've got now."

Jenny pursed her lips, staring up and over Ashley's head as she seemed to contemplate what the Vampire just said.

She opened her mouth, pushing her tongue against the inside of her cheek, before closing her eyes and shaking her head.

Slowly, the shakes turned into a nod, and she turned fractionally over to Jeremiah, her faintly glowing amber eyes contrasting sharply with her almost-grey skin in the dimly-lit apartment.

"Fine. Fine! Read me in while I take a look at just what on Earth you thought Ash should buy," she stated with an acceptance he didn't expect.

Jenny nodded once at Jeremiah, a sour expression still evident on her face as she backed out of Ashley's hand and stepped around her to rummage through the pack.

Yeah... that's not go-

Jeremiah's train of thought cut off as Ashley gave him what he could only describe as "puppy-dog-eyes", before shucking off the tan rifle bag on her back and leaning it against the couch.

She looked back up as Jenny pulled the first plastic box out of the bag and opened it, withdrawing a small, polymer-framed handgun and inspecting it.

Ashley folded her arms and stared pointedly at Jeremiah.

"Do you wanna start, or should I?" Ashley asked with a broad, teasing grin that firmly communicated to Jeremiah there wasn't a chance of hiding anything they were doing from Jenny. Either he would get to tell her, or Ashley would in his stead.

Goddamn Vampires, fuckin' manipulating everyone around them.

Jeremiah inhaled through his nose as he closed his eyes and scowled.

The more people involved, the more chances we have of getting compromised, or worse, getting ambushed.

Does Jenny even bring anything to the table that we could use besides figuring out what the hell I am?

"Fine, fuck it! Why not?" Jeremiah barked out sarcastically, raising both his arms skyward as he reluctantly agreed to spilling the beans.

"Language," Jenny waggled a finger at him without looking away from the handgun that she'd now disassembled. Jeremiah rolled his eyes as she continued to inspect each small part of the weapon without adding anything further.

"Ash, how much does Jenny know about what happened with you and the coven?" Jeremiah decided to start there, see if there was something Ashley didn't want him to talk about, or hadn't told her friend about.

"She knows... pretty much everything," Ashley shrugged and looked back to the Demoness, who had reassembled the handgun and moved onto the next one. "Was there when I escaped."

"I was shadowin' a doctor at St. Emory's Medical when she came in lookin' for help," Jenny added for Jeremiah's benefit as she began to futz around with the next handgun in the bag.

"Alright. Yeah, sure," Jeremiah grimaced and looked for any doubt in Ashley's eyes, something he could latch onto and convince her to not read Jenny into their coming activities. "Short version is, the coven that kidnapped Ashley, ol' Vasily, he needs to die. But I don't want something worse coming out of the power vacuum.

"The amount of innocent people that could get hurt from just splitting the coven in two or three parts isn't something I wanna toy with," Jeremiah inhaled and forced himself to get to the point, despite the fact that he really didn't want Jenny anywhere near what he was doing. She was an unknown, and her values might conflict with what he wanted to do.

"So, we're gonna work our way up the chain of command - at least what Ashley remembers. Kill, interrogate, rob, the works, until we can put a fuckin round in Vasily's head and dump his body in a shallow grave in the ass-end of nowhere. Hence, guns," concluded Jeremiah.

"You're goin' after Vasily?" Jenny looked up from the 1911 handgun she was inspecting.

"We're going after the whole coven. Everything Vasily has built," Jeremiah nodded emphatically as he watched Jenny's eyes glow faintly brighter. "Now, I get it if you don't wanna be a part of this. That being said, you need to stay quiet if you wa-"

"You're gonna need more ammo," Jenny pointed at the duffel bag beside the door. "Also some suppressors, maybe some drone recon. City put up this new system that tracks and triangulates gunshots outside for most of downtown and the surrounding area."

Jeremiah cocked his head and raised his eyebrows as Jenny went back to the weapon in her hand.

The addition of a citywide gunshot detection system would certainly put a damper on things for him, unless he could find a willing gun store or machine shop to make him some under-the-table silencers.

"If I'm gonna help, I might as well go all-in on this too," Jenny shrugged and locked the slide of the pistol to the rear before standing up. She walked over to where Jeremiah leaned against the counter and set the pistol on it. "You've been eyeballin' this one the entire time I was messin' with it."

Jenny exhaled a cascade of red mist from her mouth before continuing.

"Listen, I'm not the biggest fan of takin' on a

coven by our lonesome, but after what they- what he did to Ash... I have no trouble putting him in the dirt. I'm gonna give my ma' a call, see if she can provide any help for us."

"No, we need to keep at least -some- operational security," Jeremiah replied, already regretting Ashley's decision to involve Jenny in their mission. "We can't just go ca-"

"My ma' has run coups in third-world countries, eliminated criminal cartels that crossed the border, and fought off a Humanity First cell in our town that got a little too rowdy," Jenny folded her arms under her chest and stared pointedly at Jeremiah. "She's not gonna breathe a word of this and is just fine with extra-judicial work. You want to do all this in the dark, without any help, and get Ashley killed or worse because you can't handle working with a group? Well that's what's gonna happen if you don't let me get just a smidge of help."

Jenny smiled at him from a few inches away, standing almost at eye level with Jeremiah.

Wait, what? They...they went after a HF cell?

I didn't-that-well, I guess it'd go the other way, too.

Maybe something similar to what happened to my own cell?

Though, if they're that strong...that's definitely a force multiplier.

I guess...I guess the group of untrained monsters ready to fight other monsters grows larger.

Fuck it, why not just invite the entire Para community here. Really get on that platoon-sized fuckery level!

Jeremiah griped silently, staring back at Jenny as she confidently stood there, ready to shoot down any concerns he might have.

Oh yeah, this is gonna turn out great!

How long until someone gets cold feet and calls the feds down on us?

Or better yet, until Jenny calls someone who's an undercover fed and we all get wrapped up.

"Whatever," Jeremiah rolled his eyes and shook his head, stepping past the woman to inspect the rest of the firearms after snatching the pistol off the counter.

Part of him was mad that she was right and had handed him the handgun he would've selected on his own.

In stark opposition to that, it somehow made him feel better.

Perhaps she knew enough about firearms that he wouldn't have to train her like he would Ashley, who was currently struggling to lock the slide back on the polymer-framed pistol.

We're fucked...aren't we?

Please-please-please don't just rip it clean off.

Chapter 15

"Fuck, I didn't know it was possible for a Vamp to look even more like a prick," Jeremiah muttered as he stared at the social media profile of an all-too-pretty, overly muscled Vampire.

Blue eyes, blonde hair, ninety percent of the pictures on his page were shirtless.

"He does look kinda... off, doesn't he?" Jenny replied, sitting in the chair and currently running the search engine. Jeremiah watched her click through Aiden Westinghouse's profile over her right shoulder while Ashley watched from her left. "No wonder he's in charge of bringing in fresh victims. Twenty-year-old me woulda lost my mind seeing abs like that. Probably just smiles and the idiots follow him home!"

"Eh, not really my type," Ashley shrugged as Jenny clicked to the next image before turning to look up at her with a skeptical expression. Jeremiah also looked at her with a mix of disbelief and amusement.

"If Mr. Straight-outta'-playgirl ain't good enough for ya'," Jenny began with a soft chuckle, turning back to the screen.

"Then I feel real sorry for your future boyfriend," Jeremiah finished her sentence with a wry grin, as Jenny flipped the image to one of the man flexing shirtless in front of a hilltop mansion. The garage behind him was packed with three supercars, and a lifted blue truck was parked in the driveway next to him. "Must have some high standards!"

"Not like that!" Ashley bit back, giving him a small shove on his shoulder. "He's just... too pretty. Doesn't even seem real!"

"You looked in the mirror lately, Ash?" Jenny half-muttered as she continued to go through the man's social media presence. "Vampirism hit you like a truck. I mean, you were pretty before, but damn girl..."

Jeremiah looked Ashley up and down for a moment before he shrugged and nodded.

"In hindsight, should've been a dead giveaway when I first met you, Ashley," Jeremiah added as he met her eyes. A faint blush appeared on her cheeks as the corner of her mouth tweaked into a hint of a smile. "That dress the other night caught a lot of eyes."

"Wait, dress?" Jenny asked, whipping her head around to face Ashley, before snapping it around to look at Jeremiah. "What dress?"

"My blue one. I hadn't worn it in years... we went to the restaurant across from the Red Lotus to scope out the area," Ashley murmured, as if she'd been caught doing something she shouldn't have. "I... decided to dress up, it's kind of a fancy restaurant and I didn't want to be out of place."

"You went WHERE?" Jenny stared at Ashley in shock. Then she turned to Jeremiah with a disdainful look and asked: "Did you put that idea in her head? That's damn near the mouth of the lion's den!"

Yeah...not my brightest play.

Jeremiah smiled neutrally back at Jenny.

"Hey, don't just yell at him, I thought it was a good idea at the time too!" Ashley reprimanded her friend with a small shove on her shoulder, causing Jenny to look up at her with a frown. The two of them shared a look for a moment, before Jenny turned back to the computer without saying anything, continuing to scroll through the photos on the laptop.

"Hang on, this one has a location tag," Jenny leaned slightly forward as she clicked on the text at the bottom of the picture.

Aiden was flexing shirtless in front of a whitewashed mansion, a six-car garage full of expensive-looking cars was open in the background. The location tag was for an invite to a party several weeks ago, apparently at his mansion.

"It can't be that easy," Jeremiah scoffed when she clicked on the location, opening a map website. Sure enough, it actually was that easy, and the satellite map proved it.

"Looks like it is," Jenny muttered, clicking on an icon that took them down to a view from the nearby street. Panning around, she aimed it up the driveway. "Well, would ya' look at that, the idiot posted his front door up on social media for god and everyone to look at. I wonder, this neighborhood is right next to the Freeland Mountain state park. Maybe?"

Jenny exited the view by the street, zooming out and back in on the nearby forest, before bouncing around several street view locations with a thoughtful expression.

Eventually, she stopped on an overlook that seemed to have a perfect view down and into the neighborhood that Aiden lived in.

"I say we head here tomorrow. We can practically look into his garage from this spot, and more importantly, it's less obvious than the restaurant next to the club.

"I'll bring that camera I bought for photography class back in undergrad, and we can get some good pictures of what's going on," Jenny sighed and spun around in her chair, looking at Jeremiah with a searching expression. "I still have some more things to talk about with you.

"But it all boils down to letting me regularly take samples from you to study them in different environmental conditions. If your blood is as powerful as I think it is, I might be able to bribe one of the enchanters I know to produce me a copy of it. Could be able to use the stem cells for actual medical research."

Jenny shrugged as Jeremiah sucked in a breath of air through gritted teeth.

Was it not already enough to let the de-

But what's the harm, though? We've already given her samples. If she was going to create some curse or other witchcraft, she would have done so already.

If she really is going to use this for medicine, especially for humanity, imagine what diseases she could cure.

Maybe even find a cure for Vampirism?

Imagine that, a world without people like Ashley, forced to become something they didn't want to be, all because some asshole took a liking to them.

"I promise, it'll onl-" Jenny was cut off mid-word by Jeremiah.

"Fine. Just, take what you need. But I want a say in this," Jeremiah crossed his arms over his chest and stared down into the Demoness's orange eyes. "I want you to look into a cure for Vampirism. If I'm immune, and this can prevent unwanted transformations, that's your first priority."

"I'll try. The problem with that is the core nature of the disease. Or more specifically the vampirocytes," Jenny blew out a breath and shrugged. "They're both magical and viral in nature. At a certain point, even the stem cells of the gods themselves probably wouldn't be able to cure it."

Jeremiah stared at her with a sour expression for a moment, before he shook his head and let the topic drop.

Jenny said her goodbyes to Ashley and left the apartment.

By the time Jeremiah stepped out of the shower several hours later, the sun had long since gone down and Ashley had opened the blinds behind her desk.

The hallway and living room were dark, save for the moonlight spilling in. Ashley leaned on her desk with both elbows, cradling her head in her palms.

Jeremiah frowned, walking towards her as quietly as possible, trying to figure out what she was staring at. Her head twitched fractionally as he approached, clearly hearing his near-silent footsteps on the carpet.

Fuckin super-hearing.

"See something interesting?" Jeremiah asked, giving up all attempts to sneak up on Ashley, instead stopping to lean on the corner of the hallway.

"Not really," Ashley shrugged and turned slightly to face him with a half-smile. "Just spacing out."

"Uh-huh," Jeremiah nodded with a disbelieving expression. "Sure. You mind if I watch some TV for a bit? Got a decade or so of shit to catch up on."

"Yeah, yeah that's fine. Can I feed for a bit too?"

Jeremiah almost declined on reflex, but

something in her bright, hopeful smile convinced him otherwise.

"I'm kinda hungry and it's probably a good idea for me to be at my best tomorrow. Right?"

Jeremiah weighed the pros and cons internally.

On the one hand, she was right, if things went sideways somehow in their brief reconnaissance of Aiden's home, it would be better for her to be as topped off as possible.

On the other hand, just letting a Vampire - pretty as she may be - feed off him without a fight, still sat wrong within Jeremiah.

On the other, other hand, Jeremiah had agreed to feed her twice a week, and this would be the second time.

"Fine, sure," Jeremiah nodded and pushed himself off the wall.

Why am I so upset by this?

Jeremiah questioned his own emotions as he sat down on the couch and grabbed the remote. Ashley passed in front of him on her way to the kitchen, a broad smile on her face.

She's so excited to...drink my blood. But why?

Jeremiah navigated near futilely through the menus on the television. After several more seconds of scrolling, he found the cop drama he and Ashley had been watching previously and selected the resume button.

I remember when this company only did delivery.

Jeremiah smirked, mentally transposing his own thoughts with those of older people in his time.

I remember when we had to spin the phone's dial to talk to people!

"Something funny?" Ashley asked, flopping

down on the couch beside him, uncomfortably close.

"Eh, just realizing that old people might be onto something," Jeremiah snorted and shook his head as Ashley wrapped his arm over her shoulder. "I remember when this app did delivery, and it made me think of all those old-timers ranting about rotary phones."

What is she doing?

Jeremiah furrowed his brow as Ashley squeezed herself against his side, his arm draped over her shoulder.

No, no I agreed to feed her, not to cudd-

Ashley lifted his forearm and brought the knife to it, making a small incision that immediately began to well blood. Then, as the TV droned on in the background, she brought the wound to her mouth, and began to suckle gently from him.

Oh...she's just eating.

Jeremiah watched the top of her head couched atop his chest with a frown.

It-I...I mean, it's more comfortable than the other way.

Whatever, if it's the best way for her to eat, then I'll just deal with it.

Eddie loved his 'adapt, improvise, and overcome' saying.

Huh. I called Leodegrance, but I never actually tried Eddie. If I survived, I wonder if there's a chance he did too?

"Speaking of phones," Jeremiah inhaled through his nose as Ashley continued to suckle at the cut on his arm. "Can I borrow yours for a minute?"

"Hmm?" Ashey replied, not disconnecting her lips from his skin as her head turned slightly towards him.

"Your phone. I want to see if an old friend of mine is still... well, if his phone is still connected."

"Sure!" Ashley chirped, momentarily pulling back from the cut as she withdrew the smartphone from her pocket. Passing it over to him, she brought his arm back into place and continued drinking.

Jeremiah worked at dialing the number one handed, the lack of a tangible keyboard causing him to miss a stroke on the number pad. He backspaced, and typed in the number correctly.

Hopefully.

He couldn't be sure if it was a three or a two as the last digit.

Lifting it to his ear, his heartbeat thudded loudly as it dialed.

Then continued to dial, decidedly not dropping off into an out of service tone.

The line clicked and he almost began to blurt out a greeting before being let down.

"The number you have dialed has a voicemail box that is not set up yet."

Ah.

It was a longshot anyway.

Besides what would I even say?

Oh hey old buddy! Been a long thirteen years, ain't it?

How've you been? Oh me? Yeah I'm living with a Vampire and taking on a coven like some fucked up action movie!

Jeremiah grunted and shut off the phone before passing it back to Ashley.

"Hmm?" she asked again, her eyebrows raised expectantly.

"Ah. Yeah, disconnected." Jeremiah gave a neutral smile. "Eh, it was a hail-Mary anyway."

Yeah. Bad idea all around.

By the time Jeremiah's eyelids grew heavy, a couple hours later, Ashley had long since stopped eating, but she hadn't moved.

Instead, when he turned off the television, he was greeted with the soft, rhythmic breaths of a woman fast asleep.

Apparently, food comas happen to Vampires too... she's gonna wake up with one hell of a tweaked neck sleeping like that.

Jeremiah smiled to himself as Ashley rested her head against him at a steep cant. He leaned his head back against the couch cushion, and closed his eyes before exhaling.

I should get her to the bed.

Don't want her complaining all day tomorrow and asking for a midnight snack, right?

Jeremiah knew that he wasn't being honest with himself.

Shimmying just enough to let her head fall to his lap, Jeremiah scooped her up into his arms, and stood from the couch.

Have I so easily fallen, corrupted by yet another pretty face?

Jeremiah wondered, as he carried his blood-drinking roommate to her bedroom.

I've killed people for this exact sin, for staining their own soul as such.

But if I am...created, a Golem or whatever Jenny said, is anything I've ever believed...right?

Jeremiah took in a deep breath as he considered the possibility.

So many dead, and I never questioned my orders...perhaps Jenny and Ashley are the only ones, but if they were, what are the odds that they'd know each other and come into my life at the same time?

Can a soul be innocent and stained by what they are at the same time? If I'm not human, created for servitude, am I marked in the same way?

Would the immortal Judges cast me into hell because of what I am alone?

Jeremiah nudged open the bedroom door with his foot, turning slightly to enter the cramped doorway with Ashley in his arms, while his thoughts crashed against one another like warring armies inside his mind.

He'd been putting off these thoughts since Jenny had delivered her revelation to him.

He'd asked Ashley later on about what a Golem was, and had received a surprisingly lackluster response. Or at least, a response that lacked any actual useful information to him.

It boiled down to "Magical Robot" in the end.

I am an automaton, a machine made of flesh and stone.

Jeremiah leaned forward to lay Ashley on the mussed bedsheets.

How is that different than what the church teaches us?

Didn't the gods fashion us all from the stones of the highest mountains, and the mud of the lowest swamps? What are humans bu-

His thoughts were cut off as Ashley gripped his wrist and rolled over, jerking his arm with her as if it were the corner of a blanket, and pulling him down into an awkward leaning position over her.

Right...fine, fuck it. It's not like my life can get any weirder.

Jeremiah sighed and resigned himself to his fate.

Vampire cuddles it is.

Jeremiah lowered himself into the bed, careful to not disturb Ashley's gentle snoring.

After a moment, he found a comfortable position behind her, his arm still draped over her shoulder.

I...I'm going to hell, aren't I?

* * *

Jeremiah stared out over the city from the hillside as Jenny shut off the SUV's engine.

It reminded him of the views from the mountains that served as the natural western edge of Larimer.

Though here, the deep blue-green bay in the distance was a distinct difference and reminded him that he was still very far from home.

"Welp, let's see what this guy's up to," Jenny said as she pulled her keys from the ignition.

Jeremiah grabbed the binoculars off the dashboard. He opened the door and stepped out into the sunlight beyond.

They had parked in a small, deserted pull-off in a state park that overlooked Aiden's mansion.

Jenny and Ashley chatted happily behind him as he stepped up to the steep embankment that provided an uninhibited view of the city beyond, and by extension, the large development of multi-story, multi-acre mansions below.

Jeremiah brought the binoculars up to his eyes and scanned the neighborhood.

Blue, green, orange...who the fuck paints a house

orange?

Jeremiah frowned as he searched up the street for the mansion. He knew roughly where it should be, but wasn't entirely sure.

There you are, asshole.

Jeremiah found Aiden's mansion - or more specifically, the coven's mansion that the all-too-handsome Vampire resided in.

Let's see what kind of security you have.

"Ya' find it?" Jenny asked, walking up beside him.

"Yeah," Jeremiah replied, not lowering the binoculars. "These things are neat. The built-in rangefinder would make this real easy if he would just come outside and stand on his porch for a few minutes."

"Down boy," Jenny chuckled, causing him to lower the binoculars just enough to stare at her with a disapproving frown. "We're not doing anything today. Just planning. I want payback for what they did to Ash just as much as you do, but we're gonna do this right."

"Not my first rodeo, Jenny," Jeremiah reminded her calmly, watching as a man in a suit stepped out onto the second story balcony that rounded the building. Focusing in on the man, Jeremiah guessed he was a guard, especially with the slow, meandering walk he had as he rounded the corner of the building.

"One guard, second level balcony, just went around the side of the house."

"Oh yeah, I forgot, Mister 'Tough-guy-monster-hunter'. You know, if the PMC my Ma' works for went up against you guys, you'd be wiped out flat!" Jenny huffed, as Jeremiah watched a second guard exit the front door of the residence and light up a cigarette on the porch.

"Eh, probably," Jeremiah admitted, before noting the guard for the women. "Second guy, porch, having a cigarette. But yeah, we were more geared for small-scale stuff.

"I know Patrick was obsessed with only going in as a group if we had a three-on-one ratio. That being said, Leodegrance still gave me lone-wolf work from time to time."

"Okay, I know you explained some of it to me, but why is Patrick so important if Leodegrance gave you solo work?" Jenny asked as Jeremiah lowered the binoculars thoughtfully.

"Okay. So let's say you work at a normal job, right?" Jeremiah started, turning slightly towards Jenny. She nodded expectantly as he paused to look at her. "You have your supervisor, your manager, and your district manager, or some structure like that.

"My supervisor would be Eddie, my manager would be Patrick, and Leodegrance is like district management.

"Most of what I did came from Patrick or Eddie. However, from time to time, Leodegrance would contact me directly for work.

"Usually single-household targets of opportunity. Paid good, too," Jeremiah lifted the binoculars back to his eyes and looked away from Jenny as she stared at him with a suspicious expression.

"That just sounds like being a normal hitman," she pointed out, as Jeremiah noted a third guard walking around the garage.

Or maybe that's one of the earlier two.

He wasn't entirely sure, since the man

smoking a cigarette on the porch had disappeared.

"So you just killed whoever they told you to?"

"More or less. Most of the time it was because the church needed them gone, but they weren't important or dangerous enough to warrant a Templar," Jeremiah replied, looking for any security cameras on the property.

"Those guys are assholes, fuckin' pure evil," Jenny spat as Jeremiah broke contact with the binoculars to stare at her with an open-mouthed smile.

"Coming from a Demon, that's rich," Jeremiah chortled and shook his head, stepping up onto the wooden fence that stopped people from walking over the edge.

"I'm only half-Demon-Knight, thank you very much!" Jenny punched his shoulder as Jeremiah smiled without removing the binoculars.

"Your mom or your dad?" Jeremiah asked, actually curious about that. He'd honestly never heard of a Demon-Knight, but it would explain how Jenny constantly flip-flopped between being a normal college student, and having violent instincts on par with his own.

"Ma is," Jenny replied as Jeremiah continued to surveil the home. "Dad met her while working a server maintenance job for a defense contractor. She was contracted for security, and he wouldn't stop pestering her, as she tells it."

Brave dad.

Jeremiah laughed internally before freezing after realizing what he'd just thought.

No, her mo- what the hell?

Jeremiah watched an unmarked white van pull up and into the driveway of the mansion. Two guards rushed out from the front door of the house as the van parked on the side of the garage.

"Van just pulled up, guards are moving with a purpose," Jeremiah noted, still watching through the binoculars as they sprinted up to the now-parked vehicle. "Wonder what's got them so antsy?"

His heart dropped into his stomach when he saw the two figures exit the front seats of the van and move to the side door.

Shit...I've seen this movie before.

Jeremiah scowled as they opened the sliding door and pulled out a figure with a bag over their head. Then another, then a third. The entire cabal of Vampires moved their prisoners, blood slaves, or intended converts up towards the mansion.

"Change of plan," Jeremiah spun and pushed the binoculars into Jenny's hands. "We're moving now."

"Why the hell, what's got you so-" Jenny replied in an annoyed tone. "Oh... Oh shit."

"Yeah," Jeremiah growled, rounding the back of the van.

Not gonna let them do that. Not right in front of me.

Jeremiah threw open the back hatch of the SUV and opened the duffel bag zipper.

Come in from the side, hit with authority, stay mobile and keep them guessing.

Jeremiah pulled free the two halves of a rifle and snapped them together before putting two magazines in his pockets. He slapped a third inside the magwell, and chambered a round.

"Jeremiah, I don't think this is a goo-" Jenny began before Jeremiah snapped and cut her off.

"No, Jenny, it's not a 'good idea'! It's a terrible

idea!" Jeremiah admitted, stepping around her. "But it's the only idea I have. Do you wanna be the catalyst for a few more blood slaves, or heavens forbid, what happened to Ashley happening to someone else? 'Cause I fucking don't!"

"What can I do?" Ashley asked, running up beside Jenny, as the Demon-Knight med student bit her tongue and stared at Jeremiah with a sour expression.

"Dad always said willing bystanders are just as wrong as the bad guys," Jenny exhaled a faint breath of red mist. "Fine, to hell with it. In for a penny, in for a pound. Ash, take the SUV down and around, wait for me to call you at the end of the street."

"I-uh, oh," Ashley sounded dejected at the prospect of being relegated to designated driver.

"Ash, the only way down fast is through the woods. It's almost a twenty-minute drive to get to the entrance of that neighborhood," Jenny began, stepping past Jeremiah and opening a small compartment in the back of the vehicle. From it, she pulled an SMG and racked the charging handle before pulling the sling over her head.

After pulling free both mags, she handed the keys to Ashley.

"If we survive, we're gonna have at least three people to get out, and fast, before the cops show up," she continued in a reassuring tone. "I'm gonna need you to-"

The rest of the conversation was lost to Jeremiah as he stepped away before vaulting over the wooden fence. The cliff beneath him wasn't really a cliff, so much as a massive, hundred-foot steep embankment of small pebbles and dirt.

This is gonna suck.

He just knew that to be the case even as he stared downward.

"Last chance to-" Jenny said from behind him as the engine started, finishing vaulting over the fence as he looked at her. "Call it off and re-evaluate."

"Not a chance," Jeremiah shook his head with a deep inhale. "We can do something, so we will do something."

"Heh, race you to the bottom!" Jenny said with a feral smile, the red mist spilling from her mouth and nose almost like a smokescreen now. As Jeremiah formulated a plan to ask about that, Jenny leapt off the small drop, and began to slide down the side of the mountain.

Here goes nothing.

Jeremiah took a deep breath before he too, took the leap of faith.

Chapter 16

Jeremiah made it most of the way down the embankment without issue.

Most, but unfortunately, not all. At the bottom third of sliding his way down, his foot hit a root disguised by the dirt and pebbles, sending him sprawling and flopping down the final leg of the cliff.

"Hell, you okay?" Jenny sprinted up to him as he coughed up a puff of dust, facedown on the ground, where it began to level out. "Anyth-"

"I'm good," Jeremiah shook his head as he pushed himself up off the ground, looking for where his rifle had landed. Nearly a dozen feet away from him, it lay against a boulder, the finish scratched up but otherwise undamaged. "I'm good, just a little bruising. Let's keep moving."

Jeremiah scooped up the rifle and turned to face Jenny, who watched him with a mix between concern and what he believed was excitement.

Now, that's interesting...that red mist.

He watched as her breaths quickened in pace fractionally, the maroon haze deepening in both color and vibrancy.

She did that when she pointed a gun at me the other day, I wonder if it has something to do with being part Demon-Knight?

They sound like the grunts of the demonic world, perhaps...hmm, let's test this.

"C'mon Jenn," Jeremiah grinned maliciously at her, his smile widening as the faintest hint of one dawned on her face too. "Let's go kill some Vamps."

Jenny's smile widened for a brief moment as

her eyes literally flashed with orange light, despite the sunny day.

Then, she blinked, shook her head roughly, and snarled at him.

"We're killin' 'em because they're human traffickers, not because they're Vampires," she corrected, fixing him with her trademark nonplussed glare.

"Whatever helps you sleep at night," Jeremiah growled out and shrugged. He turned towards their destination and set out at a slow jog before calling over his shoulder. "You coming or not?"

If she wants to be picky about definitions, she can do that over there.

Jeremiah reasoned, as he sprinted faster through the dense undergrowth, blowing through bushes and leaping over small boulders.

They're bloodsuckers. Monsters. There might be one, two, hell, maybe even four in a million that turn against their nature, but these ones? They deserve death.

In that moment, he made a decision to end every single abomination that resided in that house.

I'll burn them out if I have to.

Jeremiah pushed himself up and over a toppled tree, as he continued to sink himself into his momentum, both physical and mental.

They're monsters, evil - nothing like Ashley. I'm gonna…I'm gonna-

His train of thought stalled as he considered that thought and grimaced.

Jenny…is right. We're going after the coven, not their victims.

Jeremiah took in a shuddering breath of air as he pushed his mind in a different direction.

This is hostage rescue, not an extermination.

I have to do this right the first time around.

"God, you're fast!" Jenny exclaimed as she vaulted over the large log about twenty feet behind him. "Left me in your dust!"

"Sorry," Jeremiah murmured, turning to face her. "Got a bit ahead of myself. Let's go."

Jeremiah began a much more sedate jog through the trees that separated him and the coven's prisoners.

The rangefinder in those binoculars said it was only about seven hundred yards away... it should be coming up soon.

Jeremiah slowed his sprint even further, to what felt like an almost tepid, agonizing pace. In reality, if he walked this quickly on the sidewalk, he would get odd looks from passersby.

What was it Patrick always said? Slow is smooth, smooth is fast?

Jeremiah heard the loud footfalls behind him transition to near-silent ones, as Jenny caught up to him and slowed her pace as well.

"See something?" she hissed from behind him as he continued with his steady pace.

"Nope, just want to do this right," Jeremiah inhaled, even as his gut demanded he charge in, that he burst into the door and open fire on the bloodsucking, disease-ridden monstrosities within.

The instinct felt... correct.

Perhaps he had sincerely underestimated the calming effect Eddie had on him, usually acting as support, or at least planning the missions alongside Jeremiah.

"When we come through the treeline, I need you to watch the left side," Jeremiah instructed, gesturing to his left side while keeping the rifle pointed forward. "We're just gonna push straight through to the door unless one of those guards catch us."

"What if they do?" Jenny asked as they approached a thick wall of green foliage.

"We kill them, and then push into the house," Jeremiah stopped to brush aside a section of the dense brush that looked somewhat cultivated. This was it, and they'd ended up coming out just on the other side of the detached, six-car garage. In front of him, he could see the parked van and the closed side-door of the house. "Alright, this is it."

Jeremiah turned to face Jenny, who stared at the foliage behind him fixedly.

He searched her face for a moment before blowing out a raspberry. Her small sub-machinegun shook slightly in her hands as she pointedly avoided his eyes, instead seeming to stare through obfuscating brush.

"Listen," Jeremiah saw the telltale signs of Jenny's nerves fraying to a dangerous level. "You don't have to be a part of this. You can go wait at the edge of the driveway and take care of anyone coming around the outside."

Jenny inhaled sharply, her eyes moving to meet Jeremiah's for the first time. She gulped, licked her lips, and looked back to the shrubbery.

"I-I'll be fine," she stuttered and lifted the SMG from a loose grasp to her shoulder, her eyebrows lowering as something harder crossed over her face. "She always said it would feel different than the range."

Always is.

Jeremiah agreed internally, nodding his head as he took her words as tacit approval. From here on out, he wasn't responsible for what happened to her. If she fucked up and got herself killed, then it was her own fault.

Except, that's not quite fair.
I'm the one forcing this, aren't I?

Jeremiah pushed through the foliage as well as his thoughts and stepped out into the shade of the tall trees beside the garage, only moving several feet forward as he stared at the side of the building with his rifle leveled.

When the rustling behind him ceased, and he judged that Jenny had made it through, he sprang into action.

"Go!" he hissed roughly, stepping off and angling his rifle to the right. He felt, more than heard, Jenny's steps beside him, hoping to whatever powers were above that she could actually handle herself in a firefight.

As they crossed the short distance between the garage and the side door of the home, Jeremiah felt his nerves string themselves tighter.

No one was watching them, otherwise they'd be shooting.

To him that spoke of one of two situations they'd find inside.

Either this would be the easiest operation he'd ever carried out, as the lackluster security represented an overconfidence that bordered on outright idiocy, or there was something so dangerous inside that it warranted little to no external security.

Jeremiah moved to the side of the door with the handle as Jenny mirrored him on the other side, the collapsible stock of her weapon rattling slightly as she breathed in short, rapid breaths. Grabbing the knob as quietly as possible with the sleeve of his jacket, Jeremiah tested to see if it was locked.

It wasn't.

Let's hope they're just idiots.

Jeremiah threw the door open.

"What the he-" a guard in a black suit stared at Jeremiah with wide eyes as he lifted his weapon at the man's head and fired. The guard's sentence cut off as the top right quarter of his head launched itself off and onto the wall behind him.

Jerking his weapon to the right, Jeremiah turned down the T-shaped hallway they found themselves in.

"No time to wait!" he shouted over the din of his ringing ears. "They know we're here now!"

Pick a direction and see it through. Don't hesitate; they have home-field advantage.

Jeremiah began to stride quickly down his side of the hallway, praying that Jenny was watching their rear.

A guard rounded the corner of the hallway in front of him, a pistol gripped tightly in one hand, just starting to aim at Jeremiah.

Unfortunately for the guard, he had wandered directly into Jeremiah's iron sights, and received several shots to the chest in rapid succession. Flopping to the floor as if he'd just slipped on a banana peel, the back of the guard's head cracked loudly enough against the polished black-tile floor to be heard over the roaring ring in Jeremiah's ears.

A faint grin touched the corner of his mouth as the macabre satisfaction of the action tickled something dark within him. As he approached the groaning Vampire clutching futilely at his chest, Jeremiah put one round through his skull for good measure. He turned the corner just in time to catch a man throw open the door to a room in front of him on his right.

This man had faster reflexes than the last two and darted out of Jeremiah's sights at the last possible second.

Instead of raising a gun, the man lashed out with a red strand of magically enhanced blood.

Now it was Jeremiah's turn to test his reflexes, dropping to his knees as the blood sorcerer's attack snapped harmlessly above his head.

Jeremiah pulled the trigger as soon as he reasoned that the muzzle of his weapon was pointed close enough to his target, then a second time.

The Sorcerer screeched and clutched at his groin, dropping to his knees before two more shots rang out from behind Jeremiah, impacting the man in his chest, then his face, which resulted in his head folding in on itself from the momentum of the last round.

"Nice shot!" Jeremiah praised Jenny's first kill, turning over his shoulder and standing up outside the direct path of her muzzle.

Her eyes were wide and her pupils were dilated, while thick red mist spilled forth from her mouth and nose.

"I... I killed him!" Jenny looked at him with a mix of fear and excitement.

"Yeah! You did!" Jeremiah smiled at her as he moved to the door the man had exited, opening it and peering down into the dim staircase. "If I were a big, bad, evil Vampire, I'd put my secret evil lair in the basement... what I wouldn't give for a flashbang right about now."

"Let me, mine has a light," Jenny offered, brushing up against his shoulder. Jeremiah stepped aside and watched as she brought her weapon up, putting her thumb on a small rubber pressure-pad on the top.

I don't think that's one of the ones Ashley bought.

Jeremiah mused as she illuminated the concrete stairwell. At the bottom was a small concrete landing, but the rest of the room was obscured by the top and walls of the stairs themselves.

That means she's got enough know-how to set up a weapon on her own. She's probably not bluffing about going to the range a lot, but this is just her first time in actual combat.

One hell of a trial-by-fire.

Jeremiah blew out the breath he was holding.

"This is gonna suck. Swap weapons with me - the first one at the bottom is gonna get lit up, I think," Jeremiah noted with a frown. "Gut says our prisoners are down there."

"No," Jenny shook her head fractionally, taking the first step down the narrow flight. "I can handle it."

Alright then, I guess she's taking point.

Jeremiah kept an ear on the door behind them after it closed. Down they went, each step winding his nerves tighter. This was the literal definition of a fatal funnel, and he knew it.

"Come down the stairs slowly!" a man's authoritative and confident voice echoed up to them. "Otherwise, I'll kill them all!"

Jenny froze mid-step, her foot hovering out over the next step. Jeremiah sighed and licked his lips.

"And it was going so well. This is why I need fucking flashbangs," Jeremiah snarled softly while thinking about his options.

Can I still get the hostages out at this point? Or

should I just...go for the kill? What's one or two hostages compared to hundreds or thousands more at this point?

No.

Jeremiah shook his head and clenched his teeth.

These are human lives...I can't just let them die.

"Listen. I have an idea," Jenny whispered to him. "Go down and distract them, try to get them looking away from the stairs. Find some way to weave the word... uh, 'grenade' into the conversation, okay?"

She's just going to leave.

Jeremiah immediately doubted Jenny's honesty, looking back up towards the door. He closed his eyes and breathed in deeply.

So what if she does? She's going to run directly to Ashley, and get her out of here - get her safe.

On that thought, Jeremiah swallowed and came to the sobering realization that his only option to really have a fraction of a chance to rescue the blood-slaves-to-be would be to trust her.

To trust a literal Demon.

Well, half-Demon, apparently.

He reasoned it out with himself, nodding as he opened his eyes.

Let's hope that Human side shows through, Jenny.

"Don't fuck me on this," Jeremiah groused in a whisper, shuffling past Jenny. "I -will- haunt you if I die."

Jeremiah took several loud steps down and shouted, "Alright, I'm coming down!"

Jeremiah put on his best 'cop' interpretation, in the hopes of throwing the Vampires off. "Clallam PD, don't shoot! I just want the hostages, and I'm gone!"

"Oh god damnit, didn't we pay you assholes enough this month?" the speaker came into view.

Aiden stood with his hands wrapped around the throat of a bleary-looking young woman, watching Jeremiah step down onto the landing.

"Toss the rifle!" the Vampire barked.

Four Vamps other than Aiden. Six hostages.

Jeremiah tossed the weapon to the side and kept his eyes firmly on Aiden.

"Clearly fuckin not," Jeremiah replied, half-raising his hands in a 'what-can-you-do' gesture. "I ain't seen no cash from your dumb ass before. Are you one of the Millay brothers?"

"I- wha-? No, who the fuck are the-" Aiden threw the woman to the side, her head cracking loudly on the pavement. Jeremiah just barely avoided grimacing at the sight and sound of it. "Okay, this is… why the fuck can't Analise get her shit together and bribe the right fucking people?"

"It's gonna be a hell of a bribe to get me to overlook seeing you drag six kidnappees into your place of residence, guy." Jeremiah began in a knowing, annoyed tone. As if this weren't an abomination, a crime against mankind and the heavens themselves. "I normally don't do shit in plainclothes, but that big van full of goodies forced my hand."

"Oh I'm sure you think it is, you goddamn pigs don't know the market value of a bribe," Aiden replied as Jeremiah slowly walked away from the stairs, as if distancing himself from the rifle. "Listen, I'm not the payroll guy, that's Analise, who I apparently need to bitch to the boss about… again."

Aiden actually rolled his eyes and sighed

exasperatedly.

"Tell you what, how does five grand today sound, and I'll go tell Analise to negotiate your new six-figure blindness side-hustle, aight?" Aiden offered, as Jeremiah walked around and leaned up against the side wall of the large, unfinished basement.

There was no cover anywhere. Just an open, concrete room with five kneeling prisoners, and four Vamps standing behind them, all of them watching Jeremiah with varying expressions from boredom to suspicion.

"I was gonna laugh at you until you said six figures," Jeremiah waggled a finger at Aiden with a smirk as they all stared at him. "Money like that can change a man's life like a grenade in a water bucket."

That's the weirdest fuckin metaphor I ever came up with.

Jeremiah held back a malicious grin as all four Vampires' expressions shifted to differing degrees of confusion.

C'mon Jenny, take the hint!

The silence stretched as Aiden stared at Jeremiah with a slack jaw, blinking as if the metaphor were as confusing as a mental flashbang.

"I... okay, you know what, I ain't even gonna question that," Aiden shook his head and raised his hands as if he were simply over this entire ordeal. "We're just gonna head upstairs, and I'mma ge-"

Aiden's head jerked sharply to the side when the loud report of gunfire started from the stairs. All further sound was drowned out as Jenny began her assault from the stairwell.

Jeremiah wasn't idle, drawing the large handgun from his right hip and pointing it at the closest Vampire as they lifted a PDW to their shoulder, facing the stairwell.

The bullet ripped through the Vampire's chest as Jeremiah moved and trained his sights on the next monster in line.

He missed the second abomination's chest, but thankfully, missed high. The bullet instead removed the front half of the woman's jaw from existence, ripping through her as she just began to turn her head towards Jeremiah.

Allowing himself to take the fraction of a second longer to train the sights on her head this time before he fired again.

Demolishing her eyeball with the slow heavy round from his weapon.

Noting that the monster on the other side of Aiden was down, Jeremiah brought his pistol to the sprawled-out Vamp on the floor closest to him, which was at this very moment struggling to push himself back up to his feet.

Jeremiah didn't let this happen.

Stepping forwards and putting two rounds into his head before surveying the room.

Jenny stood at the bottom of the stairs, fumbling to insert a fresh magazine into her weapon before successfully ramming it home.

"Where the fuck did you get a full-auto, Jenny?" Jeremiah asked as his ears somehow rung even louder.

"It's not," she mumbled, Jeremiah only really able to make out her words thanks to the movement of her lips. Her eyes were wide, and she blinked rapidly, in short, jerky motions between squeezing them tightly and snapping them back open again.

"Got one hell of a trigger fin-"

"That was dirty, you fuckin prick!" Jeremiah

watched as Aiden pushed himself off the floor, licking his lips even as the side of his head knit itself together before his eyes. "I'm gonna make you watch as I drain your girlfriend there dry. Never had Demo-"

Jeremiah shot him again.

Chapter 17

"Fuckin' pricks!" Aiden chuckled darkly, rolling his eyes, as the hole Jeremiah had put in his chest began to knit itself together again. The... thing before him extended its arms to the side as they stretched to impossible lengths. "I'm gonna drink you dry, then drop your corpses on Vasily's desk. Maybe it'll get me promoted! He's been annoyed lately and could use a distraction."

As he spoke in a raspy echoing tone, strange tufts of hair sprouted across his body, his skin became a paper-thin, near-translucent covering for the wiry black muscles beneath. Jeremiah's jaw went slack, every fiber of his muscles crying out for him to run, to get the hell away from whatever the fuck Aiden was.

This is so much worse than a normal Vampire!

Jeremiah began to slowly back up as Aiden's head lolled back and a two-foot-long tongue extended straight up from the Vampire's mouth.

What the hell is this thing? The church NEEDS to know...I have to survive an-

"Jenny, -run-!" Jeremiah snapped his train of thought clean off as he turned for the stairs.

Tucking the empty pistol into his pocket, Jeremiah sprang for the stairs, only to careen past them as his leap carried him a dozen more feet than he expected.

Jeremiah flailed his arms wildly as he tried to slow his momentum.

I...why the hell does this keep happening? Am I part rabbit or something?!

Jeremiah bounced his shoulder off the far wall

and shook his head rapidly.

Turning to look at Aiden, Jeremiah found the man's expression somewhat quizzical, cocked at an odd angle, as he watched him with pupils that rapidly dilated and shrank down to pinpricks.

Oh you're ugly, ugly.

Aiden only vaguely resembled himself, as if someone had thrown a vat of acid on his face mid-transformation into some kind of were-naked mole rat.

The mutated Vampire licked its lips thoughtfully before it leaned forward and wrapped a massive, clawed hand around the head of one of the near-comatose, seemingly tranquilized victims, picking the man up.

"Always good to have-" Aiden giggled maniacally in a hoarse tone that seemed to reverberate with itself as he gripped the torso of the man and twisted. With a pop, then a squelch, the flesh of the man's neck turned an odd shade of purple before separating entirely. "-some pre-workout!"

Aiden flung the severed head at Jeremiah with blinding speed, barely giving him enough time to leap sideways as it slammed into the concrete wall of the basement behind where he'd just been.

Jeremiah turned his head to see a massive welter of gore spread across the wall.

Fuck...okay, no, I can't let him leave. Just have to...just have to draw him upstairs and...do what exactly?

Jeremiah frantically tried to think of a solution as he scrambled to his feet and snatched up the rifle from where he'd dropped it earlier.

Shooting a passing glance to Aiden, he found the man, with the corpse upended above his distended jaw, guzzling the blood as it rained on his face.

"Hey, asshole!" Jeremiah punctuated his shout with a single round to Aiden's temple, causing the homunculus to drop the human in his grasp to the floor with a wet 'splut' sound. "Come and get me, you freaky-lookin' motherfucker!"

Not waiting for a reply, Jeremiah turned and sprinted up the steps, finding Jenny staring down from the top landing with wide, frightened eyes.

"Go go -go-!" Jeremiah waved his hand as his steps carried him higher and higher.

Who the hell has a basement twenty feet underground?

Jeremiah wondered idly as he pistoned his legs faster, talking three steps at a time.

An unearthly roar came from behind him.

The hellish shriek of an enraged abomination rattled loud enough in his ears that it caused him to miss his final step and stumble through the door.

Jeremiah shoved the bookshelf beside the door over before turning away from the door.

Grabbing Jenny as he went, Jeremiah hustled down the hallway towards what he hoped was a main area of the house. He was shortly rewarded as they entered an atrium, the two-story receiving room he believed to be just behind the front door.

"Jenny," Jeremiah used the precious seconds he had to deliver what he honestly believed were his final instructions. "I need you to take Ashley and get the hell out of here! Get to the nearest Temple of the One and All, and have them send a whole detachment of Templars. Someone -needs- to know what's going on, because that-"

A loud slam, followed by another slightly

muffled roar, sounded from down the hallway they'd just exited.

"-that thing back there isn't a normal Vampire!" Jeremiah finished, moments before the door rattled loudly again.

Jenny turned her head slightly as she looked back the way they came, taking in short, jagged breaths, as her expression jumped from a determined scowl to a grimace.

"And you?" she asked, her glowing eyes boring into his as she took a step back and checked the magazine in her weapon.

"Hold him here," Jeremiah replied, his eyes dropping to the side as he flexed his jaw and swallowed. Shakily, he grabbed a spare magazine for the pistol from his back pocket and exchanged it with the empty. "I'm gonna try and turn this place into an inferno. Dump all the chemicals I can find, cut the gas lines, and give this fucking abomination every ounce of lead I've got on me."

"What about the people in the basement?" Jenny questioned, pointedly looking back to the door as another thud sounded, followed by the rasping of wood over tile.

"They were dead before we even saw them!" Jeremiah growled, turning his body towards the hallway that Aiden would probably exit from. "We just didn't know it.

"We charged in like idiots, with no idea what we were getting ourselves into.

"Something's very wrong with the Clallam Coven, Jenny. So go tell someone, the Church, anyone that will listen."

He sighed and shook his head.

"Because we are -not- equipped to handle this,

maybe no one is," Jeremiah finished leveling his rifle as his breathing quickened.

Gas and fire, find the kitchens, turn on all the stoves. I hope this place has gas, otherwise I'm fucked.

Jeremiah cracked his neck to the side in anticipation of the coming fight before the slug coiled its way out from his gut to his leg.

After oozing around for a second, it slithered back up before going down his other leg and stopping.

Really need to get that part figured out - maybe... maybe it's my core, or whatever it was that Jenny called it.

"Fine," Jenny muttered, before wrapping the single-point sling of her SMG over Jeremiah's head. "You just make every shot count. I'll get someone down here to... deal with this."

Jeremiah felt her shove two magazines into his right pocket, not looking away from the hallway. As her steps fled, and the front door opened, he closed his eyes.

Whatever power is watching over me right now... give me strength.

With a shriek, a thud, and a cacophonous clatter, Jeremiah knew his impromptu barricade had just been unbarricaded.

Just gotta get him to follow me and not go out the front door.

Jeremiah firmed up his plan, flicking the safety off the rifle.

The creature stepped out of the hallway, slowly walking forward, as an inhumanly broad grin spread across its face.

Jeremiah decided to correct Aiden's attitude with three shots in quick succession, riding the recoil up from his chest to send a round through the creature's nose.

As the thing stumbled to the side, uttering an unholy wail as one of the long, sinewy arms reached to grasp his missing feature, Jeremiah turned and sprinted off.

Hoping to find the nearest kitchen, or at least, a closet with flammable chemicals.

Firebomb this entire fucking place!

Jeremiah's thoughts solidified as Aiden screeched again behind him, this time the pitter-patter of rapid footfalls following him was clearly distinguishable as well.

Whatever Aiden became, I'm not even sure if it's strictly Vampirism-

Jeremiah's thoughts became alien again as he dipped around a bend in the hallway.

Slowing to a stop, he turned back and leaned around the corner, lifting his sights to deliver another short barrage of fire onto the abomination as it sprinted down the hall towards him.

-it's clearly a mutation of some sort, like a Were transformation.

What kills Weres?

Jeremiah questioned, as he turned and continued running while Aiden stumbled into a wall.

Silver and fire.

Alright, where can I fi-

Jeremiah ran into an elegantly decorated dining hall and grinned, before turning toward a pair of double doors at the other end.

Jerking them open, he found himself in an almost commercial-sized kitchen with three ovens, stainless steel furnishings, and a large central steel island covered with pots and pans.

Ovens it is. Fill this room with fuckin' gas.

So decided, Jeremiah sprinted over to one of the ovens as he heard Aiden let loose another otherworldly howl. Gripping the back of the oven, he jerked it out from the wall.

A lot of these have safeties on the burners, if I remember correctly. Gotta break the connection at the pipe.

Jeremiah frowned as the oven skidded to a stop beside him.

Granted he pulled with a significant amount of force, but there was no reason why it should have moved with the speed it did.

Looking down to his hands, Jeremiah bit his tongue and decided to test his hypothesis.

He reached behind the oven's enclosure and grabbed the yellow tube he believed was the gas line, before pulling on it with a snap.

Jerking at it with a great deal of force.

As he half-expected, the flexible gas tube ripped itself apart, staying connected on either end, as the rubber that made up the outside stretched before ripping apart in the middle where he pulled.

The acrid stench of a gas leak hit his nose moments after he pulled away from the severed pipe, the air above the leak oddly distorted.

Satisfied, Jeremiah vaulted over the stove and moved onto the next one.

As he jerked it away from the wall, the double-doors slammed open behind him.

Moving faster and realizing that he wouldn't get an opportunity to work on the third one, Jeremiah snatched the cable up and pulled.

As the second line ruptured, Jeremiah was grabbed by the top of his head, jerked off his feet, and hurled across the room.

"What?" Aiden cried hoarsely with a malicious chuckle, his voice no longer even resembling human. "Were you planning on blowing me up? Trapping me in here?"

"Something like that," Jeremiah groaned, rubbing the back of his head where he'd taken the brunt of the impact. The entire backside of his body felt like coarse, broken glass, as he slowly pushed himself to his feet. "Maybe I just really didn't like your kitchen. Thought you could use a remodel."

Now that he could get a good look at the monster, he really looked Aiden over.

The thing had long, abnormally stretched arms that went past his knees, an exaggeratedly skinny torso, small tufts of brown and black fur haphazardly growing in random spots across his skin, and worst of all, a mouth of teeth that had more in common with a shark than a human being.

"What the fuck are you, by the way?" Jeremiah asked as Aiden watched him with one set of eyes, while the other two sets looked in different directions around the room. "I don't think I've ever seen something as ugly as you before."

"Hmmph," Aiden smiled, or at least, made an expression that vaguely resembled a smile. Thin, grey lips pulled back over a row of triangular, sharp teeth as all of his eyes focused on Jeremiah. "Vasily calls us Sanguis Reformatus."

Aiden shrugged before his grin stretched even further, exposing teeth nearly to his ears in a macabre display.

"I like to think of us as... Alpha Vampires," he mused, a tongue nearly as long as Jeremiah's forearm exited Aiden's mouth, licking his lips. Then, it licked one set of his eyes, in an gecko-like way. "We're just better in every way. That's why he only chooses the best of us to transform."

Lighter, lighter, I need a lighter.
Something to make a spark.

Jeremiah's mind began to work as Aiden stepped forward slowly, menacingly. His mind raced for ideas, more importantly, for a solution to the problem he'd found himself in.

I'm not...not getting out of this one, am I?
Even if I could get a lighter, I don't have time to make a Molotov or something to escape.

Jeremiah gulped and reached a hand into his pocket, pulling free one of the rifle magazines. With his other hand, he pulled the pistol from the holster on his waistband.

"What'd'ya think you're gonna do with that little peashooter?" Aiden hoarsed, leaping for Jeremiah and grabbing him by his skull again before lifting him skyward.

A gunshot might not have enough kick to set off the gas.

Jeremiah's mind kept reasoning, even as Aiden put pressure on his temples, his neck aching from the strain of supporting his bodyweight.

I hope Ashley is gonna be alright. Maybe Jenny will get stuck with feeding duty instead.

"Go ahead," Aiden laughed maliciously and met Jeremiah's eyes as he was held above the Alpha Vampire. "Put the gun to my head. Pull the trigger. See if that saves you."

"Bullets might not hurt you," Jeremiah growled, putting the muzzle of the pistol to the back of the magazine in his other hand. "But how about fire?"

Aiden's head tilted to one side as Jeremiah scrunched his eyes closed and fired.

A split second after the gunshot went off, Jeremiah heard a roar shake the earth around him, then lost consciousness.

* * *

"Darn, they really tore him up, didn't they?" a woman asked as Jeremiah lay unmoving on a cold slab. "It's gonna take a lot to fix him."

"Mmm, I mean, we cou-" a hoarse-sounding older man replied from the other side of his body before being cut off by the woman.

"We're not retiring him - he's special," the woman stated emphatically, the male voice sighing dramatically. "Just one more time, dear."

"It's always one more time. We have the parts, we have the essence, why not just let the fragments rest in peace?" the male voice questioned thoughtfully. As if he were repeating things he'd heard many times previously. "We should just make another. As much as I know you're attached to him, he's gone through too many iterations already, and it's beginning to put strain on his core. What happens if he snaps mid-operation an-"

Jeremiah groaned as his eyes snapped open, his entire body feeling like one massive, agonizing ache.

Even with them open, his world was still black.

"Jeremiah?" A voice shouted, muffled by whatever was atop him.

He tried to reply, but only managed a pitiful groan that turned into a cough as his lungs refused to work.

Something crumbled, then scraped above him, and he was acutely aware of his arm being grabbed and tugged as icy-hot pain overloaded his senses.

"I've got his arm!" the voice shouted, now less muffled than before. "Help me with this!"

"Be careful," Jenny replied in her recognizable southern drawl. "He's probably a whole bag of fracsirens, Ash! We gotta go!"

"No!" Ashley barked back as the world went from black to white under his eyelids. "I'm not leaving without him! Get his legs!"

Jeremiah lost all tension in his neck as he blacked out again.

Opening his eyes, Jeremiah felt his ears ringing as the engine of the SUV roared.

"C'mon you stubborn mother-" Jenny growled from above him as she reached a pair of pliers into his gut and pulled out a three-inch-long piece of jagged metal. "Ha! Gotc- oh, hey you're awake! Don't worry, I've gotcha'."

Jeremiah blinked again as his eyelids began to feel heavy.

In fact, his entire body felt heavy. As if an entire army of elephants pinned every exposed bit of his body to the backseat of the vehicle. The world around him grew blurry again, and then the ringing grew louder.

"Ah shit, that's no- hey, just stay with me, okay? Just stay ali-"

The world again went still.

Chapter 18

Jeremiah's dreams were fitful, chaotic, and impossible to remember. Thoughts felt fragmented and intangible, as flashes of memories that were little better than a blurry picture passed behind his eyelids, only to be immediately forgotten.

With a groan and a heavy blink, Jeremiah's mind seemed to solidify, and he awoke to an unfamiliar room.

He stared up into a polished wooden ceiling of long, six-inch-wide oak slats.

Jeremiah turned his head to the side to find the walls were also the same kind of wood.

Where the fuck am I?

Jeremiah questioned while looking at his surroundings, his eyes moving around the sparsely decorated room.

Though...at least it's not a pile of trash.

He sat up in the bed, his abdominal muscles slightly sore, along with his legs, arms, and his neck. Come to think of it, Jeremiah felt like one big bruise all over.

Lifting the white, floral-patterned blanket off of himself, Jeremiah stared down at his naked body.

His legs were dotted with angry white scars atop his tattoos, and his gut had an eight-inch-long horizontal jagged white line.

Damn...well, at least you're doing okay.

Jeremiah smirked as his morning wood proudly displayed that it was in fact, fine and unharmed.

Considering that he'd damn near brought a

section of the house down over his own head, he reasoned that a little bit of scarring was a small price to pay for taking down whatever Aiden was.

I should warn the Church...but...

"What has the Church done for me, lately?" Jeremiah finished his thought aloud, as he grimaced and panned his head around the room.

Two chairs sat next to the plush, king-sized bed that he now sat on.

Underneath him was a clean sheet of incontinence padding.

"Oh, that's right. What did the church do for me? I know what they did for me," grumbled Jeremiah. "They gunned me down in a tunnel. That was fun. Apparently, they're also completely unaware of, oh, you know, the fucking abominations that Vampires are creating around here... fuck."

Jeremiah rubbed his eyes as he felt his frustration with the current situation building.

No more stupid plans...if innocents are harmed because we have to be patient and do things right...well, then that's what has to happen.

It would've been better for us to know what we were getting into, but instead...

Jeremiah stretched his arms above his head and groaned as the ache of his muscles began in earnest.

Instead, I just charged in like an idiot.

I let my emotions get the better of me when I should've just stayed put, or called the cops on a burner. Get them to roll in with a SWAT team and do my job for me.

Jeremiah stood up and took a shaky step forward, followed by another.

I need to get dressed. I wonder if there's anything

in that closet over there, even if it's just a towel.

Jeremiah walked to the sliding closet door and pulled it open, finding it contained several sets of both his and Ashley's clothes.

Or at least, what he believed were Ashley's. There was also a small, clear plastic dresser that had his underwear and socks in the top drawer.

Convenient.

Jeremiah took his time putting on clothes, making sure to take each individual movement slowly and carefully.

He felt good.

Good for someone who intentionally dropped a building on himself, but sore enough to make him consider each action as he was taking it.

Satisfied with having dressed himself, Jeremiah moved to the door and slowly opened it. A quiet, empty hallway leading to a large living room was all that greeted him.

Wonder where Jenny and Ash are...hope they're okay.

Jeremiah stepped into the main portion of the home. The walls were all beautifully polished oak slats, sporadically decorated with small, framed paintings of different landscapes.

Hardwood polished mahogany floors were cold and smooth under his feet as he stepped into the main living space.

I wonder if this place belongs to Jenny.

Jeremiah snorted audibly at his next thought.

Certainly isn't Ashley's.

Jeremiah's gut sang out to him in that moment, letting him know that however long he'd been out, he clearly hadn't eaten enough.

Moving to the refrigerator in the kitchen, he

began to search for something, anything edible.

To both his and his stomach's dismay, the offerings in the fridge were woeful at best.

There was, however, a half-empty bag of food from a fast-food joint on the top shelf that he gleefully ransacked, demolishing the remainder of a large serving of fries before he unwrapped half a burger.

He gave it a tentative sniff, shrugged, and took a bite.

I wonder if they have any coffee.

Jeremiah opened and closed the cupboards beside the fridge.

As it turned out, wherever he was did not have coffee, though he did find some black tea in one of the cupboards, the same kind Ashley kept at her house.

Earl grey it is, then.

Jeremiah checked the water in the small electric kettle before flicking the tab at the bottom. He put the teabag in a mug he pulled out of the counter and set about finishing the burger.

As the pot began to roil and bubble, he heard muffled feminine voices from outside the door to his right.

It's probably just Jenny and Ash.

Jeremiah forcibly reminded himself in the hopes of calming his heart rate after it jumped skyward, his instinctive response was to search for a weapon.

Just calm down.

Even if it isn't, whoever brought me here clearly didn't want me dead. Or chained up.

A key was inserted into the lock, and Jeremiah brought the kettle off its pad before pouring the hot water into the mug.

"So anyways," Jenny's voice came clearly through the opening doorway, "I was trying to argue with the professor that the Troll's blo- oh, hey you're up!"

"Yeah, I am," Jeremiah smiled as the pair, loaded with plastic bags of groceries, walked into the room. "Thanks for... for patching me up."

Jeremiah forced a smile to his face as he scooped the mug of tea off the counter.

Ashley dropped the white plastic bags onto the floor and ran the short distance to him, only slowing her speed just before impact.

She wrapped him up in a tight hug around his chest, resting her head on his pectoral muscle.

"You're welcome," Jenny chuckled with a wry smile as Ash took in a deep inhale through her nose. "I'll send you the bill later."

"Bill?" Jeremiah wrapped his arms around Ashley's shoulders as it seemed she wouldn't be releasing him anytime soon.

Jenny frowned briefly at the Vampire before looking back to Jeremiah with a playful expression.

"Yeah, bill," Jenny said, placing the bags of groceries on the counter. "You owe me so many favors for all the shrapnel I pulled outta' ya', not even mentioning the stitches, tourniquets, and other goodies from my bag that I need to replace now."

Jeremiah's mind flashed back to her working on him in the back of the SUV. Like it or not, he did owe the Demon-Knight for her efforts.

He was alive and whole purely because she'd put in the work to rip the shrapnel out of him and put him back to rights.

In truth, he also owed Ashley for her resolute demands to not leave him behind.

I owe my life to a Vampire and a Demon.

Jeremiah looked at the top of Ashley's head as she continued to embrace him.

The only person who ever came to get me like that was Eddie. Not the Church, not the Templars.

Fuck this.

With how unlucky I am, there's no way I've met the only two good monste- actually, are they even monsters? Can I honestly call them that?

Jeremiah squeezed Ashley briefly before saying:

"It's good to see you too, Ash," Jeremiah chuckled and patted her back twice. "You can let go now, I'm not going anywhere."

"Sorry," she half-hiccupped, half-laughed, "I was just... I was a little worried."

"I did kinda blow myself up, so... it's justified," Jeremiah shrugged, as she stepped back, sniffled, and smiled. Jeremiah sighed, bit his tongue, and continued, "I think we should talk about the Coven. I'm no-"

"Over dinner," Jenny interrupted authoritatively, folding her arms across her chest. "We've still got a heap of groceries to haul in, along with the shit we grabbed from Ash's apartment. Think your behind is healed enough to carry anything?"

"Eh, I'll have to take it easy," Jeremiah smirked back at Jenny, lifting one of his arms to look at the scars on it. "But I can help. Where are we, by the way?"

"Galena," Jenny replied as Jeremiah stepped towards her. Turning around, she headed out the door and continued the conversation over her shoulder, "Or at least, that's the closest town. It's about twenty minutes down the road. Clallam is a couple hours west of us."

Jeremiah exited the door to find a landscape of deep green conifers that stretched skyward, dense shrubbery, and a pink-red sunset over a nearby ridgeline.

Domineering hills surrounded the valley on all sides, and birds proudly sang their song from the foliage.

Turning his head from side to side, he saw the large cabin they were staying in, had the trees cut back around twenty yards on all sides.

From what he could tell, the home was about halfway up the wall of a gently sloping valley, which was dotted with occasional homes here and there in the dense foliage.

A road sat at the end of a several-hundred-yard-long gravel driveway, and Jenny's SUV was seated at the head of a small, bulbous circle of gravel.

Looking at the home, he found it was a rather unassuming cabin. Thick wooden walls, several windows, a well-shingled roof, nothing like the veritable mansions he could see elsewhere in the valley.

"Jenny, how did you afford this place?" he asked, since the surrounding area looked more like vacation homes for the wealthy, as opposed to sensible dwellings for people that actually lived in the mountains.

"Eh, I didn't," Jenny shrugged absently continued to walk to the open rear of the SUV. "When my dad made me go to college, I managed to get a scholarship here.

"My family lives out in Georgia, and they decided that they didn't want to stay in a hotel when they came to visit me. So, they bought this place and offered it to me whenever I need to get away from the city for a bit.

"Given that we pissed off a coven, I think getting away from the city for a bit is a good idea."

"Better than trying to establish safehouses in cardboard boxes," Jeremiah shrugged and grabbed a plastic bag after rounding the vehicle.

"Darn straight," Jenny replied, handing him a bag full of bread. Jeremiah pursed his lips as he took it, then a second offered bag that had only a single item in it.

Jenny flicked her eyes to him, chuckled, and turned back to grab more bags for herself and him.

"You're not about to undo all my hard work because you want to lift something that's too heavy, alright? Technically, I don't think you should be back up again, but given that your healing is just a step beneath a Troll's, I'm gonna tolerate it. You can carry four -lightweight- bags, and that's final."

Jeremiah wanted to call her bluff, to grab the heaviest-looking bag in the trunk, but inhaled and closed his eyes.

She's right.

Jeremiah reluctantly agreed, opening his eyes and taking the next offered bag from her hand.

Look what trying to play tough guy got me in the first place. Guess there's a reason why Patrick always tried to steer us away from that.

I wonder if he'd try to kill me too, now.

The painful thought resonated with Jeremiah like a plucked chord, as he was handed his last bag and set out for the house.

All of them would. My soul is unclean - or...at least they'd think it is. Am I wrong? Were all of us wrong?

Maybe it's like Human nature...the urge to steal, to covet, to lie, but with...what did Jenny call them again? Paras? Paras.

Paranormals.

Jeremiah shifted his grip on the bags as he felt a muscle in his shoulder begin to tingle uncomfortably.

With Paras, they have the added burden of having to overcome the urge to consume, to kill, to harm humanity.

Apparently, it's just as easy for them to be a decent person as it is for everyone else.

Vampires can just go to blood banks, provided they have the money...Jenny is a Demon-Knight that does community service and is studying to be a doctor.

Maybe...maybe at some level, -we- were wrong...

Jeremiah stepped into the house and looked to Ashley, who gave him a forced, if bright smile.

She briefly lifted her hands before putting them back against the counter where she leaned against, her green eyes flicking quickly away from his before landing back on him.

How much else were we wrong about?

* * *

Jeremiah leaned back from the small kitchen table with a deep exhale, resting his hands behind his head as he basked in the feeling of being pleasantly full.

Even though the dinner was really just microwavable philly cheesesteaks and oven-baked, frozen potato wedges, he'd packed away enough to fill a small horse.

Apparently, while he'd been out, Jenny had periodically drawn blood from both him and herself, and Ashley now drank a cocktail of them from a large wine glass in lieu of food.

Jeremiah felt odd, watching her casually drink a glass of blood, giggling and talking to Jenny about college professors they'd both had in their time at the same university.

It wasn't because he felt wrong about her drinking his blood, what felt odd was that it didn't feel wrong.

Nothing about this did, in fact. Watching Jenny and Ash chat over the remnants of dinner felt like just that, two friends enjoying an evening meal together.

"So," Jeremiah interjected into a lull in the conversation, causing both of the women to look his way with expectant expressions. "We need to talk about what happened. The Coven, picking a fight with them, what happened when I was out."

"Ah, that," Ashley murmured and set her mostly empty glass down on the table. "Okay, where do you want to start?"

"Well… first. I should probably thank the both of you," Jeremiah leaned forward and couched his elbows on the table. "A lot of what I remember from after I blew the abomination up is fuzzy but… I remember some of it, and that's pretty much all you two saving my dumb ass."

"Language," Jenny added, before taking another bite of her sandwich.

"I got blown up, I think saying "ass" is okay in this situation," Jeremiah replied, opening his hands in a questioning gesture.

"Not at my dinner table," Jenny replied after swallowing a bite. "My dad made sure I was raised with manners, not in a barn."

"Fine," Jeremiah rolled his eyes as he tried and failed to fight back a grin. "But yeah. I need to thank both of you. Hell of a thing you did there, and I literally owe my life to it. But, besides that, how long have I been out? Guessing by the scars, I'm assuming a few months, at least."

"Five days," Ashley replied before licking her lips and taking another sip of her drink. "The first couple days were-well-that, that is, I worried a lot. Jenny told me you'd be okay and that you were healing quickly, but you still looked like a bloody wad of rags to me.

"Yesterday the scabs fell off, and I could hear your heartbeat strengthening."

"I thought you still had another couple of weeks to go, if I'm being honest," Jenny added after Ashley finished.

"Okay... faster healing... it's not normal to heal from that in five days, is it Jenny?" Jeremiah bit his tongue and stared intently at the table before him.

"Not in the slightest, at least, not for a human," Jenny shook her head and sighed. "Golems, from all the info I could scrounge up, are a grab-bag of magical nonsense, depending on how much effort whatever sorcerer put into creating them.

"Sometimes they're barely better than a robot. Sometimes they're given powers that would make most of the tougher Paras think twice.

"You're closer to the second end of things."

"Powerful?" Jeremiah questioned, simultaneously disheartened at the prospect of not actually being human, and relieved at the reality that his abilities had saved his life.

"Given that you didn't have a single broken bone after being crushed by a building, I'd say so, yeah," Jenny nodded with a smile and took the final bite of her sandwich before continuing. "I don't quite know how powerful, though. Golems really don't make up a large enough portion of medical science. Most of the people who make them are very cagey, and the ones that aren't, usually ain't very good at making them."

Oh?

Oh.

I suppose that makes sense.

"Normally," Jenny sighed and took a small sip of her tea as she stared at a point between Jeremiah and herself. "Normally, this is the point where I'd point you to a specialist. But I really don't know any who works on Golems. I know one gal who has experience with familiars and Zombies, but I don't think she'd be much help."

"And I'd like to avoid bringing anyone else into this, if possible," Jeremiah added, leaning back in his chair with a frown.

I guess that's the end of that, then.

Jeremiah stared blankly ahead of him as the realization set in that he might never get answers as to what and who he truly was.

If he was a created lifeform as Jenny had called it, then perhaps none of his past was truly real.

If all my memories are lies, then...the only thing that I can truly believe is real is what is right before me.

Maybe I'm programmed, maybe I have free will.

But even the Church says that the Heavens created us, created mankind.

Whatever Jenny said as his mind worked to digest his reality was lost to him.

Maybe I'm no different. I was created for a purpose I don't fully understand, by some intangible power I've never met.

But what do I do if everything I can remember is wrong? Who am I?

A hand wrapped around his, breaking the hold his internal monologue had on the forefront of Jeremiah's mind.

He looked up and found Ashley smiling knowingly at him.

"I- uh, sorry, got a bit lost in the weeds there," Jeremiah chuckled and ran his other hand through his hair. Exhaling, he turned to Jenny, met her eyes, and looked to Ash. "I made a bad call, trying to rescue those hostages.

"Most likely, the Coven will be out for blood - our blood, because I jumped in. A house that big and expensive, they probably caught me on a security camera or something."

Chewing at the inside of his cheek, he let out a short sigh.

"Jenny, we can stay here in the mountains for a while, yeah?" Jeremiah questioned, turning to face the Demoness' orange eyes.

"As long as we want. My parents won't mind," she shook her head slowly as a small grin dawned on her face. "Might catch some weird looks if they decide to drop in on us, though."

"We'll cross that bridge when we come to it," Jeremiah bit his lip, inhaled, and squeezed Ashley's hand in his briefly. "I think we should stay up here in the mountains and let things cool down in the city, at least for a bit.

"Unfortunately, I was thinking like I still had a whole team of monster hunters, supported by several detachments and an organizing group. We don't have that, it's just us," Jeremiah frowned and looked between the pair of them. "No one is coming to save us."

"As much as I really do wanna give that bastard what he really deserves," Jenny briefly flicked her eyes down to the table as her expression darkened momentarily. She looked back to Jeremiah and exhaled a faintly maroon breath. "I think you're right. Hell, I'm sure even law enforcement is looking into the 'bombing' now. A couple months of peace and quiet would be nice after that."

With Jenny's approval secured, Jeremiah looked to Ashley.

Her face was blank as she stared through his chest, blinking slowly. Her jaw flexed before she closed her eyes, inhaled, and opened them again.

"I've already waited two years to pay that asshole back for what he did to me—" Ashley trailed off, her mouth half open as she seemed to chew through her thoughts. "As long as we do kill him... I'm okay with waiting."

Jeremiah nodded his head at that.

"But-" Ashley prompted with a raised solitary finger. Then she pointed it at Jeremiah and then Jenny before continuing in a resolute tone. "We -are- going to kill him."

"Yup, he needs to die," Jeremiah affirmed, opening his mouth to continue before Jenny interrupted, reaching across the small rectangular table to take Ashley's left hand in her own.

"What we saw back there, Ash, whatever Aiden was." Jenny muttered and shook her head. She licked her lips, as if pondering what to say exactly. "It wasn't good. I know the anti-para groups love to throw the term 'monster' around all the time, but that actually -was- a monster."

"We need to rethink how we're going about this, and honestly, I'm not sure if it's something only the three of us can do."

"I… I need a drink," Ashley replied, pulling her hands out of both Jeremiah's and Jenny's before she stood, and went to the kitchen.

Chapter 19

Why can't they just play poker like normal people? Or hell, even blackjack?

Jeremiah stared at the hand of incomplete sentences he held.

There's not even...ugh, fine, I guess this one works.

Jeremiah slapped down the white card in his hand next to Ashley's selection.

He heard a snort, and turned to face the woman, her pale cheeks blushing a faint red. She reached out, flipped his card over, and patted it reassuringly.

"You're supposed to place them with the game title face up, Jeremiah," Ashley giggled and took another sip of the swirling liquid in her glass. Jeremiah knew it was a combination of his blood, vodka, and a fruity mix. A combination that thinking about made his stomach flip end over end.

However, the smile on Ashley's face, and the faint tinge of tipsy pink on her cheeks beat back the mild revulsion he still felt towards her consuming his blood. "That way she doesn't get a chance to read it beforehand."

"Oh for goodness' sake you two, can you hurry it up already?" Jenny griped from where she sat across from Jeremiah on the other side of the coffee table, in the wrong direction on her chair, which she'd stolen from the dining room table. "Sitting like this is uncomfortable."

"You could've just spun the whole chair around, Jenn," Ashley giggled, leaning back into the small sofa that she shared with Jeremiah. "You didn't have to sit the wrong way."

"I didn't wanna risk the hardwood floor! It's pretty!" Jenny huffed, folding her arms across her chest as she pointedly kept looking the other direction. "You two done over there yet?"

"Yup! We're ready for you," Ashley replied as Jeremiah watched Jenny with a smirk before she stood up, spun, and sat back down in the seat. She leaned forward and snatched the three cards off the table.

"Alright, so. We have... 'what you don't know about a powered mechsuit could kill you' - okay, Jeremiah, this one isn't even funny," Jenny looked up from the cards with a bewildered expression as she set them down on one knee. "Really, throwaways this early in the game?"

Jeremiah replied by schooling his expression and saying nothing, desperately trying not to give away the fact that he had not, in point of fact, played that card.

Instead, he had played "Dmitri, the Cosmonaut Love Hammer" in lieu of anything better in his hand.

I don't think I told Jenny about the gundam yet. Ashley knows, though...

Jeremiah maintained eye contact with Jenny's searching gaze.

"I dunno, Jenny," he shrugged, holding his poker face as he leaned back into the sofa next to Ashley. He folded his arms behind his head and groaned contentedly. "Is it a throwaway?"

Ashley chose that moment to snort loudly into her glass, causing Jenny to turn a confused expression on her instead. Then, Jenny rolled her eyes and pointed at the other white card.

"Alright, fine. Dmitri wins," Jenny folded her arms across her modest chest and shot Jeremiah a self-assured expression.

"Thank you very much!" Jeremiah replied, snatching the black card up from the table and adding it to the other one on his side of the sofa.

Ashley began to giggle maliciously as Jenny stared at them with a slack jaw, tonguing the inside of her cheek.

"So that was a throwaway, just not from you," Jenny noted, pointing an index finger at Jeremiah as he took another sip of his beer. He looked over the bottle at her as a grin broke through his poker face.

"More of an inside joke. I don't think I brought that part up when I told you about my past, but yeah," Jeremiah nodded once and set his beer back down on the table. "The ambush that led to my gap in memories, well, one part of that was the big fucking gundam-mechsuit-whateverthefuck that shot at us right before we escaped.

"Honestly, pretty damn terrifying, and if the government has those… well, how long until they try to use them on us?"

"I'm not so sure that's the Feds," muttered Jenny and shook her head, cocking her head to the side as she seemed to work to remember something. "I remember my ma' talking about a mercenary outfit she used to work for. Apparently, they had some tech that was swinging way above their weight limit. An 'inter-planar PMC' is the term she used, if I'm remembering correctly."

"What the hell does inter-planar mean?" Jeremiah folded his arms across his chest and frowned at the demoness as she took a drink from her small glass of whiskey. Jenny sighed contentedly, set her glass down and bit her tongue.

"Okay... so you know about all those science fiction movies and TV shows with people traveling between parallel universes?" Jenny asked, fixing Jeremiah with a level stare.

He nodded slowly in reply.

"Those exist," she continued with a chuckle. "We call them planes. They're not really parallel universes, more like different states of reality. Parallel universes don't actually exist, that's just silly."

"I dunno, Jenn, that sounds a lot like a parallel universe to me," Jeremiah replied quietly, his thoughts dancing around his head as he internally debated whether or not the Demoness was lying to him.

"I don't really understand the differences myself, but that's what I've been told," Jenny said with a shrug and looked to Ash. "Ready to be the judge, Ash?"

"Uhhh, yep! Let's see," Ashley murmured, pulling a black card off the pile before leaning back in her seat. "Uh, hehe, what makes me wet?"

"Okay cool, let's circle back to the whole other universes bit," Jeremiah waited until she'd finished talking to engage Jenny again. "You can't just waltz in, tell me other universes exist, and then give me absolutely nothing to go off of."

"I mean, I can, if I actually don't know anything," Jenny countered, and folded her arms across her chest and licked her lips while maintaining direct eye contact with Jeremiah. "I only know what I've been told, which more or less amounted to what I told you plus a 'don't worry about it' and a 'focus on the world you live in now' from my 'ma, okay?"

Jenny pointedly leaned forward and smacked a white card on the table, not breaking her staring match with Jeremiah.

"Trust me, I've asked. She doesn't wanna talk about where she's from. You now know as much as I do," maintained Jenny.

Jeremiah inhaled, pursed his lips, and broke eye contact with Jenny before sorting through his hand, selecting a card, and putting it on the table next to Jenny's.

"Calm down, you guys," Ashley chided, causing Jeremiah to look over and see her "staring" at him with her eyes squeezed shut. He cocked his head, opening his mouth to reply when she continued. "Both of your heartbeats just skyrocketed, and I'm pretty sure it's not because you just had the sudden urge to rip your clothes off."

That's...fair.

"This is a card game, we're supposed to be relaxing, not interrogating each other for information. We're on the same side!" Ashley opened her eyes to stare fixedly into Jeremiah's. She then turned to Jenny and quirked a brow. "We've probably got the entire coven after us, and I don't need you two constantly one step off of killing each other!"

"I wasn't planning on it," Jeremiah argued and leaned back on his side of the couch, raising his hands in a gesture of mock surrender. "Just a little miffed because I thought I wasn't getting the whole story."

"Okay, in my defense," Jenny began, causing Jeremiah to look her in direction. She also had her hands raised in a similar gesture. "How many times has Jeremiah thrown hands because he didn't have the full story?"

"I don't know if I deserved that one-" Jeremiah got out before Ashley interrupted with an expectant stare, opening her eyes pointedly as if kindly bidding him to continue his argument. After a moment of his silence, she nodded, delivered a smile that made his heart skip a beat, and snatched the cards off the table.

Instead of returning to her side of the sofa, she ended up leaning against his side, resting her head on his shoulder as she thoughtfully inspected the offered cards. Then, Ashley lifted her head and tilted her ear towards the door.

"What was that?" Ashley asked, pushing her tongue out one side of her mouth thoughtfully.

"What was what?" Jeremiah glanced over his shoulder to where Ashley was tilting her ear.

"Sounded like something crunching... Gravel?" Ashley replied in more of a questioning tone than as a clear answer.

Jeremiah shot to his feet and rounded the couch to peek through the window beside the door.

A large, black SUV was creeping steadily up the driveway.

Fuck. Shit! It's the Feds! Did Vasily bribe the Feds too?

Is the entire fucking government on his payroll? Goddammit!

Okay. Fine.

I guess we're going tombstone on this.

"Where'd you put the guns? That looks like a Fed if I've ever seen one!" Jeremiah asked, stepping back from the door and turning to Jenny.

"I put 'em in the closet." Jenny nodded her head to the side as she stood quickly up and also looked out the window. "Hold up for a second before you go nuts, you paranoid gunslinger. Let's see what happens first."

"Jenny if we give them ti-"

"If it's the feds, we're all in jail anyway, or dead if you start blasting."

"So, calm. Down."

Jenny didn't even look at him, instead batting her hand down at him as she watched out the window.

"See?" Jenny declared a moment later. "They're just turning around. Probably didn't expect our driveway to be so long. They're already leaving!"

Jeremiah chewed at the inside of his lip as he stepped up beside Jenny and peered through the other side of the window.

She was right.

The SUV was already steadily making its way back down the driveway, only its taillights visible.

Jeremiah sighed and shook his head when he made eye contact with a very smug Jenny in the next moment.

"Okay... false alarm," Jeremiah held his hands up to either side of his head in a gesture of mock surrender. "Still a bit shook up over blowing myself up, I guess."

"Uh-huh. And it's got nothing to do with who you are as a person?" Jenny eyed him with a disbelieving raised eyebrow.

"Hey! Since it's not the Feds after all, can we get back to the game?" Ashley questioned cheerfully, meeting Jeremiah's eyes with a bright smile as he looked back. "Cards are burning a hole in my hands."

With a long-suffering sigh, Jeremiah snorted and nodded, sitting back down in the couch a moment before he was joined by Jenny.

"Okay, so... what makes me wet?" she asked rhetorically, plucking the first card from her lap and holding it next to the black one. She snorted, then began to laugh before reading: "'Gay thoughts!' Okay, you're kinda right. Let's see what the other one is... okay fuck whoever this was.

"'Half-assed foreplay', no thank you, I had enough of that in high school."

Ashley rolled her eyes and set the black card on the table with the card atop it. Jenny leaned forward and snatched it up with a malicious grin.

"Really, Jenny? I thought you had the gay thoughts one," Ashley murmured.

"And why'd you think that, Ash?" Jenny questioned, waggling her eyebrows as she stuck her tongue out the corner of her mouth and bit it.

Ashley stared at Jenny with a squint before she inhaled, shook her head, and passed the deck of black cards to Jeremiah.

"Your turn!" she said quickly, with a bright smile on her face that barely disguised nerves that had been plucked by Jenny.

Am I missing something here?

Jeremiah wondered, taking the cards from her hand and pulling free the top one.

Did...did something happen between them that I don't know about? Does Ash play for the other team?

That would explain why she's so comfortable sleeping next to me. No sexual interest there whatsoever.

That prospect shot a pang of sadness and jealousy through Jeremiah that he really didn't want to consider the implications of, so he hurriedly read off the card in his hand without thinking.

"Women like... blank," he read off the card in

his hand as Jenny and Ashley both began to search through their hands of cards.

Jenny's eyes remained on Ashley for a split second longer, though, and Jeremiah looked at her with a frown.

I'm definitely missing something...but...what?

He closed his eyes and waited until two distinct sounds of cards hitting the table before him sounded.

When he opened them, both of the women were watching him with saccharine, teasing grins.

"Okay," he began after leaning forward to grab the cards. "We have... 'just the right amount of mayonnaise'."

Mildly bewildered, he looked up between the two of them with furrowed brows.

"Am... am I missin-oh, oh that kind of mayo," Jeremiah felt it when the double entendre hit him square in his head. He began to try and force back a chuckle, which failed as he broke into a laugh. "Okay - what's the other one?"

Jeremiah picked up the next card, smirked, and tried to figure out which one of his companions it had come from.

He looked to Ashley, who wore an expectant, if entertained grin as she swayed slightly back and forth.

Okay...she's tipsy. A little too tipsy.

Jeremiah turned to catch Jenny's eye as she took a sip from her small tumbler, watching him with an expression that tread the line between giddy apprehension and mischievous glee.

"Women like 'big tits and a can-do attitude'," Jeremiah read the cards aloud and leaned over to set the cards on the table. "It's okay, so do I."

"Oh -hic- is that what you want?" Ashley giggled, grinning as she leaned towards him. Jeremiah turned and stared down at her with an amused grin for a split second before blinking, then blinking again. Ashley hooked a finger on the front of her blouse and pulled down slightly as her alcohol-induced blush deepened. "Big boobs and a good attitude? Becau-"

"Ashley, knock it off," Jenny snarked from the other side of the coffee table, folding her arms across her chest as she stared at the Vampire with a frown and a quirked eyebrow. Ashley licked her lips before she broke out in a fit of exuberant, drunk laughter.

"What's so funny?" Jeremiah asked.

"B-Both of you!" Ashley got in between roiling laughter, as she danced her green eyes between Jeremiah and Jenny. "Your heartrates shot so high at the exact same time!"

Jeremiah took in a deep inhale of breath before rolling his eyes. Ashley, of course, would be Ashley. Apparently, when alcohol was involved, her bubbly nature devolved into dangerous flirtation.

* * *

Jeremiah picked the box of dehydrated potatoes off the shelf, considering it for a moment before shrugging, and put it in the shopping cart. Compared to the offerings from the bigger stores in Larimer, the small-town store was severely lacking.

Hell, Jeremiah had never even heard of the franchise before, but reasoned it might be something localized to the pacific northwest.

Jenny walked around the corner of the aisle

and dumped a frozen chicken into the basket before she set a jug of milk much more gently on the top portion of the cart.

"Oookay—" she trailed off, biting the tip of her tongue as she stared at the pile of groceries. "I think we've got everything. Can you think of anything we're missing?"

"I can think of a few things we're missing, but none of them are food," Jeremiah quipped back, leaning on the handle of the cart. Jenny rolled her eyes, even as the corners of her mouth tugged up.

"I know, don't worry, we're headed to the liquor store after this," Jenny replied before snorting once and chuckling. She raised her hand to the back of her head and scratched an itch as she continued. "Who knew Ashley would go through a bottle of vodka and two things of margarita mix in less than three weeks?"

"Eh, in her defense, I'm pretty sure she's just adjusting to her new job," Jeremiah shrugged absently as he pushed the cart forward towards the check-out. The only thing that popped into his mind was the fact that she'd decided to get a job while they were up here. "I don't think she likes being a gas station attendant."

"I mean, she was most of the way through her degree in finance before she got expelled," Jenny replied with a half-hearted shrug. "I think she's just struggling with her reality not matching up with what she expected from life."

"She can join the club," Jeremiah snorted as he pulled up to the self-checkout, before beginning to scan items. "If you told me a year ago - well, a year ago for me - that I'd be shacked up with a Vampire and a Demon, I'd've probably tried to shoot you."

"Shacked up... you make it sound like we're married," Jenny said teasingly, as she began to bag the items he passed towards her, before returning them to the cart.

"I mean, have you seen the way Ash has been acting since the... uh... explosive situation?" Jeremiah threw out and looked up from scanning the jug of milk to catch Jenny's eye. She stared at him with furrowed brows, her head cocked at a slight angle.

"She has been feeding from both of us pretty regularly," Jenny added with a frown before biting her lower lip thoughtfully. She shrugged and looked at him with an unreadable expression. It looked to him as if she were fighting something down. "I've been trying to get that woman to let me take her on a date for over a year now, so I'm not gonna tell her no if she wants to put the moves on me."

"I think you misunderstood," Jeremiah replied as he scanned the last item and passed it to Jenny. "If she was just putting the moves on you, that would be one thing. The problem is that she's acting really flirty to both of us. I really don't know what to do with that."

"Yeah, I noticed that too," Jenny agreed with a growl. Then she shrugged before nudging Jeremiah away from the scanner with a hand. "Move, ya' big lug, I need to pay."

"Of course, I'm sooo sorry for standing in your way," he replied with a hefty dose of sarcasm, stepping back and away from the register. "I clearly need to learn how to read your mind."

"Oh, kiss my behind," Jenny replied, getting in front of the small display. She started tapping at it without looking at him.

Jeremiah looked down at the movement and

took a moment to appreciate the tight jeans Jenny wore that showed off the wide flare of her hips beneath the black cardigan.

I mean, I might consider it...if you were human.

Jeremiah thought, running his tongue along his teeth.

Wait. -I'm- not human. I can't stain a soul I don't have...I think.

"Really?" Jenny asked in a low tone. She was peering at him over her shoulder having clearly caught him looking. There was a faint shimmer to her eyes that gave him pause. "Really, Jeremiah? What happened to Mr. Prim-and-proper monster hunter? When I met you, I'm pretty sure you debated trying to kill me right there."

"I... absolutely did," Jeremiah confessed with a smirk. "Even after leaving, I contemplated going back there to firebomb your ass."

"Goodness, glad to know I ranked so highly in your to-be-killed list!" Jenny exclaimed, pulled her card from the small slot and put it back in her purse. She paused for a moment, then chuckled softly. She sounded genuinely amused. "Makes a gal feel real nice about herself."

"Sue me, it was my first time seeing through a mask! I didn't even know you guys existed," Jeremiah shot back half-heartedly as they left the store. Jenny left him to push the cart behind her. "I was more surprised that everybody else wasn't trying to kill you because of what you were, least of all that priest."

"Eh, Father Thomas just runs the charity, I don't think he even knows about Paras," Jenny replied as they reached her SUV. "He's a-"

Jenny paused and pulled the back of her vehicle open after a small chirp sounded.

"Good person, but a little too preachy for my taste. I know it's his job and all, but I'm mostly just there to help people and boost my resume," Jenny shrugged absently as she began to pull bags from the cart. "He's sad that I can't help out for a while, but I just blamed my final semester of grad school, and he's dealing with it."

"Mmh, okay," Jeremiah replied thoughtfully as he pulled the last bag from the cart and stuffed it in the back. He closed the overhead door before shoving the cart into the nearby return. "How's that going by the way?"

"Grad school? Eh - been a bit bumpy lately, but thankfully the professors have an online option for me," Jenny replied as she stepped into the driver's seat of the vehicle. Jeremiah soon followed, entering the passenger's seat and buckling his seat belt. "Hardest part for me is my thesis, I really don't know what to do for that."

"Yeah, I'd love to help but unfortunately… well, I don't know shit about your degree" Jeremiah chuckled as Jenny pulled them out of the parking lot.

"Sometimes it feels like neither do I," Jenny turned onto the highway before quickly taking the next exit. Jeremiah remained silent, not having a good reply for what she said as she turned into the liquor store parking lot.

Silence settled in quickly in the gap in conversation. It remained heavy and omnipresent until they stepped into the liquor store.

"Alright, I'm gonna go get the whiskey and vodka, can you find the mix that Ash likes?" asked Jenny, turning her head towards Jeremiah with a small smile. "Really wanna be in and out quickly."

"Yeah, I can do that," Jeremiah nodded and

turned to split off from Jenny before looking back to her and asking: "Meet back here when we're done?"

"Jerry, I can practically see you from the other end of the store; we're both taller than the shelves!" Jenny folded her arms across her chest and snorted once as a teasing grin split her lips, though he once again noted there was a shine to her eyes. "That concerned with losing me?"

Only person I really remember calling me that was Eddie...

"I mean, kinda," Jeremiah shrugged, walking backwards towards a shelf full of colorful bottles that vaguely resembled the mixers that Ashley enjoyed pairing with their blood. "The two of you are all I've got."

That sentiment touched a nerve deep inside himself, and he spun, letting the statement hang.

I've been a bad friend.

I should try and call Eddie again, maybe Sarah.

Maybe he's changed too.

If all I've got is those two, maybe a call to him to check in would help.

I survived a belt of rifle ammo being emptied into my chest, maybe he did too.

Right?

Walking towards the aisle, he tried to quiet his spinning thoughts.

Part of himself wanted to scream and hide somewhere dark and deep for relying so heavily on those two.

For trusting a Demon and a Vampire.

God, Eddie might just try and hunt me down if he is still alive.

The majority of him, however, completely disregarded that logic.

Over the past two weeks just living with them at the cabin, he'd begun to view them as people, as women.

He should trust them, hell, they knew where he slept. One of them even slept beside him most mornings.

Weird fuckin schedule, though. Sleep from two in the morning to eleven in the day.

He chuckled at his relatively easy adjustment to "Vampire time" as it were.

Eh, what can you do.

Now, which one is the kind Ash likes? Isn't it the peach-pear one? Or was it the mango-tini, they both look the sa-

"Now that's something ya' don't see every day," a high-pitched, almost melodic voice said from right next to him, causing Jeremiah to jump slightly before spinning to face the speaker. A pale-skinned, golden-haired woman with blue eyes stared up at him. Her monochromatic eyes seemed to flash slightly as Jeremiah instinctively reached to his hip. "I wouldn't."

Jeremiah froze at the way her voice went from curious, almost excited, to cold in an instant.

His hand hovering above the gun on his hip, he met her narrowed blue eyes.

Something about the fact that she didn't have pupils, irises, or sclera, unnerved him to his core.

"I'm not looking for trouble, you just caught me off guard," Jeremiah replied levelly as her head moved to one side. She licked her lips once, turned her head down to his waist, and lifted it back up to his eyes before grinning wickedly.

"How about we both promise to not do anything stupid," she ran her tongue on the underside of two distinct, elongated sets of canines, before lifting one of her hands from behind her back, revealing an angry ball of blue, swirling electricity.

Okay...this is one of those...out-of-my-depth moments Ash and I talked about.

Jeremiah stared wide-eyed at the casual display of magic before him.

Not blood magic, not sleight of hand. An actual, honest-to-the-gods display of elemental magic. He lowered his hand from his hip and maintained eye contact with the diminutive woman before the magic snapped out of existence.

"I don't think I've seen a Golem so far away from civilization before," her smile shifted to genuine again. "Or at least so far away from any Wizards. Is that little Demoness over there your owner?"

Owner? Why the fuck would I have an owner?

Chapter 20

"What makes you think that I'd have an owner?" Jeremiah asked, letting his hands move down to his sides and remain steady. He didn't want to spook the strange creature.

Trying not to look obvious, he also glanced around the store and what was near him.

On the far end of it, studiously focusing on a shelf of shooters, was Jenny. No one else was in the store but them, as far as Jeremiah could tell.

The odd, nonhuman woman, watched Jeremiah with narrowed eyes and an intrigued grin.

The completely featureless ice blue eyes seemed to analyze him, tracing up and down his body. She blinked one set of eyelids, then a separate, translucent set that remained closed for several seconds before opening again.

"You really don't, do you," she murmured, her words trailing off as her smile widened. "Your tether… it's snapped off. How are you not dead?"

She stepped up to his chest, getting uncomfortably close in one fluid movement, before placing a hand above his heart.

"Hey, nice to meet ya', I'm Jeremiah," Jeremiah tried with an even tone, trying to avoid pissing the magician off. He slowly lifted his right hand toward her.

The woman's eyes snapped down to his extended right hand and she surprisingly grabbed it with her left hand.

She started shaking it vigorously and incredibly awkwardly, without removing the one from above his heart.

"Eredeniz," she stated with a bright smile, before releasing his hand and returning to focusing on his chest. "You can call me Denise, though."

"Well, Denise, is there a reason you're uh, getting handsy?" Jeremiah replied, taking a step back, to which Denise kept her hand raised and simply stepped forward, putting it right back where it was before.

"Your core, I'm trying to see if I can mmm... fix it," she replied, sticking her tongue out of the corner of her mouth before narrowing her eyes again. "Well, that's not supposed to be there."

"I wha-GAHH!" Jeremiah smacked her hand away as his chest felt like a spike of fire had been thrust into it. "What the hell, lady?"

Internally, Jeremiah debated reaching for the pistol at his hip, but decided against it as he remembered the crackling magic from earlier.

Jeremiah pulled his hand away from where hers had left a small, hand-shaped stinging sensation with a scowl.

"Oh no, your core is really bad," she muttered, biting her lip and taking a step towards him, to which he stepped back. "Though, it does explain why you're hemorrhaging essence. You look like a blasted spotlight."

"Okay, cool, stop trying to set me on fire from the inside," Jeremiah replied, continuing to evade her outstretched hand.

"You're too damn bright! I can't blink without you blinding me!" she half-whined as Jeremiah stepped out from the aisle before rounding into the next one. She shot him a pointed stare, continuing to approach him with an outstretched hand. "Now stand still, I'm just trying to plug the leak!"

"Excuse me, Ma'am, but what on earth do you think you're doin'?"

Jeremiah almost exhaled an audible sigh of relief as Jenny's voice projected around the liquor store.

It wasn't quite a yell, but the Demoness did put some weight behind her words, enough to freeze the winged, magical humanoid in her tracks.

Jeremiah turned fractionally, wary of taking his eyes off the whatever she was, longer than it took to pass Jenny a nervous glance.

"Your little boytoy here is leaking essence all over my store! It's too damn bright, and I can't focus on my studies!" Denise gestured with an open palm at Jeremiah, the myriad of bangles on her wrist jangling loudly. "I'm just trying to find the 'off-switch' so to speak. His core-"

"His core is damaged, finding his 'off-switch' might turn him 'off' for good!" Jenny stated firmly. She stepped forward and swatted Denise's hand down, away from Jeremiah's chest. As Jeremiah took another step back, Jenny stepped forward and put herself between Denise and himself. "Stop meddling, I don't need you to get involved. We're working it out."

"Oh? And what enchanter family are you from?" Denise asked with an innocent expression and a tone that positively dripped with pointed, sharpened sarcasm. "I didn't realize Demons were branching out into the market, I thought you all stayed relegated to mercenary work."

"Mercenary work pays the best, and no, I'm not an enchanter," Jenny shook her head as she stood steadfastly between them. The pain in Jeremiah's chest steadily began to decline in intensity, fading to a dull, small ache in the background. "I'm a—well, I'm almost done with my doctorate in paranormal medicine."

"Oh, that's so cute!" Denise said with a broad smile. "A normal almost-doctor who thinks she can fix a broken creature of magic! That's like a car mechanic trying to fix a jet engine!"

Denise began to giggle maliciously before sidestepping.

Jenny stepped with her.

"Miss, we're just trying to grab some drinks and be on our way," Jenny said in a calm, level tone, as Jeremiah watched her snake a hand behind her back. She pulled up the edge of the button-up flannel she wore and rested a hand on her pistol. "I'm gonna tell you once, real politely-like, to quit whatever Fae nonsense you're trying to pull on my friend here. I've got it well in-hand."

"Oh, I'm sure you keep him 'in-hand' quite often," Denise shot back as Jeremiah took a moment to analyze her.

The shorter woman barely hit the five-foot-high mark, if that. She wore a bright green, frilly blouse, patchwork, oversized pants, and a large yellow scarf. On the blouse was a small, golden name tag, denoting her as someone who worked at the store.

Denise brushed a lock of bright blonde hair behind a long, pointed ear and frowned at Jenny.

Jeremiah took a step back and put his hand on his own gun. He couldn't see Jenny's face, but he did see the faint red mist floating up beside her cheeks.

Red mist means...she's about to get violent, right?

Jeremiah questioned the woman's body language. He looked down to her hands and saw them balled into fists.

Yep, violence. Fighting a sorcerer, gotta get ready to move quickly. If she's got magical bullshit, I need to split her focus, try to keep her busy.

Jeremiah rested his hand on his pistol, ready to draw and fire as quickly as possible.

"Eredeniz Kyna Oona Lerevan!" a brassy feminine voice called like a trumpet from Jeremiah's left. Jeremiah turned his head to see a lithe, slender woman who was by every description, just an older version of Denise. "What do you think you're doing?"

"I'm trying to help them, mother!" Denise whined, quickly stepping back from Jenny and hunching her shoulders. She took a deep breath, seemed to set her jaw, and then gestured to Jeremiah with an open hand. "Look at him! He's so bright! I can't fo-"

"That is -no- excuse to badger our customers, darling," her mother answered cooly, with a weighty pressure behind her words. "Clearly they do not wish for your aid, so you must not give it. You were not asked, you were not called upon. Go into the office, we will speak later."

Denise frowned at her mother for a split second before huffing audibly, turning, and quickly walking towards a door in the back of the store. As the door slammed shut behind her, the older woman brushed a lock of blonde hair behind her ear, blinked, and shook her head.

"I apologize for my daughter," said the older woman. Then she gave them a tight smile before walking past them to the register. "She hasn't yet hit thirty, and has too much of my dear late husband in her for her own good."

"She came on a little strong," Jenny replied with a sigh. "Jeremiah, did you get Ash's drink?"

"Uhhh," Jeremiah replied intelligently, looking between Jenny and the woman at the counter. "Uh no, she caught me before I could grab it."

"Go grab it, please?" Jenny asked with a thin smile. "Ash won't be happy if we forget that."

Jeremiah nodded and went back to searching for the mixer the Vampire preferred to pair with their blood.

As he went back the register, he saw Jenny was smiling politely. The woman behind the counter said something in a knowing tone that he couldn't make out.

Jenny's smile became positively wooden for a moment, as both her and the woman passed a glance to him simultaneously.

Denise's mother quirked a brow at Jenny, eased her head to the side, and asked something with a self-assured smile as Jeremiah approached.

Jenny shook her head rapidly.

"Well, in any case," Denise's mother added after he got into earshot. She pulled a large, flat box from under the register as Jeremiah stepped up beside the Demoness. "I do need to apologize for my overenthusiastic daughter. She is still coming into her powers and has yet to learn how to apply her abilities within social norms. Please, do forgive her exuberance."

Jeremiah bit down on the tip of his tongue to hold back the scathing words that leapt to the forefront of his mind.

Inhaling, he considered how he actually wanted to handle this situation, instead of what his gut instinct told him to do.

"As long as she doesn't try to set me on fire again," Jeremiah exhaled and shook his head with a scowl. "I'll be fine."

"She tried to -what-?" asked the older Fae. She stared at Jeremiah with wide eyes. Then one set of eyelids blinked, then the other, before looking quickly away and shaking her head.

"It felt like she was setting me on fire from the inside… I don't know if it's what she was actually trying to do, but that's what it felt like," Jeremiah murmured, rubbing the spot on his chest where Denise had laid her hand. It still itched uncomfortably. "Hurt like a mothe-"

"Language-" Jenny reminded him firmly before he could finish. Jeremiah froze mid-sentence and stared at her.

She stared pointedly back at him, her orange eyes practically daring him to challenge her. He debated going through with it before a faint pinkish-red mist trickled almost imperceptibly from the corner of her mouth.

Given her mood, that would only exacerbate the situation.

"Well, anyway," Jeremiah turned back to the older Fae with a forced smile. "Hurt a lot, and I'd like to, well, not have that happen again."

"I assure you, it will not," promised the older woman as her eyes flicked from Jeremiah to Jenny and back again. The corners of her lips tugged up in a demure, barely visible grin. "Though, she was right on one account. You are… hemorrhaging essence around my shop. Since I am an Alchemist by trade, I will add this as a gift, an apology for her antics."

The woman pulled a small brown phial from

behind the counter and set it in the large flat box.

"Along with these," the woman added with a noticeable grin, pulling two handfuls of shooters from behind the counter before she added the items they'd selected to buy into the box. The tiny glass alcoholic bottles clanked against one another. "You two have a lovely night."

"But we haven't paid ye-" Jenny started to argue as the woman waved a hand to cut her off.

"I would rather have return customers than immediate money," she said with firmness and smiled warmly at them. "In a small town like this, reputation is everything, and I value mine."

Not wanting to look a gift horse in the mouth, Jeremiah smiled politely, scooped up the large, open-faced box into his arms, and turned to leave.

Jenny made a small squeak, as if she were about to say something, but sighed and clicked her tongue.

"Alright, well, thank you ma'am," Jeremiah heard her say as he stepped through the automatic doors. "It was nice to meet ya'."

Jeremiah set the box on the hood of the SUV as his mind worked through what he'd just experienced.

That…was actual magic. Not Vampire blood-bullshit, not a party trick, just a casual ball of lightning on a Tuesday evening.

He ran his hands through his short hair as he stepped back from the vehicle.

How did I miss all this…how did we miss all this?

We were throwing down with Weres and Vamps, thinking that was all there really was.

What good is a rifle against a ball of fucki-

"You doin' alright?" Jenny asked from behind him. Jeremiah exhaled a deep breath and put his hands on the hood of the vehicle.

"Yeah, just—" Jeremiah chuckled darkly and shook his head. "Didn't expect to see actual magic in my lifetime. Bit shocking to seen it thrown around in a liquor store because I'm 'too bright'."

"Eh, magic practitioners are a little cracked," Jenny offered as the car beeped next to Jeremiah. "She was actually nicer than a lot of the enchanters I've met. Their heads get too big for their shoulders."

"When you can throw around lightning as casually as a lighter," Jeremiah started with a chuckle before he grabbed the box of drinks. "It makes sense."

"Still not an excuse to act like a pretentious prick about it," Jenny replied as Jeremiah set the box on the backseat. "But I get it. I remember the first time I saw magic being used as a kid, by one of my ma's coworkers. Started up a campfire in their front yard with a ball of fire. I wanted to learn, but I just don't have the ability."

"Yeah, I guess," Jeremiah replied, rounding the car to climb into the passenger side.

The ride home was silent, save for the quietly playing radio crooning an eclectic mix of classical, country, and synth music. As they pulled to the end of the long driveway, Jenny sighed loudly and put the car in park.

"So," she said turning and looking to Jeremiah with a weary smile. "Wanna drink about it?"

"You have no idea," Jeremiah answered quickly and looked at her with a soft chuckle and a deep nod.

* * *

"So, anyway, I'm just looking this woman in the eye, trying my darndest to not call her an idiot in front an entire ER!

"I told her three times that I was just there shadowing the doc, and no, I couldn't just give her more morphine because she bonked her burn against the side of the bed!" Jenny laughingly said and rolled her eyes, pushing the two-seater porch swing back before she picked her legs up off the floor and came swinging back towards Jeremiah.

"I mean, I don't blame her," Jeremiah replied with a grin, downing one of the shooters in a single swig. "Burns ain't fun, let alone ones that bad. How the hell do you even get gasoline all over yourself like that?"

"Apparently," Jenny murmured, rolling her eyes before they settled on Jeremiah again. "She and her meth-head friends thought fireworks were just black powder and gasoline. So they made a trip to the local hardware store, sporting goods store, and the gas station."

"So they just made a fuckin pipe bomb?" Jeremiah asked incredulously as he grabbed the next shooter. He was minorly nonplussed that he still didn't feel tipsy, even after seven of them. Jenny, on the other hand, clearly was feeling the effects. "I think I made something like that to bomb a Vamp nest once upon a time."

"Oh yeah?" Jenny's smile turned into a scowl in a flash. "What'd they do? You blow 'em sky high for the crime of being a para?"

Jeremiah sucked in a sharp breath and licked

his lips before he unstoppered the shooter and downed the off-tasting contents in one quick drag. He looked off to the side with a frown and exhaled.

"No. That time... well, one of them drained a teenager from the local high school," Jeremiah replied quietly. "Looking back, it's one of the few kills from my days as a hunter that I... don't regret. We knew they did it, and we took care of the problem while the feds and police just sat on their hands."

"Are you sure it wasn't just a witch hunt? Trumped up nonsense because someone got ticked off from sharing a block with a couple Vampires?"

"Yeah. I am," Jeremiah said, and met Jenny's hard orange eyes with a resolute glare of his own. "It feels weird to say, but I regret almost everything I did back then. I killed people that didn't deserve it, people like Ashley."

Even as he brought it up, there was a whisper at the back of his mind.

A lurking specter that haunted him.

Jeremiah gulped as the admission sank into his psyche, having finally said it out loud to someone else.

He smacked his lips and looked down at the shooter in his hands with a frown, the bad taste of the drink not leaving his tongue.

In his hand was the small tincture he'd been gifted by the liquor-store alchemist. Shrugging, he set it on the banister and grabbed an actual shooter.

"I know that now," Jeremiah admitted before downing half of the shooter in a sip. "But that doesn't change the fact that I also killed fucking monsters that absolutely deserved it. Fuckers like Aiden, like Vasily. Killing monsters that deserve it? That's not wrong."

"Heh," Jenny snorted and rolled her eyes. "You sound like my mother."

"Probably a smart lady, then," Jeremiah put forward with a grin, as she shot him a withering glare that broke into the smallest hint of a smirk.

"She was born in hell, Jerry," Jenny deadpanned, downed her shooter and extended an open hand to Jeremiah. He thrust a small bottle of something pink into her hand before she leaned back into the seat. "I really don't think you should use her as a role-model for starting fights."

"Eh, she made you, so she can't be all bad," Jeremiah countered before mentally locking up.

Ah, there's the alcohol.

He desperately tried to come up with something to follow his accidental compliment.

Let's hope she just ignor-

"Jeremiah, if I didn't know any better, I'd think that was a compliment," Jenny's eyes snapped to his as a playful grin split her lips. "And I know you'd never compliment someone like me, that'd go against everything you stand for."

"Woah, pump the brakes there. I wouldn't want to piss off the armed, Texan Demon-Knight!" Jeremiah declared and raised his hands skyward in a gesture of mock surrender. A smile he tried to stop spread across his face nonetheless.

"Ooooh, them's fightin' words," Jenny growled and pushed herself up from the swing and stepped before Jeremiah, waggling a finger. "I am an armed, Georgian, Demon-Knight, thank you very much!"

"Eh, they're basically the same state," argued Jeremiah. He couldn't resist prodding her, as something dangerous flashed behind her eyes before she tilted her head to the side. She stared intently into his eyes with raised brows and an expression that practically demanded he retract his statement. "Flat, hot, humid."

"Do we need to have it out right here in my front yard?" Jenny questioned as her eyes narrowed and faint red mist floated away from her nostrils. "Are you really gonna compare my beautiful state to west Louisiana like that?"

"I just did," Jeremiah leaned in close to her orange eyes. "What're you gonna do about it?"

Jenny seized the front of his shirt and jerked forcefully as she walked with purpose towards the front steps of the porch.

"I'm gonna give you ten seconds to come up with an apology," she said archly, pulling him along behind her as Jeremiah gave genuine consideration to whether she was serious. "If you don't, I'm gonna teach you a lesson about manners."

"Gotta love the casual domestic abuse here," Jeremiah tried to pry Jenny's hand away from his collar as they went, but couldn't manage to break her hold on the fabric.

"We ain't married, it ain't domestic abuse," Jenny quipped back, grinning wickedly over her shoulder before she took the first step down. "It's just abuse, nothing domestic about it yet."

Yet?

"Yet?" Jeremiah's foot hit the paving stone walkway that lead to the gravel driveway. Now on solid ground, he brought his arm down on her hand and smacked it away.

"Okay, you know what?" Jenny spun around as her hand left his shirt, watching him with a playfully sour expression. "You can apologize –after–

I'm done handing you your ass."

Sidestepping around her, Jeremiah walked until he felt soft grass and earth under his shoes. He brought his hands before his face and shot her a teasing grin of his own.

"You never know, I might just hand you yours," he replied as she strode confidently towards him. "Maybe you need to be put in your place."

"Put in my place?" Jenny stepped onto the grass and stripped off the blue jean jacket she wore, tossing it to the side. "And where would that be, now? Making puppy-dog eyes at you every darn day like Ashley does?"

Jeremiah didn't have time to reply, or even think about that, as Jenny stepped forward and swung a fist towards his head.

Even tipsy, like Jeremiah suspected she was, Jenny's haymaker left him barely any time to duck under.

Jeremiah brought his fist up and into her abdomen before sidestepping and bringing his elbow down onto her back and jumping several steps back.

Taking a breath, he watched Jenny and seriously considered calling the fight then and there.

"Okay," she coughed once, straightening out and rubbing her abdomen. "Not bad. I think this sweater gave me rugburn, though."

Jeremiah's eyes went wide as Jenny grabbed the hem of her shirt, then pulled it up and over her head. The pale moonlight cast cascading shadows down the toned, chiseled muscles of her upper back and shoulders.

I don't think I've ever seen her work out, where the fuck did those come from?

Jeremiah stared in mild shock before her long

black hair fell back down to the midpoint of her back.

Tossing the garment to the side, Jenny turned to face Jeremiah.

For the first time in his life, he was happy to see a woman had chosen to wear a bra that day - he didn't need to deal with any more distractions from the fight

That didn't change the fact that Jenny's toned abdominal muscles were on full display beneath the sports bra she had on.

Looking back up to her face, Jeremiah gulped deeply.

He'd picked up on the fact that whenever she was about to fight, or thinking about fighting, red mist poured from her lips. Most of the time it was faint, like a small waft of smoke.

But now?

Right now there was a veritable cascade of dense red gas pouring from her lips.

Jenny charged him, going from standing completely still to a full-on sprint in a single pace, before she slammed into his ribs with her shoulder, bringing them both to the ground in a rolling sprawl.

When they rolled to a stop, Jenny straddled his waist and pinned his hands to the ground, breathing heavily as she stared wide-eyed at him, her long, dark hair shrouding the rest of the world from his view.

He sputtered once a wayward lock of hair caught in his mouth and tickled the back of his throat.

"Ugh," she let one of his hands go and wiped a fleck of spittle off her cheek. "Now that was just unc-"

Jeremiah took the opportunity with his right hand freed to reach under her chest, grab her opposite ribs, and pull. As he pushed with both his knees and pulled with his free hand, he managed to roll Jenny off of him.

Deciding to take the opportunity to get the upper hand, he rolled atop her, cocked his arm back, and froze.

Jenny stared up at him with a hard-to-read but excited expression.

Her semi-pained and confused smile seemed to communicate a mix of anger, confusion, and glee. Now breathing heavily as well, Jeremiah dropped his raised fist and placed his hand beside her head, staring into her dilated orange eyes.

"Decided to tap out alrea-" She started with a self-confident, teasing smile as a wave of impulsive emotions slammed into Jeremiah. Cutting off her words mid-sentence, he leaned forward and kissed her.

Chapter 21

Jeremiah pulled his lips back from Jenny's, blinking in confusion as the sudden desire that overwhelmed him faded slightly.

He swallowed audibly as her eyelids fluttered briefly. She slowly opened her mouth, then closed it with a small snap.

Jenny sucked in a sharp breath as her orange irises darted down and to the side before snapping to his face again.

She licked her lips as small tufts of the red gas that smelled like a combination of acrid smoke and perfume blew up, only to be sucked back in again.

Narrowing her eyes, Jenny took in a breath, like she was about to start a long-winded sentence.

She drove her fist up and under his ribs painfully, forcing the wind out of his lungs before grabbing his shoulders with both hands, and jerking him over.

Again, Jenny landed atop his hips, pinning his arms beside his head.

"Really?" she questioned in a tone that sounded equal parts rhetorical and genuinely bewildered. "After all that nonsense about me being a Demon-Knight? You insult my home, damn near get me killed, damn near steal the woman I've been waiting two years for, and then think you can just... -kiss me-?"

"I... well," Jeremiah stuttered, not quite understanding the immediate desire he'd had himself. "I thin-"

"Jeremiah, I know you're a Golem, and

probably didn't have no mama to teach you some damn manners," Jenny interrupted him brusquely. "So I'm gonna teach you some right-damn-now."

She leaned incrementally forward and the air around Jeremiah filled with red smoke.

From nearly an inch away from his nose, Jenny watched him with narrowed eyes and a snarl before leaning down further.

She brushed her lips against his ear.

"When you want to kiss a lady, you goddamn ask first," she drew out in a razor-sharp whisper. "I'm gonna give you one, and I do mean one single chance to try that again."

Then she lifted her head back, hesitated, then leaned down to the other side of his head. "You will put the right words together... and -ask-. Like you mean it. Like it wasn't a mistake."

Okay...what...uh, what did I just do?

Jeremiah tried to put the pieces in order in his head and heart of what exactly had come over him.

I just kissed a Demon.

A fucking Demon-Knight. And she's...into it?

Jeremiah noticed the rising problem in his pants as Jenny leaned back and sat her rear end firmly in his lap.

She watched him with an arch expression, her maroon skin almost glowing in the moonlight.

The horns that rose from her head reflected the bright full moon above them inside the slight fog that crept around them.

Jenny's mouth moved around as if she were trying not to chew her tongue out. Or as if she were reconsidering her actions and the current situation.

Slowly, she tilted her head to the side, her horns glistening as she did so.

I...fuck it. I'm already going to hell, so why not just go with it.

Jeremiah watched the toned, athletic Demon staring intensely down at him.

Might as well just dive right in. See what the heretics like so much.

"Seriously?" she snorted, as her expression shifted to a deep, derisive frown. "All that talk, all tho-"

Jeremiah seized her by the hips and pushed off the ground with his legs. She was distracted, so this felt like the right time to manage it.

He threw his shoulders with as much force as he could muster and successfully put himself in nearly the same position as before.

Atop Jenny with his hands resting beside her head.

Her eyes were wide and bright as she breathed heavily, the red mist spilling from the edges of her lips and pooling on the ground beneath her head, whirling and swirling complex patterns through the unkempt green grass.

"Jenny," Jeremiah leaned his head forward and pressed his lips to the edge of her ear and whispered as she'd asked, "Can I kiss you?"

Jenny exhaled a shuddering breath into his ear as he felt her nod softly against his cheek.

"Yes," she let out in a soft groan and leaned into his cheek, breathing out a soft, "Please."

Jeremiah pulled his head back slightly before he brought it down against Jenny's lips. The kiss before had been exploratory, gentle.

This one wasn't.

He began to pull his lips back, only for Jenny to chase them down with her own, before grabbing the front of his belt and pulling him down forcefully.

He broke the kiss to take in a sharp intake of breath when he felt his pants loosen, then get ripped down to his thighs.

"Uhhh," Jeremiah began, his eyes fluttering open at the same time as Jenny's snapped wide. "I mea-"

Jenny smiled wickedly as she rolled him onto his back, taking advantage of Jeremiah's moment of confusion, just as he had.

She sat atop his lap, grinding herself down against his hard shaft with lidded eyes.

"You mean what?" She paused mid-grind to open her eyes and glare down at Jeremiah, a blatant demand written in her expression.

Each and every breath was a cloud of red mist that was impossibly hard to miss.

If he was going to call this off, find some reason to not sleep with the Demon on her front lawn, he had to do it now.

If he did so, there was no guarantee she wouldn't go back to trying to knock his head off.

She waited, the same expectant, forceful expression written on her face as she rolled her hips fractionally again.

Goddamn, that's hot.

Jeremiah inhaled deeply as he placed his hands against Jenny's waist.

Her skin was soft, smooth above the toned muscles of her sides and abdomen, almost inhumanly so.

"Just wasn't expecting you to jump straight to this," Jeremiah said, and smiled up at her as he gave in to her, helping pull her hips against his in time to her movements.

"Are you trying to not get laid?" she snapped, standing up and out of his grasp.

Jeremiah worried for a moment that she was actually serious and was about to leave him half-naked in her front yard.

Instead, Jenny pulled her jeans down to her ankles and smiled.

From there, Jenny didn't seem to desire any foreplay beyond what they'd already had as they enjoyed each other on her lawn.

What caught Jeremiah very much by surprise was how vocal the Demon-Knight was, whispering words of encouragement as she ground her hips atop his, and challenges in the few times he managed to get atop her.

With both words and moans, she encouraged him as their rhythm and cadence changed. The changes in beat of their carnal dance were punctuated by their changing positions, as Jenny seemed to enjoy the exchange of power.

When she was atop him, she rode him like a prized stallion, rolling her hips in slow, methodical pushes that brought Jeremiah agonizingly close to bursting.

When Jeremiah managed to get atop her, she acquiesced to his pace, though there was always the promise that she could and would take control at some point.

The changes felt wild and distinct, similar to their earlier fight.

They vied with one another for a momentary advantage that neither truly held onto for very long.

When the end came, she was in the driver's seat.

Jenny's moans hit a frenetic, frantic point

before they cut off abruptly and suddenly as she tensed up atop him.

The visual and physical stimulation of the beautiful, otherworldly woman hitting her climax atop him brought Jeremiah's own to bear, giving him no chance to warn her.

Jenny collapsed onto his chest, nuzzling her head into his throat as she took in deep gasps of air.

"Your," she started breathlessly as one of her horns brushed his cheek. A red stained breath washing over his face. "Fault."

Yeah, my fault.

Jeremiah rolled his eyes and fought back a smile.

Said the literal Demon.

* * *

Jenny was dead to the world as Jeremiah closed the door to her bedroom.

Somehow, she'd managed to stay asleep after passing out atop him. She hadn't even stirred as he moved her off him, carried her inside, and tucked her in.

Jeremiah had briefly debated crawling into bed beside her but decided against it.

His mind was nowhere near quiet enough to sleep, despite the pleasant empty feeling that pervaded his body.

Well. That solidifies things.

Jeremiah opened the front door of the cabin and took a deep breath of the midnight air.

He was reminded of the mountains that towered over his old home, and his previous life.

Oh if you could see me now, Eddie.
Did you live through that ambush too?
What about Patrick?
Both of them would probably shove a silver spike into my temple for what I've done.
But...nothing about that felt wrong.

Jeremiah grabbed one of the few remaining shooters out of the box precariously balanced on the porch railing.

He stared up through the hazy air to the stars above and shook his head with a sigh, realizing that he was wrong.

Something had, in fact, felt wrong.

I'm not blind. Ashley has...a thing or something...for me.

This...this is gonna upset her...isn't it?

Jeremiah grimaced and took a swig of the pink drink.

He didn't understand fully why the prospect of not waking up to the woman again drove a spike of fear, guilt, and apprehension into his gut.

The idea that in the very near future, he wouldn't be waking up to the smiling Vampire stroking his cheek after she got home from her job at the nearby gas station, her hair a mess after she pulled it from an organized bun.

The thought hurt.

So the Church was right.

Jeremiah shook his head and took another drink as a short, snorting chuckle left his mouth.

Shouldn't fall for a monster...I'll only hurt myself.
Just not in the way I thought.

Jeremiah stared blankly into the trees surrounding the cabin like a towering wall of darkness at the edge of the lawn.

"So, three weeks is all it takes, huh," Jeremiah muttered to no one as the darkness felt like it closed in around him. "Three weeks to go from monster hunter to monster fucker, and not even the right monster.

"Not even the one who took you into her home when you had nothing, who had every opportunity to slit your throat and drink you dry, but asks, every time."

And...I just threw that all away, didn't I?

Jeremiah shook his head and blew out a raspberry as he stepped off the porch in a small hop.

He stepped out onto the grass, walking in small circles, with his hands interlaced above his head, as he mentally chewed at how to get himself out of this situation.

"Ah, there you are!" called an oddly familiar voice from behind him, breaking the still night air. Jeremiah froze, pulled his hands off his head, and spun.

A man in his late forties stood several paces away, his hands in the pockets of a well-tailored tweed suit. The stranger lifted his right hand to scratch thoughtfully at the short salt-and-pepper beard.

"Now that's... curious," he remarked, reaching up to adjust his round, thin-framed glasses.

"You're trespassing," Jeremiah informed the man, placing a hand on the pistol at his hip. "Road's that way. Leave."

"Mmm, were it so easy... goodness, what was this iteration's name again?" asked the man to himself. All the while he continued to stare at Jeremiah, as if analyzing a confusing puzzle. "You're not still named Jié, are you?"

"Who?" Jeremiah squinted at the confusing man who watched him with unnaturally pale blue eyes.

"Mmm, as I suspected. Well, at least we know that safeguard works. Though, I do wonder why you selected this iteration, though," murmured the man, answering none of Jeremiah's questions. It was as if he barely heard Jeremiah, riding a train of thought that he alone was on. The stranger paused, looked briefly to the cabin, then down the road, and snorted. "Ah, young love. Were it so easy to be happy. Come, Jose-no… James? Ah, Jeremiah!"

The stranger snapped his fingers as a smile and flash of recognition sparked on his face.

"Come on, Jeremiah, we have places to be. My wife has been worried sick ever since you disappeared," the man grumbled slightly and snapped his fingers towards the treeline. A whirling, static-covered oval of purple opalescent energy grew from a speck the size of a grape to nearly eight foot high. "She won't shut up about it either. She always was too sentimental about our Golems, worries about them like children."

"Who the fuck are you?" Jeremiah demanded, drawing the pistol as soon as he was able to tear his focus away from the entrancing magic to his side. He trained the sights on the skull of the man, thumbing the safety as he stepped back.

"That's the wrong choice, son," said the man with an expression that was neither scared, nor angry.

He was amused at the handgun Jeremiah brandished at him.

"Stop."

The words hit Jeremiah like a freight train and

froze him in his steps.

"Good," the man said and walked slowly towards Jeremiah, stopping at arm's length away. The muzzle of the pistol was less than an inch from the stranger's skull. Jeremiah worked to move, to flinch, to even blink. "Give me the gun."

Jeremiah, against his will, lowered the weapon and placed it in the outstretched palm of the stranger.

The man smirked, hefting the weapon several times in his hand with a subdued grin before he looked back to Jeremiah.

"Well. That's rather nice looking. I'm not exactly a... hmm... firearms connoisseur, but I like the design," the stranger mused rhetorically. "Would you believe that crossbows were originally labeled as a religious crime? Ha. Crossbows, slings, and bows.

"The more things change, the more things stay the same."

Laughing softly, the older man seemed genuinely amused.

"Other than me. My oh my have I changed.

"Well, I'll keep this until you calm down, though I think I should remind you-" the stranger drawled.

He lifted the pistol to the side of his head and fired. The large-caliber, slow-moving round splintered against the stranger's skull harmlessly, and he lowered it before tucking it into the waistband of his slacks.

He looked to Jeremiah with a self-assured smile.

"I'm sorry, son, you can't hurt me, but you can certainly tick me off. Come along, now, follow me. Well, or ruin my clothes," he explained with a shake of his head.

Compelled by some unseen force, Jeremiah's legs moved of their own accord towards the portal as he followed the man across the yard.

The stranger scratched at his head absently, then with slightly more force before snorting once.

"Forgot how much that itches," he murmured, approaching the oval, then stepping through.

"Jeremiah!" Jeremiah heard Jenny shout behind him.

Apparently, whatever happened with the portal had nullified a small amount of the stranger's control.

Jeremiah turned over his shoulder as his legs carried him forward to see Jenny standing on the porch, naked as the day she was born with a submachine gun in her hands.

"Jenny!" His front leg reached the portal. "Run!"

Jeremiah stepped into the kitchen of a home that looked straight out of an old movie.

His bare feet stood on cold, maroon tiles as his eyes scanned the room.

White cabinets and appliances, chartreuse green walls, and a red-topped counter with several tall stools pushed up against it.

The stranger shucked off his jacket and put it on a small, standing coat rack in the corner.

"Cookies?" the man asked with a smile on his face. "I made them this morning. I was experimenting with a new recipe; decided to change up the flour to egg ratio. Personally, I think they came out delightful!"

Jeremiah nervously followed the stranger's finger to the counter, where a wide metal tray held a myriad of chocolate and sugar cookies. He looked back to the older man's eyes and then around the room.

"Ah, right!" he declared, as if he were struck by a sudden epiphany. "Speak freely, Jeremiah."

"Where the... where the fuck am I?" Jeremiah questioned, unable to move anything but his head.

"Ah, you're on my personal plane," the man answered unhelpfully, as he smiled widely and gestured for the tray of sweets. "Grab a cookie. I think you'll like them."

Jeremiah took two steps forward, retrieved a singular cookie, and returned to his position.

Standing stock-still, unable to move anything but his head again, he thought about what to ask the stranger, who was apparently a god.

"There a reason you decided to kidnap me?" Jeremiah asked in a tone that demanded nothing, not wanting to piss off the reality-warping man.

"But of course, though it does speak to how damaged your core is if you don't remember anything yet," remarked the man as he slapped his hands together and sat down on one of the stools. "Come, sit."

Jeremiah complied, walking over and sitting at the stool beside the man.

"Mmm, so I did a quick scan of your memories. I take it you already know you're a Golem?" asked the man, to which Jeremiah nodded scowl. The man sighed and looked at his empty wrist. Then back to Jeremiah. "Lovely, that's another long-winded explanation off my to-do list.

"Which is already long enough as it is. I have to kill that damned angel, finish cleaning the bathroom, and get that roast in the oven in time for dinner. Thankfully, Tiff should be home soon, and that's the whole reason I dragged you here."

The stranger sighed, blowing out a raspberry in the process as he ran a hand through his salt-and-pepper brown hair.

"I am Reixhitz. Though I guess I go by Reix now mostly, so you can just call me as such if you like. I pulled you from the prime because my darling wife won't stop worrying about you and where you'd gotten to," explained the man. "Oddly enough, about two hours ago you just... popped back up onto my radar inexplicably. It was a surprise to say the least."

"You know... you could've just waited until morning and knocked on my door like a normal person," Jeremiah tried not to sound condescending towards the god-like being. "Or you co-"

"Unfortunately, that wouldn't work with my schedule. Tiff should be home shortly, in the next few minutes in fact, and then I have to get back to work," the man interrupted before raising a hand to forestall Jeremiah's reply. "Under better circumstances, yes, I would agree with you.

"However, I was already at a stopping point, and you had finished with your... ah... haha... activities, so I figured that now would be a decent time to get this out of the way. It'll finally g-"

A loud whooshing sound and flash of purple light came from the doorway behind Reixhitz, cutting his sentence off.

"Ah, lovely. That would be her!" Reixhitz smiled brightly. He turned partly around and gestured toward Jeremiah with his hands. "Darling! I found him!"

"You fou- Oh! Oh, thank God! Is he alive?" a woman's voice carried through the building, sounding like it was moving.

"Quite so, Tiff. He's here right now, actually!" Reixhitz replied, not taking his eyes off the doorway. "Though, he's reverted to an earlier iteration because his core was damaged! Lost his memories and the like."

A beautiful woman in her late thirties stepped through the doorway behind Reixhitz, wearing a concerned frown. She stepped into the room and pulled off the shawl draped over her shoulders, before setting it on the coatrack next to Reixhitz's tweed jacket.

Something itched in the back of Jeremiah's mind. Seeing them together, he knew he knew them, but not from where.

"Oh," she whispered and stared at Jeremiah. Her eyes narrowed before turning to Reixhitz. "Didn't we last let him out nearly a decade ago?"

"Over," Reixhitz replied. "Though I am thoroughly confused by some of his choices. It seems like some of the other iterations blended into this. He's managed to collect the attention of two young ladies - a Vampire and a Demon-Knight, if I'm not mistaking what I got from his memories."

"Oh, where are they?" she replied as her frown turned into an intrigued grin. She turned to Jeremiah and cocked her head. "I'm Tiff, by the way."

"Jeremiah," Jeremiah nodded with a forced, nervous smile. "I'd shake your hand, but I've kinda been locked in place since your husband here kidnapped me."

"He did –what–?"

Chapter 22

"Yup! Just walked right in when I was in the middle of... well, talking to myself," Jeremiah explained with a chuckle, as the all-powerful god that looked a lot like a bookworm suddenly folded in on himself.

Hunching under the withering glare of the woman who was, apparently, his beautiful wife.

The woman's gaze softened as she looked back to Jeremiah, then turned to ice as she tried to bore a hole through the back of Reixhitz's skull again.

"Was kinda' terrifying," Jeremiah added. "I told Jenny to run as I was involuntarily walking through the portal... at least, that's what I think it was."

"You pulled a gun on me, you don't get to make it sound li- OW!" Reixhitz cut off abruptly as Tiff smacked him on the back of his head. "I don't think I deserved that one."

"You did and you know why, Reixhitz," Tiff replied archly, folding her arms under her chest. She continued to stare at Reixhitz archly as she continued. "You decided to waltz in and pull the whole 'Torment of Sanity' shtick again, didn't you?

"Jeremiah, tell me, how exactly did my husband introduce himself?"

"Well, I si-" Reixhitz began, before Tiff snapped her eyes back to him. As if sensing the stare, Reixhitz inhaled sharply, said nothing, and stared at Jeremiah with a mildly panicked smile.

Smart move, buddy.

Jeremiah forced down his own smile at the

man's predicament and felt zero sympathy. He had gotten himself into this situation, after all.

"So I was standing in the front yard, talking to myself," Jeremiah began with a deadly smirk, watching Reixhitz wince, apparently in anticipation of his story. "Reixhitz here shows up, says 'there you are!', and I tell him to leave. He keeps talking about me, to me, as if I wasn't there-"

Tiff closed her eyes and inhaled sharply before nodding and mouthing "yep" inaudibly. She shook her head and watched Jeremiah with a smile that held a wickedly sharp edge, but clearly not for him.

"Of course, I tell him to fuck off, because hey, he's trespassing at two in the morning, and I draw my gun.

"Reixhitz there tells me to stop, and suddenly, I can't move," Jeremiah's grin widened as Reixhitz grimaced and looked off to the side. "Somehow makes me follow him through a portal here, and - then- tells me who he is. Well, his name at least."

The woman lets out a long suffering sigh, as if this wasn't new, or really even unexpected. Instead she just looks to Reixhitz and waits.

"I had to be quick, and you didn't seem willing to be helpful. Considering that you're barely a week from turning into a small essence bomb-" Reixhitz stated and turned back to Jeremiah with a frown. He reached forward and made a small grabbing motion at Jeremiah's chest.

An odd sensation overcame Jeremiah as he suddenly found himself floating several inches above Reixhitz's hand.

Looking back to his body, Jeremiah saw himself staring blankly ahead, unmoving and unblinking.

"Goodness, they really messed your core up, didn't they?" whispered the man.

What? Who?

Jeremiah couldn't speak, but felt his thoughts echo loudly through his existence.

Looking to himself, he frowned.

He could see a slithering, warping, spiky mass, hovering above Reixhitz's hand. In regular intervals, cones of black liquid extended out to sharp, six-inch points, before retracting to small, rounded mounds on the gelatinous orb.

I...is that me?

"Yes, it is. It's you. Well, more specifically, it's your core," Reixhitz replied, poking at a spot on the blob. Jeremiah tried to flinch away as pain overwhelmed his senses, as if someone were sticking their finger into an open wound. "Ah, that's not good."

"What isn't?" Tiff leaned over her husband's shoulder, cocking her head from side to side as she stared into the blob.

"See that, there?" Reixhitz pointed at a spot on the blob's side before looking up to Tiff. She squinted and leaned forward before blinking and shaking her head.

"No... no I don't. Why?" she replied, pulling her eyes off of Jeremiah to look at Reixhitz with a frown.

"Exactly. There's supposed to be a bit, a fragment there... and, well, there's not," Reixhitz stuck his finger into the blob again, sending another jolt of pain through... well, Jeremiah's consciousness. "He's missing a whole blasted fragment, and he's not dead, though he probably should be."

"I told you he was special," Tiff looked at her

husband with a nervous smile. "How can we fix him?"

"We... we can't," Reixhitz shook his head slowly as he stared at Jeremiah's blob with pursed lips and a furrowed brow. He made a soft humming noise, shook his head and sighed. "Like I said before we dispatched him last, he's gone through too many iterations as it is.

"This is it. I can't make any more meaningful changes. As an intelligence asset, he's... he's done. There's nothing else I can do to push this along."

An intelligence asset? Iterations? What the fuck do you mean?

Jeremiah thought aggressively at Reixhitz, hoping his gut instinct was right.

Care to fucking explain anything? At all?

"I can't even restore his native memories. He's... well, he's this now," Reixhitz continued, as if he hadn't heard Jeremiah. Which was, honestly, possible. "Really, it's impressive, given that this iteration was relatively aggressive and mostly controlled by de Sable's fragment. Which... happens to be the fragment that got destroyed.

"Speaking of which, I assume you've had some rather erratic personality and mood swings?" Reixhitz questioned almost absently, still painfully poking and prodding at different locations on Jeremiah. "Maybe some offshoot trains of thought that seem like they're not exactly yours?"

I...

Now that you mention it, yeah, I have.
Ever since I woke up at the dump.

"Ah, well, you'll still have them after I'm done, but-" Reixhitz cut off abruptly as a small bolt of bluish-yellow lightning arced painfully from his finger to Jeremiah's core. "It'll be a lot less. The soul fragment that got forcibly removed from your core was more or less the head honcho.

"So you've been comparable to a ship without a captain, if that makes any sense. After I patch this hole and run a new connection, you should be a lot less... mmm, Unhinged? I feel like that's not the right word."

"No... Unbalanced?

"Ah, Erratic! Yes, you should be far less erratic from this point on."

Reixhitz ran his finger along one side of Jeremiah's core, and Jeremiah readied himself for a rush of pain that never came.

Instead, a small flash of blue-orange light radiated out from below Reixhitz's finger, and suffused Jeremiah with a pleasant warmth.

This is nice and all, but is there any way we could do this inside my body?

Jeremiah thought at Reixhitz, as the sensation faded from his grasp.

Really not into being popped out like a damn toy battery.

"Unfortunately not," Reixhitz murmured, continuing to analyze Jeremiah's core. "This is a delicate process, and you're distracting me. So shush."

"Don't tell him to shush like that," Tiff chided, raising a hand to slap the side of his shoulder before she paused and seemed to reconsider.

She lowered it back to her side before resting her hands on her hips, as she watched whatever it was Reixhitz was doing to Jeremiah's core.

"He's probably just concerned that you'll break him, or kill him," she guessed.

"Mmm," was all Reixhitz responded with, seeming focused on poking and prodding painfully at Jeremiah's core.

After another minute or so, he exhaled a ragged breath and grunted again.

"That's as much as I can really do. I plugged the essence leak, which was the biggest worry I had upon seeing you," admitted Reixhitz.

With a sigh, Reixhitz leaned back forward and shoved his hand towards Jeremiah.

Jeremiah blinked, then blinked again, as the feeling of being in a body felt somewhat unfamiliar.

As if his short stint as a disembodied amorphous blob had been his whole existence.

Jeremiah moved his hands, opening and closing them into tight, balled fists. He frowned and looked up at Reixhitz.

"I don't feel any different," Jeremiah admitted, furrowing his brows and rolling his shoulders, trying to find something, anything, that had come from the odd, out-of-body experience. "Was that really necessary? Getting pulled out of my body like that felt fuckin' weird."

"You wouldn't - I didn't actually do much," Reixhitz shrugged and leaned against the back of his stool. "When I designed you, and your counterparts, I made you with a net-zero system balance. More or less, I restored that. There is, however, a problem."

"Net-zero?" Jeremiah asked, raising a brow and pointedly ignoring the final part of Reixhitz's statement.

"What do you mean there's a problem?" Tiff shot at her husband, causing him to look towards her over his shoulder with a small frown. Reixhitz then turned back to Jeremiah, sighed and nodded at him.

"Net-zero in your case means that you ambiently take in as much essence from your environment as you use to exist.

"At least, exist without using anything special," Reixhitz clarified slowly, seeming to mentally chew over every piece of information before delivering it. "In short, you'll exist in your current state perpetually, provided you don't use any of your abilities. I've stabilized your core, but you're left with roughly twenty percent of your total power."

Reixhitz scratched thoughtfully at his short beard, as Tiff looked nervously between him and Jeremiah.

Tiff inhaled deeply, grimaced, and shook her head.

"I have to go call a friend," she kissed her husband on the top of his head, straightened, and smiled at Jeremiah before turning and exiting the room.

Reixhitz blew out a short breath, and leaned forward, grabbing Jeremiah's left wrist.

"We don't have much time, so I'll make this brief," Reixhitz said in a hushed tone, tilting Jeremiah's hand over before rotating it back. A small, translucent spike emerged from the place where his wrist became his palm. "Do -not- tell Tiff about this.

"Given the nature of who this iteration is, I fully expect that you won't just be content to sit down and play house with your girlfriends, so-"

"Not my girlfriends," Jeremiah interrupted, earning an amused stare from the man across from him. Jeremiah sighed before continuing: "Alright, one of them might be-"

"Anyway," Reixhitz murmured softly, speaking over him. He was shaking his head and holding a hand up to stop Jeremiah's rebuttal. "This… version of yourself. It's probably the closest to a war Golem that we ever used.

"Normally, you worked for us as an infiltrator, a spy. This one was different, as I'm sure you've gathered, we needed you to infiltrate Humanity First. Particularly one of their more radical and violent cells in Larimer.

"But they wouldn't let just any old person off the streets in, so we needed to make sure you'd… fit in. Or fit their need," Reixhitz explained while he chewed at his lower lip.

His brow furrowed as he seemed to stare into a void between them.

"And so, we tried something we hadn't before. We added a soul fragment to your core. You 'became' someone else," he whispered. As if it wasn't something he wanted to entirely admit. "I'm sure you remember your kidnapping at the hands of Vampires. That happened, both to you and not to you. It happened to a part of you, and Humanity First sought you out.

"That's how I know you won't let sleeping dogs lie. And so, inevitably, when you use the abilities I've given you, you will find your… battery to give it a name, slowly being drained.

"Instead of letting you just die when you hit that end point, which would get me put in the doghouse by my dear wife for a century at least, I've given you a way out. The only one I can. If only to preserve her smile knowing that you're running around out there."

Jeremiah blinked, staring at Reixhitz, as his brain worked to churn through the several tons of information that had just been dropped on his head before being seemingly ignored.

As if his past was simply a fact to be revealed and dismissed.

"This shunt will allow you to drain the cores of other Golems directly into your own," Reixhitz pointed a finger at the translucent spike that extended from his wrist. "Shove it in, drain them, and you'll more or less steal their life force. Add it to your own battery, so to speak."

"So what?" Jeremiah asked sharply at that batch of information, as it left a bad taste in his mouth. "I'm just a Golem Vampire, then?"

"Yes and no," Reixhitz nodded his head from side to side thoughtfully. "Vampires have to drink to survive. If you were to just... sit at home and be a househusband to those two like you have been, you'd be completely fine.

"Net-zero, remember? In terms of essence, you'll be completely fine as long as you live life like a normal Human. You don't have to drain others to live. It's a choice for you, and one that you might have to make if you want to continue fighting Vasily."

Jeremiah felt the gears of his mind grind away on that one for a moment.

No compulsion.

I'm not forced to do it.

So...if I found a Golem working for someone like Vasily, I could just...drain him.

Like killing any monster, or their servants.

Just, instead of a bullet, I just give them the tube.

"I can live with that," affirmed Jeremiah with a single nod. Then leaned back as Reixhitz released his hand.

"Good, Tiff would be apoplectic if you

couldn't," Reixhitz whispered under his breath and shook his head. "Part of the reason we stopped using Golems for wetwork is because she kept getting attached to them.

"Especially once she began to help make them. Come to think of it, I think you were the first one I let her help me create. She views you all like an army of grandchildren, in addition to her own grandchildren."

Reixhitz smiled in an odd way, looking down and to the side briefly before slowly rocking back and forth.

"Well, I'm getting off track," Reixhitz mumbled with a grin. Then he waved his hand dismissively. "In short, you can live your life as you see fit. I have no more work for you.

"You were the last of my Golems that we still sent into operations. The rest we all gave normal human memories and sent them about their lives.

"Now, let's get you home, preferably before Tiff comes back and draws you in for an hour-long conversation to try and discover all she can about you again."

Jeremiah chuckled quietly as Reixhitz shot him a knowing smirk.

"Or before your two bookends start to worry too bad," he added with a devilish laugh.

Jeremiah rolled his eyes and sighed, before a small grin broke through on his face only to fall away quickly.

Suddenly, he remembered his other problem.

That being his activities with Jenny the night before.

Reixhitz waved his hand, and a glowing purple oval formed several feet away from them.

Jeremiah shook his head, kicking that problem to the back of his mind.

He still had questions for the man who was, apparently, his creator. This was a chance few ever got as far as he knew.

"But... what do I do? What is my, well, purpose?" Jeremiah inhaled deeply as Reixhitz turned to face him with a frown.

The older man grimaced, opened his mouth, and closed it again. He then shook his head and looked back to the portal before sighing.

"I have no more instructions for you, no jobs," Reixhitz answered after a moment's consideration, staring into the swirling morass of spellwork. "Your purpose now is the same as anyone else's. To live your life as you see fit."

With a click of his tongue, he raised his eyebrows momentarily.

"Now, if you're asking my advice on how to live your life, that's a lot more difficult," Reixhitz continued and turned back to Jeremiah with a thoughtful expression. "Personally, I'd recommend that you go home, kiss both the girls that - from what I gathered in your recent memories - both seem somewhat smitten with you.

"Build your life from there, let them care for you and guide your heart in much the same way my Tiff has mine."

"How?" Jeremiah asked, swallowing hard before adding, "All I can think about is killing monsters. In the past two weeks, I've just felt on edge all the time because I'm doing nothing!"

"Then kill monsters," Reixhitz remarked easily with a shrug. He gave him a muted grin at the small outburst, before offering Jeremiah his pistol back.

"But... I can't. Not anymore," Jeremiah said and shook his head, grasping the pistol as the thoughts that had been brewing over the past weeks bubbled to the surface. The thoughts became words and left his lips before he could rein them in. "Every time I look at a Vamp, or a Were, or even that snake-lady in town, I don't see a monster anymore. I just see a weird-looking person.

"But that... itch, it's always there, and it won't shut up. Like I should always be searching for a-" Jeremiah continued before Reixhitz waved his hand dismissively, instantly shutting Jeremiah up.

Whether this was from magic or not, Jeremiah wasn't sure.

"I like to think that I'm somewhat careful with my words, Jeremiah," Reixhitz started, and turned his body to squarely face Jeremiah. He stared at him with a resolute expression, before smacking his lips once and quirking a brow. "I don't remember telling you to hunt non-humans. Did I say to go out and kill Paras, Jeremiah?"

Jeremiah opened his mouth briefly as the question hit him like a ton of bricks. He squinted at Reixhitz, before closing his mouth slowly and gulping.

"No, you didn-"

"Exactly, I didn't," Reixhitz cut him off again, an authoritative edge to his voice that practically demanded that Jeremiah shut up and listen to his diatribe. "I said to kill -monsters-. Men like Vasily, like Aiden? Those are monsters.

"This is why I said you wouldn't be able to sit down and play house."

Reixhitz said with a short chuckle.

"You were created to be this way, Jeremiah,"

the older man said and smiled widely. "So go, kill monsters. Be what you were made to be, but be careful.

"Don't get the people you care about caught up in your foolish crusade to kill some overpowered nonsense causing trouble in your city. Fight things at your level."

Looking to his bare wrist, Reixhitz blew out a breath and shook his head.

"Alright, that's my fatherly advice quota for the century, off you go!" said the man.

He placed his hands on Jeremiah's shoulders and with a forceful shove that the skinny, shorter man had zero business using, sent Jeremiah flying through the portal.

Jeremiah instantly realized that something was wrong.

Instead of the portal merely blinking him into existence back home, as it had coming to Reixhitz's home, he was lost in a sea of vibrant, staticky violet.

It swirled, enveloped, and enraptured him for a period of time that felt almost indiscernible.

"Fuck!" he heard Reixhitz shout after a moment, or an hour, he wasn't sure.

Thunder clapped and rumbled across him, and he stumbled forward as he felt gravel under his feet.

He blinked rapidly as his heart thudded in his chest, trying to figure out where the hell he was. As he looked around the large, rectangular rooftop, he was at least confident that he was alive.

That...what the hell happened there?

Jeremiah wondered as he took a pensive step forward, then another.

Satisfied that everything was working fine,

and there were no immediate injuries to his person, he stepped around a large AC unit to find himself staring out and down into a cityscape.

Something went...really wrong with that, didn't it?

After a brief moment of staring confusedly at the landscape, he managed to figure out roughly where he was.

He made eye contact with a unique and familiar building in the distance and turned slightly to face the bay.

Well that's the space needle. And we've got the bay over there. At least I'm somewhat close to home.

As it turned out, he'd manage to land in downtown Clallam.

Really wish there were still payphones around here. That's gonna be a hell of a walk.

Chapter 23

Jeremiah opened the front door of the office building he'd found himself in, to a busy morning street.

Pedestrians passed in front of him like a tide, a haphazard overflowing river of humanity. Notable in the crowd, at least to Jeremiah, were the dozens of non-humans that went about their business.

Paras.

As he took a few short moments to watch the sea of people from the top of the office building's steps, Jeremiah shook his head.

The people ranged from human-adjacent, to overwhelmingly monstrous in some cases.

And yet here they were, dressed in the same clothes, with the same no-nonsense expressions written on their faces, as they went about their morning business.

Reixhitz was right.

Jeremiah took a deep inhale of the rank downtown air and chuckled.

And a fuckin' asshole.

Just throws me out because he's behind on chores.

Fuck you too...dad.

Jeremiah smirked to himself before starting down the steps.

He was rather amused at the odd glances he got while walking down the street. Jeremiah was, after all, still wearing his jeans and a thin, white t-shirt. He was also wearing no shoes. Downtown.

The morning was brisk enough for the average person to wear a jacket of some sort, but Jeremiah imagined the odd looks were aimed more at the plethora of tattoos and his bare feet.

He pursed his lips and debated trying to hail a taxi - he had to get back to Jenny and Ash somehow, after all.

He exhaled a breath when he realized that he, in fact, also didn't have his wallet.

Need to get that old man to learn how to open a portal where it's supposed to go.

Jeremiah frowned and shook his head.

Though...that didn't feel like he accidentally plopped me down in the wrong place. It felt more like... something went haywire. Like he lost control of the portal.

If I was being used to gather intelligence, does that mean he has enemies?

He seemed like he knew what he was doing with portals, not like someone who would lose control in a calm situation like that.

Jeremiah jumped slightly as a long, boxy car parked next to him roared to life and drove off with a screech of tires.

He frowned at the square brake-lights of the older vehicle, as they disappeared into the throng of traffic, bobbing and weaving between other cars.

Maybe...maybe I was shot down - or whatever the magical bullshit equivalent would be.

Maybe he did open the portal correctly, but I just got hit by an inter-planar surface-to-portal missile. Does that even exi-

A thunderous blast of pressure hit Jeremiah like a truck, sending him stumbling to the side.

The brisk pace of the throng of people that flowed in two directions suddenly became a cascade of fleeing, screaming people, as the blast echoed around the buildings and city blocks.

With a shove, then a short jump, Jeremiah stumbled into an alley, out of the mass of sprinting, shouting people.

What the hell was that?

Jeremiah's mind screamed out as he stared around, as more and more people crowded the sidewalk, pointedly running away from where the sound had come.

It sounded like a bomb - and a big one too.

People driving towards the direction of the explosion stopped their cars, opened their doors, and began to run away. Jeremiah bit down on his tongue as he stared at the panicked faces of the people fleeing... something.

Is...is it a fucking nuke? Did we just get nuked?

Jeremiah's heart began to beat even faster as he moved up to the corner of the alley and peered around, just in time for a billowing wave of dust to pour down on him and obfuscate his view.

Okay...lot of dust, but no mushroom cloud. Probably just a normal bomb.

Jeremiah pulled his shirt up over his nose as the cloud pressed in around him.

He was only able to see several feet in front of him, but the wave of people slowly began to diminish in numbers. It went from a blasting firehose of humanity to a steady stream, and finally, fell away to a trickle after a minute.

The dust cloud also began to fall away, being blown by gusts of wind through the buildings.

Now he could see a whole twenty feet in front of him.

People are gonna be hurt by something that big.

Jeremiah inhaled and grimaced.

I should go and help...see if there's something,

anything I can do. First responders probably won't be there for a bit anyway.

Jeremiah lowered the shirt from his mouth and stepped out into the mostly empty sidewalk.

The occasional person still ran, or in one case, limped away down the sidewalk.

Jeremiah began to slowly run towards the apparent disaster site.

The dust grew thicker as he went.

Turning his head from side to side, Jeremiah grimaced and realized that he'd have to wait it out just to be able to move slowly through the pale, off-tan cloud of microscopic debris.

Don't wanna run past it.

Jeremiah continued to pan his head from side to side, blinking away grit and other nasty things that he didn't want to think about.

Suddenly, the dust grew thicker and more intense, as a powerful gust of air pressed against his front, to the point that he actually closed his eyes and turned away.

Holding a hand before his face, he waited for the apparent windstorm to die away, when suddenly, it became little more than a strong breeze.

Jeremiah opened his eyes in confusion to find himself suddenly standing in clean, un-contaminated air.

Half a block in front of him stood a massive pile of rubble, along with several people.

One of them was a woman with long pointed ears, her arms extended wide to either side as she pumped what looked like blasts of condensed air from her palms.

She's...she's using magic to clear the cloud.

Jeremiah looked up and saw that they were

standing in a small dome of clean air, with cascades of dust billowing down the edges like a waterfall. Grimacing, she looked to the other three members of her group.

"I'll hold it up as long as I can!" she shouted at her team, nodding towards the smoldering rubble, "This is a big spell to keep up an extended operation. Do what you can before it fails!"

"On it!" the man bellowed as Jeremiah began to run towards them. "Anne, shift and see if you can sniff anything out. Lil', you ready to lift some heavy shit?"

"Yut!" said a mountain of a woman beside the man. She crackled her knuckles and began to unbutton the camouflage uniform top. Now that Jeremiah looked, they all wore military uniforms.

"How can I help?" Jeremiah projected his voice as he approached the group.

The man turned to Jeremiah with a briefly shocked expression before it shifted to one of appraisal, then dismissal.

"If you're not willing to get your hands dirty, or care about asbestos poisoning, then leave," he said and held a hand out to the woman he'd called Anne, as if bidding her to wait just a moment.

"If there's people in there, innocent people that just got blown up? Yeah, I'm willing to get my hands dirty," Jeremiah said and stared back at the man. "The more time we spend bullshitting while your fuckin' sorcerer tries to hold the spell up, the more people we lose."

"Fuck it. Fine," the man barked and pointed a hand at the pile of rubble in front of them. "Get going you two. New guy, you're with me."

As soon as the man uttered his orders, Anne

growled and grew several inches.

Patches of silken grey hair began to grow across the exposed portions of her skin, and Jeremiah understood suddenly why there were elastic portions sewn in different increments across her uniform.

As she shifted into a full-sized Were, her clothes didn't rip as Jeremiah had seen in the past.

Instead, the uniform adjusted to her new measurements as she threw her head back and howled.

In a burst of speed, she sprinted full tilt for the pile of rubble that was once a building.

"Speedy Were," grumbled the mountain of a woman apparently named Lil', nonetheless doing so with a broad grin. Immediately, she started stripping the camouflage jacket off her broad shoulders, and revealing the sleeveless tan shirt underneath.

She chuckled loudly before slamming her fist into her palm and set off sprinting thunderously towards the rubble.

The man snorted, running a hand through his jet-black hair, before he turned to Jeremiah and nodded his head sideways after the pair.

"Alright, here's the deal," the man began as Jeremiah looked at his chest. Finding a name emblazoned there, along with an all-capital "U. S. MARINES", Jeremiah identified him as Aders. "You and I will be retrieving the casualties those two find, carrying them back to the sidewalk, and repeating.

"If they're wounded bad enough, I might have to stay behind and try to provide aid. In which case, nut up and carry the next casualties to me."

Jeremiah initially debated trying to argue with the man, and point out that he, too, had had medical training in the past, and then decided against it.

Aders walked towards the rubble with confidence and spoke authoritatively.

It was clear that the man had experience with events like this in the past and understood how to take charge of the situation.

"Understood," Jeremiah nodded once as the soldier glanced over to him with a raised brow. Aders grunted and faced forward again.

"Captain! I got a live one!" Anne half-howled, half yelled from about halfway up the towering mountain of debris. "About... five feet down! I smell a lot of blood but can't tell if it's theirs!"

"Lily! Get on it!" Aders shouted at the massive woman, who had already made it a quarter of the way up the pile. He smacked the back of his hand against Jeremiah's chest and gestured towards the Were. "Come on, hustle up!"

Aders began to jog towards the pile and hit the bottom chunk of concrete at speed, using it to propel himself up a dozen feet in short order.

Jeremiah put some spring into his step, reaching the base of the pile as the Captain neared Anne.

Fuck that guy's fast.

Jeremiah jumped up the first piece of fractured concrete as sirens began to sound out distantly.

By the time he reached the group, Lily was in the process of lifting another massive hunk of concrete above her head.

She threw it with a loud, percussive shout, sending it flying down to the front lawn of the building.

"Should've fuckin' listened," Anne growled, tearing through the smaller debris with a focused intent. "We told them that some shit like this was gonna happen. Blew up a fuckin Fed office... how the hell did they even get the explosives for this?"

"Dunno, Sergeant," Aders shook his head, grabbed a basketball-sized hunk of concrete and hucked it aside. "We tried to warn them, SIGINT tried to warn them, but the senator just didn't want to listen.

"Same shit, different day - we get to clean up their mess."

As Aders said the last, he did it with a dark chuckle.

Jeremiah leaned down to grab a chest-sized hunk of concrete that Anne had flung behind herself in her frantic digging.

Lifting it to his knees, he pushed it up and away, sending it tumbling down the hill.

"Arm! Got an arm!" Anne called, tugging slightly on a dust-covered limb that seemed to materialize from the debris.

Jeremiah leapt into the short hole that she'd dug, and began to help uncover what was apparently, a person.

Lifting up a chunk of concrete, he uncovered a small pile of dust that the Werewolf immediately began to dig through.

After what felt like an agonizingly long period of time, she withdrew the head of a woman, who coughed a puff of white dust into the air.

As they continued to dig through the rubble, they uncovered more and more of her body, until finally she was lifted free.

"Got her legs!" Jeremiah called, preparing to lift the overweight, middle-aged woman.

"Let's get her down!" Aders shouted, sliding into the hole beside Jeremiah, and grabbing her underneath her shoulders.

Jeremiah grabbed her ankles, as that was the only part of her legs not coated in a thick layer of bloody dust.

Moaning something unintelligible, the woman's head lolled back as they carried her down the slope, taking each sliding step arduously slow to avoid losing their footing and sending their rescuee careening down the steep embankment.

Jeremiah and Aders made it to the bottom and carried the woman's limp body another few yards before setting her down on the grass.

"Okay, alright... let's see," murmured Aders as he gripped the woman around her neck and slid his hands down before pulling away and looking at them. Nodding, he moved to her armpits, then between her upper thighs. "No major bleeding."

"Eh, her pulse seems alright," Jeremiah added, pinching the woman's wrist. "Looks like it's all superficial."

"Alright, good," Aders remarked and stood up. He blew out a breath. He nodded once at Jeremiah and extended a hand. "Tim."

"Jeremiah," Jeremiah replied with a small smile. He smirked at Jeremiah before passing a glance up the mound of rubble towards the two women at the top.

"Viola, how you holding up?" Tim questioned loudly, turning to the dusky-skinned, long-eared woman that held the dome of clean air for them.

"It would be easier," the woman growled as sweat dripped off her face, "if I didn't have to -talk-!"

"Elves, man," Aders said quietly and shook his head before nodding sideways towards the rubble again. "Let's ge-"

He cut off as the sirens suddenly sounded less distant, turning towards the direction of the sound. After a few seconds, an ambulance, then a fire truck, pulled onto the block and turned directly towards them.

"Fuck… shoulda' just stayed enlisted," Aders murmured, shaking his head. He turned to Jeremiah with a frown and pointed back towards the mound. "Get back up there and work with my team on retrieving casualties. I'm gonna take a few minutes down here and direct their manpower, alright?"

"Good luck with that," Jeremiah wished with a smirk before heading back towards the destroyed building.

The Captain grumbled under his breath as he began to jog in the opposite direction of Jeremiah - towards the approaching vehicles.

Jeremiah couldn't make out what was said as his foot met the first chunk of concrete, but he could absolutely tell what was being conveyed.

Captain Aders was taking charge of the situation and giving orders to the approaching first responders.

Time to go play search and rescue with the fucking Werewolf, I guess.

Jeremiah snickered to himself as he climbed ever higher.

* * *

Heavens this place turned into a circus real quick once the dust settled.

Jeremiah had long since been sidelined after

dozens of crews of firefighters, police, EMT's and agencies with acronyms he'd never even heard of swarmed the scene to search for injured and dead people in what was left of the building.

Initially, he was intensely worried about the three letter agencies on the scene, but it seemed that for the moment, they had significantly higher priorities than any lingering suspicions of him.

Beyond the mountain of rubble and crushed bodies in front of him, the swarms of news crews around the scene being cordoned off by lines of tired-looking police officers were something far more immediate and pressing for them to worry about.

Let's play count the news vans! One, two, two hundred...

Fuck, I'm going to have to make a side trip up to Canada just to lose anyone who saw my face on TV. I'm so far -over- the radar right now, they might not even think it's me.

That would just be too obvious.

That, and I'm covered in..whatever the fuck this dust is.

"Sir!" a diminutive, green-skinned man approached Jeremiah, wearing a backpack on his chest. "Water?"

Jeremiah lifted his head from where he rested on the stoop of a building across the street from the blast site, watching as the small army of police, firefighters, and EMT's searched for survivors.

One thing that surprised Jeremiah to no end was the fact that well over a solid third of the people scrambling on the rubble weren't human.

After the initial blast, people had begun to stream in, offering their help in any way they could. Some were human.

Others weren't.

"Yeah, thanks," Jeremiah offered a small smile as what he believed was a Goblin reached into the pack and withdrew a plastic water bottle before scuttling quickly away. He opened it, greedily slurping at the ice-cold liquid that seemed to ease his rasping throat.

Whatever was in that building...that dust sure isn't good for me.

Jeremiah shook his head and sighed before leaning back against the stone plinth.

"Yeah. Understood, sir," he heard Aders say into a cellphone pressed against his cheek as he walked slowly towards Jeremiah. "zero-eight-thirty tomorrow. We'll be there."

He pulled it away and tapped the screen.

"Mind if I borrow that?" Jeremiah asked with a tired smile as Aders continued to walk towards him, though quicker. "Need to phone a friend."

"Not this one," Aders replied, stuffing the phone into his breast pocket. He pulled a second phone out of a pocket on his left arm and held it up. "Government issue. This one's my personal cell, you can use that."

"Thanks," Jeremiah accepted the offered device as the Captain sat down beside him.

"Don't mention it," Tim groaned and leaned back on the steps beside Jeremiah.

Jeremiah stared blankly at the dial screen in his hand and tried to remember Jenny or Ashley's number.

Fuck, I've really been slipping, haven't I?

He chided himself as he tried to rip apart his memory to the day Ashley had returned with a small cell phone for him.

After a longer-than-comfortable span of seconds, he thought he had the right number. Dialing it, he waited and got an out-of-service tone.

Switching the last two numbers on a gamble, Jeremiah dialed again. This time, it didn't go to the void. After a few seconds of steady ringing, the line clicked audibly, and Jeremiah nearly exhaled an audible sigh of relief.

"H-hello?" Jenny's voice came over the line. "Who is this?"

"Hey Jenny," Jeremiah smiled widely as he heard her take in a sharp inhale of breath. "How a-"

"Where on Earth have you been? Me and Ash have been worrie- no, you can talk to hi-" Jenny's high-pitched reply was cut off as she argued with someone that Jeremiah could only believe was Ashley.

After a second of muffled arguing, he was proven right.

"Jeremiah? Are you alright? What happened? Jenny says you got kidnapped and pulled through a portal or something!" Ashley blurted over the line, her tone an odd mix of excitement and concern.

"Yeah, Ash... I'm fine. I'll tell you more about what happened when I get back," Jeremiah smiled as he replied, something about her tone warming him to his core. "Right now I'm in downtown Clallam. Think... well, can you guys send me a cab or something?"

"Oh yeah, I can do that, I'll order it right now!" Ash replied before the phone emitted several soft popping noises, followed by muffled speech.

"Well, she's excited," Jenny breathed out with a chuckle as the phone was apparently handed back to her. "For what it's worth, I'm glad you're safe too. Now where are you?"

"Downtown Clallam. Across from the old Fed building," Jeremiah answered before adding: "The same one that got bombed an hour or two ago."

"Jeremiah," Jenny replied with a clear question in her tone.

"Dunno who did it. I just helped with the search and rescue but got kicked out as more and more firefighters and police arrived," Jeremiah answered the unasked question clearly on her mind. "I'm covered in dust right now and it would be real nice to get home and take a shower. How soon can you guys have a cab here?"

"Eh, I can take you home if you need a ride, bud," Aders offered abruptly, causing Jeremiah to look over at the man, who appeared to be napping on the steps. His hands were folded behind his head, his eyes were closed, and for all intents and purposes, he wasn't moving. "Don't have anything better to do, and I bet my team is gonna be stuck with the cleanup crew for another few hours, given their abilities."

"You sure?" Jeremiah asked with a raised brow. "I live a couple hours outside of town."

"Eh, it's fine," Aders replied without moving anything but his hand, and only for a dismissive wave. "Even if I'm late, my team knows how to hurry up and wait.

"Besides, taxis won't be coming anywhere near this place for about a day, probably. Maybe longer if the investigators want to get uppity.

"You helped me carry that super fat lady down, so I'll help you get home. Seems like a square deal."

"Uhhh, well," Jeremiah replied into the line, shrugging as he decided to accept. "Looks like I just found a ride actually."

Chapter 24

"Take a right up here," Jeremiah instructed, pointing a finger to the county road that eventually led to Jenny's cabin. "We'll be on this road for a solid five, ten minutes."

"Roger," Aders reported with a nod. He scratched at the stubble on his face as he idly hit the blinker. Setting his right hand back on the steering wheel, he slowly turned down the dusty paved road and sighed. "You did good today. You Ex-military? Law Enforcement?"

"No," Jeremiah answered and shook his head slowly. He wedged his tongue between his teeth as he considered how to answer the question. "Just worked with a guy who was for a... long time. Taught me everything I know about, well... pretty much everything I know."

"Mmm," Aders grunted, briefly looking over to him with a frown, before staring back out the front of the vehicle. "Seems like he taught you right. Your dad?"

"Never knew my dad. Well... I think I met him right before the bombing, but it's complicated," Jeremiah answered maybe a bit too honestly. "The guy who actually taught me what I know, a lot of it was wrong."

"I dunno, bud. When that bomb went off there were probably... give or take, two thousand people in a square mile around it," Aders clicked his tongue and seemed to consider his next words before adding, "Sure, people eventually trickled in after the first responders got there, but out of that crowd? Only you and my team ran towards the blast.

"I'm willing to put some money on the idea that there were several police, and probably some off-duty Joes from the base in that crowd too."

The captain shrugged noncommittally, perhaps at his own words, as he stared out the front window of the vehicle with a sour expression.

"And they just up and ran. Waited until they thought things were clear before they came back. It's the smart move," the captain admitted, though there was a clear accusation to the words.

"But not the right move," Jeremiah finished where Aders had let the statement hang. A small smile teased the corner of the Captain's mouth as he began to nod slowly. Aders rolled his head to the side and clicked his tongue.

"Point I'm gettin' at is that the guy who taught you couldn't have been all bad," Aders redirected and waggled a finger at Jeremiah with a chuckle. "Ya' see, people don't hear a bomb go off, see a tidal wave of dust, and think 'Yeah, I'mma go fuck around in that' naturally. That's something that has to be taught, trained into you."

"Yeah, well, I dunno if it was worth it. The women I live with, one of them I tried to kill when I met her, and the other I threw a hissy fit at in a soup kitchen because she wasn't human," recounted Jeremiah. He shook his head and let out a breath. "And now I live with them. I don't have a fucking driver's license, any hope of a real future, but those two take care of me for some reason I'll never understand."

"Mmm, HF?" Aders asked, turning his head to look at Jeremiah with a raised brow.

"I was, yeah. Not anymore," admitted Jeremiah.

A strange thought flickered across his mind that he was being unordinarily chatty with the man. In some way it didn't feel abnormal either though.

It honestly reminded him of talking with Eddie in a way.

"Fair enough. I had a brief brush with them a few years back. Considered joining up, was an odd time in my life," Aders admitted with a laugh "My first run-in with the para world in any way I recognized was in the sandbox.

"Desert Elves had a platoon from my battalion pinned down and cut off from reinforcements. My unit was supposed to be playing QRF for them, but red tape got in the way.

"Somehow, third platoon went way off course during a routine search operation in Kazmandi and ended up crossing the border. Based on what I could figure, a big sandstorm hit and fucked with their nav equipment."

"And you're telling me this... why?" Jeremiah asked curiously and watched as the soldier stared out over the dashboard, clearly remembering something that wasn't left in the past.

"I'll get to that. So anyway, we keep trying to get permission to cross the border to get our boys out, but command can't risk starting a war with a nuclear-armed nation just because of fifty men. Hell, we can't even go in and drop supplies with a medivac chopper," the captain said and raised his eyebrows.

His shock remained with him long after it happened.

Aders chewed on his lower lip, staring out the front window darkly.

"So we get to wait over three weeks. Listening to the comms of the dudes stuck in a crumbling, thousand-year-old fort, as their buddies die all around them, trying to get command to just let us cross four miles of mountain terrain and get our men out," Aders continued, his voice slowing down. "In the end, command sat on their asses long enough that one dude going fuckin' Rambo on the local tribes was what brought them back.

"Guy killed so many Elves, so effectively, that the tribes just let them go.

Aders looked over to Jeremiah with a hard-to-read expression.

"There were only three of 'em left at that point. Three Marines and a flag," he continued, looking back to the road ahead. "That one Corporal did what two bitchy nations couldn't, and he did it by killin' Elves.

"Now, I was fresh outta boot camp back then, and as all impressionable lower enlisted are bound to do, I got the wrong message.

"Wanna solve problems around the world? Kill the non-humans."

Jeremiah watched Aders curiously, not understanding where this was leading to.

"Imagine my surprise when I put in a packet to go special forces, and suddenly find myself surrounded by Paras.

"Get shot, boom, all of a sudden, I've got some Werewolf carrying me back to the corpsman, who as it turns out, is a damned Elf.

"Got my ass pulled out of more fires than I can count by Paras just... being Paras," Aders shrugged before chuckling. "I like to think of them like a machinegun. Give a human a big fuckin gun and they can go kill dozens, maybe even hundreds of innocents.

"Or they can defend a home from an army of people that want their skull on a pike.

"Alternatively, they can just box it up and let the damn thing collect dust in a safe, no better, no worse than anyone else."

Aders tapped the side of his head, looking away from the road to turn to Jeremiah again with a smirk.

"What matters is up here. There's other things too, but... well, considering it sounds like you've got two Paras who you say have taken a liking to you, I'm sure you know just as well as I do. They can be rather different in how they show it," he finished with a short laugh and a wink at Jeremiah.

"I thought fraternization was illegal in the military," Jeremiah caught his drift. He was genuinely curious now.

"It would be, unless you get yourself caught in a multilateral shitstorm of geopolitical bullshit that your commanding officer drops on your plate, and now you have to deal with the consequences," Aders griped with a smile as Jeremiah raised a finger towards a small gap in the trees ahead.

"Up there," Jeremiah directed as Aders nodded and hit the blinker.

"Mmm, nice place," Aders noted as they pulled into the driveway. "Would love to get some land like this one day."

"Me too, it belongs to Jenny. More specifically, to her parents," Jeremiah noted as the van pulled to a stop. Again he felt like he was giving away too much information, but it just lined up too closely with how things went with Eddie. This felt entirely natural. "Ash had an apartment in the city, but we're uh... taking some time away that's looking more and more permanent."

"Running from something?" Aders asked, panning his eyes around the property.

"Got in a fight with a coven and pissed them off.

"Actually... you might be more equipped to deal with it than we are," Jeremiah said with a spark of inspiration, as he realized that although he couldn't pick a fight with a supernatural bullshit Vampire, the soldier beside him might have enough juice to take them down. "The coven in Clallam. Ran by a dude named Vasily."

"Hang on, I'm the grunt here, aren't I supposed to be recruiting you?" Aders asked with a quirked brow and looking to Jeremiah.

"I mean, typically. But you could just consider this a random tip you got," offered Jeremiah and threw his hands up in mock confusion. "But seriously, something fucked is going on with them.

"Lotta cops apparently on their payroll, and a Vamp that we were fighting fuckin... changed. Shifted, like the most fucked up Were transformation I've ever seen.

"Took multiple rifle and pistol rounds to the dome, and healed like it was nothing."

Jeremiah paused, considering his words. He really did feel like he was throwing way too much at Aders but he couldn't stop himself at this point.

"We can't handle it. But I'm sure you know someone who can," Jeremiah finished, staring at the captain.

The man didn't actually say anything in return, he just stared at Jeremiah for several seconds.

"Just saying, take a look into them," urged Jeremiah with a nod of his head, then he opened the door and stepped out of the vehicle.

Surprisingly, Aders also stepped out of the van, scratching his stubble thoughtfully as he seemed to consider what Jeremiah had just told him.

"No promises, but I'll pass it along," Aders confirmed and stepped around the front of the car.

He extended a hand to Jeremiah.

Jeremiah accepted the handshake, smiling back at the man.

When he withdrew his hand, in his palm was a business card.

Jeremiah frowned down at it before looking back up to Aders.

"If something goes sideways and you need help, give me a call. Call it a favor owed for me not having to haul people down by myself," Aders remarked as he stepped back towards the driver's side of the van. "If you find more intel on this coven, drop it in that email.

"I'll see it and pass it along to whoever I think needs it. Can't promise anything though. Need read receipts for read receipts to confirm the receipt.

"Then they ask why you never sent it and suddenly you're wondering if it's still in your damn outbox."

With that being said Aders stepped into the van and closed the door.

The engine started up, and he backed out of the parking spot. Just before the van began its way down the driveway, the passenger side rolled down and Aders yelled:

"Good luck with your girlfriends!"

"Asshole," Jeremiah muttered with a grin, rolling his eyes and taking the first step onto the porch.

He extended a hand to knock on the door but froze.

In a way, this was his home. Why did he feel like he needed to knock?

Shrugging, Jeremiah opened the door and walked in to find Ashley sitting down in the recliner.

She was immaculately put together right now. From hair, to makeup, to even her clothes, she was as picture perfect as could be.

Other than the near massive pout and sorrowful expression she had on her face. One that left him feeling guilty without even knowing why.

Jenny was sat down on the sofa, her hands pressed between her knees, and staring down at the ground. She didn't lift her head up to even look at him.

Her focus was her feet and little else.

"You hurt me, Jeremiah," she drawled and then wrinkled her nose. "Close the door. You'll let in the bugs."

His heart quivered in his chest as he heard the words. They struck him far deeply than he honestly expected them to.

In a way he didn't think was possible, in fact.

"Do you know how, Jeremiah?" she pressed, her pretty face watching him with eyes that looked almost ready to tear over.

"I... ah... that... Jenny and I-we... that is—" his words failed him, and he stood there floundering. Feeling as if he desperately wanted to go back to the blast site and dig for survivors.

That felt infinitely easier at the moment.

"Yes. You and Jenny. Though... I feel a little better, since it's obvious you know why I'm hurt. Don't you?" she asked, the pout slowly fading.

Erasing itself as she watched him.

"Pretty sure of it, yeah," Jeremiah confirmed, though he really didn't know how or what to say.

"Well... that's good then. Then please have a seat. It's obvious we have some things to talk about," Ashley said, pointing a finger in Jenny's direction, then Jeremiah's, then to herself before repeating the small triangle. "Because the two of you surprised me. Ah, not that you two did what you did, but it was sooner than I expected.

"I wasn't quite ready for what happened which... well... it's a bit of my fault. But still! I thought maybe I would get to be... well... well, anyways. We— we should talk, yes."

"Uhhh," Jeremiah got out dumbly, licking his lips and feeling very much like he was out of his depth.

Jenny didn't respond or even move. Whatever was happening, she'd clearly gotten some type of conversation directed at her before this.

Given her posture, it didn't look as if it were terrible, but it had clearly been out of expectation.

"Can I shower first?" he tried, wondering if he could possibly catch a chance to think.

"Nope!" Ashley replied with a warm smile. She lifted one hand and pointed several times at the couch.

When he went over and sat down in it, she lifted her hand again and motioned him toward Jenny. He slid closer to her, then did so again when Ashley kept motioning to do so.

Now much closer to Jenny, Jeremiah looked to Ashley.

Looking pleased with herself, she got out of the recliner. Walking over to the kitchen table, she grabbed a chair and dragged it back to sit across from them.

Or more accurately, directly in front of the two of them.

"Goodness, you really are dusty," Jenny noted with a frown as Ashley planted herself in the chair.

"Playing in asbestos for a few hours will do that to ya'," Jeremiah confirmed with a small bob of his head. Ashley glanced between the two thoughtfully as she wore a pleasant, unreadable smile on her face.

When nothing more was said, Ashley's smile grew by several degrees, then she sighed. Getting up she moved to him and hugged him tightly.

"I… I'm so glad you're okay. Despite everything else, regardless of anything that happened, I'm truly… truly glad you're okay," whispered the Vampire. Hugging him with enough strength that it actually made him wheeze.

Whatever tension that'd been between them up to this moment was gone in that simple action. Jeremiah found himself hugging her back.

"Thanks. I was… I'll be honest, there was a minute there was I was pretty nervous," admitted Jeremiah.

Ashley grunted at that, squeezed him harder for just a moment, then, surprisingly, laid a kiss on his lips. The faint lingering taste of her lipstick left him guessing as to what it was.

She sat back down on the chair heavily and looked to the two of them with a wide smile.

He was no longer sure about what was even happening.

No matter how hard he flogged his mind to get into gear, he couldn't seem to catch it. The gears were slipping faster than a blown-out transmission on a chewed-up truck used for a driving school.

"Okay, so! This might be a little awkward to talk about, but frankly, I think it's the best choice for us, as a group," Ashley murmured and leaned back in her seat. She crossed one leg over the other, brushing an errant lock of pale brown hair out of her green eyes. All signs of her being hurt were gone. "And frankly, with us being the only people that have each other's backs right now, I feel like doing everything possible to keep us together is important."

Jeremiah sat there listening, though he was a bit concerned as well.

"Part of this is on me, I knew you two would come about eventually, but I didn't expect it to happen so soon," Ashley admitted, and folded her hands in her lap. She focused pointedly on Jeremiah. "And I'm gonna get this out of the way at the start; I'm upset with both of you. Not mad, just upset.

"Jeremiah, I've been practically bombarding you with massive fucking hints for two weeks now, that I know you've picked up on.

"I've listened to your heartbeat skyrocket when I flirt with you, and I've certainly noticed all the peeks you sneak at me when you think I'm not looking."

Jeremiah leaned back in his seat, folding his arms across his chest, trying to search for a way to deny what she was accusing him of, but dropped the thought process when she arched a brow.

Her smile went from warm to blisteringly cold, as she apparently saw right through him. Jeremiah licked his lips, sighed, and then nodded twice.

"Good," she said, her smile becoming genuine again. She turned her head the other way, her hair spilling around her shoulder as she looked at Jenny. "As for you, Jenny, I know I've turned you down for... a while.

"That wasn't because I didn't like you. It wasn't because I was disinterested, or—" Ashley inhaled deeply and seemed to compose herself. "I wasn't in a good headspace. Frankly, it took you and Jeremiah running face-first into problems that wouldn't have even been yours if you hadn't met me to snap me out of it.

"At first, I felt torn because I managed to catch feelings for both of you at the same time."

Ashley was most certainly in the driver's seat, and no one responded at all.

"Not even little ones either," Ashley confessed with a frown. She shook her head and ran her tongue underneath an elongated canine as she stared deeply into Jenny's eyes. "And so, I worried about pursuing either one of you until I noticed something.

"The same pulse, the same fluttering rush of blood away from your brains that I could smell, that I could hear whenever you looked at me?"

She paused in her monologue to let loose a giggle.

It had a predatory edge and she leaned forward. Giving everyone looking a lovely view down her blouse.

"That. That right there. That increase in your heart rate. It was happening when you two looked at each other," she murmured. "When you argued over something pointless, or when you accidentally bumped into each other after Jenny hopped out of the shower the other week.

"That beat was there."

Ashley leaned back in her seat and extended

her hands towards Jeremiah and Jenny, as if delivering a revelation.

"I like the both of you, you two like each other, and the both of you like me," she said, as if that were as simple as it needed to be. Her smile grew blisteringly bright levels. "We have two choices at this point: either we can have a normal relationship, and one of us will always get hurt, or, my idea. We throw caution to the wind, tell society to go fuck itself, and be honest."

"Ash," Jenny began, raising a finger to ask a question. "Are you suggesting that we… all date each other? Just to be clear."

"That is exactly what I'm suggesting, Jenny," Ashley snapped her fingers and pointed at the Demon-Knight. "Everybody's happy that way. Depending on what the coven does over the coming weeks, and when we decide to go after them, we might not have long together.

"I, for one, want to make the most of that time. I want the both of you beside me, holding me as I fall asleep, and waking up to your arms around me."

Initially, Jeremiah recoiled at the idea, then froze.

Wait no.

Jeremiah internally smacked down his train of thought.

Ash is right. These two women have done practically everything for me when no one else would.
If they want to…split me, then I'm going all-in.
Besides.
Two girlfriends.
I would be a prissy idiot to turn that down.

"Jenn?" Jeremiah turned slightly to look at the

Demon-Knight, who chewed at her lip thoughtfully. "How do you feel about this?"

"I'm... I'm not—" Jenny trailed off as she shrugged, chuckled absently, and shook her head. "I'm not opposed, really. I'm a little concerned that this is just going to be the overcomplicated, too-many-steps path to the same destination as just making a choice now and sticking with it. What if we get jealous, or—"

Ashley darted forward and planted a small peck on Jenny's lips, before repeating the gesture for Jeremiah with an equally brief kiss. Sitting back down in her chair, she looked between both of them.

"Jeremiah, did me kissing Jenny make you jealous just then?" Ashley asked with a knowing smile.

"Uh... no," Jeremiah shook his head after a moment's consideration. In truth, he had felt something at their brief kiss, but it certainly wasn't jealousy.

"Jenny, were you jealous when I kissed Jeremiah?" Ashley asked after nodding at Jeremiah's reply.

"I mean... nah, I wasn't," Jenny shook her head thoughtfully. "More than anything, I think I kinda... liked it?"

"Good. Now, the both of you, kiss each other," Ashley demanded, making a small smooshing motion with her hands, miming the two of them coming together.

Jeremiah looked over to Jenny at the same second she turned to him, a faint blush appearing on her cheeks as she murmured the word "okay" under her breath. Leaning in, Jeremiah kissed Jenny's soft lips for a fraction of a second longer than he had

Ashley's.

"See?" Ashley said brightly as they parted, gesturing towards her chest. "Not jealous! Turned on a little bit, but I'm not jealous, or upset."

Ashley pushed herself off the chair and knelt down in front of Jeremiah and Jenny as she grabbed both of their hands at the same time, holding them tight against her chest.

"I know it's weird, I know it's not conventional, but neither are we," Ashley said, looking from person to person with hopeful eyes. "I want both of you by my side for a long time, and for us to experience what life has to offer… together. So, what do you say?"

"Alright," Jenny was the first to answer, exhaling a deep breath and shaking her head with a smile that grew brighter by the second. "I'm willing to give this whole thing a shot."

Jeremiah took a moment longer, digging deep through his mind as he considered the ramifications of what he was about to do.

"Yeah… all-in."

Jeremiah nodded once and Ashley squealed excitedly, flinging her arms out wide and drawing the both of them into a deep embrace that only managed to smush Jeremiah's head next to Jenny's, and both their faces buried in Ashley's bountiful chest.

This… this is about to get really weird, isn't it?

Chapter 25

Jeremiah stepped out of the bathroom, rubbing his still-damp hair with a towel, as the smell of freshly cooked food filled his nose.

Jeremiah was suddenly aware of how hungry he was, practically moaning when he smelled the seared meat and spices.

Apparently, his rather hectic day had both sapped him of energy and caused him to completely forget his hunger, which now reared its ugly head by way of aggressive stomach growls.

Pausing to toss the towel back onto the bathroom vanity, Jeremiah set out for the kitchen and grinned when he saw Jenny carrying a large steel bowl piled high with spaghetti to the table.

Ashley swayed her hips as she stirred the pan full of sauce and meatballs on the stove, music playing quietly from the phone sat beside her on the countertop.

Despite what Jeremiah would have assumed, he'd discovered that Ashley had a knack and love for cooking.

Frequently, he'd found himself being pushed out of the kitchen while making the pair breakfast for doing it "wrong".

All Ashley required to dine with Jenny and Jeremiah was a little of their "sauce," as she referred to it, poured over the meal.

"Mmm, I think that's good enough!" Ashley said, doing one final stir of the meatballs before pulling the pan off the stove. She turned off the burner and walked over to the table to set the pan on a small pad. "Perfect timing too!"

Ashley smiled up at Jeremiah as he walked to the table and sat down.

Taking a seat shortly before Ashley, he pursed his lips thoughtfully while reaching out for the bowl of spaghetti and serving himself before passing it to Ashley.

"So," Jeremiah said, and broke the brief lull in conversation as he scooped several meatballs onto his plate. "I feel like we need to talk about what happened to me last night."

"I... thought we already had that figured out," Ashley murmured with a smile and looked at him in a hard-to-read way.

"Not that part," Jeremiah answered, and shook his head as he passed her the meatballs and sauce before continuing, "The man who... kidnapped me, wasn't just anyone. He's my... creator? Dad? Eh, something like that."

He paused to consider his words, then gave up on thinking about it.

"Also met his wife, who seems to have all the common sense between the two of them," Jeremiah added with a small shrug, as Ashley's grin brightened by several degrees. "But yeah, mom and dad, or at least the closest I can get. Since they made me."

Jeremiah slowly began to mix his sauce and meatballs into the spaghetti as he thought of what to say next, having failed to completely process the events of the day himself.

"Well?" Jenny asked, causing him to look up at the woman seated across from him. "What else? He just ups and kidnaps you with zero darn explanation and that's all you ha-"

Jenny cut off abruptly as Ashley reached over

and gripped her hand, giving it a small squeeze while she lowered her left hand towards the table.

Clearly directing the Demon-Knight to calm down.

"I'm sure he's just working through it himself, dear," Ashley added after a moment's pause, before turning to Jeremiah and nodding.

Jeremiah took this as tacit approval to continue and inhaled a breath.

"So... the uh, the Fae at the store were right. My core was pretty messed up apparently and the best Reixhitz and Tiff could do was to put more or less the equivalent of a band-aid on it," explained Jeremiah. He took a bite of the food and quickly followed it with another, before swallowing and continuing. "I was pretty close to turning into a walking bomb, at least from what he told me. I'm good, I'm stable now, but... I'm running on a low battery.

"As far as I understand-" Jeremiah took another bite, swallowed, and frowned. "If I do any more high-energy stuff like blowing myself up... well, I won't have long."

"You don't say," Jenny added with raised brows and a barely hidden smirk.

"I know, right?" Jeremiah smiled back as he took another bite. "Almost like that's bad for you or something. A healthy diet of explosions apparently isn't a good thing, and for most people, would be a once in a lifetime event."

Jenny rolled her eyes as Ashley seemed to consider what he'd said carefully, pouring a small ramekin of blood over her meal like gravy.

"What does this mean for us?" Ashley asked, balling the spaghetti on her fork and taking a bite.

"I don't really think it means anything's changed," Jeremiah said and shook his head thoughtfully. "We're still gonna have to lie low for a while, not take any major risks that we can't afford.

"Once the... blow-back dies down about what we did to Aiden, we'll start digging into the coven more, that's if the Fed doesn't work to take it down on its own."

Ashley inhaled, leaning back in her seat as she chewed thoughtfully on a meatball. She closed her eyes and licked her lips before exhaling and nodding quickly. Then, a smile broke through her expression, and she looked between Jeremiah and Jenny.

"As... as long as I have you two, I'll be happy," Ashley said with distant eyes and a bright smile.

"Hear, hear," Jenny added, lifting her soda can skyward. Jeremiah chuckled and brought his glass of water to her drink, then to Ashley's.

Don't get the people you care about caught up in your foolish crusade.

Jeremiah remembered Reixhitz's warning as he began to drink. Maybe what'd felt half-hearted about at the start was more real than he'd thought.

* * *

Jeremiah awoke the next morning feeling incredibly refreshed.

Sitting up in the bed, he looked to the two women still fast asleep next to him, as the sunlight backlit the curtains of the room.

The cool, soft skin of Ashley's back was

pressed against his right side, and Jenny's warm figure was against his left.

She took slow, deep breaths, looking serene in a way she rarely did as he internally worked out how to extricate himself from the small pile without waking them.

Eventually, he managed to escape through wriggling and contorting himself between the two women.

He sat on the foot of the queen-sized bed for a moment, scratching at the short beard on his cheeks thoughtfully.

We're gonna be here for a while, it looks like.
I should get a good routine going.

He idly thought, standing up and grabbing a pair of sweatpants from the dresser.

Been a while since I had a good run. That'd be nice, actually.

When Jeremiah returned from his run half an hour later, he felt odd. His "morning" exercise had been a struggle.

Not a struggle to maintain his speed, but a struggle to feel winded, to feel like any physical exertion was happening at all.

It had ended with him sprinting at full tilt for the final mile and only then did his heart rate increase in intensity.

The fuck did Reixhitz do to me?

Jeremiah considered his newfound endurance as he approached the front door of the cabin, the brisk morning breeze blowing ice into his veins.

Sweat and cold breeze.
Always a good way to cool down after a run.

He opened the door and found both Jenny and Ashley sitting at the kitchen table, drinking from steaming mugs and simultaneously turning to look to Jeremiah with bleary eyes.

"Morning you two. Or uh, afternoon," Jeremiah smiled at his girlfriends while closing the door behind him. "Sleep well?"

"Mmmm," Jenny grunted and took another sip of her coffee.

"We did!" Ashley grinned back at him as she took another sip of the dark liquid in her mug. "You?"

"I was certainly—" Jeremiah pursed his lips and nodded slowly. "Comfortable."

Jenny narrowed her eyes and glared at him, and Ashley began to faintly blush.

"Good. I'm glad! Now, tonight is date night," Ashley declared and nodded firmly.

Jeremiah walked over the refrigerator and pulled out a carton of eggs from beside a bag of blood. Setting about making "breakfast" for himself, he strolled over to the stove and turned it on.

It didn't take him long at all to be finished, since eggs were the simplest thing in the world to fire-off.

"Jeremiah?" Ashley asked in a small voice as she placed her burrito on the table in front of her, looking up at him with a smile. "Could I... get some fresh blood for this? The stuff in the fridge is kinda starting to go stale. And uh... coagulated. It gets clumpy."

"Uh, yeah, sure. Let me just go get the good knife," Jeremiah agreed with a nod and walked to the bedroom.

"I'll get the equipment for a blood draw set up later today," Jenny offered as he walked away. "Get some fresh supply for you. I know it's been a week or two since we really got one going. Though we'll need to be a bit more sparing with the anti-coagulant till I get more. So… more frequent blood draws."

Jeremiah returned to find that Ashley had unwrapped her burrito mostly, and was sitting sideways in her chair, clearly waiting on him with eager eyes. He approached, handed her the knife, and left his arm hovering above her burrito, staring fixedly into the wall beyond.

By this point, he'd become accustomed to her partner-feeding on him whenever they watched TV, and her habit of sprinkling blood on everything she ate.

Still, the act of dangling a bleeding limb above her food was a decidedly uncomfortable moment for him.

As the blade kissed his skin, he took in a slow inhale of breath and let his skin be split just beyond his wrist. He waited for close to a minute, opening and closing his hand as his blood dripped onto the meal beneath until softly, gingerly, Ashley kissed the wound.

Then she licked it several times.

When she removed her mouth, Jeremiah looked down to find the cut sealed shut, before Ashley pulled him gently, yet firmly down.

She kissed him on the lips, then the cheek, then whispered in his ear,

"Thank you. I know how weird this is for you."

Ashley released his arm as Jeremiah straightened back out, smiling beatifically up at him.

She's too damn cute.

Jeremiah emptied out the skillet of his eggs, flicked them into the tortilla, then grabbed his seat.

Date night is gonna be fun... speaking of which-

"So... what was the plan for date night?" he asked, before swallowing a bite of burrito, earning a nonplussed look from Jenny.

"I'm honestly not sure," Ashley began, throwing her head to each side thoughtfully as she happily chewed on a bite of her sauced burrito. "Anything in the city is off the table... but there's not much to do here in town."

"What if we did something during the day?" Jenny asked with a thoughtful expression, looking between Jeremiah and Ashley. "National forest land is just down the way."

"They've got a bunch of designated shooting areas there. My ma' goes all the time whenever she visits."

"What if we go there, bring the guns and some targets and just—" Jenny pursed her lips and frowned before shrugging. "Blow off some steam? We have the guns, and we have the ammo."

Jeremiah thought back to the closet in their room stacked with duffel bags full of ammo, beneath a small pile of rifles.

Looking to Ashley, he found her seeming to chew through that information slowly.

"I'm not opposed... but how would we make that a date?" Ashley asked after a moment, looking to Jeremiah and Jenny. "Would that really be fun?"

"I mean, there's something really satisfying about mag-dumping," Jeremiah replied with a wide grin. "I wonder if the hardware store in town sells exploding targets?"

"Oooh! We've got some junk in the shed out back!" Jenny added with a rapidly broadening grin. "I think there's an old microwave in there, and a couple of TVs! We could fill them full of tannerite and see who's the first to hit them if we can find a big enough range!"

"That seems like a terrible idea," Jeremiah noted with a wide grin. "I can't wait."

"Uhhh... what's tannerite?" Ashley asked, looking between the two of them with a nervous, confused expression. She wrinkled her nose as Jenny grinned even wider and leaned forward.

"So, it's this powder, right? You mix it up, set it a ways away, and shoot it," Jenny explained with bright eyes and a feral smile. "If you hit it, it explodes!"

"That sounds... dangerous," Ashley murmured with raised eyebrows and pursed lips.

"Well, yeah!" Jenny agreed and shrugged. She rolled her head to the side, the faint red mist beginning to pour from her nose. "I mean, it's guns and explosives. The danger is half the fun!"

"At least we've got a good medic on hand," Jeremiah added and leaned back in his seat, his burrito finished.

"That we do," Ashley allowed with a fractional nod before licking her lips and shrugging. "Okay, you know what? I'll give it a try. If you two think it will be fun, then it's probably going to be fun."

Jenny pumped her fist and grinned, leaning back in her chair before quickly finishing off her burrito.

"Okay, I'mma head into town and see if they have any," Jenny said before pointing at Jeremiah. "Can you... walk her through some safety stuff and dry fire beforehand, so when we get there, we can just set up the targets and go off?"

"Yeah, I can do that," Jeremiah nodded and grinned. "I'll walk her through the basics first, and then teach her how to clear each one we have."

"Sounds good!" Jenny pushed her seat back, stood up, and kissed Jeremiah and Ashley before she grabbed her jean jacket off a small coatrack by the door, and exited the house.

"So," Jeremiah said, grinning at Ashley as she pushed the last, gargantuan bite of burrito into her mouth, freezing stock-still as she watched him with wide, deer-in-the-headlights eyes. Leaning forward slightly, she swallowed and followed it up with a large gulp from her mug. "Wanna go play with some guns?"

* * *

Jeremiah pulled the phone away from his ear with a frustrated sigh.

It was his fourth attempt to call Eddie, and he'd found that it no longer rang, now it just went straight to voicemail. Perhaps after all these years the number had in fact changed, and Jeremiah was just aggressively bothering some random nobody in Larimer.

That, or Eddie just didn't want to talk to him.

Well, I suppose I am acting kind of like the psychotic ex. If he is really there, he might be busy, or maybe he wants nothing do to with what HF was back in the day.

Jeremiah shrugged, turned the key in the ignition, and exited the SUV.

He did have a mission to complete, after all.

Walking through the parking lot, Jeremiah stewed bemusedly at the reality that he'd been more or less conned into this by his girlfriends.

The sliding doors of the local "supermarket" slid open ahead of Jeremiah.

The fact that one could even consider it that said more about the nature of the mountain village than anything else. The store was barely even a quarter the size of a small supermarket in the city.

Ideally, it would have all the things he needed to fulfill his end of the bet.

The bet he'd lost at the shooting range of all places.

As it turned out, not only was Jenny a better shot than him, but she also plotted with Ashley, resulting in his inevitable loss in an impromptu target-shooting competition.

The end result left him being in charge of making a semi-lavish dinner for the women.

Jeremiah snorted and smiled sideways to himself, fondly annoyed at the devious play, as he leaned down to pick up one of the small baskets with a folding handle beside the door.

Gonna be the best steak and potatoes you've ever had, Jenny.

Make you feel bad about playing dirty and making me use that crappy revolver.

A cashier who was decidedly inhuman glanced up and over a newspaper in their hands. If Jeremiah had to use a word to describe the person, he would put his finger on the "zombie" category.

In truth, he didn't know what the person was, or even what gender they were, but something about the cold, cataract-white eyed stare, made Jeremiah feel unsettled. Alarm bells rang out as the person cocked their head to the side and continued to stare fixedly at Jeremiah.

Jeremiah broke eye contact first, pulling his eyes back to the front and towards the aisles, as a creeping chill climbed its way down his spine.

It's just a para. They're not trying to hurt you, they're just working their day job.

Jeremiah made a sharp right turn and headed for the produce section, working overtime at quelling the sudden burst of paranoia he felt. He suddenly wished he'd worn a hat and a hoodie, maybe even some sunglasses despite it being sunset.

Something to cover his tattoos and give him a shred of anonymity.

Jeremiah shook himself out like a wet dog before grabbing several of the largest potatoes he could find in the display. He glanced up and over the tubers and caught a woman that looked human watching him with a confused expression, as if debating whether or not he was a threat, as she put a box of pre-made salad into her cart.

Ah..yeah, normal people don't twitch out in the market like a crackhead.

She brushed a lock of hair up behind her ear and gave him a neutral smile before quickly walking away.

As calmly, sedately, and inconspicuously as he could, Jeremiah made his way over to the meat section of the store, some of his irrational fears being quieted as he picked through several rows of mouth-watering steaks.

He selected four of them that looked the freshest and put them in the basket on his arm.

Absently, Jeremiah glanced over to the door of the store and had to press down the instinct to dart for cover.

A Clallam city police officer stood in the door. He wore body armor, and seemed to tower over everything around him. The officer's head was just several inches shorter than the top of the sliding door.

Walking at a casual pace, Jeremiah stepped up to the end of an aisle, acting like he was contemplating buying one of the many rolls of paper towels, as he watched the officer around the edge of the display.

He transferred the basket of groceries to his left arm and hooked his thumb over his belt on his right hip.

Right atop his gun.

Jeremiah knew the pistol at his hip most likely wouldn't pierce the armor of the officer, who just stood by the front door menacingly.

So...I think I could find a way out the back, but if there's already officers here for me, they probably have the place surrounded.

But how did Vasily find us? And why did he send police on his payroll after me too?

An almost comically smaller police officer stepped up beside the towering man before heading towards the counter. She had sergeant's stripes on her arms and seemed to exude a casual confidence as her partner followed her like a puppy on a leash.

Jeremiah watched as the mountain of a man patiently waited for the diminutive woman beside him to pay for her cigarettes, and then followed her back out the door.

Jeremiah exhaled a deep sigh of relief and pulled his hand down the front of his face, realizing that he'd just nearly pulled his gun in a supermarket over nothing. Just two officers buying cigarettes.

Miles away from their jurisdiction.

For some reason.

I should keep an eye out for more... there was no real reason for them to be here, this far out of town.

Chapter 26

Jeremiah exited the supermarket after triple-checking the list prepared by Ashley and Jenny.

Just one more stop... this oughta be fun.

He threw the bagged items in the back of the SUV, closed the door and entered the driver's seat.

Let's hope this goes easier than last time. Really don't want to have to shoot the lightning-bitch on date night.

A short drive later and Jeremiah was parked in front of the liquor store, staring up and over the steering wheel through the windows of the shop.

He slowly panned his head from left to right, searching for the diminutive, blue-eyed menace. Jeremiah blew out a breath and shook his head, seeing only Denise's mother at the counter.

Here goes nothing.

Rolling his eyes, he stepped out of the car.

As the door slammed closed behind him with an unobtrusive tinkle of bells, Denise's mother looked up from the counter.

Her face blossomed into a wide smile.

"It's good to see you again!" she tilted her head to the side as her monochrome, glowing blue eyes seemed to search him. "You look like you're doing better. I take it the potion worked?"

"I'm sure it did but just not in the way anyone expected," Jeremiah murmured slowly, pausing to look at the list his girlfriends had sent him with. "Just in a roundabout way. About an hour or two after I drank it, my... dad? Creator? The guy who made me showed up to chat. Apparently, my core was pretty close to blowing up."

Jeremiah shrugged and began to walk towards the aisle that held Ashley's preferred mixer.

"So I was right," He heard the woman say under her breath from behind him. Jeremiah searched for the mango-strawberry flavor that the Vampire preferred when he heard a small clatter behind him as the woman exited the register area. "Did your maker tell you anything? Are you working for them again?"

"I don't really think any of that is your business," Jeremiah answered, then faced the Fae. She stopped at the end of the aisle and folded her hands demurely in front of her waist.

"At a passing glance, no, it isn't," she shook her head slowly and watched him with an amused smirk. "That being said, this store is... more than just a place for those seeking to quench their thirst."

"Mmm, cryptic," remarked Jeremiah. He held her gaze for a moment, then looked back to the alcohol. "And here I thought all the legends about Fae being tricksters was just bullshit."

"Partially," she noted after a moment's pause with a slight edge to her voice. "We do love our deals."

Jeremiah grabbed the bottle that he was searching for and began to walk to the other side for Jenny's preferred wine.

"Golems need essence to survive," the woman noted behind him, causing Jeremiah to momentarily halt his steps.

"Built with a net-zero system balance, ma'am," Jeremiah informed her, turning fractionally to the woman. "I'm more than happy to just sit still and do nothing. Live my life.

"Besides, I'm probably gonna stop coming here if I keep getting bitched at by the two of you."

"I'm not... -bitching-," she replied in a tight but polite tone, as he heard her footsteps approach him. "I'm offering additional services to a member of the community. Golems are like any other species or machine, they need regular maintenance.

"Humans go to hospitals, the Wood-Elves go to their shamans, and Golems are no different.

"If your maker has offered more than I can provide, I understand completely."

Listening, Jeremiah didn't say anything. He was now regretting being as forthcoming with information as he had been.

"That being said, most enchanters tend to be... rather emotionless to their creations," the woman continued in a smooth, calming tone, "I see that you have carved out a chunk of life for yourself.

"You have a clear partner in that lovely young Demon-Knight. If your maker is different and has offered you what you need to survive on your own, that is well, and I will not take offense.

"But, if there is, in fact, something that you need that they will not provide, please, contact me."

Jeremiah turned onto the aisle that held the wine Jenny liked and paused in front of a display.

"I... I can eat other Golems," Jeremiah confessed and flicked out his wrist. He showed her the translucent spike. "Drain them like a Vampire. According to Reixhitz, my core is so fucked up that there's no other way to charge me up, except to pull from Golems. Like popping the batteries out of a remote and putting in fresh ones."

"Oh... that's odd," she noted as Jeremiah looked over with a frown.

"Yeah, me and my fucked up, weird little world," Jeremiah remarked before looking back to the rack of wine and selecting a bottle. "Personally, I'd rather not deal with a messed-up dilemma of draining another person like me just to keep using flashy powers that I don't even understand. So now I'm just going to do my best to live like a normal human being. Hell, that's what I'm doing here-"

Jeremiah lifted and shook the mixer in his hand demonstratively.

"-date night. I got volun-told to make dinner for the two of them, and this is the booze portion of it," he continued with a shrug. He grabbed a bottle of wine that he believed was his target. "I'm trying to just live my life while I can, with the two women who've decided to put me back together after I woke up homeless in Clallam."

"There's two of them?" the woman asked with a small, barely audible giggle.

"Yeah. Vampire and a Demon-Knight," Jeremiah added with a small grin and an absent nod, before looking back to the smiling, ageless, yet matronly woman. "Not sure why they've both taken a shine to me after I was such an ass, but I can't complain."

"I'm sure you can't," agreed the woman. Her large blue eyes stared deep into him as an understanding smile tugged at the corners of her mouth. "I would like to make you an... offer, however. No strings attached. And you're welcome to say no at any point in time."

Jeremiah stared at the rack of wine thoughtfully as he considered what negative effects could come from accepting a Fae's offer. Inhaling sharply before blowing out a breath, he shrugged.

"I'm listening."

"Golems are unique to their creators. The way magic flows through their bodies, their mental capabilities, even their appearance, is all tailored by their creators for a purpose.

"I can give you a tincture, for free, that would allow me to better understand you and how you work," she explained. Jeremiah furrowed his brow, as the offer sent all kinds of alarm bells ringing in his gut. "From that point, if there is something I can do, I will be able to craft potions specifically for you and your needs.

"They might be as simple as a maintenance routine. Perhaps I can find some solution your creator couldn't as well, and we can undo the damage to your core."

"That sounds... a lot like giving you the keys to making me your slave," Jeremiah replied archly, fully turning to stare at the lithe woman as she brushed a lock of hair behind a long, pointed ear.

"You would be... correct, but wrong as well," she agreed, nodding with a neutral expression on her face. "Though I would ask, when you allow a mechanic to work on your car, do you not give them your keys? You trust them to not drive away into the sunset with your vehicle, and why is that?"

"Because they don't need a fucking car. They need customers. Also, I'm not a damned car!" Jeremiah shot back, folding his arms across his chest with a sour expression.

"Correct. On all counts," the woman answered, folding her arms across her chest in a mirror to Jeremiah's stance, and he began to feel something radiate from her. "Jeremiah, I have lived in this forest for a long time.

"I was already old when Europeans rediscovered this continent. I assure you, I do not - need- a war Golem.

"When people from other cities, nations, and continents come to visit my home for my wares, I charge them exorbitant prices because I need not worry about their distant lives."

Old as old could be, I guess.

"But you live here. As I also chose to do many centuries ago, you have decided to make these woods your home.

"In truth, if you find yourself as enraptured by these mountains as I am, I may still run this shop when your grandchildren leave home to find their own lives," said the woman with a building of power to her words. The aura around her began to dissipate as she exhaled a deep breath. "I care for those whose descendants may ask for my aid, because I am not an island. There are things that I need as anyone else. Food, water, shelter, and friendship."

Jeremiah gulped deeply as she smiled sadly and the power that seemed to pour out of her cut off abruptly.

"My help will not be free, but the cost will be fair," she said after a brief pause, looking at him with a resolute, unreadable expression. "As I sell alcohol at the market price, I will not trick you into an underhanded deal. What I offer for free is a consultation of sorts. I will tell you what I find wrong, and then you are free to accept my aid or not."

Jeremiah looked into her eyes before he closed his own. With a deep exhale, he slowly began to shake his head, and then nodded.

"Sure, fine. Fuck it, why not?" He declared, threw his arms up beside him and rolled his eyes.

"Lovely. I will be by your home soon to drop off the tracing tincture," she smiled brightly as Jeremiah adjusted his grip on the bottle of wine. "Are you ready to check out now?"

* * *

Jeremiah checked his watch and nodded before pulling the tray of foil-wrapped potatoes out of the oven.

He briefly glanced over at his phone before continuing with the next step of the recipe.

Two distinct sets of footsteps exiting the bedroom - which he had not been allowed into for the past hour - caused him to turn fractionally to talk over his shoulder.

"Finally de- duh... woah," Jeremiah trailed off and snapped his head back around to see if his eyes had, in fact, lied to him.

Ashley smiled radiantly, looking between him and Jenny, her hands placed on the hips of her green dress.

Ashley looked positively dazzling in a tight-fitting, deep emerald dress that hugged tight to her upper body before flowing out around her wide hips.

The shape of the dress emphasized Ashley's substantial bust, and seemed to deliberately draw his eyes to her cleavage, which was actively threatening to spill out.

But what Ashley proudly beamed at, however, was Jenny.

Jeremiah followed the Vampire's eyes to a sight that he honestly didn't expect to see.

The usually informal, jean-wearing Demon-Knight, refused to meet his eyes as her maroon skin began to flush a deep rusty red.

"I... I think this is a bit too much..." Jenny nervously fluttered her hands in front of herself as Jeremiah took in long eyefuls of the elegant dress she wore. The black and turquoise number clung tight to her, as if she was sewn into it. Primarily, the satin material was a vibrant black, from the high collar down to her hips. The loose hanging shoulders and the material under her waist gradually transitioned into a bright turquoise, that both contrasted and emphasized the color of her skin, which practically glowed in the dim light of the candles he'd decorated the table with.

"He's actually speechless," Ashley noted with a somehow-brighter grin as Jeremiah gulped deeply. Jenny blushed ever deeper and brushed a lock of midnight-black hair up and over one of her horns when she finally made eye contact with Jeremiah.

"You're starin'," Jenny said, a small smile tugging at the corner of her lips.

"Uhh -ahem- yeah," Jeremiah sucked in his lips and nodded, momentarily forgetting to breathe. "Yeah I am."

"See?" Ashley chirped excitedly, grabbing Jenny's arm and leading her to the table. "He likes it. You look beautiful!"

"I feel... wrong," Jenny drawled with a small chuckle, allowing Ashley to sit her down at the table. "Gussied up like a belle just... ain't my thing."

"Exactly," Ashley noted as Jeremiah physically couldn't take his eyes off of the two beautiful women. "That's what makes this special. Otherwise, it would just be our boyfriend making a nice dinner for us. But tonight is our first date as a... mmmn, thruple.

"We should remember this night nearly as much as ou-" Ashley froze stock-still and ran her tongue along her canines as she seemed to reconsider saying something. "Well, it should be memorable. Jeremiah, how's dinner coming along?"

"Looks good, smells even better," Jeremiah replied, turning back to the food in a way that kept his eyes on the two as long as physically possible. "You two look... well, I don't really have the right words for it."

"I can suggest a few, if you like," Ashley chimed happily from right behind him, and Jeremiah turned to see her peeking around him at the food he was working on. She leaned forward, grabbed the pepper shaker, and began to add it in small, deliberate amounts on the steaks sitting in the pan before him. "That smells... right."

Ashley stood up on her tiptoes, kissing his cheek before patting his bicep reassuringly and returning to the table. Jeremiah snorted and shook his head.

It seemed no matter how much effort he put into cooking, Ashley would always be there to help him get it just that little bit better.

Jeremiah paused and grabbed the bottle of wine on the counter, pouring it into a glass before he set it aside.

He walked over to the fridge and grabbed one of the chilled, drink-sized bags of blood that Jenny had drawn from him and herself earlier. He shook off the odd, conflicting feelings it gave him as he opened it and drained half of it into a tall glass, before he grabbed the fruity mixer that Ashley had requested.

Their drinks completed, he brought them over to the table and set them down in front of the two women.

Jenny reached for her glass, but Ashley subtly rested a hand on her thigh, as Jenny's hand froze midway to the glass, then returned to the table.

Jeremiah briefly frowned at the byplay as he returned to the counter and began to set up their plates with food.

Over Ashley's, he took a pre-prepared ramekin of spices and poured blood into the mix. Stirring it with a spoon, he was satisfied that it was mixed properly, and he drizzled it over her steak and baked potato.

He smirked, nodded, and grabbed the women's plates first.

He set them on the table and grabbed his own, along with a beer from the fridge, before sitting down across from them. Now, with a positively glowing smile, Ashley reached for her glass and picked it up.

"To the people who've made my life have meaning again," she said, lifting her glass high above the center of the table with Jeremiah and Jenny following suit, clinking their glasses together. "I'm so happy that you're in my life."

"Hear, hear," added Jenny with a deep blush and a broad, toothy smile.

Jeremiah took a deep pull of his beer and sighed contentedly as he set it on the table, savoring the rich, almost-chocolatey flavor of the stout.

"This looks amazing, by the way," complimented Jenny, cutting into the steak and taking a bite. She paused chewing after a moment, inhaled deeply and leaned her head back over her seat before swallowing. "Oh my god... I would kill for this steak!"

Jeremiah's smile spread across his face of its own accord.

Ashley took a much smaller bite of her steak after dipping it in the sauce, chewing thoughtfully. Jeremiah cut into his own as he awaited her opinion as well.

She swallowed and began cutting off another piece as she ran her tongue along her bottom lip.

"Perfect," Ashley commended pointedly, before bringing another bite to her lips.

Jeremiah took his own bite and had to agree. The recipe that Ashley had provided him with had decidedly not steered him wrong.

The perfectly seared, medium-rare steak, practically melted on his tongue, and filled his mouth with a firework of flavors.

Something odd began to well up inside of Jeremiah, an odd confluence of emotions and feelings that he'd been putting off and individually compartmentalizing over the past week. It was an immediate and powerful feeling that seemed to suffuse his entire body with warmth and pleasant calm.

It was new, confusing, and alien to him, in a way he struggled to rationalize to himself, and he shrugged it off before taking a bite of the baked potato.

Jeremiah cut another piece off his steak while his mind screamed in every direction, seemingly unable to make a coherent thought as he missed what was being said by the two women.

I...what is happening to me?

* * *

Chapter 27

Jeremiah blew out a long, heavy breath, setting down his fork next to the empty plate.

A veritable tsunami of tiredness slammed into him when he leaned his head back over the top of the wooden chair. He closed his eyes and smiled to himself while Ashley and Jenny bantered happily across the table from him.

"Ah, ah, ah!" Ashley giggled as he felt her spoon rap with muted pain on his knuckle. "You don't get to fall asleep now!"

"I was just resting my eyes," Jeremiah lied, opening his eyes, he rolled his head back forward and found Ashley grinning archly at him. Jenny watched him with a doubtful smirk and a raised eyebrow, clearly doubting his reply. Jeremiah chuckled, blinked slowly, and finally nodded. "Okay. Maybe dinner is hitting me a little hard."

"Well, I mean, we could go to bed early, right, Ash?" Jenny looked over to the Vampire with a hard-to-read grin as Ashley giggled quietly. Ashley flicked her eyes to Jenny, then to Jeremiah, and a blush colored her cheeks slightly.

"I think that's a good idea, Jenn," Ashley replied with a smile in her tone. "It's past your bedtime anyway."

"That's right!" Jenny pushed her seat back and stood up as Ashley mirrored her. "A good sleep schedule is recommended by most doctors, after all."

Now Jeremiah was absolutely certain the pair were up to something.

He watched the two of them with narrowed

eyes, pushing his seat back and standing up. As he rounded the table, both of the women extended their hands to him, before pulling him towards the bedroom.

I...is this what I think it is?

Jeremiah's heart thudded loudly in his chest as he happily followed along with the giggling beauties. Ashley's eyes snapped to him, and she ran her tongue on one of her elongated, sharp canines with a heated grin.

I'm pretty sure this is exactly what I think it is.

Ashley flung open the bedroom door as she jerked Jeremiah, then Jenny through.

With surprising strength from the diminutive woman, he was half-pushed, half-flung him onto the bed, allowing him to see Jenny frozen in place, her eyes nervously flicking between Jeremiah and Ashley.

Jeremiah pushed himself up onto his elbows as he watched Ashley walk behind Jenny, trailing a hand along the much taller woman's shoulder.

"She looks gorgeous in this dress, right?" Ashley wrapped an arm around Jenny's broad hips and leaned her head on the Demon-Knight's arm.

"I think you both look beautiful," Jeremiah answered honestly with a broad grin. Ashley's eyes narrowed for the briefest of moments before her eyes flicked down and back up to Jeremiah's face.

"Oooh, good answer!" the Vampire replied with a playful smile. She leaned fractionally forward before continuing in a tone that dripped with desire. "But there's a surprise that you don't know about yet."

Jeremiah raised his eyebrows and turned his head questioningly when Ashley reached up to the back of Jenny's collar and began to slowly undo a zipper. As the satin high-collar of the dress began to fall away, it revealed that underneath, the Demon-Knight wore an alluring set of black lace lingerie.

It was simple, without any of the complex straps that were common with smallclothes that looked to draw the eye, and merely served the purpose of accentuating what Jenny already had.

Jeremiah's breath caught in his throat as he watched her blush deeply, her hands attempting to flutter up nervously before Jenny pulled them back down to her sides.

She closed her eyes, took in a deep inhale, and looked back to Jeremiah, red mist beginning to trickle out of her mouth.

"You made us such an amazing dinner, that I thought we should have a gift for you as well!" Ashley began with a proud, bubbly smile. She stepped in front of Jenny, resting one of her hands on her shoulder and turning slightly over her shoulder to ask of the other woman, "Zip me, dear?"

"I... yeah," Jenny's smile was broad, somewhat listless, and her eyes seemed to jump, between Jeremiah's noticeable tent and Ashley's stunning figure in a dress that emphasized what she naturally had. She reached forward and pulled down the zipper at the back of Ashley's emerald dress.

As the fabric of the top part of the dress clearly loosened, Ashley pulled it forward and extracted her arms from the straps of the number, revealing that underneath, she was not wearing a bra.

Dear gods...

Jeremiah blew out a sharp breath, finding himself unable and unwilling to draw his eyes away from the sight of the two beautiful women. Jenny stood in stark contrast to Ashley, with her tall, athletic figure. Where Jenny had defined muscles that coiled around her legs, shoulders and abdomen, Ashley seemed almost plush by comparison.

His palms began to itch as he took in deep eyefuls of her hourglass figure, working his way up to her eyes after several long moments. Ashley gripped Jenny's hand, and started towards Jeremiah with that achingly-pretty, fanged smile he now expected from her.

As it became abundantly clear to Jeremiah, what Ashley wanted most in the bedroom was control. Over the course of an hour, she dictated, orchestrated, and controlled their passion with the skill of a maestra, and Jeremiah found himself being passed between the two women, and the two women seeming to pass themselves to him.

As the final moments came, Jeremiah felt himself get close with his pulse pounding quicker. He struggled to bring himself back from the ledge, but no amount of idle thoughts of puppies and grandmas could change the fact that he currently had a curvaceous Vampire atop his face, and a muscular, fast-moving Demon-Knight riding his hips.

Mere moments before the proverbial dam broke, Jeremiah felt Jenny rise off of him, leaving him twitching, and achingly close to a release that seemed like it wouldn't arrive. Ashley climbed off of his face and into his lap, pinning him to the bed, as a breathless Jenny laid down beside him. He informed Ashley how close he was as she sank down on his member, which only seemed to draw out the Vampire's desire more.

Even as he patted her leg to warn her, the woman merely bucked her hips harder, as Jenny began to kiss his neck and whisper encouragements in his ear. Like a literal devil on his shoulder, she practically begged him to fill her, to give Ashley the reward she'd earned.

Jeremiah obliged.

* * *

Jeremiah blinked heavily as he took another long, deep drag of the bittersweet coffee.

He blew out a deep breath and savored both the flavor and the feeling of the warm mug in his hands while he stared listlessly at the top of the kitchen table.

Soft footsteps echoed off of the hardwood floor from the bedroom, causing Jeremiah to force his eyes up.

Jenny walked out of the short hallway, yawning and blearily rubbing her eyes. He blinked hard several times as the sight of her wearing nothing but his shirt and the lacey panties from the night before sent a jolt of sudden energy through his body.

"Morning," he greeted with a half-smile, taking time to appreciate the effortless beauty she flaunted.

Something about the simple combination of his worn shirt hanging loosely over her curves only served to draw his eyes more.

"We stayed up too late… and drank too much," Jenny grumbled, stumbling to the pot of coffee after grabbing a mug.

Jeremiah frowned, trying to remember exactly how much he'd had to drink the night before.

He'd had at least four beers on his own, but felt absolutely nothing.

No hangover, no headache, not even dehydrated.

"Maybe you did," Jeremiah agreed with a chuckle, and then another sip of his coffee. "I'm feeling just fine. A little tired, but hey, we did go to sleep around... ah... whatever. It doesn't matter. We were definitely up late.

"Will you need me to tuck you back into bed?"

"Mmmn screw off," Jenny groaned and sat down at the table. "You didn't have to deal with a cute, bossy Vampire spending an hour and a half playing makeover-queen on you."

"Point," Jeremiah agreed with a smile. He nodded before taking a long pull of his coffee. "You... you looked beautiful though. I'd say the view was worth it."

"Mmmm, I'm sure," Jenny growled and wore an expression that seemed to simultaneously combine a proud smirk and a disgruntled scowl. "I don't think I'm gonna get gussied up like that for a while though.

"Takes too much effort. I mean, let's be honest, I'm gonna end up naked anyway, why can't I just wear sweatpants and some cute underwear?"

"Good mooorning!" Ashley practically sang as she barged into the kitchen, also wearing one of Jeremiah's shirts. The baggy flannel from the thrift store that was over-sized even for him fit her almost as comprehensively as the dress the night before.

Well, it would if she actually decided to button the front.

Jeremiah watched the curvaceous Vampire stroll through the kitchen, grab a small, covered mug from the fridge, and open the plastic-wrapped top.

She passed by Jenny, kissed her on the top of her head, and then rounded the table to sit beside Jeremiah.

Ashley snaked her arm through his before leaning her head on his shoulder with a contented hum.

"How'd you two sleep?" Ashley asked in a cheery tone and Jeremiah caught the sidelong wince from Jenny. She was apparently still sensitive to sound.

"I slept fine," confirmed Jeremiah with a teasing grin, continuing to stare at Jenny. "Our tough Demon-Knight over there can't handle her booze though, I thi-"

"Oh, screw off, I can handle it fine," Jenny hissed before wincing and continuing in a much smaller voice, "Maybe I just had a… a little much. I was nervous, okay?"

"Hey, I ain't gonna fault you for needing a little liquid courage," promised Jeremiah. "I -am- gonna give you shit for being grouchy this early, though, it's killing my vibe."

Ashley snorted into her mug of blood laced coffee before giggling and snuggling close to Jeremiah.

"Your vibe?" Jenny asked with an arched eyebrow and a small eyeroll. "What's that? Psychotic brooding in the corner?"

Jeremiah clicked his tongue and raised his mug towards the Demon-Knight with a smug grin before downing it in one go.

The powerful, velvet-soft feeling from the night before returned as he watched Jenny grin, clearly despite some effort to stop, as Ashley continued to snuggle into his arm.

The morning was blessedly calm and quiet

with the trio enjoying relaxation around the cozy mountain cabin.

They watched TV, talked, and did something that felt relatively unfamiliar to Jeremiah, they simply enjoyed each other's presence without worry of the outside world and issues of the recent past.

The brief bliss was shattered several hours later when a sharp knock sounded from the door.

Ashley cocked her head towards the entryway. Jeremiah and Jenny both had much sharper reactions, snapping their heads towards the door and back to one another.

"You expecting company?" Jenny questioned almost rhetorically, pushing herself up from the couch.

"No, I'm fuckin' not," Jeremiah growled as Jenny half-ran to the bedroom and rounded the corner.

"Uhhm, where are you two going?" Ashley whispered loudly, following them to the bedroom.

"Ash, we aren't expecting guests. That means that there's a pretty good chance that whoever's at the door isn't someone we want to have at our door," Jeremiah said before catching the battle rifle Jenny flung at him. He racked the bolt on the side of the weapon as Jenny pulled out her submachine gun.

When the fuck did we get one of these?

Jeremiah stared at the long, heavy rifle in his hands with a frown. He shrugged and pushed past Ashley into the hallway with the weapon at the low ready.

"Okay, wait you two!" the Vampire hissed, squeezing around Jeremiah and putting both her hands against his chest. "It could just be our neighbors, or a package that got delivered to the wrong address.

"I'll open the door, while you two wait here, okay? If I think there's danger, I'll drop and you two can... do what you do, okay?" Jeremiah suggested.

"She... she's got a point," Jenny said and tapped Jeremiah on the shoulder while looking pointedly at him.

"Yeah..." Jeremiah exhaled deeply and loosened his grip on the rifle. "Yeah she does. Opening the door armed to the teeth is probably a bad image. Jenny, can you get set up on the other side of the couch? If someone comes through the door, you and I can get a good L-shape going if you're there. Ash, you answer the door, see who it is."

"On it!" Jenny agreed, moving near-silently and quickly towards the other side of the living room.

"It'll be okay," Ashley whispered, placing her hand over Jeremiah's heart. She offered him a brief, nervous smile, and turned for the door.

It was going too well...looks like the other fucking shoe has finally dropped.

Jeremiah's heart pounded faster as he came to the conclusion and Ashley placed her hand on the doorknob.

Vasily fucking found us. I always thought Vampires needing an invite was a stupid legend, mayb-

"Hello. Can I help you?" Ashley asked politely as she opened the door, cutting Jeremiah's train of thought short.

"Oh, well... maybe I have the wrong address. I'm looking for Jeremiah," came a high-pitched, slightly accented voice replying cheerily. A voice that he knew.

"Oh, that's my boyfriend. Is everything okay?" Ashley asked with a giggle. She smiled at who

Jeremiah believed was Denise.

"Is he here? I have some items for him from my mother," Denise replied as Jeremiah sighed, rolled his eyes, and leaned the rifle up against the wall before stepping out.

"Hey, Denise," Jeremiah said in a mildly sour tone, making eye contact with the blonde-haired Fae.

"Oh there you are! And look, your core is so much better!" Denise said as her monochromatic eyes seemed to size him up. Then surprisingly, doing the same to Ashley. "And here I thought you had the warm and fuzzies for your little Demon. Who is this enchanting beauty?"

"I'm Ashley!" the Vampire replied brightly, extending a hand to shake. Denise briefly shook it, and then brought it to her lips, kissing Ashley's knuckles.

Jeremiah frowned and sucked his lips behind his teeth as he watched the sight in mild confusion.

"Okay, no, nope," Jenny said, rounding the couch and waggling a finger at the Fae, who released Ashley's hand with a malicious, self-confident smirk as she peeked around the door. "No, uh-uh, you stay aw-"

"Ah, there you are! It's so lovely to see you again! Are you going to threaten to shoot me again?" Denise murmured with a wicked smile for the Demon-Knight while Jenny pushed herself between the two diminutive women.

"I might if you keep acting like a- a bitch!" Jenny snapped back, which somehow caused Denise burst into loud, exuberant cackling. "What's so funny?"

"I'm sorry, just the – hehe – the image of a six-two Demon struggling to say bitch is just-" Denise cut off again as another bout of giggles spread through her body. "-it's just funny, that's all."

"I'm sorry that I put the moves on your woman. That's all very confusing, by the way. Is she your woman, or are you Jeremiah's?"

"We're all dating each other!" Ashley said enthusiastically, poking her head around Jenny's much taller frame.

What the fuck is happening?

Jeremiah remained silent, staring at the three women with a half-open mouth and a squint.

"Oh? Oh that's lovely, congratulations! Now, with formalities out of the way, may I join you inside?" Denise asked with a nod at Ashley, before sighing, reaching into a small leather over-the-shoulder bag and pulling out two small phials, a notebook, and a pen.

"Why?" Jenny snapped back, red mist beginning to pour from her lips.

"Because, my mother has offered Jeremiah a consultation," Denise replied confidently, looking into the intimidating larger woman's eyes with a smile. "His maker may have tried to fix him, but we're here to see if there's anything we can do on our end. My mother got busy with some powerful clients from out of town, and has sent me in her stead."

"Trust me, I've already got diagnostics being ran on him, there's nothing you can offer that actual medical science can't offer better, cleaner, and safer," Jenny growled while folding her arms across her chest. She glared at the Fae with a feral glare.

Denise's eyelid twitched briefly and she cocked her head even further to the side.

Something dangerous flashed behind the Fae's glowing monochrome-blue eyes as she blew out a breath.

"Well, you didn't do a very good job before, now did you?" Denise's deadpanned and her smile broke into a glare. "He was pretty close to turning into a walking essence bomb, all because your 'tests' and 'science' couldn't pick up just how fractured his core was.

"So I'm gonna stick with the medicine and alchemy that has worked for my family for a thousand years, m'kay?"

The Fae licked her lips and leaned slightly over to look at Ashley.

"Though, as much fun as this little bit of verbal jousting is, I would actually like to come in," she said to the Vampire. "Believe it or not, I do have your boyfriend's best interests at heart."

Jenny opened her mouth to respond but was interrupted by Ashley pulling on her arm and stepping past the cantankerous Demon-Knight.

"You're more than welcome to come in and run any tests Jeremiah agreed to, but-but if you're here, you're going to be nice to my girlfriend, okay? Stop pushing her buttons. We have enough stress as it is," Ashley declared while raising her hand to forestall the Fae's entry into the home.

"I... very well, I understand," Denise smiled and nodded deeply at Ashley. "I will be civil, so long as she is."

"Jenn? Please?" requested Ashley.

Jenny turned and looked at Jeremiah with a frustrated, questioning expression. After a brief moment of thought, he gave her a small nod.

"Fine. But you keep the nonsense to ya'self, okay?" Jenny muttered with a defeated expression. She turned back to the Fae and stepped back.

"I will if you will!" Denise replied with an absolutely plastic smile. "Now! Here's what we'll do-"

Why did it have to be her?

Jeremiah all but screamed mentally to the heavens as the Fae entered the room.

I guess the other shoe really did drop after all.

Chapter 28

Jenny dropped into the recliner across from Jeremiah with folded arms and a flat stare.

Jeremiah blew out a breath, trying not to appear nervous when Denise pursed her lips, idly pointed a finger to one of the chairs at the dining room, and sharply arced it towards the ground in front of her.

With a loud screech and groan of wood sliding over wood, the chair was sent flying across the room by some invisible force, sliding to a stop beside the Fae.

Not even waiting for the motion to completely finish, Denise flopped down onto the chair with a contented sigh.

She leaned forward and placed a blue-labeled, thumb-sized tincture in front of Jeremiah, before clicking her pen twice and opening her notebook. The other bottle rested in her lap.

"Okay, so," Denise began, shaking a lock of curly blonde hair out of her eye while smiling over at Jeremiah. "I'll give you a brief rundown of how this is going to happen before we get started, just so there are no surprises. It seems like you three are a little... mmm, jumpy, after all."

There was a pregnant pause that no one said anything into.

"And personally, I'd like to stay living and with a clean record.

"Now, this phial contains a tincture that acts like a tracer for magical pathways through the body. It'll allow me to see where, when, and how your body pulls in and dumps essence.

"While that's happening, I will be sketching what I can see to take back to my mother for further diagnosis," explained Denise with a toothy smile for Jeremiah.

She pointed at the small bottle on the table.

"If you would be so kind, please drink that. The second bottle beside me is just a neutralizer, so you don't look like a large, vascular, neon sign to other magic users after we're done," she finished with a wave of her hand.

Jeremiah frowned, but shrugged and grabbed the first bottle regardless. He pulled the cork out and drank the acrid-tasting tincture. It felt like it burned his throat on the way down, and he had to force back a cough.

"God, could you make these taste worse?" Jeremiah groaned with a grimace, smacking his lips audibly.

"Oh stop being such a baby. You can handle a little bitter," Denise replied, clicking her pen several times and watching him curiously.

Then, she began to sketch, drawing small lines, curves, and occasionally, intentionally smudging the ink with a thumb.

"Well-" Ashley broke the several minute stretch of silence with a forced smile. "Can I get anyone anything to drink?"

"Mmmm," Denise pursed her lips and dotted her pen several times on the page before moving a thumb across the top. "Do you have any tea?"

"We do, actually! Jenny is actually a big fan of tea!" answered Ashley with a nod of her head.

"Oh? Lovely! What are my options?" Denise asked, her smile growing by a degree or two, actually looking genuine to Jeremiah.

"I'll bring the boxes over and let you pick!" Ashely pushed herself out of the sofa and moved towards the kitchen, before returning with several boxes of tea.

Denise hesitated, her pen holding steady over the sketch as if she needed to get something down. Then she threw a glance over her shoulder.

She had a thoughtful expression and wrinkled her nose, a smile curling her lips.

"Oh, the one on the end please. The blue box. It's one of my favorites, may I have some?" Denise asked politely, resting her sketch pad on her lap.

"I'll get it ready!" Ashley grinned and added, "It's Jenny's favorite too."

"Oh, is it now?" Denise purred and turned towards the Demon-Knight with a teasing smile for a brief moment. It lasted only a moment before she turned back to Ashley. "She has good taste."

To Jeremiah, it felt like there was more to that sentiment than just what she'd said out loud.

Apparently, Jenny agreed, since she scowled, rolled her eyes, and folded her arms against her chest even tighter.

Denise continued to sketch on her pad while Ashley got the kettle going on the stove. After a few minutes, Ashley returned with three cups of piping-hot tea.

She handed one to Denise, one to a clearly irked Jenny, who managed to grumble a quiet 'thank you' and moved to hand one to Jeremiah.

"Ah, Jeremiah, could you refrain from drinking the tea until I'm done with my sketch?" she glanced up and over her sketch pad with raised, questioning eyebrows. An apologetic smile bowed her lips. "I don't think it would interfere with the tincture, but I'd prefer to not risk it."

Jeremiah shrugged, placing the tea on the short coffee table between them.

After another couple minutes of sketchwork, Denise snapped the notebook closed with a loud pop and sighed.

She sipped her tea, exhaled contentedly, and set the mug down on the table.

"Okay, now it's time for this, and yes, you can enjoy your tea now, thank you for being so generous with my request. I'd almost recommend drinking the tea after the next phial as... well... I'm sure it won't taste wonderfully," Denise pleasantly murmured and smiled at Jeremiah.

She leaned forward and pushed the small phial towards him over the table.

This move caused the shirt, which in reality seemed more like a large collection of interwoven swaths of silk, to spill outward, giving Jeremiah a brief, but lovely view.

He blinked, looked away, and reached for the glass, at the same time making eye contact with Ashely, who watched him thoughtfully.

Realizing that the momentary acceleration in his heart had been caught by the Vampire, Jeremiah decided to ignore it.

Jeremiah upended the small flask into his mouth and grimaced at the bitter taste before setting it back on the table and retrieving the tea.

"Have you ever thought about... flavoring these?" Jeremiah grouched after taking a drink of the tea. Denise watched him with an amused smirk, arching a skeptical eyebrow before replying.

"Jeremiah, it's medicine. It doesn't need to

taste good," stated Denise while fighting against her smile to keep it from getting bigger. "Though, I can tell you some interesting things about yourself, just from what I could see here today."

"I'm listening," Jeremiah replied neutrally. Something in her voice sent alarm bells ringing through his head.

"Though, hmm. I really don't know if I should," Denise mused and tapped her lips thoughtfully with a fingertip.

"Why not?" Jeremiah asked after a momentary sharp inhale, realizing that this was probably going to be some form of trap.

"Fast. Cheap. Good," Denise said in a thoughtful tone, locking eyes with Jeremiah on the last word. "You must always choose two at the expense of one, right?"

"Oh for Pete's sake," Jenny started angrily before being interrupted by Denise.

"You see, my mother made the agreement with you. However, I did no such thing. You can wait for her prognosis if you like. It might be a couple of days, however. Possibly more, if I'm not mistaken." Denise admitted and rested her palms on the hardback sketchbook, pressing it into her waist.

Jeremiah felt like the trap he expected was indeed true. Except he was considering stepping into it depending on the condition.

"She will be good, and cheap," Denise continued, a pointed, malicious grin spreading across her face. "But not fast. And given that you three seem to be hiding from something, I would guess that time is of the essence, regarding what our war Golem here can do?"

The Fae glanced between the other occupants

of the room as Jenny grit her teeth and snarled:

"What do you mean 'our'?"

"Oh, sorry, must've just been a slip of the tongue," Denise waved her hand dismissively and continued.

She stuck her tongue out, caught it with her teeth, and wrinkled her nose.

"So, I can give you a… mmm, early access diagnosis, if you will.

"Since I'm assuming none of us want quick, cheap and bad, this won't be… inexpensive," clarified Denise.

"Also, what makes you think we're hiding from something?" Jeremiah shot after she paused to take a breath.

Denise didn't respond immediately.

Instead, she just watched him.

Staring at him for several long seconds.

With a polite smile, she arched her finger and opened her hand with a flourish, as the battle rifle Jeremiah had leaned against the hallway wall earlier jumped into her hand.

She laid it across her lap and ran a finger along the receiver of the weapon.

"People who aren't hiding from something, or worried that someone might find them, don't answer the door with a gun," offered up the Fae.

"Battle rifle," Jenny corrected the Fae with a snarl, seeming to be halfway to throttling the smaller woman.

"Mmmn, semantics and really… it doesn't matter," murmured Denise a moment before she tossed the weapon over to Jeremiah with surprising ease.

"What's your fucking point?" Jeremiah

snapped back, setting the long, heavy rifle beside the sofa.

"That I know how much you need my help, or at least, strongly suspect. With that in mind, would you be willing to hear my offer?" Denise asked and leaned forward.

She smiled beatifically at Jeremiah, an expression that certainly didn't match the surely predatory nature of the deal she was offering.

Jenny scoffed loudly and rolled her eyes while Denise continued to stare fixedly at Jeremiah with unblinking eyes.

Jeremiah sucked in a deep breath, sighed and shook his head before it turned into a nod.

Fuck it, I can always say no to it, right?

"Alright. Let's hear it then," Jeremiah allowed, meeting her self-confident smirk with a flat expression.

"I find you interesting. Your construction is… unique. And artistically well done. You will tell me your story over dinner.

"Alone, just you.

"Though, I'm completely fine if your Demon-Knight here watches through a scope from several hundred yards away," Denise waved her hand dismissively, as if the thought of being watched by a sniper wasn't even a concern.

Given how Reixhitz had reacted to a gun, as well as Aiden, Jeremiah wondered if his faith in firearms was a touch over-rated.

They didn't seem as wonderful as of late.

"After we have our picnic, I'll tell you all I can understand about the mechanics of your body. Seems like a fair trade, if not overwhelmingly in your favor, no? A story for a story," summarized Denise.

"What's the catch?" Jenny groused, watching Denise with a snarl.

"Catch, there's no catch," Denise promised in a way that sounded incredibly forced. She was apparently a terrible liar and only needed to be confronted to collapse.

"Your... ah... well... your heart rate is sky high," Ashley argued, giving Denise a pained smile while biting her lower lip. "That just doesn't really fit not having a catch. Now does it?"

Turquoise wings fluttered out from her back and began to twitch as if debating taking flight, he was caught off guard.

Jeremiah couldn't pull his eyes away from the dazzling, butterfly-like wings. His eyes traced along the edges of the seven-foot wingspan that threatened to hit Jenny's face.

Is...is that why they wear those weird hippie clothes? Because it allows them to hide their wings?

Jeremiah was intrigued by the sight before him. Then, Ashley's eyes darted to him before moving right back to Denise.

"No catch," Denise uttered in a near-breathless tone, glancing nervously between Jeremiah and Ashley. It was odd that Jeremiah could tell when she was looking at him, given she had no pupils, sclera, or iris to speak of. But somehow, he always knew when the near-luminescent blue orbs that were her eyes landed on him. "Just information for information."

"And?" Ashely asked with a pointed, smiling stare.

"And... I just want to talk to him more," confessed Denise with a frow. She looked away and blew out a breath before continuing in a blurt,

"There's no interesting guys here! It's just kids, people that are already married, and retirees! I work in the store, study and study and study, and do nothing else!"

Ashley seemed to accept that and made a soft clucking noise with her tongue. She slowly moved around the table and sat down next to Jeremiah.

She folded her hands in her lap before resting her head against Jeremiah's shoulder.

"I'm fine with it. Jenny?" asked Ashley after a few more seconds of consideration, shrugging against Jeremiah.

"What? Why on Earth would I be okay with this sleazeball of a woman running off with our man?" Jenny shot back with a dumbfounded expression, slowly shaking her head.

"I..." Denise exhaled, bit her tongue, and inhaled before continuing. "I'll sweeten the deal. You guys have problems with... something that I'll probably learn about later. Magic, for all it's worth, is just a very complex, creative way of solving problems.

"If you accept the deal, you can consider me... 'on retainer' so to speak.

"My help will not be free, but my consultation, my time? I will answer when you call and offer solutions to the best of my ability."

"Denise, do you have a phone number?" Ashley asked, after sharing a long, unbroken stare with Jenny. "I think the three of us should talk privately and get back to you on your offer."

"I... I, yes I do!" Denise's expression went from hard-to-read to a pleased smile in a flash, and she pulled the device from her pocket to hand over to Ashley.

* * *

Where the fuck am I?
Jeremiah stepped out of the SUV in the deserted trail parking lot.

He checked the phone's GPS app again with a frown, confirming the coordinates sent with Ashley's text.

The discussion between himself, Ashley, and Jenny had been more of a 'talk Jenny out of disappearing a Fae' conversation, than an actual back and forth on whether or not they should take the Fae's deal.

At least for the first half of it.

The second half, after they had managed to calm down the somewhat-incensed Demon-Knight, had been interesting to Jeremiah.

As soon as he brought up the utility of having a sorceress such as Denise on hand, and how that could possibly aid them in their fight against whatever the Vampires like Aiden were, and generally in regards to eliminating the coven, something seemed to shift in Ashley.

She went from an almost wishy-washy attitude about including Denise, to become an ardent supporter of the Fae becoming involved in their fight, much to Jeremiah's confusion and Jenny's dismay.

And so, after inevitably winning the debate, Ashley had sent Jeremiah here.

The sun was just beginning to set in the mountains behind him as he pulled the battle rifle out of the back of the vehicle, along with a couple of spare magazines for his pockets.

"Time to go find a fucking Faerie in the densest forest I've ever seen," Jeremiah grumbled with a grimace. He looked towards the trailhead and the trees that seemed to arc over the top like a perpetual green hallway.

Jeremiah really wished that he had night vision goggles as he began to walk down the path.

"Should just be a half-mile in... why couldn't she have just met me in the damn parking lot?" Jeremiah muttered, clicking on the small flashlight he'd brought with him.

The forest seemed to close in around him and the wind blew strange sounds around the overgrown trail.

Tilting his head, Jeremiah frowned when it seemed like the dark trees beyond whispered something inaudible, just out of reach of his senses.

The trail ended.

A flat plane of trees sprang up before him, like an indomitable wall of interwoven, twisted wood.

In truth, Jeremiah had almost walked directly into it as he meandered with his head on a perpetual swivel.

"That's... that doesn't look natural," Jeremiah grunted and shook his head slowly, placing his hand on the twisted pine trunks before him.

"It is and it also isn't," a bright voice said from behind him, causing Jeremiah to tense up sharply.

Slowly, he turned to face the speaker.

Denise stood with her hands folded demurely in front of herself, her wings fully extended behind her.

They flapped once, the last glimmers of sunset casting strange flashes of reflected orange and pink light off the turquoise membranes.

"You look... interesting," Jeremiah noted the bright yellow dress she wore, far out of her usual style of clothing. "Aren't you cold?"

"Freezing, actually," Denise admitted with a chuckle. She continued to stare at Jeremiah with a satisfied grin. "I usually try to hide my wings, since the mask doesn't do an amazing job of... that.

"But, every once in a while, I do get to go out without having to worry about hiding them. It's refreshing. Though that does make it hard to wear things that cover my shoulders."

"Mmmm, sure," Jeremiah answered flatly, looking around the end of the trailhead. "Any particular reason you wanted to meet in the ass-end of nowhere?"

"Any particular reason you decided to come armed to our little picnic in the woods? Doesn't the lovely Demon-Knight have my head in the sights of a rifle already?" Denise replied to his question with one of her own.

"Because you wanted to meet in the middle of nowhere, at night. Like a psychopath." Jeremiah retorted, unconsciously adjusting the holster in the waistband of his pants.

"Mmm, perhaps I was worried about Miss Jenny showing up, and didn't want to involve the townspeople in the inevitable firefight that would ensue. Being out here is just... easier," Denise offered with a shrug of her shoulders.

"Jenny's at home. So is Ash," Jeremiah replied, raising his hands in a calming gesture of mock surrender as he watched the Fae roll her fingers fluidly, as if contemplating summoning the lightning at that moment. "They decided we should hold up our end of the bargain. Now, are you gonna hold up yours, or do I need to walk back to my car?"

"No, you don't have to do that," Denise sighed and rolled her eyes with a playful smile before dropping her hands to her side. "I'll be 'nice'."

Jeremiah grunted, but continued to watch the Fae approach him with a noticeable sway to her hips.

"Shall we?" she asked and waved a hand over Jeremiah's shoulder to the wall of foliage, causing him to turn back and look.

The blockade was gone.

All Jeremiah saw before him was a dark, foreboding trail of hard-to-see dirt in between towering, ancient-looking pines.

With a frown and a confused stare, he turned back to where Denise stood.

Only, Denise wasn't there.

He groaned when he saw that the wall of foliage had simply migrated to the other side of the trail, blocking any chance he'd had of escape.

A quiet giggle emanated from deeper in the trees behind him, causing Jeremiah to whip his head around, and pull the pistol out of its holster.

He pointed it down the path in front of him, turning on the small flashlight on the underside, which output a significantly brighter beam than the one in his hand.

"Oh come now. Don't be like that.

"I have everything ready for you, come on in, please," Denise said with a pout clear in her words. His reaction clearly hadn't exactly been friendly.

Jeremiah blew out a breath, scowled, and rolled his eyes.

I never should have come here!

He groused inside of his mind, taking his first step down the path.

I'm in fucking danger.
She's a Faerie after all.
A God damn trickster.

Chapter 29

"You know!" Jeremiah shouted into the still woods. "You could just… talk to me like a normal damn person!"

He stepped carefully, heel to toe, down the dark path ahead of him. Jeremiah kept his pistol at the low ready as he panned his eyes right and left.

"But this is so much more fun!" Denise giggled omni-directionally, the sound seeming to surround him.

"What fun would life be if everything was just… handed to you? Of course we could just… talk like normal people, have dinner and swap information. But would you remember that? In a decade, a century, would you remember a mundane, boring," Denise teased. "And you pulled a gun on me. I'm a little hurt."

"Denise!" Jeremiah shouted into the woods, snapping the Fae's monologue off. "Cut the shit!"

The entire forest around him seemed to grind to a halt at his command.

Even the breeze itself seemed to ebb in intensity, leaving Jeremiah alone with the mild tinnitus in his ears.

"I came here because you offered help, and for some unknown reason, Ashley convinced me it was a good idea!" Jeremiah continued shouting into the silent trees around him, looking for a woman who wasn't there.

"If you're gonna keep up this cryptic 'find-your-way-out-of-a-maze' bullshit, then I'm just gonna pick a direction and fuck OFF!" cried the lone man in the woods.

Like a silent thunderclap, the trees around Jeremiah creaked, bristled, then stilled.

He narrowed his eyes and slowly spun in a circle, looking for anything that could be construed as a threat. As he completed his spin, he found himself standing at the edge of a candlelit clearing in the trees.

Before him was a table made from a still-living tree that bent horizontally, then back vertically again.

Roots sprang from the ground, flattening almost two feet above the mossy forest floor to create benches.

The whole ten-meter circle honestly reminded him of a normal bedroom, if one somehow managed to convince the forest itself to grow directly into furniture.

"Y-you're serious, aren't you?" Denise asked in a small voice from his right.

Jeremiah jerked his head over to look at her with a scowl, planning to continue his rant.

Instead, his words died on his lips.

Denise wouldn't meet his eyes, instead seeming to fold in on herself as she clutched the upper portion of her right arm with her left.

Jeremiah didn't reply, instead staring at the diminutive Fae with a slack jaw and narrowed eyes.

"Yeah, I'm fuckin' serious," Jeremiah snapped back, though quieter than before. "What the -hell- is your problem?"

"I just thought... I thought it would be fun," Denise mumbled and shrugged absently. Continuing to refuse eye contact. "You get to find your way through the exciting labyrinth I prepared, and then at the end, there's this lovely dinner ready, and... I thought you'd have fun."

"Denise, why on Earth would you think I'd have fun with that?" Jeremiah sighed and rolled his eyes as he re-holstered the pistol. "If my first response to someone knocking unexpectedly at my door is to grab a damn rifle, what do you think trapping me in some bullshit maze is gonna do?"

"I thought you'd have a good time. Like a little puzzle, a fun game. We could have some witty banter and learn more about each other. But no, you wanted to yell at me," Denise huffed, folding her arms across her chest as her entire demeanor began to shift.

Jeremiah sighed and pinched the bridge of his nose as Denise finally made eye contact, with a self-assured, flat stare.

He rolled his eyes before extending a hand towards the all-natural table.

"Can we just get this over with?" He asked in a sour tone, as Denise's jaw dropped in an expression of mock shock.

"My, is that any way to talk to a lady?" she questioned with a frown that turned her mouth downward tugging at the corners of her mouth, a pearl necklace appearing around her throat. Jeremiah sighed again as she clutched at the illusory jewelry. "I even went through the trouble of making us dinner!"

Jeremiah slowly began to shake his head, his immediate snarky reply dying on his lips, gradually turning into a throaty chuckle.

Whatever...if she wanted me dead, I would be.

* * *

Jeremiah swallowed a bite of the rabbit stew, savoring the tangy and slightly spicy flavor that permeated his mouth. He blew a breath out over his warm, tingling tongue, and continued his story.

"So after the place went up, Jenny and Ash brought me up here. And we've mostly just been living life in the cabin since then," Jeremiah said with a shrug and loaded another bite onto his spoon.

Which had more in common with a wooden ladle than a normal eating utensil.

Jeremiah shrugged and took another bite, pointedly -not- bringing up his interaction with Reixhitz and Tiff.

As much as Denise had managed to push his buttons upon entering the forest, she'd definitely managed to change his heart through her cooking.

"Okay, but what happened with your maker?" Denise asked, apparently catching his pointed avoidance of the conversation with the Torment of Sanity. "Your core was repaired somewhat, and I am absolutely sure it wasn't you or your girlfriends that did that."

"Well," Jeremiah muttered with a wince. Gritting his teeth and looking away, before he glanced back to the glowing sapphire eyes of the Fae. "Yeah... the same night you went full crazy sorceress on us-"

"Hey!" She half-heartedly chided, waggling her spoon at him. "You were too damn bright, I just wanted to help and you two went for your guns-"

"Well, he kinda showed up and kidnapped me, did some magical bullshit I don't understand, and threw me back into the world. Something went wrong... I think, and I ended up landing in downtown Clallam instead of back at the cabin,"

Jeremiah continued, completely ignoring the argument Denise made. "Just in time for a big ass bomb to blow up a Fed building too."

"Oh, it wasn't just a Fed building," Denise countered with a quick shake of her head. The ever-present teasing smile disappeared from her face. "As far as my mom can tell, it was -all- of them.

"Outside of a few outliers that somehow got missed, all the major Fed buildings, other than the capitol itself, went up."

Jeremiah sharply inhaled, his spoon frozen halfway to his mouth.

"Uh... all of them?" he asked with his brow fully skyward, leaning forward as he set the spoon back in the wooden bowl. "As in... the whole government is gone?"

"Mmm, most of the bureaucrats, yes," confirmed Denise with an absent-minded shrug. As if the revelation was utterly inconsequential. "The talking heads are still around for the most part."

Jeremiah felt his jaw drop and his mouth hang open. He rested his elbows on the "table", staring at a point between himself and Denise.

This... this is gonna get bad, isn't it?

Jeremiah considered the repercussions of the Federal government essentially being gutted.

It's gonna be like the troubles all over again, but all over the states.

"What about law enforcement?" Jeremiah asked almost absently while his mind chewed at the reality of the situation he was sure to come down the pipe.

Not for the first time, he was glad to be living, however temporarily, in the mountains and away from civilization.

"Well, I did say bureaucrats bit it, didn't I?" Denise replied with a pleased smirk. She took a drink from a large wooden mug beside her meal, letting out a content moan before continuing, "But all that is irrelevant. You were saying about your maker?"

"That's not irrelevant! You can't just drop something like 'the Fed's gone, anyways' on me in casual conversation!" Jeremiah scoffed, raising his hands skyward in frustration.

"Why not?" Denise asked with a genuinely confused expression on her face. "It's not like they really do anything, besides being annoying and yelling at me about practicing magic in a national forest."

Yeah, that would be how the Fed are this far out.

Jeremiah considered the mass removal of the government idly, before deciding to let it lie with Denise.

The ramifications of the mass bombing could be discussed later, with Ashley and Jenny.

"So, I've told you my story," Jeremiah began a new train of thought, picking his spoon back up and preparing his next bite. He was deliberately ignoring her questions about Reixhitz for the time being. "Now it's your turn. What's the diagnosis?"

Denise sighed dramatically before snapping her fingers and holding out her hand next to her head.

A moment later, a leather-bound tome appeared in her hand, slowly fading into reality from seemingly nothing.

She smiled, opened the book and set it on the table before Jeremiah.

"As you can see, your essence flow is… unusual," Denise started, pointing at an incredibly well-sketched drawing of Jeremiah sitting on the couch earlier. The odd part, however, was the clear, vascular flow in green and blue colored pencil along his arms, legs, and chest, that looked almost like blood vessels. "Like most Golems, it goes to your major organs and muscle groups, but also seems to connect to your skin, facial structure, bones, and, oddly enough, two points in your forearms."

"That would be these," Jeremiah interjected, flicking out the Golem-draining wrist spike. "Something my maker gave me when he realized that he couldn't just recharge me after fixing my core."

"Oh… oh my goodness, so mother wasn't lying to me," Denise half-murmured, half-exclaimed as she stared at the translucent protrusion. "Well, that explains the circuit of essence running there."

"Yeah," Jeremiah nodded absently as he pulled the small spear back inside himself. "According to my creator, if I wanna just sit by and live my life without using any of the abilities he apparently gave me, I can do that.

"But if I want to pick a fight with the assholes after us, and stand a chance of winning - well, I'm gonna have to figure out what those powers actually are first."

He paused and considered how much to relay. Then decided it wouldn't harm him.

"But if I use them, I need to find other Golems and drain them, like some kind of fucked up Vampire," Jeremiah finished, tapping the back of his spoon against the twisted pine table.

"Well, if it helps," Denise offered, after the silence began to grow longer, "you are by far the most advanced Golem I've ever seen. Most of your ilk are… automatons at best. They do the tasks that their owner assigns to them, and that's the end of it.

"For some reason, whoever made you - this 'Reixhitz¹, I'm assuming from what my mother told me - gave you the single most complex core and essence channels I've ever seen."

Denise clicked her tongue, pursed her lips, then shook her head. As if dismissing a thought that'd lingered in her mind.

"It's like, if the vast majority of Golems are a model T, you are an advanced F-one race car," Denise suggested, looking up and to the side as she spoke. "After all, you have more going for you than just the essence capillaries running along more than the usual places."

"More than... wait, what do you mean the... usual places?" Jeremiah questioned with a frown.

"Yes, like I said before, major muscle groups and organs are the standard. But apart from that, you have them running all along your skin, through your facial structure, bones, and ligaments," Denise clarified with a smile, blinking translucent horizontal lids as her monochrome blue eyes seemed to trace down his body.

Before Jeremiah could come up with a response to her words, she continued her explanation.

"But you've clearly been wired up with a purpose beyond advanced strength and speed. They gave you a high level of self-governance and decision-making capability, which in itself is unusual.

"The subcutaneous essence capillaries are honestly what interests me the most, as they seem to be near-universal across your body," mumbled Denise, though the last almost sounded more to herself.

"Could... you put that into English, please?" Jeremiah asked with a raised eyebrow.

"In short, for some reason, your skin itself is magically powered," Denise bounced her head from side to side thoughtfully as she took her next bite. "I could make a guess as to what the purpose of that would be, but honestly it would just be conjecture at this point."

"Well, your guess would be better than mine," Jeremiah shrugged and swallowed the final bite of his stew. "Hit me."

"Like physically, or—"

"You know what I meant!" Jeremiah shot back at the wryly grinning Fae, who brushed a lock of hair out of her eyes nonchalantly.

"My guess is that it has something to do with changing the appearance of your skin, or alternatively, it could be a healing-slash-hardening function for defense," offered Denise with a wave of a hand.

Appearance...like...my face in the water.

"Given the fact that you're apparently managing to keep two lovely girls wrapped around your finger, I'm sure a hardening function is at least part of it," suggested Denise with raised eyebrows.

Jeremiah sighed exasperatedly as he stretched his arms above his head.

"Back to the point," Jeremiah redirected after letting out a deep yawn. "You have any idea on how I can trigger the abilities? Reixhitz really gave me nothing to work with here, so I'm mostly just trying to come up with some hint as to what I can do."

"Honestly, your best bet is to just... experiment. Try to just instinctively do... things," Denise suggested and gave him a noncommittal shrug. "I wish I could be of more help there, but unfortunately, I am not my mother. She has expertise that I have simply yet to acquire."

"Speaking of your mother, where is she? I was honestly expecting her to show up to do the thing, not you," Jeremiah asked before taking a drink of water from the wooden mug.

Then he put it down and sighed.

"This whole deal was between me and her, and I'm honestly a little pissed that she just dipped on me," he continued when Denise didn't add anything.

"Clients from out of town," Denise answered with an annoyed glare at the table, her lip curled into a faint snarl. "Honestly, I just enjoy any excuse to avoid them.

"She was going to visit you after they'd left, most likely in a few days. I offered to take care of the grunt work for her, specifically the consultation and examination, so I could have a reason to get out of the house while they're there."

"Oh boy, what'd they do to piss you off?" Jeremiah chortled, smirking over at the scowling Fae.

"Existed," Denise spat with a disgusted look on her face. "They just... ooze everywhere.

"Every time I'm around and they say anything, I just feel like I've had a bucket of grease and grit dumped all over me."

"Sounds like they're some real sleazeballs," Jeremiah nodded reassuringly at Denise, who was opening and closing her hands in front of herself, as if literally feeling a disgusting mass around her.

"They are. At least your Vampire has better manners," Denise said with a sharp nod and a smile.

"Yeah... Ash-" Jeremiah snorted and shook his head as a deep warmth suffused him, a smile forcing its way through to his lips. "Ash changed a lot of my world view. Made me realize there was more to life than just... killing things because I think they might be a threat."

Denise's grin was subtle, but present as Jeremiah took in a deep inhale of breath, and then froze.

"Wait, what do you mean 'my' Vampire?" Jeremiah shot back as an icy chill crept its way up his spine.

"Well, I mean she is your girlfriend after all," Denise's expression went from sly to confused in an instant. "It's not really that much of a stretch to call her your Vampire, now is it?"

"Oh, thank fuck," Jeremiah exhaled a breath of relief before chuckling nervously. "For a minute there I thought you were saying your mother's guests were Vampires too."

"I mean, they are. From what I understand, they've been coming to my mother for alchemical research for decades now," Denise said, her words sending a jolt of electricity down Jeremiah's spine. "They're some important coven from the city, show up every now and then to have my mother make them tinctures and the like.

"Always leave me feeling like I've just been oozed upon when they visit. I wouldn't put it past them to be criminals of a sort."

Jeremiah pulled his phone out of his pocket, and tapped through the menus, eventually landing on Ashley's name.

He hit the dial button and pressed it to his ear as Denise scoffed in the background.

"A phone call during our dinner? So ru-"
"Shut it!" Jeremiah snapped literally and

metaphorically at Denise, lowering his hand to the table as the phone tried, then failed to connect. "Damnit, no signal."

"Of course not, we're too far awa-" Denise began to clarify the obvious.

"Denise," Jeremiah interrupted, hanging up the unconnected line. "What are the Vampire's names?"

"Uh… I'm not sure actually, at least not for the lead ones," Denise slowly shook her head as her expression grew ever more concerned. "Why?"

"Did you not listen to me earlier? We're being hunted by a coven from Clallam. Unless these guys are from another country or something, I'm guessing there's a good chance that they're the coven that's trying to -kill- us," Jeremiah hissed, his mouth hanging open as his brows went up.

"Ah," Denise said with an odd look, her mouth turning to one side as she apparently made the connection Jeremiah just had. "I think these Vampires are… somewhat local. I think… the one who simps for the one in charge is named… Veronica or something? I honestly don't remember."

The name didn't ring a bell to Jeremiah, but he still pushed himself out of the bench and ran his hands through his hair in frustration.

"Though, the one who always tries to hit on me, I know his name," Denise complained with a grumpy tone. "It's Aiden… something."

"Fuck!" Jeremiah shouted, snarling and baring his teeth. "Shit! Goddamnit!"

He began to jog down the trail that he thought lead to his car.

"Wait!" Denise shouted after him, as a loud buzzing noise came from behind. "Where are you going?"

"Home!" Jeremiah snapped back, lifting his head to see Denise literally flying above him. "That fucker I blew up? That was Aiden."

"Well, I'm sure everything will be fine! It's not like they know you're here, otherwise they would have gone straight to your cabin first. Wouldn't they?" Denise offered, floating slightly in front of him now.

That was a good point, and it gave Jeremiah a small piece of hope that his duo and himself could just stay at a hotel for a day or four until the coven left.

But the majority of his mind was still set on the fact that somehow, Vasily would discover their presence before Jeremiah could return.

"Not chancing it," Jeremiah shook his head as his heart thudded in his chest. "Even if we're fine, I'd much rather catch a hotel a few hours away and wait for the coven to dip."

"Fair. Off we go then," Denise agreed and waved her hand before Jeremiah nearly upended his stomach, as reality bent before him. As the mirage-like shimmer stabilized, he found the dark, winding trail was no longer present.

Instead, a short, slightly curved trail to his car sat before him.

"We?" Jeremiah slid to a fast walk a dozen feet from the SUV.

"Yes, we. You think you can just leave dinner early on me?" Denise grunted out and dropped out of the sky on the passenger side of his SUV.

The Fae scoffed and rolled her eyes, as a smile crossed her face. "Preposterous."

"Fine, whatever," Jeremiah grunted as he

opened the rear door of the SUV, flipped up the seat, and pulled free a handgun stashed there. "You know how to shoot?"

"I don't really need toys. I'm the weapon," Denise murmured with a self-assured smile. Her hand came up and presented a ball of angry, crackling lightning, that dissipated to nothing after a second.

"Right," Jeremiah tossed the gun back and slammed the door before climbing into the driver's side shortly before the Fae sat in the passenger's seat.

I'm about to ride into an ambush with a trickster Fae and a gun that will do absolutely nothing...aren't I?

He shook his head and turned the key in the ignition.

We'll just...keep calling Ash and Jenny as we get into town. Hopefully they pick up.

Chapter 30

Jeremiah pulled the steering wheel of the SUV sharply as they rounded the corner of the dirt mountain road.

The vehicle fishtailed, causing one of the back tires to slide off the edge of the road.

He outright refused to let up on the gas pedal.

"You know," Denise grunted, holding tight to the oh-shit-handle with one hand, and Jeremiah's arm with the other. "I almost would have preferred just flying you there if you drive like this!"

"Don't ca- wait, you can do that?" Jeremiah asked, risking pulling his eyes off the road for a split second to glance inquisitively at the Fae.

"With how much muscle you have?" Denise chuckled nervously as they bounced over a dip in the road. "It would be -guh- more like hang-gliding.

"And I doubt that it would be faster than your damn lead foot!"

Something about the Fae's ardent critique of his driving style made Jeremiah chuckle, despite the tense situation.

"Well, I'm sooo sorry this couldn't be a lovely Sunday drive, o' queen of the forest!" Jeremiah quipped back, putting a false accent that both mimicked and over-exaggerated Denise's small accent.

"Hmm, that's better," Denise briefly crossed her arms across her chest in a mock huff before Jeremiah hit another bump. Her hands immediately shot back to the handle and Jeremiah's arm. "You still drive like a madman though."

"I drive. Like a man worried about his girlfriends! I can pull over and let you go if you want!" Jeremiah grunted, jerking the wheel around another steep corner in the road.

"As if!" Jeremiah could physically hear the eye roll in Denise's statement. "We still haven't finished our date! You're not getting away just because some creepy Vamps are in town!"

"Not a date!" Jeremiah shot back as they turned onto the paved county road. "Just dinner!"

"Would you have gone without your dear, sweet lovelies' approval?" Denise questioned in return after the engine roared.

Jeremiah glanced over at her with a raised brow and an open mouth, genuinely considering the statement.

"See?" Denise asked rhetorically with a broad, playful smile that in no way, shape, or form, matched the situation.

Jeremiah outright refused to reply as they sped down the dark mountain road, instead pulling out his phone and dialing up Jenny's number. After a few short rings, it answered.

"Oh, shit, thank god. I thought th-" Jeremiah wheezed, leaning back into his seat and blew out a breath.

"You thought... what?" A sententious Eastern European voice asked with a smile in his tone. "Mr. Nemo, I take? Or should I call you... Jerry, heart emoji, heart emoji?"

Jeremiah's heart dropped into his guts, his left hand gripping the steering wheel with white knuckles.

"Really, mister Jeremiah? Are we honestly going to play this game of silence?" Vasily questioned exasperatedly. "You act as if speaking to me will change the inevitable."

"The... inevitable?" Jeremiah replied after a further moment's pause.

"Ah, so he speaks!" Vasily laughed gleefully over the line. "And yes. The inevitable. You see, Jeremiah heart emoji, heart emoji, I was more than content to let this particular sleeping dog lie.

"As much as it pained me to lose my pet, does not a good owner smile when a stray is taken in by a loving home?"

The man spoke with a drawl that almost sounded bored.

"But then you went and targeted my business. My sweat and blood," Vasily's slow, dark chuckle ended in a snarl. "My home, which I spent over a century building from the ground up. Destroyed a multi-million-dollar mansion, killed five of my coven members, and then dropped off the face of the earth for weeks.

"My oh my, that's not even... it's like you gave up trying to knock me off my throne before you even started. I am honestly insulted!"

Jeremiah again remained silent, staring fixedly out the front window of the vehicle still speeding through the valley.

He gulped deeply, feeling like his entire body was alight with adrenaline.

"But, as providence would have it, I stumbled across this... lovely, quaint cabin you're hiding in while visiting an old friend," Vasily continued after the silence stretched for several seconds, apparently more than happy to carry a conversation on his own. "Perhaps I should buy it myself, a vacation home for after I deal with this thorn lodged in my side."

"I'm gonna fuckin' kill you i-"

"You? Kill me?" Vasily interrupted with an amused snort. "I'll admit, it's possible. You did a nasty bit of work on my village idiot. He's still in a bed recovering.

"Even for us, it's not easy to just regrow a limb or four. Let alone a massive chunk of his torso.

"In fact, that's part of the reason why I came to visit dear Maljori here. A tincture or two to aid in the healing process for mister Westinghouse."

I mean...if I survived, it's not really a stretch to assume that he did too.

Jeremiah grimaced and rounded a bend in the road.

He did survive rounds to the dome, after all.

"Why am I not surprised that his ugly ass lived?" Jeremiah replied flatly.

"What he lacks in brains, he makes up for in copious reserves of luck," Vasily noted over the line with a humorless snort. "Not that dissimilar to you, from what I gather. You also survived the explosion, somehow, though I personally attribute that to your maker's creativity and skill."

"Wouldn't know. Only met the asshole once," Jeremiah said in an exasperated tone and blew out a breath.

He glanced over to the wide-eyed and concerned-looking Denise.

"Come now, is that any way for a man to talk about his father?" Vasily asked in a thoughtful tone. Then he sighed audibly into the line and clicked his tongue. "But that's not the point of this conversation.

"You see, Jerry, you have pissed me off. First, you stab me in my own restaurant, then blow up one of my homes?

"I've never been one to leap pointlessly towards premature conclusions, but to me it seems as if you are at fault for causing these problems.

"So I'll make you a final offer."

Vasily paused for clear dramatic effect. Jeremiah, honestly, already knew what was coming.

"You for them," Vasily offered exactly what Jeremiah dreaded. "You have one hour, or pieces start coming off."

The line clicked silent.

Jeremiah pulled the phone away from his ear, gripping it like a vise before he hucked it at the dash with a wordless shout.

And I wasn't there for any of it.

Jeremiah glared over the hood of the vehicle.

Out on a damned date with another woman, and what did it get me?

My life or theirs.

My life of theirs!

Of course it is. Because that's what would happen!

Because I got involved with this monster!

It's this damn Fae!

It's all her, the damned trickster!

All she wanted was to separate me from Ash and Jenny. Because that's what monsters do!

They just want to take you apart. No different than any other monster out there.

They're all the same.

She did this to get me out of the house and... and...

Even as he had the thoughts, he realized they were stupid.

Pointless.

His rage and misdirected thoughts puttered

out the instant he put any fragment of rationality behind them.

The idea that Denise would betray him because she was a monster, to kill other monsters for the sake of being a monster, sounded ludicrous. Even to his rage addled mind he knew such conclusions were the stuff of fear.

Fear for Ashley and Jennifer.

Jeremiah slammed on the brakes without really considering it. The whole of the vehicle came to a screeching halt and partially turned to the side.

It was a move that flung Denise into the dashboard.

Jeremiah sat there, his hands gripping the steering wheel as if it were a lifeline. One that he needed desperately in the moment.

"How could they have found out?" hissed Jeremiah mostly to himself. "He found the cabin. Only a few people knew we were there. Only a few."

"Ow! That hurt, damnit!" Denise whined throatily. One of her hands pressed to her temple as she looked at him.

Sitting there, Jeremiah didn't look away from the empty blackness that he was staring at. His mind was honestly elsewhere, even as he vaguely recognized that Denise was talking to him.

"Well don't look at me. I didn't tell them anything. I wasn't even there, damnit," cursed Denise.

From sitting next to him to vanishing outright, she was gone.

Leaving only an odd sense of vertigo as the world bent back into place.

The change shook him from his stupor and he started to look around.

"-You asshole-!" Denise shouted from outside the SUV.

The Fae was hovering several feet off the ground less than a yard from the hood of his vehicle, holding crackling balls of lightning in either hand. "Do you know how long it took to do my hair like this? In the woods? Off of a hand mirror?"

Jeremiah ran his tongue along his teeth as he watched the Fae sorceress hover menacingly.

Jeremiah furrowed his brow and blinked, making eye contact with the snarling, petite, flying woman.

"If I wanted you dead, you would be!" Denise hurled one of the balls of lightning off to the side, resulting in an ear-splitting explosion and a pressure wave that caused the car to shift on its suspension, even from the nearby hillside it impacted. "Hell, even if I decided to make you be mine, I could make that happen! Your tether is just sitting there, ready to be connected and free for the taking!"

Sitting there, truly lost in his thoughts, Jeremiah just stared at her almost uncomprehendingly, even as bits of dirt and debris pattered down on the roof of the vehicle.

"Instead, I thought that allowing things to progress naturally would be the most fun, entertaining, and -polite- way to handle things!" seethed Denise.

Having a sudden thought that actually felt somewhat useful, Jeremiah slowly opened the door of the SUV.

He stepped out and just stood there. Staring up at Denise, his brow furrowed as his teeth gnawed at the inside of his lip.

"Didn't-didn't actually say it was you,"

growled Jeremiah with a flick of his hand. "Sorry about jamming the brakes. I didn't-I'm just-things are fucked, okay? They're fucked!

"I have no clue about what to do, and realistically, there's only like... five people who knew where I was. You and your mother are two of them.

"My dad-well, I don't think he really cares, and the other two are kidnapped! You were here with me so... that leaves one person, doesn't it?"

Jeremiah stood there, staring at Denise, who stared back at him.

"Your mom," Jeremiah dropped into the empty space as if it were a lead weight.

Denise paused mid-flight and squinted thoughtfully at nothing.

Pursing her lips, she sniffed once, rolled her head back and forth on her shoulders, and then shook it.

"My mother? Surely not," Denise disagreed with a low tone, resuming her slow hover around Jeremiah. He got the impression that she really was actually listening to him, however. "Though... when she's working, she does tend to get a little... mmm, scatterbrained, I suppose you could say.

"If it was indeed something she said, I would believe it to be entirely innocent.

"Innocuous.

"Brought up in conversation. That or someone might have snooped about if a workbook was left out. Though it's equally possible they smelled you, or your ladies in the store, no? Vampires have a good sense of smell," Denise suggested with a noncommittal shrug. She raised her hands beside her head in a clear 'dunno' gesture. "Those Vamps are always really nosy so it wouldn't be surprising. They tend to poke and prod into anything they can.

"We're always forced to lock our d-lock... lock our—"

Denise words slowly faded away as if she'd run out of power or letters to use.

"Shit," Denise spat out as if she were a gumball machine that just had its lever turned. She then dropped the spell from her hand and looked away with a grimace.

"What?" Jeremiah asked, watching as the spell blew away into a faint, glittering nothing.

"I usually go through the house and lock all the doors when they visit... today I was too focused on... well, getting ready for you," admitted Denise with a sigh. She rubbed her forehead as she slowly lowered herself to the ground. "Perhaps... I actually am at fault for them finding you. Though that seems somewhat... farfetched, it isn't impossible."

"They're Vampires. If they want in a door, they can just kick it down with that beefed up strength they've got," remarked Jeremiah with a long and slow sigh. Then he shook his head and looked to the ground where the spell disintegrated.

"Not if your doors are enchanted," Denise waggled her finger at Jeremiah with a smirk. "Pretty hard to get through those without bringing down the entire house unless you have the key. And I... well, I didn't lock up. I honestly didn't think anything of it, as it's happened before without an incident."

Jeremiah watched as Denise stared pointedly to the left, crossing her arms over her chest, clearly avoiding his gaze.

His mind drifted away from the colored cheeks of the diminutive woman, and back to the fact that he still had less than an hour to come up with a plan, get home, and somehow win against Vasily and god knows how many of the mutated Vampires.

"Well," Jeremiah tried, pursing his lips to the side before smacking them once and turning for the driver's side door. "Sounds like this is a conversation to have after this is all wrapped up. Stay safe, Denise."

With the curt goodbye finished, he sat in the driver's seat, closed the door, and put the vehicle in gear. Then he sighed when the SUV shifted slightly, and he saw movement out of the corner of his eye.

"Denise," Jeremiah didn't take his foot off the brake as he refused to look the Fae in the eyes.

"I told you - you're not getting out of our date that easily," Denise said with a razor-sharp edge to her voice. "Besides! This is so exciting! We're going on an actual rescue mission!"

Denise did a small, shimmying dance in the passenger seat that in no way, shape, or form matched the floating personification of chaos she'd been just a few moments before.

Jeremiah blew out a breath as an old mantra made its way through his mind.

Don't stick your dick in crazy.

"Yeah, we are," Jeremiah nodded slowly as he realized that he might have to temper the Fae's enthusiasm somewhat if he had a hope of making it out of this with both him and his girlfriends alive. "That means we need to make a good plan beforehand, and execute it properly. The most important part of this is getting Ash and Jenny out alive."

"Hmmm..." Denise tapped at the bottom of her lip as Jeremiah pulled the vehicle back onto the road and accelerated quickly. "We have an hour, right?"

"Less, now," Jeremiah shot back, pulling out his phone to check the time he'd made the call. "Fifty-four minutes."

"I might have something at my house that could help... I might have a few things, actually, " Denise offered with a thoughtful expression on her face.

"We don't have time t-"

"Oh, it's on the way back, don't worry," Denise waved a dismissive hand at him as they sped down the road. "It's a small dirt road behind my mother's shop. Less than a couple minutes out of our way."

"Denise, I'm not sure if that's a goo-"

"Do you want access to magical grenades, or not?" Denise interrupted again with a pointed, pretty smile.

Jeremiah's reply died on his lips.

He closed his mouth, inhaled, and raised his eyebrows, glancing back down the dark road ahead.

I'd like some grenades. Yes.

Very much.

"Your place it is," he said, feeling slightly better.

* * *

Jeremiah pulled to a stop in front of a Tudor-style, three-story house. He withdrew the pistol from his waistband, checked the chamber, and looked back to the lit windows of the home.

"Come on!" Denise chirped brightly, throwing open her side of the car and exiting. "Let's go!"

Jeremiah grunted and opened his door, deciding to leave the long, heavy rifle put.

He aimed the pistol at the house and slowly began to approach, watching each of the windows for any signs of movement.

"Stay quiet and keep your eyes peeled," Jeremiah commanded in a low, quiet tone as Denise seemed to be approaching the small manor without a care in the world. "We don't know who or what they left behind. I don't want any surprises, and I certainly don't want them calling Vasily."

"Hmm? Oh, right" Denise snapped her fingers before a powerful thrum of energy shook the world once, then returned with a diminished thud. "Hmm... it looks like they left two people inside."

"Can you tell where they are, specifically?" Jeremiah asked and stopped moving, more than aware of a Vampire's propensity for enhanced hearing and how they might react to Denise's soundwave.

"Best I can tell, they're both by the front door. Though I'm not sure if they're in the entryway, the library, or the lab," admitted Denise as she slowly tilted her head to the side and took in a deep breath, staring pointedly at the door.

"Alright. Let me go in first," Jeremiah muttered, nodding his head once sharply at the end. He resumed his slow, steady steps, trying to make as little noise as possible.

"Why?" Denise snapped her eyes to him with a frown.

"Because I have the gun... and I've killed a lot of Vamps before," Jeremiah replied with his sights trained on the front door of the home.

"Have you? Or are those just the memories implanted into you?" Denise asked a question that caused Jeremiah to momentarily stumble in his steps. "Also, I can use magic, remember?"

Jeremiah's eyes glanced down and to the side as he struggled to find a reply to that. He shook his head in a sharp snapping motion, hoping to shake away the uncertainty with the motion.

"Fine," he murmured, stopping for a brief second to let Denise move ahead of him. "But try and give me a clear line of fire."

"I'll try," she giggled quietly, taking the first of the steps up to the door. "I might just do all the work, though. My home, after all."

Denise threw open the door to the home, walking in with a confident saunter.

"Oh mother! I'm home!" she declared loudly while Jeremiah crept up behind her. "Have our guests left yet?"

"No, we haven't," a decidedly male voice answered, and Jeremiah heard the distinct sound of a round being chambered. "We've got orders from the boss to hold you here until a situation gets reso- -oh shit-!"

A thunderous boom emanated from the doorway in front of him, and Jeremiah sprang through, lifting the weapon skyward, only to have his eyebrows follow suit.

Two charred bodies rested on the floor, writhing and moaning listlessly while Denise chuckled maliciously.

"Pull a gun on me?" she cooed at the twin red and black pieces of meat. "In my own home?"

The Fae shot another bolt of lightning that hit

the body on the right before jumping to the left.

"Do you two not have any manners? At all?" Denise again chided rhetorically at the same time Jeremiah stepped around her and sighted the first meatsack's skull.

Or at least, what he assumed was a skull. The bodies were far beyond recognizable as people, aside from a passing resemblance to a humanoid shape.

He pulled the trigger once, twice, and a third time on the former Vampire's skull, leaving only a jagged, bloody stump where a skull once was.

He turned at his waist, aimed at the second head, and repeated the process.

"Aww, I wanted to mess with them a little more!" Denise whined, slumping her shoulders and frowning deeply. She glared at the corpses with a huff. "And I'm absolutely sure that I'm going to have to clean the mess up!"

Jeremiah pursed his lips before he let out a breath and shook his head.

On the one hand, he absolutely understood why she wouldn't want to clean up the pulpy mess left over from the heavy hollow-point rounds.

On the other, her attitude was far too chipper for the situation at hand, in his opinion.

I mean...they're Vampires. And not good ones either.

Jeremiah dropped his magazine free and replaced it with a fresh one.

Fuck 'em. Died like they deserved. Painfully.

"Yeah, sorry," lied Jeremiah, lowering his weapon when he didn't see any sign of the near-instant self-repair he'd seen with Aiden. "Let's pick up the pace. You said something about magical grenades?"

"Oh, that's just the appetizer!" promised Denise, who grinned broadly and put her hands on her hips shooting him a self-assured smile. "But I promised to be on retainer, not to be free. You want more than the bare minimum to fight a coven of mutagenic Vampires? It's gonna cost you."

"I don't really have any money," Jeremiah mumbled and held the handgun loosely at his side.

"Oh I don't want money," Denise ran her thumb and forefinger along her jaw, brushing away a fleck of blood. "I want—"

"Oh god, not this bullshit again," Jeremiah muttered as the Fae's voice drew silent. He did not have the time to play games.

"I want," restated Denise as her gaze snapped to him, her lips splitting into a wide, dangerous-looking grin. "A kiss."

"You know what? Fuck it!" Jeremiah snapped angrily, pressing his palms into his eyes before throwing them out to the side explosively. He grabbed Denise by the back of her head and forcefully pulled her lips to his.

Breaking the kiss after a moment, Jeremiah pulled his head back and stared at the blinking, somewhat confused-looking otherworldly woman.

"Now," he held his hands beside his head like blinders and continued in the slowest, firmest tone he could manage, "Grenades. Where?"

Chapter 31

Jeremiah allowed himself a moment to take in the sights of the home while Denise hummed tunelessly to herself, walking through the hallway with an odd bouncing gait.

It was like if she were trying to skip and walk normally in the same motion. Though, whether this was an expression of subdued glee from their brief kiss, or just Denise's natural chaotic and enormously tone-deaf energy, he wasn't sure.

On virtually every wall were paintings, trophies, and framed documents written in languages Jeremiah couldn't understand.

"Denise, are we actually going anywhere, or are you just using this as an excuse to show me around?" Jeremiah asked in a flat tone, peering into a room full of blown glass chemical equipment arrayed in a complex, purposeful manner.

"We're going to the armory!" Denise replied in a tone that felt drenched with bright, sunny energy.

"Uh-huh."

Jeremiah's response felt almost small in these rooms.

He followed her direction as they passed a room that was clearly a kitchen, with two sinks full of dishes, a stove, and a large stone island counter.

Denise turned to the left around a bend in the hallway, and Jeremiah followed to find himself standing in front of a small, sharply turning spiral staircase, around a two-foot-wide bronze pole, that seemed to run the entire height of the home.

"Down we go!" Denise chittered happily,

sitting on the outside rail of the staircase and sliding down the banister. "Wheee!"

Jeremiah followed with his eyes, sighed, and fought a smile while he began to walk down the steps and the Fae's voice grew ever so slightly distant as she neared the bottom of the staircase.

Arriving at the bottom, he found himself staring at three massive bronze-banded oak doors. One to his front, with the other two on his left and his right.

Denise stepped up to the door on the left, placed her hand atop a flat, mirror-polished piece of bronze, and whispered softly.

A small flash of blue light tinted the room for a scant second before the door began to groan and creak.

It clacked loudly, then began to slowly swing inward. Denise grinned widely at it.

Jeremiah blew out a breath at what he saw when he stepped up beside the Fae.

The word "Armory" definitely fit, considering the display of row after row of ancient and modern weapons resting upon large wooden racks.

"Where the hell did you get all this hardware?" Jeremiah pushed past Denise, a sideways, enthusiastic snarl growing on his face.

"My mother has been the object of assassination attempts for centuries," Denise commented from behind him as he ran a finger along an ancient-looking, gold-inlaid sword. "Inevitably, they fail. Honestly, this room is more of a garbage bin for the ones she doesn't really care about. There are several trophies in her office commemorating fights that she remembers fondly."

Jeremiah pursed his lips, nodding slowly,

remembering his talk with the elder Fae woman in her shop.

Even without her ever saying or doing anything remotely threatening, he'd felt the power roll off of her in waves. To imagine that she'd fought and won against various hit teams over the centuries wasn't a stretch by any means.

"That sword came from a Templar roughly three centuries ago," Denise informed Jeremiah when he couldn't pull his eyes away from the weapon. "It actually used to sit on her desk, until she reorganized it a few years back. I'm sure she wouldn't mind you borrowing it to free your women."

"Mnn, nah," responded Jeremiah, pulling his hand back with a sigh and soft chuckle. "Swords are cool and all, but don't really have a place in a fight these days. Nothing a sword can do that a rifle can't.

"Besides, that thing looks almost decorative," Jeremiah shrugged and moved down the line of weapons. "Fit for some asshole who rules a country and doesn't get their hands dirty. Someone with a name like..."

Jeremiah picked up a large handgun with a suppressor and massive light on the bottom. He turned it over in his hand, checked the chamber, and grunted approvingly.

"Like..." Denise prompted slowly, and Jeremiah shrugged, set the safety on the handgun, and tucked it into his waistband.

"'Unno," Jeremiah gazed thoughtfully around the room, seeing a distinct lack of anything he would classify as a grenade. "Had it for a moment, then I lost it. Where are the grenades?"

"Oh, those are over here," Denise proclaimed before she pushed past him to a small wooden box on a table in the back of the room. She unclasped a small latch, opened the box, and stepped aside.

With a frown, Jeremiah picked up one of the small leather pouches in the box.

A short string stuck out of the top of the cinched-tight leather sack. He glanced up to Denise, who was grinning at him.

"This is a bag," he stated the obvious, hoping his expression would communicate his displeasure at the complete lack of explosives he was holding.

"It is a bag," agreed Denise, smiled bright as she answered in a tone that confirmed only what he'd said. The painful silence stretched on for several seconds before Jeremiah closed his eyes and began to place the sack back in the box. "A bag filled with a lot of things that are... touchy, with certain circumstances."

Jeremiah scratched a small piece of dust out of his eye and said nothing further as he watched the Fae watch him with an unreadable grin.

"And that means," he murmured, still not getting it.

"Ka-boom!" Denise mimed an explosion with her hands, before pointing to the bag he held. "The powder in that bag will detonate and excite the naturally present essence in the air, causing it to harden into small pebble-like chunks.

"So... so... everything goes ka-blamo and nothing gets left behind! It's all atomized.

"But because of that, all those chunks get blown out in every possible direction.

"Well, that's dependent on the amount of Essence nearby, but that's beside the point.

"It's really quite energetic. Violent. I used it to clear out some tree trunks so I could plant new things."

Denise nodded her head several times with a wide expectant smile. She looked very much as if she were looking for affirmation.

"Alright," Jeremiah stuffed one in his back pocket, then another, as he continued perusing the arms room. "What else do we have in here?"

"Well, I'm assuming you're already using anti-para rounds, so nothing more than what you really already have. A couple magic swords, the grenades you have, guns from various centuries," Denise offered neutrally while Jeremiah ran his eyes along each of the shelves.

"Wait… anti-para rounds?" Jeremiah pressed and furrowed his brow. He looked at Denise to make sure he caught her eye. "You mean the kind the government uses? I thought you couldn't get those as a civilian."

"Not wholesale, no," Denise affirmed his point with a predatory grin. "However, trades aren't purchases, and sometimes people are more than willing to offer it up.

"That and… well… people tend to come equipped with them, then donate them.

"When they die."

Jeremiah blinked, took in a short breath, and held it. He was suddenly glad he hadn't actually let his bad temper get the best of him when it came to the Fae.

He pursed his lips, reaching into the waistband of his pants to pull free the large pistol he'd taken off of the nearby table.

Dropping the magazine, he grinned widely as he saw the crystalline lattice interwoven with gold and brown flecks.

"Hello beautiful," he murmured to himself with a small smirk, feeling a small weight lifting off his shoulders for the first time since dinner.

The anti-para rounds might not have any effect at all on the mutated Vampires, but it left him with a small spark of hope burning its way into his heart.

"Do you like that?" Denise asked, causing Jeremiah to look up and find her grabbing another weapon off the rack with a broad smile, before presenting it to Jeremiah with outstretched arms. "There's more!"

Jeremiah put the pistol back into his waistband and took the rifle with a smile, checking the magazine and finding the same anti-para rounds inside, this time in a small rifle caliber.

Denise then directed him to a pile of assorted gear and armor that, much like the weapons themselves, seemed to span the ages.

He withdrew the body armor that he believed went with the weapon, as the magazines inside the plate carrier matched the one in the rifle.

He had almost given up on finding a holster for the massive pistol when his foot kicked a black object out from under the no-longer-neat pile of equipment.

It skidded across the floor and revealed itself to be a holster upon its gentle impact against the wall.

Jeremiah grinned widely as the pistol slid perfectly into place.

He clipped it to his belt and moved to leave, when he realized that he'd forgotten to grab a spare mag for the pistol, and returned to the table he'd found it at.

He found two more loaded with anti-para

rounds against the back and stuffed them into the pocket of his jeans before turning to exit the room.

Then, he froze.

Jeremiah exhaled a breath and stared at the sword on the wall. His eyes ran over the foreign script on the hilt, trying to remember how to read Latin, not that he'd ever learned.

Something about leaving it behind felt wrong, criminal even.

"What... are you?" Jeremiah whispered as he lifted the sheath of the sword out of the two hooks that held it horizontal above the floor.

Put it back.

He scoffed at himself.

By the time you'd have a chance to use it, you'll already be dead.

It's just going to be extra weight. You don't need it.

Jeremiah blew out a breath, set the rifle down on the table, and buckled the belt of the sword around his hips. Grabbing the rifle again, he set out to follow Denise back up the stairs.

She leaned on the railing a few steps up, watching him with a curious expression.

She opened her mouth to ask the obvious, teasing question at hand, but Jeremiah raised his hand sharply.

"Save it," grouched Jeremiah, making a chopping motion with his arm. "I don't know, it just felt wrong leaving it behind."

Denise raised her eyebrow and rolled her head from one shoulder to the other.

"Let's go, we've gotta make a plan on the way," Jeremiah commanded, giving Denise a gentle but pointed push up the stairs. "On the clock, remember?"

"But you look so good! That armor really makes your shoulders look nice and broad," Denise whined, bouncing into the air to hover backwards up the stairs as Jeremiah climbed upwards.

"Are you intentionally this bad at flirting?" Jeremiah asked, the two going up in the dimly lit stairwell.

"Maybe I just have a thing for bad boys," mused Denise and shrugged. "Though, you're a lot cuter than the last Templar that tried to kill us. You actually talk back, instead of screaming and wildly swinging your sword around!"

Jeremiah rolled his eyes and sighed.

Sounds like Claudius.

"Anyway," he pointedly changed the direction of the conversation. "How fast can you fly?"

"Why?" asked Denise as her eyes narrowed. She dropped silently onto the main floor of the house a moment before Jeremiah's foot hit the hardwood floor.

"I need to know what I'm walking into. I was hoping you could do a fly-by without being seen. Maybe snap a picture or two," explained Jeremiah. His mind began to work at dismantling the problem at hand. "I need to know roughly how many I'm up against, and hopefully where they are. If there's a way I can get Ash and Jenn to safety without getting myself in too deep, that's what I'd prefer."

"If you're open to trying something," Denise offered with a predatory grin and a small waggle of magically glittering fingers, "I have an idea."

"What?" Jeremiah felt suspicion bubble to the surface in his gut, eyeing the Fae.

"Have you ever heard of astral projection?"

* * *

Jeremiah walked steadily up the long driveway to the cabin, slowly panning his head to scan the dense treelines on either side of him.

Two cowled figures stood at the end of the driveway, both aiming small submachine guns at him. Jeremiah slowly raised his hands.

He kept walking as they offered no challenge, no order to stop.

Keep going. Keep their eyes on me long enough for Denise to get her spell up and working.

Then go for Vasily.

Cut the head off the snake.

"Jerry Heart-Emoji, Heart-Emoji!" Vasily called enthusiastically as he entered the clearing around the cabin. "You cut that a little close, didn't you?"

Jeremiah looked around the clearing with a flat, emotionless expression.

In front of the porch steps were Ashley and Jenny, on their knees, with pistols aimed at the back of both their heads. Additionally, there were over a dozen Vampires around the home, including Vasily.

"Yeah," Jeremiah inhaled deeply, turning his head fractionally to glare at the unassuming, terrifying Vampire lord. "Spent a solid ten or twenty minutes watching the place through the scope of a rifle."

"As I had figured," Vasily smirked at Jeremiah, standing up from where he crouched in front of Ashley and Jenny.

"Jeremiah, you damn idiot!" Jenny shouted, struggling with the bindings behind her back.

"It's alright, Jenny," Jeremiah gave her a sad smile before turning back to Vasily. The Vampire watched Jeremiah with a confused and faux-concerned expression, his arms folded behind his back.

"I must admit," Vasily offered after a moment's pause, taking a deep breath before letting it out in a rush and approaching Jeremiah slowly. "I... expected more from you. An explosion, a grand exchange of gunfire, something.

"But you come before me like a scolded puppy, with no fangs to bear. This is... different from the man I so briefly met those weeks ago," Vasily scratched at the stubble on his cheeks thoughtfully, seeming to size up Jeremiah in a different light. "Are you sure you're the same man who stabbed my hand and bombed my employee?"

"Clearly fuckin' not!" Jeremiah smirked and lifted his shoulders. "You should just let us three go while you run off and look for that guy. Sounds like a real prick."

"Hmm," Vasily mused and slowly shook his head. "Perhaps an... explanation is in order, no? Jeremiah's last testament to the world, of how he fought the unbeatable and inevitably lost."

With a shake of his head, Vasily seemed to give up on the train of thought he'd been holding.

"Were it so easy for us to change the things we desire, to shift the world through willpower alone!" Vasily continued. Speaking with a voice that projected. It was as if he were delivering a sermon in front of their home. "Unfortunately, I learned long ago that power comes at the end of a dagger.

"Though, I must say, to let aside your pride and lay your head at my feet like this is... moving. Originally, I had planned on just killing these two as a matter of course, but now..."

Vasily waved a hand absently at Ashley and Jenny.

Then he stretched his arms out to each side in an odd gesture.

Jeremiah scratched his short beard with one hand, letting his gaze roll about the clearing. Everyone here had been focused on him but didn't look too nervous.

They seemed entirely confident about the situation.

"But now, I think I might actually let them go," admitted Vasily as he stared at the floor. Blinking slowly, he rested his hands on his hips. Shaking his head rapidly, the Vampire lord blew out a breath as he blinked several times. "See... anyone can be violent. Anyone can kill. Hell, I built my empire on it.

"But it takes a... unique man to sacrifice himself for the ones he values," Vasily began to nod slowly, taking two steps towards Jeremiah. "All this just makes me wish we had met under better circumstances. I do believe you would have been a valuable asset for my organization."

"You know, I think your head's gotten too damn big up there at the head of your coven," accused Jeremiah while scowling at the disgusting bloodsucker.

At the moment, he'd decided he knew everything that he needed to.

Now he just hoped that Denise had been successful.

"It's about damn time someone takes you

down a few pegs," he asserted.

"Well... that someone won't be you," Vasily smirked dangerously at Jeremiah.

Then he lunged at him.

Shit.

Hope this is enough time for Denise to do what she needed.

He's gonna try and drink me dry.

Let's leave him confused.

Just gotta open my eyes.

Feel the energy like Denise said, and open my-

Jeremiah opened his eyes with a slow, gentle inhale, and turned the key in the SUV ignition.

Well, that was fuckin' weird.

Jeremiah blinked his eyes quickly, the soft ringing in his ears began to grow in intensity.

He reached up as his lips began to feel warm and wet, wiping away the blood from his nose.

Denise had told him that projecting from this distance at that level of tangibility, even with her help initiating it, would be difficult at best.

Possibly fatal at worst.

His head began to scream at him, an aching throb at the front of his head that felt like an icepick to his brain.

He put the vehicle in drive and slowly pressed on the accelerator, driving up and over the hill.

The forest before him was dense, but not so dense that he couldn't drive through it. The problem was, for their plan to work, he couldn't just 'drive' through it.

He had to careen through it at a speed that would induce even the heartiest of Paras to clench the wheel.

As well as their ass cheeks.

"Fuckin'—" Jeremiah growled, clenching his teeth and slammed onto the accelerator.

He passed through the first gap, then the second, then had to jerk his wheel to make it through the third.

This was at best a walking trail, at worst a game trail.

And he was going through it as if it were a rally course.

He couldn't read the numbers on the incessantly bouncing and rattling dash, but he could see the hand of the speedometer standing quite nearly vertical.

Crashing through a bush, Jeremiah blew out a breath.

He felt his heart thud loudly once before it stilled momentarily and began to resume its energetic rhythm.

As if responding to his desire for reassurance.

Out of instinct as much as conscious desire, Jeremiah did something he hadn't done in what felt like ages.

He prayed.

To what god, to what pantheon or power, he didn't know.

Then he suddenly smirked.

"Reixhitz, you dead-beat dad, if you're listening, I could use a damn hand," he growled out.

The hood of the car shot skyward as he launched off a small bump in the road, sending his stomach into his throat before the SUV crashed down firmly on its wheels and sped forward, sending his gut into his bowels.

The trees grew denser around him, causing

Jeremiah to end up losing both mirrors from the doors of the vehicle at the same time the passenger side window cracked, then shattered from a passing branch.

Jeremiah saw the beginning of the dense natural shrubbery that lined the edge of the property ahead, snarled, and let loose a wordless roar.

Lost in that scream was Denise in turn screaming at him.

Chapter 32

There were few things that felt truly satisfying to Jeremiah.

Waking up to breakfast cooked by Ashley.

Watching cheesy dramedy shows and poking fun at the characters with Jenny as the sun set.

As it turned out, he could now add running over Vampires with an SUV to that list.

One of the gun-brandishing Vampires to the rear of the property bounced off the edge of his bumper as he sped straight for Vasily.

The engine roared when the vehicle rumbled over what he assumed was the body of the Vamp he'd just hit, briefly launching Jeremiah out of his seat.

Vasily watched him with a confused, concerned expression on his face, seemingly stuck in place as Jeremiah sped towards him.

That was, until a black-haired woman tackled him to the side, sending him sprawling away mere moments before Jeremiah's hood slammed into the space where Vasily had been.

It wasn't a complete loss.

He still managed to fold the woman over, then under the hood of the vehicle.

Jeremiah slammed on the brakes, wrenching the wheel to the right as it skidded to a stop, lifting the tires of the right side off the ground as rounds began to crash through the windows.

He opened the door, practically falling out of the seat onto the ground, before reaching back up and grabbing the rifle he'd purloined from Denise's home.

Taking up a position behind the engine block of the SUV, Jeremiah flipped the weapon off safe, leaned down, and aimed underneath the car.

He saw a pair of legs and two bodies writhing about on the ground.

Aiming at the still-walking legs, he shot once, then twice, before a three-inch section of the limb around the knee disappeared in a spray of viscera.

The Vampire fell flat on his face with a barely audible scream, cutting off when Jeremiah's round slammed into the top of his skull, leaving a deep trail of gore to the middle of his back.

Straightening back out, Jeremiah blew out a ragged breath.

"Come on you bloodsucking motherfuckers!" Jeremiah taunted, hoping to buy more time for Jenny, Ashley and Denise to make it up the slope behind the cabin. "Who's next? Come on, I got enough ammo for all of ya'!"

The gunfire slowly died away to sporadic, singular pops and Jeremiah heard Vasily screaming for people to cease fire.

Jeremiah turned the rifle to the side, checked the window on the side of the magazine, and nodded.

Twenty-five. Three more mags in reserve, and two for the pistol.

Jeremiah took a mental inventory, slung the sling over his head and reached into his right pocket, pulling free one of the bags and a lighter.

"Now -that- is what I expected!" Vasily's laughter-filled shout filled the clearing. Jeremiah cocked his head to the side, trying to determine the exact location of the Vampire lord. "Big! Flashy!

Loud! My oh my, you had me buying the lie the entire time!

"Was that astral projection I just saw? Immaculate work Jeremiah, that kind of skill normally takes years to perfect!"

Too bad for you, I'm a Golem.

My soul doesn't have to live in a body, bitch.

"Needed to figure out where you assholes were standing!" Jeremiah shouted back over the hood, trying to get the fuse to spark while the lighter failed to live up to its namesake. "That was a nice save by your little friend there! She one of the freaks, or will she bleed out in a minute?"

"Freaks?" Vasily questioned archly, with a bitter edge to his voice, barely contained by the self-important tone he hurled Jeremiah's way. "Do you mean my life's work? The next generation of political and military leaders? "

Politics?

Leaders?

Freaks...freaks works.

"These freaks, as you call them, are the result of over a century of magical chemistry and genetic therapy, before we even knew what a gene was!" Vasily paused dramatically, seeming to take a second to calm himself down from the rising agitation in his tone.

Jeremiah grimaced and set down the small leather pouch, his lighter refusing to work.

He took this opportunity to pop up and over the hood of the vehicle, aiming his rifle at the first silhouette of a Vampire that he could see.

He sent two rounds into the woman's chest and dropped back down behind the engine.

"To all the assholes out there, take a good look

at your buddy there!" Jeremiah shouted, completely ignoring Vasily's diatribe. "That's your fucking future!"

Jeremiah leaned back underneath the hood and put two rounds into the skull of the still-groaning Vampire.

These rounds hit like a fucking truck.

He nodded his head sideways as he eyed the side of the weapon thoughtfully.

I need to get more, a whole fucking truckload.

He heard more than a couple nervous-sounding whispers emanating from where the Vampires now stood in a wide half-circle in front of the cabin and smiled.

"Veronique is fine, thanks to decades of research and sweat on my part!" Vasily proclaimed, the whispers giving way to giggles. To Jeremiah, that wasn't a good sign, and his spine began to tingle uncomfortably.

On instinct, he sprang back from where he crouched, a pale, clawed hand carving through the air where he just was, as the hood thudded and creaked loudly.

Jeremiah fell onto his back, looking up at the creature that crouched there.

Veronique, or so he guessed from the pair of breasts and long, dark hair that spilled over her shredded clothes, snarled at him with a mouth of long, pointed teeth.

Unlike the dark translucent sheen of Aiden's skin, she was a stark, alabaster white.

Veronique's skin was smooth and hairless everywhere other than her head and was pulled taut above layer after layer of dense muscles.

She rolled her head slowly to the side while

she seemed to size him up.

Her eyes were two black slits upon a blood-red sclera and iris, narrowing to fine lines as her grin stretched to unnatural lengths in her cheeks.

"You're a jumpy little shi-" Veronique cut off the moment Jeremiah lifted the rifle fractionally and unloaded nearly a dozen rounds into her from point blank, tearing massive chunks of flesh from her body while she briefly screamed, tried to cover her face, before having a round slam through to her head.

Jeremiah pushed up to a crouch with his left hand as she flopped bonelessly off the hood and onto the ground beside him.

Having a thought, Jeremiah pulled the sword out of its sheath, crouch-walked to her slowly reconstructing corpse, and brought the weapon down into the mushy mass that would become her head.

With a shove, then another that had more in common with a push-up, he pushed the sword down nearly to the hilt, with less than ten inches of the blade sticking out of the soft earth.

"How far does this regeneration go, Vasily?" Jeremiah knelt on the freak's chest, dropped the magazine of his weapon, pulled a fresh one from the armor, and reloaded. "It can fix the body, but can it fix stupid? Your bitch seems like she's staying dead over here!"

"Oh, don't worry, she'll be back soon! As I'm sure you experienced with my head of acquisitions!" Vasily retorted while the rest of his crew grew deadly silent.

"You might be sure of that. What about your friends?" Jeremiah questioned into the still evening air.

Glass shattered and was blasted out of the cars

around him. Causing him to flinch and turn his head away partially.

Gunfire split the night, bright flashes were visible around the hood of the SUV and Jeremiah hunched lower. It'd only take a single round through his head to put this whole damn plan off.

As the gunfire abated again, Jeremiah strained his eyes to see into the dark and listen to anything he could make out.

To him, it sounded like they actually had lost sight of where he was.

Ha...eat a bloody dick.

Do vampires have extreme tinnitus? I bet they do.

Taking a chance, Jeremiah popped up over the side of the car. He dropped his rifle into position on the hood. He had a good sight picture on several of them who indeed looked surprised to see him.

In a matter of seconds, he dropped the ones he could see, as others scurried for cover. He couldn't see Vasily at all at the moment.

"C'mon Vasily! Send me another freak!" Jeremiah growled into the night, and then dropped down behind the car again. He popped the magazine out of his weapon and loaded another in.

If he got lucky, he could bait the egotistic man into revealing his position. He pointed the weapon at the twin town-cars on the long driveway that Vasily had brought with him.

"I'm feelin' violent today!" he called out loudly.

Moving across the soft, grassy ground, as quietly as possible, he approached the pair of vehicles, waiting for a vampire to show up somewhere.

He needed to keep himself moving or risk getting pinned to the car from a good angle.

After all, in the time it took for everything to happen so far, he had no doubt that they were probably moving around him now. There was no way they wouldn't be.

Unsurprisingly, and regretfully, he was right.

Off to the left, vampires were heading his way. Ducking and moving at a near silent jog along the treeline.

They'd shouldered their weapons and began firing on him. The short glimpse of him had apparently been all they needed to start firing, rather than flanking.

Damnit, I'm not an action hero!
What the hell am I doing?

Several rounds impacted his armor and sent his thoughts skittering around. He didn't want to be in this open position right now, and everything felt like an open position.

Sighting his weapon in as best as he could, he squeezed the trigger smoothly, getting several shots off on the lead vampire.

Then the second one after he felt confident that he'd put rounds on target.

Though they'd been firing just as much if not more as he had, at the same time.

Thankfully, his rounds had more punch than their SMGs.

Two more of their shots struck his armor, and then one pounded down into his waist. It was low and under his armor.

A burning white-hot pain lanced through him and left him gritting his teeth.

Wherever the anti-Para round struck, they simply no longer had a body part though. The vampires that'd been coming to flank him had been

removed from the fight.
Each of them had a fresh new ventilation duct installed on their chest. One of them looked as if they'd had their heart and lungs removed outright.
Fuck, these are strong.
Peeking up over the car he'd taken refuge behind, or more accurately, the engine block, he spotted two more breaking from the house. They were rapidly sprinting off to his right. They'd be coming around for him at some point.
His peek had lasted no more than a second before he whipped his head back down. Rounds impacted the car as well as whizzed over his head.
Panting, not wanting to think about the hit he had taken, Jeremiah realized the folly of his situation. This had been backwards from the get-go.
Damnit. Probably should have had Denise do this. I could've probably gotten in around the back with a spell from her.
She could've floated above them and just dropped balls of death magic on them.
Letting out a short breath, Jeremiah stepped to the side in a crouch, shifting his weapon up onto his shoulder again.
He sighted up a vampire that was aiming toward his general position and put two shots into them. Then dropped right back into cover.
Realizing that this wasn't the right place to be, and he was likely about to be flanked, he turned and sprinted for the nearby treeline.
Only to get knocked right off his feet and sent to the ground.
Looking up, he saw Vasily standing over him.
The shit.
Jeremiah pulled his pistol from its holster,

doing a small sit-up while he aimed it towards Vasily.

It was knocked free from his hands as Vasily leapt upon him, grabbing Jeremiah by the throat and snarling.

The veins in Vasily's face bulged from his skin, tinged an ugly brown instead of the blue that they should have been.

The Vampire hefted Jeremiah skyward, off his feet, blood dripping from the Vampire's fangs.

Not far behind him was a laid-out Vampire with a hand to their neck.

Unbelievably, Vasily had become a kin-drinker.

"Every time I try and take my time, enjoy life, and show mercy," Vasily growled, transitioning his grip to a single hand and wiping at his lips, "I'm punished."

Jeremiah's reply was a mere gurgle as he felt his heart beat against the Vampire's thumb.

"Well, that shows me the price of mercy. I'll have to remind myself of you whenever I think of being... charitable," Vasily spat out, even as his face started to shift and mottle in a strange way. Almost as if his face were about to split in half, in fact.

Jeremiah grabbed at the man's wrist and put all of his strength into breaking it.

He accomplished nothing.

"Perhaps luck brought me here today for a lesson. To find that little Fae girl's diary, full of drawings of the object of her desire by the Fate's design," Vasily snorted derisively, his lips blowing out with the force of the breath that came with it. Over his shoulder, he turned to the three remaining Vampires. Apparently the others had been killed by Jeremiah, spread out, or he'd seriously over-counted them.

"Spread out. Make sure that he was alone. I'm not entirely sure he was. There's a faint scent of... others... on him but I can't place it. Figure out where that car came from, too. Might provide us with more information," growled Vasily.

Jeremiah kicked out his foot into Vasily's belly, causing nothing but a solitary eyebrow raise from the Vampire when he looked back to him.

"Maybe it's taken me too long to learn these lessons. It isn't the first time I've been burnt by this sort of hubris, mind you. The only real answer that keeps coming back to me with earnest results is swift and complete violence," Vasily shrugged as the three vampires behind him began to move away.

With a strangled croaking noise as the result, Jeremiah tried to speak.

It was a disgusting gurgle that sounded terrible even to his own ears.

Vasily raised his eyebrows, slowly tilting his head to the side as if he were inspecting a minor mystery.

Like the back of a puzzle box when you were trying to fit in the edges.

"Mmmm? Have some last words?" asked Vasily who then surprisingly dropped Jeremiah. Only to instantly grab him up in a headlock in nearly the same fluid motion.

The rapid spin caused Jeremiah's head to feel as if it'd done the same.

Disorienting him spectacularly.

"Something I should note for the next would-be savior of the human race that thinks they're special? Any advice for me? After all, it's always good to pass on good advice you know. It's the only thing you can do with it after all. It's no use for yourself," mused Vasily with a self-satisfied grin.

Jeremiah's hands balled into fists, the first taste of air like a gentle kiss to his screaming lungs. He breathed out deeply, rolled his hand back, and said:

"You talk too much."

Jeremiah's hypodermic spike, designed for draining other Golems, shot from his wrist and he brought it over his shoulder.

Aiming for the vampire's forehead.

An odd, crunching squelch came from Vasily's skull as the spike pierced the man's eye socket.

Taking the opportunity, Jeremiah threw himself bodily backward. Attempting to break free of Vasily's grasp.

The backstep didn't get what he wanted, but it did cause Vasily to stutter step as he lost his footing.

Jeremiah launched forward in that moment and ended up squirming away from the vampire who was still screaming.

Even as he landed on the ground in a heap, Jeremiah groaned and tried to roll away.

To roll to his front and push himself up to his knees.

He'd bought himself some time, but he needed to get going and do so immediately.

Vasily clutched at his face, a wrathful grimace plastered to his lips as he snarled. He pulled his hand away, staring at his palm before placing it back and removing it again.

"Ow," Vasily chuckled absently, staring at the blood on his hand before his good eye snapped back to Jeremiah. Clearly, Jeremiah's spike had done something to the Vampire lord, since now, over Vasily's right eye was a milky blue cataract. "And so, the lesson is driven home beyond all doubt. Because nothing teaches better than pain."

Vasily spat to the side, leaned down, and grabbed the handgun from Jeremiah.

Actually, where's Denise?

She should have gotten Jenny and Ashley out by now. I don't see them...anywhere. Is it done?

Did a stray round catch her?

His thoughts churned in a circle.

When her work was done, she was supposed to have come over and helped.

Flying above and dropping explosives as well as magic, as needed.

Her absence left him feeling rather nervous.

Vasily walked the short distance to him and stood over him. Over the vampire's shoulder, he saw Denise.

She was perched atop the cabin's roof, looking like some type of fantasy-land Gargoyle. Her bright dress making it hard to miss her.

In one hand she had a glowing ball of lightning, the other clung to the roof.

Vasily followed Jeremiah's eyes.

"I should've known as much," the Vampire lamented with a shake of his head. He lifted the pistol and sighted it on the Fae.

Jeremiah put every ounce of strength he had left into springing towards the man. One arm got up under the vampire's throat and wrenched his head to the side. His other hand grabbed at the wrist that held the pistol.

Jeremiah's hand locked tightly into position, and he managed to bend it away from aiming at Denise. Slowly further and further till it was nowhere near to Denise, but went no further.

"Really?" Are you attempting to become the proverbial monkey on my back?" quipped Vasily with a chuckle. Then he jerked his arm to the side and sent Jeremiah quite literally flying over his shoulder.

He didn't go far before he slammed into the front of the town car.

Coughing as the wind was knocked out of him, Jeremiah wheezed and then forced himself to his feet.

The alarm on the car was going off loudly behind him.

Getting his hands up in front of him, Jeremiah tried to make himself as ready as he could for the vampire.

Not waiting, he drove forward and put his fist into Vasily's gut.

Once, twice, thrice, then again, he struck, before Vasily lashed out with a brutal, earth-rocking kick to Jeremiah's gut, sending him flying once again.

Thankfully, this time, he didn't hit the car.

Instead, he hit the dirt. His ribs and guts aching at the abuse as well as the gunshot that'd gone through him earlier.

A fiery ache in his head screamed at him to just stay still. To lie down and give up, that moving would be worse than accepting his fate.

A slew of thunderous cracks snapped him from his thoughts. As if they were sent from the heavens above to deliver righteous justice to Vasily.

Jeremiah rolled onto his back in an almost-uncontrolled flop. He pushed himself up and onto his elbows.

Looking over, he saw Vasily holding one arm up beside himself as lightning crackled around him.

It traveled up and down his body, circling as if

it were making a continuous circuit from hand to foot, and back again.

"You damn canary, I'll knock you out of the sky and tear your wings off!" shrieked Vasily as he began to radically shift then and there.

Denise flicked through the air over head and vanished out over the treeline to one side. She banked hard and dropped several balls of lightning.

Well, I guess I can tell where the other Vampires went.

How'd she do it quietly though?

Muscles bulged from Vasily's tailored suit sleeves, ripping the fabric. Demanding that Jeremiah put his attention on him rather than the Fae.

Soon enough, the vampire grew to stand well over eight feet in height, muscled like a professional bodybuilder.

What...I...really?

Fuck.

"To hell with this!" Vasily shouted with an incredible volume. His voice had dropped several octaves as he transformed, the scowl on his face disappearing to be replaced with a lip-less mass of teeth.

There was a strange wave of crimson liquid that flowed back and forth as well. Almost as if his face wasn't even his own anymore.

As if it weren't even solid.

The hulking figure that had been Vasily threw his hands out to either side, the bodies of his thralls shredding apart as the blood flowed from their bodies and formed into two pulpy balls. One became a large disk that Vasily climbed upon. The other separated, turning into a dozen sharp-looking spears of blood.

A new ball of crackling lightning blasted into

the back of his head.

The bolt of electricity crackled from tooth to tooth, leaping back and forth even as he looked up to Denise as she shot by.

It didn't seem that her magic was doing much at all now.

"Cute," Vasily said pointedly, looking back to Jeremiah with a smirk. Or at least Jeremiah thought it was a smirk, since his inhuman face barely resembled anything familiar.

The hairs on Jeremiah's arms rose skyward, as well as the ones on his neck. The smell of ozone permeated the air so noticeably, that even Vasily took an exploratory sniff.

Jeremiah hadn't been completely idle as the big monster watched Denise. Almost as if he were contemplating throwing something at her.

As the creature was distracted, Jeremiah had snatched up the pistol.

Fuck, fuck, please, please, do your thing, anti-para rounds!

His mind screeched, squealed, and demanded he run, even as he lifted the gun up and put the barrel just about touching Vasily's jaw.

He was just far enough away that when the man turned, he'd get it right in his face.

"Cute? No," Jeremiah stated. Vasily's head jerked around just as he expected, though the aim was off, it was more at his upper lip. "You're not my type."

Jeremiah pulled the trigger and then did his best to keep shooting rapidly.

His only goal was to buy time to get the hell out of here. If Denise was here, then her job as done. Their mission was a success.

It was time to go.

The strange goopy morass that was Vasily's face deformed, moved outward, then collapsed in on itself.

Only to split in half as the continued rounds detonated inside of his skull.

When the hammer clicked and the slide locked back, Jeremiah dropped the gun and turned to run at a full dead-on sprint.

Getting his feet under him, he didn't manage that.

It was more akin to a galloping limp that left him hobbling away with some speed.

"What'd you say last time?! Such a pretty mouth?!" shrieked Denise behind him.

Jeremiah glanced over his shoulder just in time to see Denise had stuffed one of the magical grenades into Vasily's strangely semi-solid face.

Followed by the second grenade.

Oh fuck.

Denise turned and then shot forward. She caught him up under the armpits and then began trying to drag him through the air with speed.

Given his equipment, and that he wasn't light to begin with, she didn't get him far. Or fast, even.

They slammed into the hood of a car, slid off it, and dropped to the other side.

Jeremiah rolled to one side and looked up just in time to watch Vasily explode.

Or more accurately, his head exploded.

Except the grenade did as advertised by Denise.

His head evaporated, then the explosion traveled downward, turning his upper body into meaty chunks that slammed into the ground in a

small circle.
> Standing there, Vasily didn't fall.
> Jeremiah's heart dropped.
> Vasily was going to regrow again.

Except, no sooner did he have the thought, before the explosion had faded, than Vasily started to pop and crackle. His body exploding over and over across the bloody edge of where he'd been blow apart.

Hundreds of thousands of small puffs and explosions ripped through the night air as Vasily continued to explode.

> "Oh, that's a lot of Essence. They were holding it all," remarked Denise, laying on the ground behind Jeremiah and watching as well. "It's all going off in a chain reaction. How absolutely fascinating. I had no idea of this application, but I look forward to repeated testing."

Fire began to lick upward from the center of the writhing body of Vasily as he continued to go off.

As if he were a gigantic chain of firecrackers put in a pot.

It was a chain reaction of carnage that while somewhat muted, became ever worse as it went on.

Parts of his body began to expand briefly and then pop.

Each burst flung bits of blood and viscera about even as the next went off.

As if he were slowly being deleted one bite-sized portion at a time.

In a second that felt like hours, what had once been a near-unstoppable horror caused by magic, mutagenic chemistry and disease, was gone.

Nothing was left of Vasily, save for a heavy-handed splatter of blood upon the car nearby, and a smoking pair of expensive looking shoes.

Denise sniffed once and then coughed.

"Oh, goodness. It stinks like wet dog for some reason. That's rather unpleasant. I'll have to make a note of that and see if it's only vampires that react like that," she murmured.

"Like a damn sparkler," Jeremiah whispered.

Chapter 33

Jeremiah blew a raspberry with his lips and fully stood up, scanning back and forth across the clearing around the cabin, ignoring the smoking boots.

"Nice play with that... grenade, Denise," Jeremiah said and rolled his shoulder backward. The joint popped and he let out a groan. "I'm glad you were able to make it back in time. Where'd you stash Ash and Jenny?"

"I didn't," Denise replied abruptly, shrugging at Jeremiah from where she was seated.

"You... didn't?" Jeremiah asked and turned to Denise with a scrunched, confused expression. "Then... what were you doing before you stepped in to help fight Vasily? Did they make it out on their own?"

"Well, I was trying to get back to you at the top of the hill, then back down here when you sped off," explained Denise. She looked winded as she pushed herself to her feet. Jeremiah on the other hand, felt a twinge of fear creeping up his spine.

If she didn't get them out, and they're not there on the porch, then...where are they?

"I was trying to warn you, you dense little shit, but no! You just had to speed off!" explained Denise.

Jeremiah's heart skipped a beat, feeling like the Earth fell out underneath him into a bottomless chasm.

"Your women weren't here. I came down to work my little illusion spell while you were distracting them, and I saw right through their trickery." Denise huffed and folded her arms over her chest. The words were an immediate balm to his mind, as well as yet another jolt of fear. "They do absolutely dreadful work. Plebian, in fact. Vulgar one could say. I could've done better as a toddler.

"But, by the time I managed to get back up to the top of the hill, you'd already started off to your little heroic last stand. I did tell you that this was a stupid plan, didn't I? I think I did.

"You're stupid. And those bloody holes in your shirt prove it."

Denise seemed more interested in pointing out the flaws in his plan and the failures of the coven than helping Jeremiah rescue Ashley and Jenny.

"Denise... please," Jeremiah said in a tired voice. "They're not here?"

"No. They're not here. Illusions. Even that Vasily wasn't Vasily. Though those might be his boots. Maybe. To be fair, they were a fairly accomplished Blood Mage," agreed Denise. Then she laughed and shrugged her shoulders. "And there's no need to wonder where they are.

"I'm sure my amazing self can just track them! All I need is hair! Or blood... or... well... seminal fluid. Though that one's always a bit touchy for people I find. You wouldn't believe—"

It wasn't Vasily?
They escaped then?
Together.

She said it all in a way that made finding Ashley and Jenny sound like running to the store and grabbing a carton of milk. Or finding a car that you forgot in a parking lot.

"That's all you need? Hair?" Jeremiah asked,

cutting her off as his eyebrows climbed ever skyward.

"Or blood. I did say blood. Or seminal fluids," Denise stated in such a nonchalant tone that Jeremiah couldn't decide whether to throttle her or hug her. "Then we just steal a car or get to the top of that mountain across the way."

"Top of the mountain? Why?" Jeremiah could absolutely understand stealing a car and keeping the accelerator pressed to the floorboard, but couldn't understand why they would go to the top of the nearby peaked ridge.

"Well, if they're still in the pass, which I'm guessing they are, given how long it winds for, it's all downhill from right up there." Denise pointed with a broad grin to the highest point in the ridge across from them. "I'll pick you up and we can just... glide down to them."

"You're sure this will work?" Jeremiah queried after sucking on his teeth for a moment. Her demeanor, as irreverent it may be, had actually put him somewhat at ease.

Like going to a doctor and being told you had a terminal disease, but don't worry, they had a solution.

"Nope!" Denise smiled broadly enough to crinkle the corners of her bright blue eyes. She then clapped her hands together with pop. "But it -is- the best chance we have of catching them before they disappear into the city.

"We can do a lot more in this forest than in Clallam."

Cowabunga it is.
My plan didn't work.
Time for a hail-Mary to save my failed hail-Mary.

* * *

This was a bad idea.

Jeremiah clung tight to Denise's underside, or technically her front, as she buzzed at an ever-decreasing altitude down the mountainside.

She followed a spell that only she could see.

According to Denise, the magical compass she'd spun with a speck of essence would pull at her psyche in the direction of their quarry.

He'd been forced to ditch the armor at the top of the mountain.

In fact, he'd left all his gear there, other than his pistol, his rifle, and an extra magazine for each.

Everything else was sacrificed for Denise being able to glide along the pass.

Though she'd clearly had a nervous look on her face when determining their weight.

"How far?!" Jeremiah shouted into the roaring winds of the dark night sky.

"C-close!" Denise shouted.

Jeremiah could feel her chest heaving as he clung to her like a life preserver, his arms wrapped around her waist, and his legs locked behind her knees.

Right…probably should just let her do her thing.

"Running… out of steam!" Denise half-groaned, half-whined. "There."

Jeremiah turned his head over his shoulder and looked at the ground.

All he saw was dark, empty forest beneath him.

Distantly, he felt he could see the pre-dawn light.

It was hard to tell, given they were in a pass, and in the hillside.

But the dawn was coming.

They'd spoken briefly about what to do about Vasily and the only thing they came up with was, "get him in sunlight".

Which while sounding simplistic, was also likely going to be rather difficult. Apparently, the windows of the vehicle were enhanced to provide a vampire safety from the sun.

Speaking of vehicles.

Ahead, on a turn, was a car's headlights.

"That them?" he called out.

Denise didn't reply.

Given the intensity of her gaze and her breathing, she was more or less tapped out and flying on by sheer determination.

Denise banked slightly, coming even with a straight section of the road ahead of the town car.

A straight path for a crow was just that, after all.

"How am I getting down?" Jeremiah asked. "Ahead of it?"

Shooting out the tires probably wouldn't work though, since most of the time that just left them able to drive as the tire deflated.

Car chases on TV had shown that off quite often.

"Hope you've a cushy!" Denise shouted abruptly, steadily lowering towards the road. "Tushy!"

I- what? The hell does that even mea-

Denise pushed both her hands against his

chest and shoved him free of her.

With a wordless, entirely masculine scream, Jeremiah hurtled towards the ground.

Wholly expecting his world to go black.

If not to just lose all track of it after smashing into the road like a Saturday morning cartoon.

Instead, he landed with a colossal bang.

Quite literally atop the car itself.

His impact made a massive dent between the driver's seat and passenger. The back of his head smacked into the windshield, and he swore he heard it crack.

Or his head broke open, he wasn't sure.

Sitting up, he saw the back of the car, and the road it'd already traveled.

Oh.

The car suddenly swerved underneath him, and he grabbed onto the sides of the vehicle's top with both hands.

Fuck!

The car straightened out and seemed to be trying to determine if it should speed up or slow down. The accelerator didn't sound very loud, and if anything, the engine sounded as if it were winding down.

Jeremiah snatched at the pistol he was carrying. Nearly losing it, he swapped it to his left hand.

Turning his body, he tried to gauge where the driver would be.

Given that he wasn't seated securely, with the vehicle moving and bouncing over every small thing in the road, that made it rather difficult.

He fired thrice into the roof and was rewarded when the vehicle banked hard to the left and into a guardrail.

With a horrendous shriek of metal shearing off, it came free of it momentarily. Then slammed right back into it and nearly came to a full stop.

Physics was a dickhead in the best of times.

Jeremiah was flung bodily forward, screaming wordlessly into the night air, before he crashed into the upper branches of a large tree.

Only to end up falling -out- of the tree a moment later.

Nearly managing to hit every branch on the way down like a Plinko chip.

With a wet splash, he hit the ground, landing in a deep puddle that quickly began to flow over him.

Sputtering as the water went up his nose, Jeremiah sat up. His back popped like a series of firecrackers as something settled back into place.

Maybe it was a rib.

Maybe it was his spine.

Jeremiah didn't have time to fully consider his injuries as he heard an ugly groaning of metal on metal behind him.

As if the car had kept going to a degree and was soldiering on somehow.

Pushing to his feet, he realized he'd lost the rifle somewhere in the fall, likely eaten by the tree.

Nor had he kept his pistol either.

Pushing himself up, he turned and stumbled off after the car.

In that moment, he realized he was in a small creek and what he'd fallen into, wasn't a puddle at all.

There were also a pair of brake lights not far off wedged partway in the embankment.

The car had continued along the guard rail,

only to come off the road entirely just as he had.

Stumbling through the shallow creek, he made it to the car. Putting a hand on the trunk, he steadied himself.

In the strange light of neither dawn nor night, he could see a massive branch extending from the front of the passenger's side of the cab.

Wanting to act now, since regardless of who the passenger was they'd likely be injured, he moved. Shambling through the muck of the creek-bed, he clambered over to the right side of the car.

He felt for the latch on the rear right door and attempted to open it before it was flung open, painfully impacting his ribs.

"Ah," Vasily declared with a grunt. He stepped out of the backseat of the car as Jeremiah stumbled backwards into the hillside running up to the road. "It's you."

Vasily glanced up above himself to the sky momentarily with a mystified expression, before looking back to Jeremiah.

"I'll admit, I did not expect for you to simply... drop out of the sky on me," murmured Vasily in a confused and clearly surprised tone. He brushed what looked like a piece of dashboard off of the arm of his suit.

"After all, one expects vermin to crawl from the woodwork, not swoop in like a diving falcon," Vasily exclaimed with a thrown hand up at the sky above. Then he looked at his wrist and stared daggers at it.

"And this! This... this is... ahhhh. You've ruined yet another suit," Vasily complained and showed the torn sleeve toward Jeremiah. "Look! You... you filthy, nasty little thing. The fact that you're here means you've probably slain poor Travis. No?"

"Yeah," Jeremiah grunted out and climbed to his feet, dirt and bits of grass falling away from his back and arms. "I took care of the little surprise party you left at the cabin for me. Even the blood mage."

"He died bad. Like a god damn candle on a cake."

"Shame," Vasily remarked and then shrugged his shoulders. He didn't seem torn up about it as he glanced around the valley. "Oh well. There will always be another blood mage. A steady diet of other vampires is all it takes after all.

"So what was your intent with all this? Drop in, gun me down like some kind of action hero?

"I don't see a gun on you, so surely it can't be that. Come to barter with me for the women?"

"I... yeah? Yeah. Something like that I guess. I certainly wasn't going to just let you drive off into the sunrise though. Sure as shit not that," Jeremiah remarked and put a hand to his neck. He pushed at it and turned his head to the side, and got a solid crack out of it.

Oh fuck that feels better.

Come on, Denise, where'd you get off to?

I could really use some air support.

A ball of lightning or something. Or better yet, find where I dropped my rifle and pistol.

"Boldness is the way to a woman's heart, Jeremiah," Vasily shucked off the suit jacket and tossed it atop the crumpled roof of the car, when a muted thud sounded from the trunk. "In another life, I feel as though you would have made a phenomenal employee. Even a friend perhaps. You've got that... eager... attitude one looks for in henchmen."

Trunk noises.
Can't see the girls in the back seat, or the front.
That...means they're in the trunk?
Jeremiah took several steps back.
Realistically, Vasily was an existence beyond him at the moment.
"It's a pity you've become a thorn in the side of my lovely organization. You've forced my hand in this."
Vasily grunted and then his skin began to bubble and his body writhe underneath the surface.
He was shifting.
Fuck. Fuck, shit, okay.
Draw him away.
Fight him until the sun comes.
Vasily's transformation abruptly halted halfway through, while a glowing blue streak slammed into him with a thunderous crackle.
As if whatever hit him had activated a hidden spring underneath the Vampire, Vasily launched vertically into the air and over Jeremiah's head.
Jeremiah glanced to his left briefly.
Denise was standing some ways off, already readying another ball of lightning between her palms.
Nice timing.
Keep him busy, Denise. I need to get the girls out of this trunk.
Jeremiah hurried around the front of the car and ripped open the driver's door. He fumbled in the dark next to the leg of the headless driver's corpse for the trunk release latch as another crack of lightning sounded, echoing and reverberating through the mountain pass.
He pulled at a latch.

Nothing happened.

He pulled at the latch again with more force and he heard something at the front end of the car slam home.

Ah. The hood.

Jeremiah moved his hand to the left, found another latch, and was rewarded with a satisfying pop from the trunk of the car.

"Help would be greatly appreciated!" Denise called out in a loud voice from his right and above him. It sounded near the street.

The sorceress hurled what sounded akin to her cackling balls of power. A resounding thud followed after, along with a boom.

As Jeremiah rounded the back of the car, he found both Jenny and Ashley in the trunk. Jenny was bound wrist to ankle and gagged, while Ashley had a number of handcuffs locked about her wrists.

They went down in a chain toward her ankles and were numerous there as well.

Jeremiah put his hand to the bindings around Jenny and launched the spike out of his wrist. It neatly separated a number of the strands on the first pass.

Withdrawing the spike, he did it again and managed to cut the rope free entirely this time. Lining it up to the point that it wound down to the binding that went to Jenny's ankles, he repeated the process.

It took only seconds and Jenny was free.

Not bothering with the gag, he instead leaned over and tried the same process on the handcuffs that held Ashley down.

They clanked against the spike but didn't bend, flex, or give way. In fact, they looked as if they weren't even made of a normal metal, the way they reflected what little light there was, in a weird prism-like way.

"Don't bother," Jenny got out after yanking the gag down. "We'll need the key and that's somewhere... uh... somewhere."

"Right," Jeremiah grunted, meeting Ashley's eyes.

She was lucid, aware, and clearly frustrated. Then she shrugged her shoulders. Or at least tried to.

Keys...keys we don't have at the moment.
Time for plan whatever.
Find the guns, make a hole somewhere in Vasily, pop him like the other freak.

"You insolent little bug! I should've had your mother killed years ago!" Shouted Vasily from the road.

The rifle was strapped to my back when I fell off of Denise...if it came off in the impact, that means it should be in the tree or under it.

"No keys, Denise is up there fighting," Jeremiah explained while looking between Jenny and Ash's face.

"I'm going to go try and find my rifle. See if you can't help Denise up there, Jenny," Jeremiah said and turned.

"And how am I supposed to do that without a gun or a sword or... anything? Harsh language!?" shouted Jenny at his back

Jeremiah sprinted towards where he'd fallen out of the tree. He was hoping desperately that it'd be right there for him, but he couldn't count on it.

Denise had the other "grenade" on her person, and other than sunlight, it was their best bet.

Scrambling about in the broken leaves and branches, Jeremiah's hands were blindly groping about for the most part.

Then he looked up as his head bumped into a shattered branch.

Only to discover it wasn't a branch.

The rifle was hanging there, suspended from a branch above. The muzzle was pointing down toward the ground.

"Ah... I wouldn't" advised Vasily as Jeremiah reached for the rifle.

Directly above him, was Vasily. He was on the side of the road and glaring down at him.

Looking up into the ugly, twisted face of a half-changed vampire turned true monster, Jeremiah tried to work out what to do.

Jeremiah heard a strange and low rumbling but refused to take his eyes off the Vampire. It felt like the moment he did than, he'd have the creature draining him like a juice-box in the hands of a toddler.

Vasily began to glow a pale yellowish-white as they stared at each other. Then his head whipped to one side and looked up the road.

In the next moment, Vasily just wasn't there. Vanishing from sight entirely.

A flash of taillights and a bright chrome bumper was all Jeremiah saw.

Was...was that a big ass truck?

Jeremiah snatched the rifle out of the tree, pausing to break the branch that held it, and activated the flashlight on the front of it.

Though it flickered wildly, as if the bulb was about to go, it worked.

Scrambling up the hillside, he got to the road.

Looking left, he saw nothing, then looked right.

Some yards down the road was Vasily, looking quite mangled. As if he had not only been hit by the car, but like he'd gone under it.

Jeremiah ran up somewhat closer to see Vasily more clearly. He was still breathing, amazingly enough.

Lifting the rifle up, he simply unloaded the rifle into the body. Firing until the magazine went dry outright. Blood and viscera had been splattered about by the heavy-hitting para-rounds.

Before he could even say anything, Denise sprinted past him.

Whatever was going through her Fae head, he had no idea.

"Denise—"

Even as he tried to voice his question, Denise acted.

She shoved the grenade into Vasily's body. The fuse had already been lit somehow. In the next moment, she looked to him.

"Run," she commanded and then teleported off.

Not waiting, Jeremiah turned, sprinted, and leapt over the nearby guardrail.

There was no time to even confirm where he'd be landing.

A boom sounded off behind him, even as he crashed to the river-rocks below.

Shaking his head, Jeremiah pushed himself to a standing position and looked back to the road above.

He could hear a similar crackling noise to what'd happened with the Blood Mage, but it didn't quite sound the same either.

"He isn't a blood mage," advised Denise. "He

isn't... full of Essence. It won't work in the same way as it did for the not-Vasily."

There fizzling, crackling, randomized pops slowed fairly quickly, then stopped.

It felt too quick compared to the lengthy continuous explosion of the other grenade.

Damnit. She's right isn't she.

Jeremiah pushed himself up on the embankment to peer over the guard rail.

Something hideous twisted its way along the roadway, lit up enough to see by the hazy pre-dawn gloom.

An inky maroon mass of twisting viscera that slowly shaped itself into something that only vaguely resembled a living thing.

"You... damn... bastard," growled the misshapen mass of blood and gore. "Do you... know... how much... that... hurt?"

As Jeremiah turned and looked to the smoking bag of broken bits of bone and guts, he saw it rise up.

Hideously, a head formed on the underside. Made of shattered bones and torn flesh, it congealed in a way similar to a pudding hardening.

A mouth he hadn't noticed was stuck there in the center of it, along with one single eye.

"It'll take me... weeks... to look normal... again," squealed what was left over of Vasily. Two appendages that most assuredly weren't arms, snaked out of the writhing mass of biological material and stuck to the ground. Two more came out of the rear of it. All four seemed to be made of everything and anything.

Jeremiah swore he saw what looked a lot like a stomach being used as a foot.

"I'll have to... drain... an entire... community,

just to be... able to... sleep!" screamed the distorted mouth.

"Oh my fuck," Jeremiah said without realizing he'd done so. He pressed a hand to his forehead and hazarded a glance behind himself.

Denise was standing there beside him. She looked wrecked.

She had dark bags under her eyes, there were massive sweat stains under her arm pits, and her hair was wild and unbound.

Jenny was beside her, and she really didn't look much better.

What I wouldn't give for another truck to come right about now...

"I think... I think the grenade did its job... but also eliminated things that were holding him together. Maybe?" surmised the Fae. "I don't even know what he is anymore. We just... how far off is the dawn?"

"Five or something minutes," whispered Jenny.

Five minutes? How the fuck do we hold that off for five minutes?!

"No, I don't have any idea," Jeremiah said, deciding to push an idea at Vasily. Maybe he could get him talking again. "Would you like to explain to me just what you did? How you managed that? Pretty sure those bombs killed the other super vampire. Clearly you're a step above."

"I'll let you know... in the future... sometime," growled Vasily. A fifth, and then a sixth appendage snaking out from the blob. He looked something more akin to a spider at this point than a human. "In the... future... I'll see you... very soon. Until then."

Not bothering to wait around, Vasily turned,

and skittered off the road, then veered into the trees. The strange limbs propelling him at an intense speed that Jeremiah didn't think he could match at a dead sprint.

*

"Fuck?" Jenny offered, apparently breaking her taboo on curse words in that moment.

Epilogue

"Welp, that's gonna be a problem." Jeremiah bit down and chewed at the inside of his lip as he watched the spot in the trees where the clump of organs named Vasily had skittered off into. "But, it's a problem for us to solve later."

"I've seen some wild things in my day, Jeremiah, but that was…" Jenny blew a breath out through tightly pressed lips. "Something else. Vasily shouldn't've been alive like that. I dunno if I could even call that livin'."

"Yep. Fuck that. Fuck that and the car it rode in on." Jeremiah turned over his shoulder and glanced at the pair of women behind him. "Where's Ash?"

"Still in the trunk," Jenny tossed her head back towards the wreckage of the car. "Told her to stay put.

"Saw the sun was comin' up, didn't want to risk her gettin' burnt. She wasn't wearing any sunscreen when we got grabbed."

Jeremiah glanced up the mountain pass and nodded to himself. The sky above had gone from the blue pre-dawn glow to a vibrant orange sunrise, though the sun itself still sat behind the mountains.

"Denise," Jeremiah glanced over to the Faerie who looked like she was in the middle of spacing out, staring past him with a thousand-yard stare. Several moments after he spoke, she blinked, shook her head rapidly, and looked to him with raised eyebrows. "After you get a few minutes to rest and recuperate, can you go grab Ashley some of the SPF-nine-thousand from the cabin?

"As pretty as this pass is, I don't think any of us would really enjoy waiting here until sunset."

Jeremiah had changed his question at the last moment, deciding to ask Denise to go on the fetch quest for sunscreen -after- she'd had a moment to rest.

Really don't want to get caught by a patrolling deputy with the corpse in the front seat.

Pretty sure there's a way to tell that his head was vaporized by a bullet and not the crash.

"Of course!" Denise smiled and seemed to partway come back to herself as a playful smile grew to life. "But, since you ruined our date, I want a do-over. I don't think having to rush off on a rescue mission before I even got to show you dessert counts as a date!

"I worked so hard on the raspberry tarts. I even picked them fresh this morning."

Denise crossed her arms across her chest and glared at Jeremiah with an expression that felt like a midpoint between a scowl and a pout.

"Or yesterday morning now, I suppose."

Jeremiah blinked and turned his head fractionally to shoot a questioning expression at Jenny, who snorted and rolled her eyes.

"You and I both know that this'll end up being Ash's decision." Jenny smiled in a way that looked like a smirk then turned back to the car in the ravine. "I say we let her decide. That woman runs over both of us in an argument anyways."

Jenny began to walk down the embankment towards the crashed town car, waving for Jeremiah and Denise to follow. Jenny then crawled into the open rear door of the car and scrambled through the seats to the other side. Denise followed just after, but instead of sitting in an actual seat, she squeezed into the middle and sat down on the center console, between the driver's seat and the passenger's.

Jeremiah followed a moment later, sitting down in the furthest right seat, as Jenny worked at freeing a section of the back of the seat in the middle. Seeming to find what she was looking for, she folded a section of the backboard down.

Near immediately, Ashley's head popped out like a groundhog.

"You guys look like how I feel!" the Vampire glanced over to Jenny, then to Denise, then rolled her head over to smile up at Jeremiah.

"Well, we did take on a small coven's worth of Vampires to get you two back." Denise quipped before Jeremiah could reply. "Your boyfriend is incredibly dense, and I'm sure we flew for well over a dozen miles."

"I knew it! As soon as I heard the boom, I was sure that Jeremiah had somehow come to get us." Ashley's smile grew incrementally brighter as she turned to look up to him. She twisted around in the trunk and seemed to change from lying on her stomach to lying on her back before looking back to him.

Still smiling, she rolled her head back to look at Denise again.

"I'm very glad that he had you around. From what I could hear of the fight just now, it sounds like you were instrumental in breaking Jenny and I out."

"I was," Denise grinned proudly for a moment before the grin became teasing. She looked to Jeremiah and added; "Thank you for the compliment, Ashley. It's nice to know I'm appreciated."

I...I guess I haven't actually thanked her for helping me.

She did risk her life too, and all I've done is worry about Ash and Jenny.

"You're right, Denise." Jeremiah answered the Faerie's challenge. "Thank you for everything you've done today. I don't think I would've even made it out of the cabin, let alone actually been able to save these two without you."

Jenny clucked her tongue and shook her head once with a snort. Then, she nodded.

"I guess I was wrong about you, Denise." Jenny smiled politely at Denise before she looked at Jeremiah. "What actually did happen at the cabin? I thought they left some people there to kill you before you could get a good plan in motion."

"They did." Jeremiah leaned his head against the headrest and closed his eyes. "I... took the bait. Wasted time I didn't have to spare, because I thought you two were still there."

"Because you didn't stop when I tried to flag you down, you mean." Denise huffed at him, drawing a snort of amusement out of Jenny.

"Yeah, he's not exactly the most flexible person when his heart is set on something, is he?" Jenny chortled back at Denise before she let out a long, deep sigh. "Well, regardless of anything else, I'm glad you were here tonight."

"So... what should we do now?" Ashley asked after Jenny let her sentence hang. "Vasily found the cabin, and we're not made of money... we can't just go and buy another house, or stay in a hotel for the next few years."

"Eh, when we get back to the phones, I can give my family a call. I know my grandpa always says that there's a home for any of his grandchildren on his plane." Jenny offered as Jeremiah continued to rest his eyes.

He was tired.

Everything felt bruised.

But the feeling of getting Ashley and Jenny back, regardless of Vasily's escape, gave the soreness a positive flare.

Like aching muscles after an intense workout.

I...Reix said I was built for intelligence gathering, not fighting, originally. Maybe...maybe I should find a way to hunt down Vasily and his henchmen, but give their location to someone more equipped than me.

Become a spy, or a watchman, or something like that.

Dig up information and kick it off to someone who's actually set up to deal with something like that.

Reixhitz's plea came into his mind.

Don't get the people I care about caught up in my foolish crusade.

Well, dad, it looks like I should take your advice after all.

"Just take the fight to Vasily. It's not like the cops will be able to do anything with all the Feds being dead." Denise offered in a diplomatic tone.

Jeremiah opened his eyes again and watched Denise as she beamed wildly at Jenny and Ashley.

Jenny scratched at her cheek and Ashley inhaled sharply.

"I... would much rather make sure Vasily never hurts anyone ever again than run... as scary as the idea of taking him on is." Ashley said a moment later with a barely present bite to her tone.

Though...is fighting Vasily even my crusade in the first place?

Am I being selfish by not wanting to chase him down and just live my life with those two?

Jeremiah gulped and stared at the back of the seat in front of him, which still had a large branch shoved partway through the back.

I'm not the only one with an axe to grind against Vasily.

I'll let them decide.

If they want to fight them, then I'll do this the way we should have from the start. How we thought to do it, if I hadn't rushed in when I saw those dead people walking.

No protracted gunfights, no last stands.

Car bombs, sniper rifles, and dark alleys only.

Shouldn't let them see us until they're about to die. And preferably, not even then.

"That's... fair," Jenny replied to Ashley a moment later, slowly nodding her head as she seemed to chew through the idea. "Would you mind if I still got my family involved though? I think we could do with some hardware, even if it's just supplies like armor, drones, and ammunition."

"Drones?" Jeremiah pursed his lips and looked at Jenny with raised eyebrows. "Your parents have drones? Like Afghanistan, drone strike drones?"

"No, well..." Jenny tilted her head to one side and made a thoughtful expression. "I don't think they do. They might have a friend, or a contact that can get us one, but I'm talking about the pocket ones. Fly 'em up high and watch things for us.

"I know my dad has used 'em for surveillance sometimes, and he's a hobbyist when it comes to 'em."

The shit we could've pulled in Larimer with some of those...

"Ash, are you absolutely sure that you wanna chase Vasily down? He's gonna be coming after us with some force after this." Jeremiah looked down to the achingly pretty, green eyed Vampire beside him. "It might not end pretty. It might put us in jail, or worse."

"I don't want to live on the run for the rest of my life, Jeremiah." Ashley stared resolutely up at him, an inner hardness behind her eyes. "Even if he doesn't chase us, I don't want to let him walk.

"The law let him go.

"I'm not going to."

I...alright then. Hell or high water, looks like we're going to keep hunting for Vampires.

Overpowered, hyper-aggressive mutated Vampires that are already out for our blood.

Jeremiah looked down to Ashley with a wicked grin as a thought entered his mind.

I wonder how many enemies Vasily has. I wonder if there are any covens of Vampires like Ashley.

A Vampire counter culture.

Maybe I could get some packs of Weres on board too.

A whole coalition of monster-hunting monsters.

Like humanity first, but for anyone willing to fight for what's right, and aimed against truly monstrous monsters, rather than just any and all paras.

"Ash, you said you went to a support group in the past right?" Jeremiah asked as his grin widened. "For paras that got turned against their will?"

"Well... it wasn't always against their will, sometimes they were just separated from their pack, or struggling with new instincts they didn't have before, but yes! I know a few others who are in the same boat as me, why?"

"If we're going after Vasily, I think we need more than just us three –"

"Four," Corrected Denise archly.

"Than just us four." Jeremiah continued after the brief interruption. "As much as I really don't want to risk more people getting involved and drawing the eye of a three-letter agency, I think those agencies have a lot more to worry about than little old us right now.

"We need people. They don't need to be fighters, but we need people who think the same as us, to take on a coven that big. When we're this out-gunned, even having a couple of people who just act as lookouts for us could be the difference between life and death."

Ashley tilted her head fractionally as her eyes seemed to flash.

"You... you want to make para humanity first, don't you?" the corners of Ashley's lips tweaked up at the sides as her eyes seemed to sparkle. "Just instead of killing innocent non-humans, you're going after Vasily."

"I don't think it's a terrible idea," Jeremiah shrugged his shoulders, secretly pleased she had figured his thoughts out precisely, and looked to Jenny who wore an expression between concern and excitement.

"If we run it more like a mercenary company than terrorists, we might be able to really do some good." Jenny nodded once as a smile also grew on her face. "My great aunt actually uses her PMC to hunt down criminal organizations and take them for everything they're worth.

"I think I could talk her into sending down a team to us to help pro-bono. Or at least to help us teach, as I'm guessin' a lot of the paras we'll be talking to don't have any training."

"Oh! Lovely!" Denise brought her hands together in a singular clap. "I can make more of the grenades! That chemical formula is always so fun to titrate!"

With all three of the women on board with the plan, Jeremiah slowly nodded to himself.

Vasily's not gonna know what hit him.

Thank you, dear reader!

Well, I hope you really enjoyed reading Turncoat's Truth! If you did, please consider adding a review, commentary, or even messaging me to chat about it!

Feel free to join in on the chaos and fun of my discord server at: Victor E. Krabin's Discord

Patreon: https://www.patreon.com/CRABWRITES
Keep up to date - Facebook: https://www.facebook.com/profile.php?id=100093235821560
HaremLit Group: https://www.facebook.com/groups/haremlit/
Mailing list: http://eepurl.com/izprpc

If you enjoyed this book, and somehow haven't already - Consider jumping feet-first into the other books by **William D. Arand**, here: https://www.amazon.com/stores/William-D.-Arand/author/B01AY7PSG4

Additionally, if you're in the mood for something disconnected from this story in all ways, consider checking out my alter-ego - **A. D. Krabis**, here: https://www.amazon.com/stores/A.-D.-Krabis/author/B0BB89TZC2